By KARA NASH

With Caitlin Ricci: Dare to Risk

Published by DREAMSPINNER PRESS
www.dreamspinnerpress.com

By CAITLIN RICCI

Blood Slave
Country Strong
Cuddling (Dreamspinner Anthology)
With Kara Nash: Dare to Risk
For the Asking
His Lion Tamer
Marked by Grief
Reckless
With Cari Z: Worth the Wait

A FOREVER HOME
Rescuing Jack
Of Monsters and Men

A PLANET CALLED WISH
To the Highest Bidder
Fantasy for a Gentleman

THORNWOOD
One More Time
About Last Night

Published by Harmony Ink Press
Crush
First Time for Everything (Harmony Ink Anthology)
Weathering the Storm

Published by DREAMSPINNER PRESS
www.dreamspinnerpress.com

KARA NASH & CAITLIN RICCI

DARE TO RISK

Published by
DREAMSPINNER PRESS

5032 Capital Circle SW, Suite 2, PMB# 279, Tallahassee, FL 32305-7886 USA
www.dreamspinnerpress.com

Dare to Risk
© 2016 Kara Nash & Caitlin Ricci.

Cover Art
© 2016 Anna Sikorska.
Cover content is for illustrative purposes only and any person depicted on the cover is a model.

ISBN: 978-1-63477-410-9
Digital ISBN: 978-1-63477-411-6
Library of Congress Control Number: 2016902768
Published July 2016
v. 1.0

Printed in the United States of America
♾
This paper meets the requirements of
ANSI/NISO Z39.48-1992 (Permanence of Paper).

PROLOGUE

KADEN BARKER swiped the back of his dirt-covered hand over his eyes to brush away his tears as the preacher finished saying his words over Tobias Wilson's coffin. For the past few years, Tobias had been like another father to him, and it was hard to admit that the old gentleman was really gone now.

Beside him, his two best friends, Trent and Samuel, put a hand on each of his shoulders. They'd all grown to know and love him over the last few years working on Tobias's dairy farm, but it was Kaden who had been closest to him and who had taken care of him toward the end.

"It doesn't feel real," Trent whispered beside him.

Kaden shook his head. It was all so surreal. Tobias had been slowly declining for the past several months, but Kaden never expected to go into Tobias's room and find him lying there motionless on the bed. "He'd been smiling with us only the night before." There was no warning. Tobias went up to bed, and the three of them stayed downstairs in the living room talking and watching late-night TV.

He had no idea what to say to make his best friends okay again. He wasn't even sure if he was really ready to process Tobias's death himself yet. But they still had their contracts on the farm, for now, and the few hundred dairy cows in the pastures behind them weren't going away anytime soon.

The cool evening breeze whipped through his hair before he put his hat back on and came forward to lay his hand on Tobias's coffin. There were people from the funeral home standing nearby, respectfully waiting while they said their good-byes to Tobias before they would lower him into the ground.

"Good-bye, old man," Kaden gently said as he leaned down to place a kiss on the coffin. "Thank you for giving three Kiwis a chance."

CHAPTER ONE

Two Months Later

BRAN WILSON shook his head when he saw who was calling him. *I really don't need this shit right now,* he thought to himself as he swiped his finger across the screen, answering the call from a Montana land developer he'd only recently met but who had already begun to be a pain in his ass.

"What is it that you want?" Bran snapped at him.

"Sir, there's a problem...."

The little man, Frank Conns, had been given a lot of power when Bran called him a few weeks back, looking to sell an immense plot of land. He could have easily not been the man for the job, and he likely wasn't, but he was the only one who had answered Bran's call in Montana.

Bran rose from his desk, a sleek, glass modern masterpiece from a high-end furniture store down the street, and went over to his window that looked over Central Park. The view usually helped soothe him, but not when he was faced with stupidity.

"What could possibly be going wrong? I want to sell your buyer hundreds of acres. He'll make a profit on it from turning it into houses, condos, or whatever the hell else it is that he wants to build in Montana. I really don't care what anyone does with it, as long as he buys it for the price we already agreed upon."

"Yes.... Of course you're right. There's just this man."

Rolling his eyes, Bran wondered why the world was full of so many idiots that seemed so ready to flock to him. "Frank, deal with it, or I'll find someone who can."

Bran heard yelling on Frank's end of the call and wondered what the hell could be going on there. "He has a shotgun. How am I supposed to get him off your land when he has a shotgun?"

"Call the police?" Bran suggested. Really, was there no one sane in Montana? He was half-convinced everyone crazy rushed right over there, if Frank was any example of the people who lived there. Generations of his family had owned the acres of land, but they were hardly anything to brag about, as far as Bran was concerned.

"I did." Bran heard Frank start up his car, one of those electric ones that hardly made any noise, but still sounded like a microwave working. "They aren't exactly friends of land developers either. I'm afraid he'll only speak to you. He's camped out on your grandfather's ranch and refusing to leave."

"Who is?" Bran asked him, wondering who this lunatic could possibly be who seemed to frighten Frank so completely.

"His name is Kaden Barker. Big guy with an accent and a shotgun. You can't miss him."

Bran sighed. From Manhattan to Montana on short notice was going to be a hellish plane ride, and expensive because he refused to fly coach…. Bran turned away from his view of Central Park and went back to his desk to order his tickets. "I'll be there tomorrow."

KADEN KEPT the shotgun cocked against his shoulder until the dust settled behind the weaselly little man driving down the farm track. The bastard intended to develop a casino on Tobias Wilson's land and apparently his grandson, Bran, who Tobias had talked about constantly, couldn't give a shit about that. After Tobi's passing a few months ago, Bran inherited the small dairy farm from his granddad, although the man hadn't even bothered to show his face at the funeral or on the farm since. Which is why Kaden hated his guts without ever having met the guy.

When the little blue car's tires hit the tar seal on the main road, the tension drained out of Kaden's body, and he lowered the weapon. He would do what he could to carry on the dream of the man he'd loved like his own blood, but if Bran kicked his ass off the place, there wouldn't be much he could do.

A scuffle of feet behind reminded him his two workers had witnessed the whole thing. The smiles on their faces as he turned around assured him they approved of his actions, and he chuckled.

"Righto, show's over. Back to work, you two."

"Hey, boss, you should've hurt him just a little bit." To get the day's dust out, Trent shook his shaggy blond hair, his blue eyes almost hidden behind the too-long wisps. At six foot two, he was tall and wiry, but strong as hell.

Beside him Samuel unfolded his meaty arms off his barrel of a chest. Gray eyes glinted in the morning sun, the expression in them colder than ice and a stark contrast to his black hair.

"Little?" Samuel grunted. "I'll wring his neck next time he shows up here."

"I wanted to hurt him so bad, but it would land our asses in jail, and that would suck." Kaden scanned the area around them—the milking shed and adjacent concrete yard, the surrounding paddocks and barns. He loved this place. If he had the means, he would buy it and make it his own, but with all his assets held up in his home country, New Zealand, it would be a few years before that could happen.

"Come on, let's get that feedout wagon loaded. The cows are waiting." As Samuel and Trent walked off to go do as he asked, Kaden opened his truck door and stored the gun behind the seat.

Why anyone would want to sell his grandfather's legacy, Kaden couldn't understand. The farm had been in the Wilson family for generations and the pride and joy of the men who had worked it. Literal blood, sweat, and tears had produced the successful dairy operation, and he would do what he could to save it.

AFTER SEVEN hours spent on planes and in airports, Bran was more than ready to get his business in Montana over with. He paid the high price the taxi driver demanded for driving him two hours away from the airport and stepped out of the air-conditioned car. Montana was still as desolate and heartbreaking as he remembered it being. With a sigh he shook his head and walked onto his grandfather's property. He hated this place and the memories he had of it, right down to when he'd spread his father's ashes over the south pasture.

Bran pushed those memories as far back as he could and headed toward the old farmhouse. It hadn't changed much in the years since he'd fled the place in search of the much greener pastures of Manhattan, but somehow he'd expected it to. The yellow paint, once so vibrant from the pictures he'd seen when it had first been built in the early 1900s, had faded considerably until it was barely more than a cream color with more paint peeling off of it than actually staying on.

He was more than ready to see the whole thing torn down and made ready for a casino. There was a man sitting on the cracked front steps leading up to the stained glass door. His grandmother had helped build that door, but the land had swallowed her up as well.

"Are you Kaden Barker?" Bran called out to him as he pulled his black suitcase behind him. It rattled over the gravel and dirt and kicked plenty of it up on his black slacks, further irritating him since he knew there was nowhere for him to get his clothes dry-cleaned here.

"No, who are you?" the man asked him as he rose from the steps.

Bran wasn't about to start answering the questions of a low-life farmhand. "You have three minutes to get Mr. Barker for me."

He didn't look impressed at Bran's snappish ways, not like the people in Manhattan did when he ordered them around. They were always so quick to obey him. This man simply stood there staring at him with a bottle of beer held loosely in his hands.

"Why?" he asked Bran.

"Because, unlike my agent, you will listen to me, because the police will come and throw your ass off my land," Bran nearly yelled at him as he tried to hold back on his growing frustration and rage.

"Can I help you?" The rich calmness of the sexiest voice Bran had ever heard rumbled from somewhere behind him.

Bran tried not to let his reaction to that voice, or the tightness in his gut, reflect in his voice as he turned to face a gloriously shirtless man wearing only loose, dirty jeans, and a beat-up cowboy hat, along with some scuffed boots.

"Unless you are Mr. Barker, no."

"And what if I am?" The highest quality Swiss chocolate was no match for the gorgeous brown eyes looking back at him with challenge. Confidence, strength, and raw masculinity oozed from every pore on the man's body. Bran hadn't prepared himself for this.

Bran narrowed his gaze at the man and stepped toward him, trying to intimidate him even though he had a good four inches and at least five years, if not fifty pounds of muscle, on Bran. "If you are Mr. Barker, and not just some Australian idiot wasting my time, then I suggest you pack up your things, call yourself a taxi, and get off my land."

The other big lug behind him coughed, but Bran ignored him. A small muscle started ticking in the jaw of the sexy man standing in front of him. "Now those are fighting words, mate! I am not an Australian, so get your accents straight, yeah. I'm a Kiwi, and in case that doesn't ring a bell or high school geography seems to be a distant memory, it means I'm from New Zealand. Two completely different countries separated by lots of water."

Bran wanted to roll his eyes at the man's reaction but thought it might have come across as childish. "Whatever. Still haven't told me your name, not that it really matters much. You—" He looked to the man that still stood with a beer in his hand by the steps. "—and your… friend, are both trespassing on my farm. I want you gone. Now." If the man was going to respond to him in any fashion, he didn't get the chance as Bran's phone began ringing. "What?" he snapped into it.

"Fucking hello to you too, asshole," Chris, his lawyer and best friend since college, replied.

Bran shook his head and looked away from the Aus—New Zealander. Fuck it, the Kiwi. He was too good-looking to stare at for long without risk of drooling like an idiot. "Not a good time, Chris. I'm kicking some wannabe cowboys off my land."

"Damn. I was hoping I'd catch you before you got to the farm. I've been calling you."

He had seen a few missed calls but figured it was Chris wanting betting advice or something equally time wasting, and a return call could wait until this business at the farm was concluded. Apparently he'd been wrong.

"My phone was off since I was on the plane, and I figured I'd call you after I was done here. What was so important that you needed to talk to be before I got to the farm?"

"You're not going to like this, Bran. Not at all. You can't kick him off. Kaden Barker, you can't throw him off the land. Nor the other two ranch hands, Trent and Samuel. I just looked over your grandfather's will, and if you force them to leave, then you'll forfeit any right you have to the land, the money… any of it. It'll go to some fucking charity."

Chris was right. He hated every bit of that idea. "Of course my grandfather would do that. He was far too soft for his own good. Fine. How long do I need to let them stay here? Three days to pack up their shit and get off my land?"

"Five years. This is a fucking nightmare, Bran."

Bran closed his eyes as a litany of curses ran through his mind, most of them directed at his late grandfather. "Any alternative?"

Chris laughed unhappily. "Either they stay there for the next five years, or however long it takes them to naturally quit or die off on their own, or you live on the land and work it for thirty days. That's it. There are no other choices. He had a really good lawyer do this will for him."

If Bran wasn't so angry in that moment, he might have wondered at what kind of a will would make his friend, who had years of experience in one of the busiest law firms in Manhattan, sit back in awe. As it was, he could barely form a coherent thought that didn't repeat the word *fuck* with little other variance in it.

"Find me a loophole. And quickly. I don't want to be here any longer than I have to be," he said before he hung up on Chris and turned back to the Kiwi who was still glowering at him. "Mr. Barker, I assume?"

"Yes, I'm Kaden. What do you want?" The frown made Kaden look dangerous.

Bran bit back his anger as he lifted his chin to Kaden, refusing to be intimidated by him. "My grandfather's will demands that I spend the next thirty days here, participating in the farm... activities before this place can be sold. While my lawyer works to find me a loophole out of this stupidity, I suppose we'll just have to get along, because I will be selling this land for far more than my grandfather ever thought possible. A glorious casino will sit on this godforsaken barren land, and you, and your two friends, will be back on the first flight out of here."

"Are you fucking blind? Look around you. This land is everything but barren, and the fact that you can compare what your family has worked so hard for with money, shows what a shallow asshole you are. You can't attach a monetary value to something precious, but I can see such a sentiment is foreign to you." The next moment a smile broke out on the angry man's face. "I can see Tobias knew that about you and outsmarted you at your own game. Bloody brilliant!" With that, Kaden stepped around him and opened the screen door before entering the house.

"Oh yes—find a bed somewhere. The master bedroom is mine, and don't you dare put your money-grubbing hands on the doorknob to your grandfather's room. You'll wish you hadn't." The screen door slammed shut with an echo as the last words reached his ears.

Dumbfounded to be threatened on his own property and told where to stay in his own house, Bran turned to the tree stump of a man standing a few feet away from him. "Is he for real?"

"Any more real and you'd lose those two pretty front teeth of yours, mate. Don't push him. It always ends bad when that happens." The man walked down the porch steps with heavy thuds before disappearing around the side of the house. What sounded like a motorbike started up, and the man drove past on an ATV, heading down one of the dirt tracks to who knows where.

Bran stood staring at the door like an idiot. All of a sudden he felt the exhaustion of the long flight, the stress of work and the farm business. As if he hadn't had enough, his granddaddy gave him a kick in the gut from the grave. Years ago, Bran had made it clear to Tobias he had no desire to be a farmer or to live on a farm, ever again.

Annoyed, and barely able to control his anger and frustration at the entire situation, Bran followed him inside. Being back in the home he'd grown up in was not a pleasant experience for him, though any time he spent there had been admittedly brief after he'd moved out at sixteen. He remembered counting down the days until he graduated high school that year and moved in with his mother. At the time she'd been an ad executive in Manhattan, which was probably why he'd stayed there even after her death.

He staunchly ignored the man sitting at the table as he headed up the stairs, his heavy suitcase clopping behind him on each of the steps. If any of them had been good people, they might have carried his bag up for him, he reasoned. But they were filthy ranch hands with no manners and even less class. He was looking forward to being done with them as quickly as possible.

He walked past the faded wallpaper and the old photos, many of himself as a child growing up on the farm, as he headed up to the second floor landing. The master bedroom was off limits, of course, because Kaden was a selfish prick. It didn't matter how long he'd taken to move his things in there after his grandfather's death, Bran knew, it was more that he wasn't the owner of the farm and yet had taken over the space that belonged rightly to him.

"Fucking perfect," he seethed as he turned and headed into his childhood bedroom, which was barely more than a closet and currently full of excess boxes and other useless random crap. With a shake of his head, he tossed his suitcase onto the bed and coughed as a light layer of dust lifted into the air. He was still coughing as he pulled out his inhaler and took a puff of the medicine he needed to be able to breathe correctly again.

Taking a few deep breaths, he looked at the dust and items stored around him. For tonight they'd have to stay. He was too damn tired to take care of it now. Unzipping his luggage with the intention of finding a towel and his toiletries for a much-needed shower, he jumped when a less than friendly tone addressed him through the door.

"Seeing as you interrupted our work this afternoon with your untimely arrival, get your ass out here so we can go finish up at the milking shed. The yard needs to be hosed down, and now is as good a time as any for you to learn. I'll see you down there in five minutes."

Bran's shoulders slumped forward, and he stared blindly at the contents of his suitcase. Fighting with Kaden at this point would be fruitless, and Bran knew the quicker he got the job over and done with, the quicker he could have his fucking shower.

The oldest clothes he had packed were a faded pair of jeans and a plain black T-shirt, which he changed into before storming from the cubicle of a room. Outside the door he found a pair of nameless gumboots, and after shaking the collected dust, twigs, and leaves out of them, he shoved his feet into them and clomped down toward the cowshed.

As soon as he entered through the little side gate, Kaden reached overhead and pulled a string, which started the water pump before he shoved the large blue hose into Bran's hands.

"The whole yard, the bails, and the pit need to be cleaned. Best you start." With a mocking smirk on his devilishly handsome face, the bastard walked off. He obviously didn't think Bran could hack it. He so loved to prove people wrong.

Twisting the front end of the nozzle, Bran watched the water spew out, almost jerking the pipe out of his hands. Madly groping for it, he managed to secure a strong grip and aim it at the concrete by his feet. Cow shit splattered him from forehead to ankles.

"For fuck's sake!" Spitting wildly to ensure no crap had entered his lips, he blinked through whatever stuck to his eyelashes and centered the powerful stream of water farther forward at a slight angle, and finally the manure started to shift. A delirious sense of accomplishment rushed through him.

About forty-five minutes later, he wanted to lie down in the mixture of poop and water to sleep. He could barely keep his eyes open. Trying his utmost to usher the last bit of watery crap into the drain hole, he stumbled over the hose lying on the ground and lost his grip. The hose instantly became a demon snake from hell about to beat him to death.

Bran tried to jump on it to keep it grounded, but it moved faster than he did. The heavy weight of the powered hose slammed into his hip, spraying water all over him before arcing into the air for another shot. This time the damn thing headed for his face, and he threw up his arms to protect himself, but the beating never came.

Slowly lowering his arms, he saw the hose lying on the clean concrete a few feet away. The powerful water turned off. Looking behind him he saw the three men watching and laughing at him. Kaden's hand still held the string of the pump in his hand, and he had come to Bran's rescue by turning the flailing hose off.

Having had enough humiliation for one day, he turned around and walked right past them out the gate and up to the house. His feet swam in his boots filled with water, but he honestly couldn't care less. Still, he didn't want to risk there being a mess for Kaden to blame on him and then make him clean up, so he kicked off the boots before going inside.

The delicious aroma of pasta sauce and basil assailed him when he jerked open the door and stormed into the foyer. His stomach growled intensely, but he had no intention of facing those three idiots again tonight. He'd rather starve.

He grabbed his toiletry bag and made a beeline for the bathroom. Once there he looked around with amazement. His grandfather must've enjoyed a few luxuries in his older days because the room had been renovated since Bran last visited. A large walk-in, wet floor shower sat in one corner. Several spray jets emerged from the tiles of the cubicle, and a seat had been fashioned against one wall.

Bran reached in and turned on the water, holding his hand under the spray until the temperature suited him. He stripped off his dirty, sodden clothes and stepped into the warm water. A groan of enjoyment left his chest. When last had he been this exhausted?

He took his time shampooing and conditioning his hair and washing himself. The heat soon made him sluggish, and not wanting to pass out in the shower, he switched off the water and stepped out. He reached toward the hook behind the door, but his towel wasn't there, nor anywhere else in the room. In his hurry to get away from the other men, he'd forgotten his towel in his room.

Only a small face towel hung by the basin. "Oh, hell no." Walking out of there naked was a hell of a lot more dignified than trying to cover his ass with that small square of terry cloth.

CHAPTER TWO

KADEN KNEW he shouldn't have been surprised by just how long a shower the city boy could take. He'd been selfish in everything else, so it only made sense that Bran would use up as much well water as he possibly could on himself.

Samuel snickered and helped himself to another serving of spaghetti. "Did you see his face?" Samuel laughed between bites. "All that cow shit might have been an actual improvement."

Trent howled with laughter, and Kaden grinned before digging into his own meal. But something was missing. "I think this calls for some bourbon," he declared as he rose from the table. Of all the things he'd fallen in love with in this country, bourbon was definitely near the top of the list. His friends gave a cheer, then went back to eating, as he headed up the stairs.

He was two steps away from the top when he saw Bran come out of the bathroom, dripping wet and completely naked. He seemed to freeze for a moment once he saw Kaden but then stormed past him, slamming the bedroom door behind him. But not before Kaden had caught a view of a rather nicely shaped arse. Grinning, he went into his bedroom and grabbed an open bottle of bourbon before heading downstairs again.

"Was that Bran slamming the door?" Trent asked him.

"Yeah." Kaden pulled down some glasses and poured them each some. They'd saved Bran a little dinner, but as they began to drink and continued to eat, it became clear that he wasn't coming down. So they split the rest amongst themselves. There was no reason to waste Samuel's good cooking.

Apparently full, after three large servings, Trent pushed his empty plate aside and put his elbows up on the table. "Only here a few hours and already he's more trouble than a bull during mating season. I don't like it."

Samuel shook his head, silently adding in his agreement of Trent's assessment.

Kaden nodded. "You're right. Not much we can do about it, though. You heard him. He stays on for thirty days, then we're gone." And the land was sold. It was something he'd been trying hard not to think about all day.

"It's shit," Samuel growled.

It was easy to agree with him. "That's enough misery for tonight," Kaden said, finishing off the last of his drink. It burned going down, but it made him feel a fraction better. They got up together and made short work of the dishes before he said good night to the guys at the front door.

"Do you want us to stay?" Trent asked him.

Samuel shifted his weight on the rickety steps and added, "In case he gives you any trouble tonight."

The idea of Bran actually giving him anything more than a headache was pretty laughable, but Kaden did appreciate that his friends were worried about him. "I'll be fine. See you both in a few hours." They didn't groan about the work as a child might, and as he expected Bran to in the morning, instead they nodded to him before riding away on the ATV down the dirt trail that connected the farmhouse with the little cabin they shared.

Kaden stood in the doorway for a few long minutes, savoring the quiet sounds of the farm as it slept. There were a few birds that were up that late, mostly hawks out hunting, but the land was largely silent. He enjoyed the peace and the way, in the darkness, everything seemed so right. It made him sick to think of a casino stretching out across the hectares. It would be a monstrosity. He tried to focus on better things, like calving season, but his mind kept coming back to the inevitable.

He went to bed a little while later, with miserable thoughts chasing him into his sleep.

AT FOUR thirty the next morning, the alarm on his phone went off, and he groaned as he rolled out of bed after a restless few hours of sleep. Before Tobias's death, he'd slept fine, but since then he'd been unable to stay asleep at all.

He showered quickly, not minding at all that the creak of the old pipes as hot water passed through them would likely wake Bran up. If the noises from the shower didn't do it, then him banging on Bran's door as soon as Kaden got dressed would definitely get him up. No one got to sleep in on the farm when there was work to be done.

At four forty-five he was dressed and standing in front of Bran's door. He tried knocking, at first, then banging. When it flew open, he expected Bran's irate expression, but not to see him dressed, and certainly not to hear him barking obnoxiously into his phone like one of the coyotes that frequented the farm near sunset.

"It's nothing, just one of the farmhands giving me my wake-up call like I'm an incompetent child who can't tell time. Find me something, Chris," he overheard Bran say. He could have left him there and trusted that he would come down when he was done, but Kaden didn't trust him anymore than he would a rattlesnake near the chicken coop.

"Work's starting," he said over the sound of whoever was talking just as loudly into Bran's ear. He couldn't make out the words, but the tone was obvious. Kaden wasn't the only person Bran annoyed.

Bran shot him a disgusted look. "And order me some clothes…. What kind? I don't know. Here, one second." Kaden was suddenly treated to the flash of a camera as he stood there, impatiently waiting for Bran to get off the damn phone so they could get to work. "There, that's the hand. Something like that…. No, you cannot have him. I don't think he comes in your size."

Kaden snickered and shook his head, but while he might have been amused at some unknown person finding him attractive, his patience was not endless, and there was plenty of work to be done. "Get off the phone, or I take it away from you," he warned Bran.

"Fine," Bran shot to him. "Chris, just do as I ask. Clothes, and find me some way to discredit my grandfather's will. He was old, likely senile, he drank, a cow probably kicked him in his head a few times. Find me *something*." He hung up the phone before turning back to Kaden. "Happy now?" He sat back down on the bed.

It was too early in the day to kill him, Kaden knew, but that didn't mean he couldn't be as hard on him as he possibly could be. "Your grandfather was a good man. You should have more respect for him."

Bran snorted as he laughed and got up from the bed he'd been sitting on to put on his shoes. "A good man? What do you, someone who only worked for him, know of it? I was his grandson, I knew him for all thirty-two years of my life, and you're going to tell me he was a good man?" He pushed past Kaden, who was trying very hard not to slam him into a wall for his attitude, before stomping down the stairs.

"Oh yeah, this next month is going to be a joy," Kaden said sarcastically to himself as he followed the biggest, most egotistical asshole he'd ever met, down the stairs to the kitchen. Where he found Bran sitting at the dining room table as if waiting for someone to serve him breakfast. "What do you think you're doing?" he snapped at Bran.

"Where is breakfast?" Bran asked him, just as nastily.

Kaden shook his head and snickered. "Out there in the chicken coop. Get up. There's work to do." Bran moved so slowly that Kaden wanted to pick him up by the back of his shirt and haul him out of the kitchen, but he resisted the urge and tried his best to find some lingering patience somewhere inside himself as Bran got up and went through the front door, which Kaden propped open to air the house out as soon as they were gone.

"Did you get a good view last night?" Bran snarked at him as they walked toward the chicken coop. They wouldn't be stopping there to collect the eggs and go right back in and eat them, if that was what Bran thought they were doing, but it was on the way to cowshed, and the chickens did need to be fed.

"Of your arse?" Kaden replied. He wouldn't pretend to be ignorant around him, and as Bran walked in front of him, it was easy to let his gaze fall right back down to Bran's butt as he walked around in jeans that were far too nice for farm work, but fit him just right.

Bran turned around so that Kaden was forced to look at his face and denied a look at his backside. "Or my dick. You could have gone away and given me some privacy. If you weren't an asshole."

Kaden shrugged. He wouldn't deny looking. "You were the one parading around like we're in some nudist resort. You want privacy, take a towel in with you."

Bran was still walking backward, so he didn't see a pile of feed pans behind him. When he fell over them, Kaden left him there to rot as he started tossing crumbles of food in for the chickens. Bran was getting to his feet and looking embarrassed and angry when Kaden was done with them.

Trent was in the middle of ushering the last few cows into the yard before shutting the gate behind them. Kaden switched on the lights in the shed and the pump room before turning on the milking plant. He made sure a new filter sock was in place, aware of Bran hovering behind him.

"Here are some milking aprons and vinyl gloves. I suggest you wear them to keep yourself from being splattered with muck like yesterday." He chuckled.

"Thanks for showing me these when I needed them." Sarcasm dripped from every word.

"You didn't ask."

Bran followed him as he walked into the milking area and climbed down the three steps into the pit. Cows lined up both sides, some dripping with milk.

Kaden glanced at Bran as he grabbed the first set of cups. "Look and learn, mate." He reached between the cow's back legs and attached a cup to each teat, before moving on to the next one. After cupping ten cows, he looked at Bran over his shoulder. "Your turn."

Skipping five animals, he left Bran to it and moved farther down the line and carried on. Bran surprised him by efficiently cupping the cows left to him before joining Kaden farther down the pit.

When Trent descended into the pit a few moments later, Kaden and Bran had a rhythm going, and it was working pretty well.

"Do you wanna go do some other chores, Trent? I think we can handle this." Kaden arched an eyebrow at the other man.

Trent grinned and nodded. "Sure thing. I'm positive I can find something to keep myself busy. See you at breakfast."

Together Kaden and Bran had a flow going, one he hadn't expected to find with Bran, or so soon. "Looks like you didn't forget everything," Kaden said as they finished up a row of cows.

Bran shrugged and got the cups ready for the next group of cows that were ready to come in. "It's coming back to me. I forgot how much I hated doing this." He pushed one of the cow's tails aside as he cupped them.

Kaden couldn't understand hating it, but then again he would probably be miserable in a big city like he knew Bran lived in. "Life for you in the city is a lot different than this, huh?"

Bran nodded and went to the next cow. Kaden had to admit that he was efficient, though he did fumble sometimes. "I left here as soon as I could, and until I got the call from the land developer telling me about you and some damn shotgun, I hadn't intended to ever come back here."

"Why were you in such a hurry to leave?" Kaden asked him as they finished up with the row.

He saw Bran's shoulders tighten and his expression sour. "That's not your business. I'm not your friend so don't try to become mine."

That was easy enough, Kaden figured, since he couldn't stand Bran. "You aren't half-bad when you've got your mouth shut while you're working. Or when you're naked."

He saw Bran's cheeks flame as he shot Kaden a glare. He wasn't going to pretend that Bran hadn't been walking around naked and maybe the reminder would get him to wear a towel when he came out of the bathroom next time. He was tempting, when he wasn't being a pain in the ass, and Kaden didn't need someone like him parading around naked and distracting him from his work for the next month. Not unless he could gag him so that he didn't have to listen to him whine. Bran had a way of being annoying without even seeming to try.

"We're done," Kaden called out as the last of the cows were released from the milking shed. "This place needs to be hosed down. All walls, all floors. Cold rinse, then hot acid wash. Then cold rinse again to remove any traces of chemicals. We do a hot alkali on Mondays and Thursdays. Read the instructions if you don't know how. Think you can do that?"

Bran sighed loudly. "I don't exactly have a choice."

Kaden smirked and moved to turn on the water. "No, you don't." He didn't mind supervising Bran in the least, and though the sour expression was still on his face when he was done, it was better than seeing him covered in cow shit, or smelling like it, as he had the night before.

"I hope you threw out your clothes from last night," Kaden called to him as Bran began hosing everything down.

"Two-hundred-dollar outfit, gone just like that," Bran confirmed for him.

Kaden shook his head at the tone Bran was using. He sounded more upset about whatever clothes he'd been wearing the night before than Kaden had heard him sound when talking about his grandfather, a man who had talked about Bran all the time. Admittedly it wasn't always positive, since he resented Bran for refusing to work the farm, but Kaden was sure that Tobias had loved his grandson up until the day he'd died.

"You're done. Let's go to breakfast," Kaden called to him when the milking shed was clean. Bran looked relieved and hurriedly took off his apron and gloves.

When they reached the house, the delicious smell of bacon, toast, and eggs reached Kaden's nose. "Damn, I'm starving." Bran's stomach growled loudly beside him as if it agreed. "You must be too after skipping dinner last night."

Bran quietly followed him into the house and the bathroom where he waited his turn to wash his hands and forearms clean of any remaining dirt. Kaden took his seat at the table as Trent put the large bowl of scrambled eggs down on it.

Expecting Bran to be his usual cocky self during the meal, Kaden almost felt disappointed when the subdued man joined them and helped himself to some food. Kaden ate slowly, savoring the break before they had to get back to work. He kept looking at Bran, though, who was being unusually quiet. Well, as far as Kaden knew, he was being more quiet than usual. But, really, he'd known the guy less than twenty-four hours, and there was no telling what he was really like.

"You did good out there," he told Bran.

Bran glanced at him. "I don't need you to tell me that I can put cups on a cow's teats."

Beside him, Trent looked like he wanted to say something, but Kaden put his hand over Trent's wrist, stopping him. He saw Bran look between himself and Trent and knew that the gesture hadn't gone unnoticed, but Bran didn't say anything as he quickly finished eating and got up to wash his dishes in the sink.

"Come get me when there's some other piece of work that needs to be done," he said before storming up the stairs.

"He's a piece of work," Samuel grumbled. "What is his problem?"

Kaden shook his head as he heard Bran lie down right above them. The old house wasn't that good for hiding sounds, and a few minutes later, he heard Bran talking on the phone with someone. He sounded angry, and Kaden went back to eating.

"I can't believe he was related to Tobias. Bran is a little shit. And Tobias…."

"Tobias was a good man, who loved the animals, and the land," Trent filled in for him.

Trent was right. Tobias had been the best kind of boss to them. And now Bran was there to piss all over generations of his family's life. Kaden couldn't believe it.

After breakfast was over and they'd cleaned up their dishes, he went upstairs to fetch Bran again. His door was open, so Kaden pushed it a little farther open with his foot and found Bran on his laptop.

"Hi. The horses need tending to. And we need to check the fences."

"I can't deal with the horses," Bran said as he kept typing.

Kaden folded his arms across his chest. "Why not?"

Bran turned to look up at him. "Because I'm allergic to them. Because, if I happen to have an allergic reaction out here and my injection doesn't work to stop it, there isn't a hospital within a hundred miles of this godforsaken farm. So I'll go check fences. But I'll do it in half an hour when I finish this negotiation."

"Negotiating for a new personality?" Kaden snapped at him.

Bran shook his head and turned back to his computer. "No. For a multimillion dollar company. I'm going to break it up into little pieces and sell it off to whoever wants it."

"And the people working there?" Kaden should not have been surprised that Bran would be so callous about destroying a company, which was probably important to someone out there, just as Tobias's dairy operation had been to him.

"They were fired months ago before negotiations started. I don't like complications like that hanging around when I'm trying to buy out a company." Bran shrugged, the hardships of other people clearly meaning nothing to him.

"Heartless prick," Kaden muttered before turning away. "You've got ten minutes before I drag your skinny ass back outside."

"You didn't think it was skinny when you ogled it last night," Bran struck back, but Kaden chose to ignore him. It was either that or smacking the man upside the head, and at this point Kaden tried to avoid violence as much as he could.

CHAPTER THREE

EXHAUSTED, LATE that evening, Bran barely pulled himself through the front door. He was sore from working on fences, from milking more cows, from fixing the chicken coop… from doing far more labor than he could ever remember doing in a day. The smell of barbecuing steak hit him square between the eyes, and his stomach revolted.

Staring at cows all day, milking them, and feeding their babies meant he couldn't fathom having a piece of that on his plate. Not tonight anyway. Normally he could have a steak rare, then ask for more, but tonight it wasn't going to happen.

"Dinner," Kaden called to him.

Bran shook his head and took out his phone as he headed upstairs where he collapsed on his bed. He slipped off his shirt while the slow Internet tried to find him somewhere that delivered. Usually he disliked delivery food, but he didn't have the energy to keep his head up while eating in a restaurant. And he didn't have anything left that was nice to wear, or any more shoes that didn't seem to have cow shit permanently ground into their soles just from walking around the farm.

Having his shirt off felt better, and he stretched his arms over his head while the delivery website loaded. Nothing was within distance, so he found a Thai place and called them, hoping for the best.

"Hello, take out or delivery?" the man on the other end of the line asked him.

"How much for you to deliver to the Wilson dairy farm off Route 29 and County Road 221?" Bran asked him as he rubbed his hand over his face.

"Uh…. According to my map that's over an hour drive. We don't deliver that far out."

Bran shook his head. "No. How much for you to deliver to me?"

"The food would be cold…," the guy tried to argue.

Despite the man's reluctance, Bran knew what his money could make people agree to. Nothing horrible, he wasn't a mobster or anything like that, but he did enjoy nice things and getting his way.

"I'll order something cold. And I don't really care how much it'll cost either. Just bring me food. Everything cold off your menu. And don't skimp on summer rolls. With extra peanut sauce. God, I'm hungry." And he was particularly miserable because his stomach growled, and his head began to swim as his exhaustion combined with hunger and his lack of sleep.

"One hundred and thirteen dollars. And twelve cents," the man on the other end of the line said, almost sounding apologetic about the price.

Of course it was. Not that Bran could bring himself to care very much at that point. "Sure. Here's my credit card number." He rattled it off when the man was ready. "So how long?"

"Hour and a half to two hours." Again he sounded apologetic. Bran wished he would stop that. He had known what to expect when he placed his order.

"Fine. Thanks."

He hung up the phone and lay down to wait for his food to come, but Kaden stood in his doorway, watching him like a perv. "What?" he barked at Kaden.

"You need to eat dinner," Kaden told him.

"I took care of it." Bran closed his eyes and folded his hands over his stomach, right above the waist of jeans that were a bit too big for him and hung around his hips. He might have been showing too much, especially since he hadn't bothered to put on briefs that morning, but since Kaden had already seen him naked and Bran was too tired to care, he didn't bother to do anything about it even though his blanket wasn't more than six inches from his hip.

He heard Kaden move away from his doorway. "Put your shirt back on," he called back, making Bran smile. If Kaden had an issue with him not having a shirt on, when he was in his own room resting at the end of a horribly hard day, then that was his problem.

When the food arrived, a good two hours later, he found the three of them drinking together in the living room while watching TV. The living room was right next to the front door, so seeing them, or being seen by them more accurately, was unavoidable. He also hadn't bothered to put his shirt back on when he had come down to answer the doorbell.

"Who is it?" Trent called to him.

"My dinner." Bran opened the door and smiled at the wary delivery driver. "Hi. Thanks for coming out here." He had some cash on him and quickly handed it over for a tip. He wasn't filthy rich, not like his best friend's father was, or that the amount of money he traded in would lead people to probably believe, but he enjoyed his life and didn't worry about things. There was certainly no need for him to hang on to the cash when he could use it to make the driver's two-hour round trip less miserable and make him more agreeable to delivering in the future.

"Thanks. The owner said that if you wanted to, you could order from us again anytime," the driver told him.

That was comforting, especially if these ranch hands insisted on eating steak more often. He could handle bacon or sausage in the morning, but in general he largely ate sushi and salads when he was at home and when entertaining clients. Occasionally he would indulge in red meat, but the only person he even ate fried food—or pasta, for that matter—with was Chris.

He went to the dining room table and started laying out his dinner. He didn't even really know what he'd purchased, but as soon as he found the summer rolls, he stopped opening Styrofoam containers and dove into them. He could see Kaden watching him from the living room as he also looked at the TV, but most of his attention was on Bran.

"What?" he called to Kaden, annoyed at the staring after he'd finished off the sixth roll.

Kaden shrugged. "Didn't think you could eat that much."

Bran slurped some cold noodles into his mouth and tried to ignore Kaden, but it was hard to do when Kaden kept looking over at him every few minutes. "Seriously, it's not a fucking peep show, you pervert. Look somewhere else."

He saw Kaden blush, only a little, which was a bit satisfying, but Samuel gave him a glare like he should be watching himself, or his mouth, which was such utter bullshit since Kaden should be the one not being a creep and staring at him while he ate. He ate as much as he could, which was barely a fifth of what he'd ordered, then found a place for the rest in the fridge before starting to head back upstairs to his room.

"You can watch TV with us. You don't have to hide in your room," Kaden called to him when he'd already started up the stairs.

Rude or not, Bran had no interest in spending time with the three of them. He had to when he worked, because he was sure his grandfather had put some kind of clause into the will to make sure he was actually productive for this month, but that didn't mean he wanted anything to do with them otherwise.

He left his door partially cracked, to get some airflow in, and opened up the single window in the room as well. It was nice, now that most of the dust was gone from it, even though it was still ridiculously small for a bedroom. There was no getting over how incredibly cramped his childhood room was. As a kid, and even a teenager, it hadn't been impossible to deal with. But now, being back in here, there was just too much there, and he felt like his memories of the place were nearly suffocating him.

It was still fairly early for him, though the lack of sleep from the night before and knowing that he'd probably have an early morning again, made him decide to call it a night. He fucking missed his own bed, though, especially as he stripped off his pants and lay naked between the hard sheets. They weren't his sheets, it wasn't his bed, and the lumpy pillows were not anything like what he would have had for himself.

Before he was fully asleep, he heard the stairs creak behind him and turned over in bed to see Kaden coming up to the landing and turning off the light that was right outside of his door in the hallway that ran between their rooms and the bathroom. If Kaden saw him looking back at him as he paused outside of his partially open door, he didn't say anything. And if the sheet happened to slip down his hip a little, Bran didn't bother pulling it back up.

BEING FORCED to wake up at four thirty in the morning was shit, and by the second day, Bran was pretty much over it. He'd woken up to a text that told him his clothes would be there sometime that morning, and that there was nothing in his grandfather's medical records, which Chris assured him he'd gained access to completely legally, that would let him disqualify the will. That bit of news had left him feeling annoyed even before Kaden had come over to pound on his door.

"I'm awake," he said, throwing a pillow at the man.

Kaden looked irritated, and Bran felt the same way. "Then get up."

Bran sat up but didn't get out of bed. That was mostly because he was still naked under the thin sheet, and Kaden was standing in his doorway. "Find me something else to do. Something that doesn't involve milking the damn cows or mending fences or some other tedious task that hurts my hands."

"Excuse me?"

He'd heard him, Bran knew he had, and at four in the morning, he wasn't up to repeating himself, so he groaned and flopped back down onto his lumpy, awful pillow.

Of course Kaden wouldn't simply leave him the hell alone. No, that would have been too easy. Instead he came into Bran's room and yanked on his sheet. "Get up. You have work to do."

Bran grabbed Kaden's wrist with his right hand and squeezed him as hard as he could, making the other man stop. "I'm naked under this sheet, so unless the work you want me to do is suddenly as your personal fuck toy, I suggest you get the hell out of my room."

Kaden blanched and pulled back, which was gratifying for Bran, and even more so when he stumbled into the wall in his hurry to leave the room. Once Kaden had closed the bedroom door, Bran took his time getting out of bed. He figured Kaden wouldn't be coming back in to bother him anytime soon, so it was nearly six by the time he'd gotten dressed, found a pair of clean socks that matched, and finished answering the e-mails he'd received overnight.

When he came downstairs, he actually had the house to himself, which was a hell of a relief. But that didn't last long as Kaden came back in a few minutes later while he was microwaving some water to make instant coffee. It was a poor substitute for the lattes he generally enjoyed in the mornings, but he'd take what he could get right now.

He lifted his eyebrows at Kaden, waiting for him to tell him how late he was, how he wasn't going to wait around for him, or whatever other utter bullshit the ranch hand liked to spiel, but he didn't say anything as he came over and started making himself some coffee too.

"The cows are good," he said, as if he expected Bran to care how a bunch of cows were doing.

Bran shrugged and sipped his lukewarm coffee. The stupid microwave hadn't even made the water all that warm, even though the mug was nearly too hot to handle.

"Sorry I came into your room," Kaden continued.

Bran snorted and finished off his coffee. "No, you're not. You're sorry that you almost pulled the sheet off me and saw me naked. Again.

If you could have dragged me out of bed and shoved me into the milking shed, you would have." He rinsed the mug out and put it in the sink.

Kaden gave him a little smile. "Guilty. You do need to get out there, though. We're oral drenching for parasites and giving trace element vaccines today. On all three hundred head of cattle. Straight after they've been milked."

"Sounds lovely," Bran said sarcastically as he headed toward the shed. He remembered bits and pieces of caring for the cows, but just the things his grandfather or his father had shown him. And after a while his mom hadn't permitted him to do much at all. She had been the overprotective, loving sort of parent that he felt his father never was. And his grandfather had been far more focused on the cows and his farm to really bother with a kid running around.

It hadn't all been a miserable childhood, he remembered as he followed Kaden to a large barn with chutes set up in it that would hold the cows still while they worked on them. He remembered playing with a dog they'd found loose by the road when he was five. He'd named the dog Smoke, because he was a dark gray beast with fluffy fur. He'd had a pony, once, before his allergies had really kicked in, and had galloped him all over the fields, chasing the cows until he'd gotten in trouble for bothering them during calving season.

And then there had been the times with his mother where they would sit quietly together, and she would make him tea, and they would read side by side on the old swing that used to hang on the back porch and overlook the bull pen. Those had been the good times, the ones he had focused on when he'd been reminded of this place and all its awfulness. But those memories had been few and far between, especially after she'd left and told Bran that he couldn't go with her to live in New York City.

"Looks like somebody finally decided to get up," Trent called to him as they approached.

Bran hoped the cow Trent was currently cupping would kick him in the head. "What do you want me to do?" he asked Kaden instead of responding to Trent's taunt.

"We'll start on this side, and you follow me down. As soon as Sam and Trent take the last set of cups off, I'll drench them into the sides of their mouths, and you can jab them after I'm done. So, we'll work down the rows in this narrow walkway in front of the cows. We'll do each row that way until they've all been done. Or you can drench? Which are you more comfortable with?"

Neither, was the right answer. But Bran could tell that Kaden expected him to do something, so he said, "Injecting. I guess." It was either wrestle the cow's head into a position where he could slip the drench nozzle down to the back of their throats, or stab the cows with needles. In that scenario he would much rather not fight the massive beasts. His whole damn body already hurt from head to toe, and he didn't need to add to that.

Kaden gave him a nod, and they started. Despite the early hour, it got hot quickly. Or maybe it was that he was doing something that was actually physical, but after an hour of it, he had his shirt off and kept having to wipe the sweat out of his eyes.

"Why couldn't he have been a rabbit farmer?" Bran grumbled as the completed row of cows walked out.

"Because there's no profit in rabbits?" Kaden suggested before he went around to the opposite row and continued the treatments.

Bran shook his head as they got to work. "I've got news for you, there's no real profit in cows either. Nothing that is livable anyway."

"I don't know about that," Kaden growled in exertion as he drenched the next cow while its head was tightly lodged in the crook of his arm. "Your grandfather seemed to do pretty well for himself."

If his grandfather's finances were that impressive to Kaden, Bran had no doubt selling the place off would be a good thing because he knew the margins his grandfather had been living on, and they were measly. The bank had sent over his grandfather's records when he'd been named the heir of the estate, but not executor of the will. That honor went to some lawyer he'd never met but had talked to a few times over the phone. He operated out of an office a few hours west of the farm. Apparently good lawyers were just as scarce as decent delivery restaurants when it came to the farm.

"My grandfather was a stingy old bastard. The only bit of money he ever put into the place that wasn't spent on cows or even more equipment, which, let's face it, is mostly worthless junk now, was put into that ridiculous bathroom of his," Bran snapped at him. The heat, plus how little he actually enjoyed physical labor, was working to make his temper much easier to lose. If his clients could see him now, they'd likely have no idea what was wrong with him, since he was normally so cool under pressure, but being back in this place, with these people, was already driving him over the edge.

Samuel's head suddenly popped up from the pit where he cupped cows, his dark brows pulled together in a dark vee. "Hey, don't be an asshole about it. Kaden did that whole bathroom for your grandfather himself. With his own money."

Bran looked from Samuel to Kaden and waited for him to deny it. He said nothing, so that was as much of a confirmation as he figured he was going to get. "It was a waste of money. If you were going to invest in the house, there are other, better, rooms to spend the money on that would have brought you a better return on investment if any of the money from the sale was going to go to you. But that won't matter at all when it gets torn down in less than a month anyway."

Kaden shook his head at him. "You are such a selfish prick. Don't you ever think about anything but money and how much you're going to get when you sell off this land to build a damn casino?" Bran opened his mouth to argue with him, not that he had any idea what he would have said since Kaden was right, when Kaden glared at him. "Go. You're dismissed for the day. I don't want to see you down here again until tomorrow."

That was more than fine with Bran, and he bent to pick up his shirt from where he'd left it in the dirt. "Good to know that all I have to do to get out of work is piss you off. Thanks for the tip." He gave them all the finger as he marched back to the house. Not even seven in the morning and he was done for the day, which was perfect as far as he was concerned. He showered, then wrapped a towel around his waist and headed back downstairs to have some of his leftover Thai food for breakfast.

The doorbell rang as the three of them were coming in an hour later, probably for breakfast. Bran knew he should have put some pants on, but he'd been too engrossed in a news article about the rising cost of real estate in the city to notice much aside from that his Thai food didn't taste nearly as good the second day around. His towel slipped a little as he got up from the dining room table to answer the door, but at least it stayed on. He said nothing to them as he opened the door, though the cute delivery guy did give him a pretty thorough once-over.

"Mr. Wilson? I have a package for you," he said.

The cheesy line, so typical in the porn he watched sometimes, made him smile, and he kept one hand on the towel, holding it tightly around his waist so that he didn't end up flashing them all, as he signed for the box Chris had promised him.

"There you go. If you want, I can bring it inside for you. I could put it in your bedroom," the delivery guy offered suggestively.

Being hit on was a nice change from being treated like an incompetent child running loose around the farm, but he wasn't really in the mood to entertain that offer. "Thanks. But I think I can manage one little box of clothes."

"Sure thing." He stepped back, making Bran crouch down to get it if he wanted it since the guy was clearly not going to make things easy for him. He played these games plenty well himself back home, and while he was down there, practically on his knees in front of the delivery man in only a towel, he looked up at him and licked his lips a little. The guy blushed, and Bran was left grinning and barely holding back a laugh as the guy backed away as if afraid Bran was going to bite him.

Only he figured out it wasn't him that the delivery guy was trying so hard to get away from when he got up and ran smack into Kaden's chest. "What the hell? Don't stand right behind someone!" he snapped at Kaden before stepping around him. "Shit! Were you raised in some kind of a shed or something?"

"You shouldn't let people talk to you like that," Kaden called to him as Bran grabbed his towel with one hand and tucked his box under his arm with the other before heading up the stairs.

Bran rolled his eyes, but he did stop on the stairs to look down at Kaden, who hadn't moved from his place in front of the open door. "Like what? Like I'm an attractive gay man in his thirties wearing a towel? Here's a tip. Don't try mothering me. It won't work out for you."

Kaden pursed his lips together, and Bran kept climbing the stairs. He used his shoulder to push the door closed, then tossed the box onto the bed. He could hear the three of them talking downstairs, probably about him, but he tried hard to ignore their voices as he opened the box of things he so desperately needed.

There was a note on top, simply saying *Love you too, Asshole,* which Bran promptly tossed aside in favor of the goods Chris had sent him. The jeans were nice, though cheaper than he normally wore. They'd probably be ruined by the time the month was over, so he supposed he could deal with the coarser fabric until then.

Some socks, a few pairs of red briefs with hearts on them in a size too small for him made him roll his eyes, but it was the bright neon pink, purple, and orange shirts that had him gritting his teeth. Whatever, he had to wear them since he had nothing else. The jeans fit, the socks were good quality, but in addition to being the ugliest colors known to man, Bran found out that the shirts were also at least a size too small for him. He looked like he was trying to qualify for one of those bodybuilder magazines with all of his muscles exposed. He took pride in his body, but he wasn't about to go around wearing shirts that made it look like he craved attention and was flamboyant to boot. How in the hell were the three men downstairs supposed to take him seriously while he was wearing skintight neon pink?

He stomped down the stairs, his phone already in his hands and dialing Chris before he got out of the house. "What the fuck? Do you hate me or something?" he snapped at Chris as soon as his best friend picked up.

Chris laughed at him. "So it sounds like you got the box of clothes. And the shirts. You like them? I thought they were very you."

Dirt flew up from his shoes as he paced. "I'm going to strangle you. I swear to God, Chris, I am going to fucking murder you when I get back home. Pink? Purple? You thought pink and purple would be good colors for me? And the fit...." He shook his head and looked down at his stomach, where his very visible abs were. "Seriously? What did I ever do to you?"

Snorting, Chris said, "Well, in this conversation you've threatened to kill me. Twice. If I didn't know how much you hated to get dirty, I might actually be afraid, though just a tiny bit. It is you we're talking about here. Maybe you should be nicer to the people that you ask for favors from if you want clothes that will actually fit you correctly. Maybe then more people would like you."

Bran went over and leaned his arms on one of the fence posts as he looked out at a bull grazing in his pasture. "I don't want people to like me, you moron. I want to be back home, in my apartment, with my own bed and my own coffee. I'd settle for a hotel right now. One of the good ones. I'm not desperate enough for random cum stains on the sheets yet."

"Is it that awful? Really?" Chris asked, suddenly sounding concerned.

Bran turned his head at the sound of the back door opening and watched as Kaden and his men headed back out to do more work. "Yes, it's horrible. They're Neanderthals. They probably poisoned my grandfather to make him die faster or something."

"You don't actually believe that."

Bran looked away from Kaden and the others to focus on the bull again. At least the bull didn't have the troubles Bran was currently experiencing. "No. I don't. And besides, if they did, what does it really matter to me? Not like I cared about him."

"I know. Look, Bran, I love you, but I do need to get some work done. You're not my only client, and you can't call me every day during working hours when you decide to have a hissy fit."

"I'm not a child. I don't have fucking hissy fits," Bran grumbled.

Chris chuckled. "Yes, you do, but I adore you anyway. Find some way to get along with the barbarians. They must be good for something. At least the one was decent to look at. Go get laid while you're there. And look for a box tomorrow. You'll like what's in it this time. I promise. No more awful shirts. A few things that will probably fit well too. Now, who loves me?"

Bran grinned. "I do. Don't let Manhattan burn down without me there. Please? I miss being home so much. This place is horrible."

"Manhattan will still be here when you get back in less than a month. Stop being a baby. Find something fun to do."

That made Bran snort as he shook his head. "Fun? You've clearly never been to Montana."

"No, I haven't. But go be a cowboy, well, no. You're allergic to horses. Even the ones that pull the carriages make you start sneezing like a crazy person if you get too close to them. They have guns there. Go shoot something. Have an orgy. Rob a bank. Bran, really, I don't care what you do. Just find a way to get through the next month without losing your shit. Okay? Don't make me worry so much about you."

"Okay." One good pep talk from Chris and he felt like he could get through at least the next few days, if not the rest of the week, without wanting to strangle someone. "Thanks."

"Uh-huh. Go have fun. Bye."

"See you." Bran hung up the phone and thought about what Chris had said, about going to have fun while he was there. It seemed like an impossible task on the farm, but still he walked around, because being in his room all the time felt claustrophobic, and eventually found his way over to a large pasture where the heifers grazed peacefully. He didn't go in with them because he wasn't that interested in smelling like cows all afternoon, but he did climb up on the fence, prop his foot up on the railing to get comfortable, and laid his hands over his knee as he watched their behavior.

It all seemed so serene, and yet his head and heart were in turmoil. This place, these people fucked with his head, and he needed to leave. Soon.

Chapter Four

WHEN BRAN walked into the kitchen the next morning for his cup of coffee before milking, Kaden did a double take. Then he didn't know if he should laugh or cry. Bran wore an ordinary pair of jeans, but on his upper body, a neon pink T-shirt appeared spray-painted onto his skin. Right above the waistband of the jeans, a tanned band of skin peeked out, despite Bran continuously pulling the fabric down while making his hot drink.

"Not one fucking word, thank you very much," Bran said with his back to Kaden.

When he turned around, Kaden tried not to look but failed. Horribly. Despite Bran being a conceited dick and annoying the living shit out of him, Kaden's eyes and body didn't care one bit what his brain seemed to think. Beneath the glaringly loud shirt, Kaden could see the outline of two hard nipples. The morning could be cool in Montana after all.

A sexy, inny belly button showed above the denim button, and Kaden felt robbed when the fabric stopped his visual feast from continuing farther down.

If Kaden could hate everything about Bran Wilson, his life would be incredibly easy, but since the man's unwelcome arrival on the farm, Kaden had been fighting a battle almost daily. He was no hypocrite and avoided lying to himself—Bran turned him on. Big-time. If this outfit was a joke, Kaden for one didn't find it funny at all.

"Where's the other half of your shirt?" When he made eye contact with Bran, a blush stained the man's neck and face.

"Hell hath no fury like a gay best friend scorned…," Bran offered in explanation.

"Aaah. Your friend, Chris, I presume? It looks like you piss off a lot of people." Averting his eyes to try to get his libido under control, Kaden downed the last of his own coffee and got up to rinse the cup.

Bran snorted. "No, many piss me off. Depends which way you look at it."

Kaden walked past him and barely managed not to stare. "Time to go. You're gonna be so uncomfortable working in that all day."

"At least I have a breathing hole," Bran deadpanned. Kaden couldn't help it, he laughed.

The morning milking went smoothly without any problems until the very last row. One cranky heifer kicked her cups off several times, and Kaden watched as Bran reached to drag them out from under her feet. She stomped around restlessly and stepped on Bran's hand, keeping it pinned underneath her hoof.

"Fucking hell!" the man yelled before slapping her rump with his free hand, causing her to shift her weight and lift her foot off his fingers. By the time Bran cradled his right hand with his left, Kaden stood beside him.

"You need ice on that immediately, or your hand is gonna be twice its size in a few minutes." Kaden reached out to have a closer look, but Bran flinched away from him with a horrified look on his pale face.

"Go up to the house. There's ice in the small freezer above the fridge. I'll finish up here."

"Thanks." Bran turned around and left the shed.

Kaden hurried as best he could to finish up the work. He worried at the extent of damage Bran's hand would've suffered with the cow's full weight on it. In most cases there was swelling and bruising, but seldom any broken bones. Hopefully that would be the case with Bran's injury.

With the shed cleaned, he ran up to the house. He found Bran in the kitchen, sitting on the counter with his back and head leaning against the wall behind him, while his hand soaked in the ice water filling the sink beside him.

Bran's eyes were shut, the pain visible by the small lines pulling at the corners of his full mouth and the frown drawing his dark brows together. Kaden haltingly approached and stood before Bran's spread thighs. He wanted to move between them but held back.

"Hurts like a bitch. I know," he offered lamely.

The left side of Bran's mouth lifted in a half smile, and he opened one eye to look at him. "Do you speak from experience?"

"Many experiences." Kaden stepped closer, now feeling the heat of Bran's body radiate through the fabric of his jeans. "Let me see."

Bran lifted his hand out of the ice, and Kaden grimaced. All the fingers except for the thumb were swollen, and below the skin, the dark bruising had begun to show.

Kaden gently caressed his thumb over the back of Bran's hand. Bran's sharp intake of breath made him jerk his gaze back to his face, afraid he'd caused more hurt by the gesture. Bran's eyes were wide open, his lips slightly parted as he breathed deeply.

The vulnerability in the stare undid him. He placed Bran's hand gently back into the icy water and stepped fully up against the vee of his thighs. He cupped Bran's face and kissed him. A soft touching of mouths. Feeling. Probing. Breathing.

When Bran's tongue snaked out to lick the top of his lip and flicked against Kaden's, all rational thought left him. Twisting his head, Kaden took full possession of Bran's lips, which parted with a soft moan of want.

Bran tasted wild… and wicked… and far too good. Kaden sucked on his tongue and explored his mouth. Bran let him be the aggressor until Kaden's right hand lowered to one of those tempting nipples that drove him crazy all morning.

Bran's legs clamped around his hips and dragged him closer. A wickedly talented tongue slipped into his mouth and stole his breath. Damn. The man knew how to kiss. The click of ice blocks sounded, and the next moment a wet hand gripped his shirt at his waist.

"Ow. Dammit!" Bran's exclamation broke the spell. Not for Kaden, but clearly for himself, because he shoved Kaden back and cradled his sore hand against his chest like a weapon between them.

"I'm sorry." Kaden knew his apology could have double meanings, but he wasn't apologizing for the kiss. Nothing that spontaneously good should ever be apologized for.

"It's not your fault. I've taken two painkillers, and I'm gonna go lie down for a bit to see if this throbbing will go away." If the situation hadn't been so awkward, Kaden would've joked and asked him which throbbing he referred to, but now wasn't the time.

His own dick throbbed too, but so did his heartbeat and his head. What a mess. He was attracted to the one man on this earth he should hate with his whole being. A man who stood for everything Kaden couldn't: greed, selfishness, pride, disrespect, disregard, and deception. Someone who felt nothing for anyone but himself, and still Kaden couldn't deny the attraction.

"Okay. I'll see you later."

BACK AT work he went through the motions, eternally grateful Samuel and Trent weren't there to grill him for answers. Very little fazed Kaden, and his two best friends knew that well. Kaden had met Trent when they started primary school together at their rural farm school not far from where they lived. Amongst the snotty little bullies and giggling girls, they had smiled at each other with two gaps where their two front teeth were to appear months later and stuck together from day one. Samuel on the other hand, moved onto the neighboring farm next to Kaden's parents' land a few months later.

In the rural countryside, sound traveled for miles at night, and it didn't take long for Kaden and his family to know that life on the neighbor's farm wasn't easy. One day while swimming naked in a creek at the end of their property, Kaden and Trent stumbled across a dirty, tired Samuel sleeping in the long grass under the shade of a tree hanging over the small stream.

The tear streaks and bruise on one cheek spoke volumes, and so did Kaden's mother when she threatened Sam's parents with a baseball bat if they ever laid a hand on that "poor, beautiful, boy" again. That had been the end of Sam's beatings, because he practically moved in the next day and never left, except to show his face to his parents every now and then and to get fresh clothes for school. At the age of fourteen, Sam's parents moved away, and he didn't go with them. As far as Kaden knew, he had never seen them again. Was it coincidence that all three of them turned out to be gay? Who the hell knew, and who cared. It suited them just fine.

Kaden didn't remember life without his two friends in it, and he wouldn't be able to hide this thing with Bran from them for very long. Trent could sometimes have his head in the clouds and be completely oblivious, but very rarely did Samuel's sharp gaze and perceptive nature miss anything of importance.

BRAN LAY in bed until he heard the doorbell ring. Clutching his hand to his chest, he went downstairs to see who it was but sighed as he saw the same deliveryman standing on the porch. Like Kaden, this guy noticed his shirt, and how little it left to anyone's imagination. Unlike with Kaden, Bran actually kind of minded the way this man's gaze lingered on him.

"Hi. Did I get something?" Bran asked him, his voice holding none of its usual snap. He couldn't manage it with his current pain.

"Yeah." The guy gave him a wide smile as he offered him a smaller box than the one Chris had sent him the day before, but the label still had Chris's perfect handwriting across the top. Bran knew what the parcel contained, and he couldn't wait to get a different shirt on.

Bran signed for it, then took it with his free hand, and waited for the guy to leave, but he wasn't as fast as Bran would have preferred. "You alone right now?" the delivery guy asked him, and Bran rolled his eyes at the creepy come-on.

"No. Bye. Thanks for the box." He closed the door in the guy's face before he could say anything more. "Creep," Bran muttered as he headed back upstairs. He really fucking loved Chris, he decided, as he opened up the box and found not only a few nice, plain black T-shirts inside that would be baggy enough to be comfortable on him, but also a bag of his favorite chocolates. He carefully changed his shirt, because of his hand, but once the other shirt was off and replaced with one of the new ones, he felt so much better as he curled onto his side and laid his head onto the lumpy pillow.

He was halfway through the bag of chocolates when the three of them came in for lunch. Since he'd binged on the chocolates, he wasn't all that hungry, but he was tired of lying in his room and not doing anything, so he came down to the kitchen and sat at the dining room table with them. It was fairly easy to be near Trent and Samuel. He didn't suddenly want them. But Kaden he couldn't look at without feeling heat creep up his neck and go to his cheeks.

"How's your hand?" Kaden asked him, interrupting Bran's attempts at ignoring him sitting at the same table.

He'd been hiding it under the table, not wanting to show off the swelling or the bruising. "Fine." He should have brought down a book or something else to focus on and distract himself from Kaden. The man was an ass with no class, but what a nice ass it was. Bran forced himself not to think about it. Or the way Kaden's mouth had felt against his, all rough and possessive. He licked his lips subconsciously as his thoughts began to wander to whether that would translate into how he'd be in bed. Would Kaden take control? Be rough with him there too? Fuck he needed away from Kaden. First, though, he needed some ice-cold water.

"That one heifer, seventy-one, I've put her in the paddock behind the house. She's about a week overdue and looks about ready to pop. I hope it's not twins for a first-timer. How long until you want to call the vet in to check her out?" Samuel asked Kaden as Bran got up to get some water from the fridge. He saw Kaden watching him and ignored his heated look as he bent down to get out a drink.

He grabbed a pitcher from inside the fridge and came back out as quickly as he could. With Kaden sitting right by the fridge, he wasn't more than a foot from him, and it wasn't helping.

"Give her another three days. Thanks for bringing her closer so we can keep an eye on her," Kaden said.

Samuel nodded as if he agreed, and Bran finished getting himself a drink. He escaped nearly to the stairs when Kaden stopped him. "Aren't you going to eat something?"

Damn, he'd been so close to not having to talk to him. "Already did." It was only chocolate, but Bran generally didn't eat as much as these men seemed to when he was at home. Probably because he didn't need to. He didn't really work like they did.

"You're in charge of dinner, since you can't work with your hand," Kaden told him as he started heading back upstairs.

Bran shrugged and leaned against the wall beside the stairs. "That's fine. I'll order something." Kaden made a face, like that wasn't really what he'd had in mind, but Bran wasn't about to start actually cooking anytime soon. He didn't even really cook for himself at home, unless tossing together a salad counted as cooking food.

"Any requests?"

"I didn't think all that many places around here delivered," Trent spoke up.

Bran shrugged. If it cost a little more to get food out there to them, then so be it. And if his hurt hand got him out of having to actually work, then that was even better. This was all a business trip anyway, and he'd write it off completely before he had to pay taxes the next year.

"Suggest something, or I'll order Indian food." He didn't know if there was an Indian restaurant anywhere in Montana, but once he'd said it, he was suddenly craving curry.

"Italian instead?" Kaden offered.

Nodding, Bran pulled out his phone and set an alarm for himself to remember to order food two hours before dinner to make sure it got there in time. It wouldn't be warm, but they had ways to heat it up.

"Bran?"

He turned to find Kaden not more than two feet from him, at the bottom of the stairs. "I need to go back to lying down. The pain, it's awful." His pain pills had kicked in, and it wasn't that bad, but getting away from Kaden in that moment was a necessity.

Kaden pursed his lips and took a step back. "Sure."

Bran tried not to feel like he was running away as he did exactly that. He lay down on his back, ate the rest of his chocolate, and tried not to listen to the three of them talk below. Their voices were muffled through the walls and the floor, but he imagined that they were talking about him, and he didn't like it one bit. He pulled out his phone and called Chris.

"Having another meltdown already?" Chris asked him once he'd picked up.

"Something like that."

"Wow, you actually do sound miserable this time. What's wrong?"

Shrugging, Bran sat up and went to the small window to look out. He watched Kaden and the others get on their ATVs to get back to work. "Nothing, just tired." It was a lie, and it felt weird to lie to someone he'd known for half his life like he had with Chris, but he couldn't really say what else was going on.

"The first week is pretty much over. Only a few hours left until the weekend. Hang in there for three more weeks," Chris encouraged him.

Bran nodded and turned away from the window. "Yeah. Three weeks. Thanks for the box today, by the way. Much nicer." If wanting Kaden as badly as he did now didn't end up killing him in three weeks, he could actually get through this. And then the farm would only be a distant memory and he could get back to Manhattan where he didn't feel so screwed.

"You're welcome. And I hate these stupid meetings. You know MacFarlain? He's divorcing his fourth wife. I'm so sick of handling his divorces."

"At least he pays you well," Bran said, smiling.

"Obscenely so. Call me later. And sound happier when you do."

Bran hung up the phone and tried to think of how he was going to accomplish that.

DINNER HAD been tense, followed by Bran going right back up to his room as soon as he was done eating. Kaden came up half an hour later, while Bran was trying to work but finding it impossible now that his pain medicine had worn off. It was too soon, according to the bottle, to take any more, but he was starting to think cutting off his hand might have been less painful than the stiff, broken feeling he was experiencing now.

"You don't have to hide in your room," Kaden said once he'd come to the top of the stairs.

That's exactly what he had been doing. "I'm not hiding, I'm working." Actually he was browsing his favorite chocolate maker's website to see what would be in their fall flavor collection, but while Bran was facing the doorway, Kaden couldn't see the screen of his laptop.

"The kiss...."

Bran looked away from his screen and wished he could be anywhere other than where he was in that moment.

"Yes?" he asked Kaden.

"It shouldn't have happened." And wasn't that just a kick in the gut?

Nodding, Bran turned back to his laptop. "Agreed." When Kaden continued to stand there, watching him from right outside the door, Bran glanced at him. "Anything else?"

"No." Kaden stepped away, and Bran pretended to still be working until he heard Kaden go back downstairs. He went to bed early, after taking more pain medicine, and putting some ice on his hand.

When Kaden was in his room, with the door closed behind him, Bran stopped pretending to be asleep and let himself drift back to that kiss, to the feeling of having Kaden between his legs, rubbing against him. Of being controlled, of his mouth being taken. He stroked himself slowly, enjoying the memory of having Kaden's mouth pressed against his. He'd felt more than wanted by Kaden. It was like he'd been desired, and there was a definite difference between the two for him.

His mind shifted from the memory of their kiss, to a fantasy of what he imagined being with Kaden could be like. He'd walk in the room, press him down without saying a word, and take him. There'd be nothing slow and sweet about it, just rough, needful sex, as Kaden claimed him.

Bran thrust into his hand and softly swore as he came into the shirt he had waiting nearby. He tossed the garment aside and sighed. He saw nothing wrong with having sex, when that was all it was, but he knew enough to realize that sex with Kaden wouldn't be just physical. And the attraction he felt for him, that seemed to have come out of nowhere, was enough to knock him back on his ass. He couldn't do this, couldn't give in, couldn't get out of bed and go right over to Kaden's room, less than ten feet from his own, and ask to be let into Kaden's arms, because there would be no recovering from what was building between them. Bran knew it would change him, and he didn't like change. Not one bit.

CHAPTER FIVE

WHILE THE others were outside the next morning, Bran went to go rest against a railing in a dry area of the closest pasture he could find. He'd entered through a gate, but why a thick, heavy chain kept it shut, he didn't know. As far as he could see, there were no cows in the pasture. He closed the gate up anyway, mostly so they didn't have a reason to yell at him. In the quiet moments, when he was certainly not, but probably, hiding in his room to get away from Kaden, he could almost remember the fun times he'd had while being a kid on the farm. But thinking about those times meant he also thought about his dad, and that was never a good thing.

He rested his back against the metal fence, which was easily over his head, so it had to be seven feet or more since, at a little over six feet, he wasn't exactly short. The wind, with nothing to block it for miles, whistled through the tall grass and whipped through his hair. He'd gone without mousse that morning after his shower. It didn't seem to make a difference since he didn't have to look good on the farm. He only had to work, and thanks to his hand, that meant ordering dinner. Despite the meals being pricey and the options limited, he'd choose the ten minutes he spent on the phone over the hours they took caring for the cows any day.

Pushing himself away from the fence as it started to get too warm on his back, Bran walked along beside it. It was a large pasture, maybe for pregnant heifers or young calves being weaned. He didn't remember the farm's layout well enough to know for sure. And there was no telling what had been changed since he left. He turned away from the north pastures once he started heading in that direction. He wasn't ready to go back there or to even look in that direction. That wasn't happening.

"Bran!"

"Oh for fuck's sake," he muttered to himself as he turned his head to see Kaden running toward him. "Can't I have five minutes alone?"

"I'm not working with the cows today!" Bran shouted back, lifting up his bandaged hand to remind Kaden he was still taking it easy.

"Get out of there!" Kaden shouted at him as he kept running.

Well, at least he was pretty when he ran, Bran thought as he ignored Kaden and kept walking. He wasn't working until his hand was better, and they could all kiss his ass if they thought differently.

The next moment Bran went flying as Kaden ran into him with the force of a milk tanker loaded to capacity. A surprised cry left his lips before changing into an "Oomph," as he came to a sudden stop. Unable to catch himself with his injured hand, he fell chest-first into the heavy metal railings of the fence and shuddered as he slumped down, putting his uninjured arm around his probably shattered ribs.

He glared up at Kaden. "What the ever-loving fuck is your problem?" he seethed.

But Kaden wasn't answering him. Instead he grabbed Bran's arm, and dragged him as quickly as possible, even when Bran stumbled, out of the pasture.

"My problem?" Kaden nearly shouted back at him. "Is that you were in the pasture with the meanest, most aggressive bull on the farm. And he could have killed you!"

Bran wouldn't have believed him, if he hadn't seen a massive black bull storm over a slight hill and look right at them. The beast breathed hard, telling Bran he'd had him in his sights on his way to do exactly what Kaden said. Despite the seven-foot metal fence between them, Bran still shied back. He'd never liked bulls very much, and that one looked meaner than most.

He tried to stand up but gasped when lifting his uninjured hand up to the railings brought pain shooting down his side, straight into his ribs. "Shit," he gasped.

"What, are you hurt?" Kaden asked him, reaching for his shirt, likely to pull it up. Bran didn't want to give him that chance.

"Again?" Trent grumbled. Samuel just shook his head.

While Bran focused on Trent and Samuel, Kaden managed to pull his shirt up a little. It wasn't much, only enough to be able to see his ribs before Bran figured out what he was doing and smacked Kaden's hands away.

Despite the pain he forced himself to his feet without help. "I'm going back inside."

"Did I.... Is that from pushing you to the railing?" Kaden asked him, his voice soft, the worry clear in his expression as he moved against him.

Bran pursed his lips and stared him down. "Oh, you mean when you threw me at a giant metal barrier and I couldn't stop myself from crashing into it because one of the fucking cows screwed up my hand? Yeah, it is from that. So thanks."

Kaden's face fell. "I was trying to protect you from the approaching bull."

"Don't," Bran said, moving away from him.

"Don't what?" Kaden called when Bran had managed to get a few feet between them.

"Anything," he shot back. He stormed into the house, grateful to be away from them, and took out some ice to make himself an ice pack. At this rate, they would need a damn freezer full of the stuff to nurse his injuries. No one followed him in, thankfully, and he went upstairs to call Chris. He desperately needed to hear his best friend's voice while everything seemed to be going to shit around him.

"Howdy," Chris said, making Bran smile despite the pain he was in.

"Don't do that. You sound awful."

Chris laughed. "Okay, deal. I was trying it out. So, anything horrible happen already today?"

There was so much to tell him, but Bran didn't want to get into it over the phone. And really, there was nothing that Chris could have done about it. "I needed to hear your voice." That wasn't a weird thing to say between them, not really anyway. "Needed someone friendly. You know?"

"You sound miserable. You okay?"

He really wasn't. "I shouldn't have come back here. It's just... I hate this place. I hate everything about it. I'm exhausted all the time." And in pain, but Bran wouldn't say that to Chris and make him worry.

"Bran, is it really worth it? The money, I mean? You could come home. They'd have the next five years on the farm, and then you could burn it to the ground if you wanted to. I'd even help you find a place that rented one of those big yellow things that we see along the highways sometimes. Not the bulldozers, but the other things with the scoops? Anyway, not important."

Bran heard the stairs creak as Kaden came up. He stood in the shadows outside of Bran's door, and Bran turned away, hoping he'd leave after a few minutes. He wished that just once he could have a little bit of privacy in the house.

"It is worth it. I'll be here for another three weeks, and then I will sell this property and leave and never, ever come back to Montana. I might not even leave the East Coast for a while. We might have to vacation in Miami or something this year."

"Okay. If you're sure," Chris said, sounding like he was still a little worried and not believing him.

Bran tried to smile, to force as much lightness into his voice so that Chris would stop worrying about him. He had his own issues to deal with. Bran was grateful they'd been able to talk between what seemed like his endless meetings.

"I'm okay. See you."

"Bye."

Bran hung up the phone and turned his head to see Kaden still standing there in his doorway. "Don't be creepy." None of his usual venom was in his voice. He simply didn't have the energy for that much of an effort.

Kaden came in, and Bran watched him come around the bed. "I wanted to check on you. Can I see your ribs now? Or are you still hiding?"

Shrugging, Bran reached down to the bottom of his shirt, because he sure as hell wasn't going to give Kaden permission to undress him, and lifted it up enough so Kaden could clearly see the large purple bruises already forming over his ribs.

Kaden shook his head and reached out to touch one of the large blotches marring Bran's side, but Bran shoved his shirt down before Kaden could put his hands on him again. It wasn't that he didn't want Kaden's touch. It was that he wanted him too much and didn't want to lose himself in another of Kaden's kisses.

"I'm sorry. I didn't mean to do that to you."

Bran nodded. He'd never thought it had been intentional. "I know."

"I didn't want the bull to get you," Kaden continued to explain.

"Yeah." Bran heard the back door open, and Trent and Samuel come in. "Break time?" he asked Kaden, who nodded.

"A quick lunch, then back to the cows. What are you going to order us for dinner?"

Bran gave him a little smile, because he was glad none of them had any illusions about him cooking for them. "Sushi."

Kaden made a face. "You do realize you're in Montana right? We don't exactly have a lot of ocean around here."

He hadn't considered that, since he was used to the freshest sushi imaginable. But now that he'd said it, he didn't want to give Kaden the satisfaction of being right. "Then make your own food. I'm ordering sushi."

"Suit yourself," Kaden said, backing away from him. "Are you coming down for lunch?"

Bran shook his head. Having Kaden so close to him, in the kitchen, where he could still feel Kaden's hands on him…. No. He wouldn't be going down for lunch.

"Fine. Do what you want."

Waiting until Kaden went back downstairs, Bran took some more pain pills and closed his eyes as he waited for them to kick in. A few hours later, he was trying to rest when he heard a strange sound. Carefully rolling off his bed, he looked out the window, trying to determine where it was coming from. Unable to see anything, he went into the bathroom, pushed open the window, and looked out.

There, in the paddock behind the house, was the cow he remembered Samuel mentioning before. The overdue heifer—and she was not happy, judging by the pacing going on. Bran decided to check on her, not wanting something to go wrong on his watch. The stairs appeared endless, and every step an agony as he walked. He went out the back door, then approached the fence where the heifer walked up and down restlessly. As she turned around, he saw there was trouble brewing. A thick gelatinous discharge hung out of her, but the yellowy color meant the calf was in distress.

"Fuck! Does all this crap have to happen in one day?" He swore under his breath as he headed to the farm storage room by the milking shed as fast as his sore ribs allowed. He didn't have Kaden's number, or the others', to be able to call them for help.

In the storeroom he knew what he was looking for the moment his eyes touched on it—the calving rope. His father had taught him how to use it the same day he told him the signs of a cow having calving trouble. How to spot it and how to fix it. Never in a million years had he thought he would apply that knowledge. Until today.

He also grabbed a sturdy rope to restrain the cow and some veterinary lube before hurrying back to the paddock. Being as quiet as possible, as not to startle her, and have to chase her across the pasture, he let himself in and, holding out his good hand, came up to her.

"Hey, cow," he said awkwardly. She appeared too dazed from pain to bolt, and she let him touch her. "That's a really big baby in there."

Working quickly, he fashioned a halter type knot in the extra rope and slip knotted it around the fencepost, giving her a bit of room to move so she didn't panic.

"Come on, cow, you and me gonna do this," he said. "There. Now, this is going to suck. I'll tell you that right now. And I haven't actually ever done this myself. But my dad—" He shook his head as thinking about him hurt. "My dad showed me this. I was ten, so bear with me. And please don't kick me. I'm bruised enough for one week."

Throwing the calving rope over his shoulder he pulled up his shirtsleeve as far as it would go and covered his arm with lube. He wasn't able to find the long gloves he would have preferred to be wearing. Quietly, he came up behind her, touching her on the rump to let her know he was there. She shifted a bit and flicked her ears but stayed put. He gritted his teeth and cautiously worked his hand into her, closing his eyes to concentrate on determining its position. At the same time, he tried hard not to think about how gross it was to have his arm, past his elbow, up the backside of a cow.

He shuddered at the smell, but focused on trying to find the calf's feet. "Okay, I found… something, maybe," he told the cow, who moaned quietly at the extra intrusion in her body. Every time she had a contraction it felt like his arm was being crushed in a vise, including his already tender hand, but he fought through the pain. He managed to find the calf's one foot, and identifying the little hocks at the back, he knew it was a back foot. He moved around to find the other. When he did, he realized it was positioned wrong. Okay, he could handle that.

Trying to picture it didn't really help him figure out how the calf was lying, so he used touch and hoped that he wasn't hurting the cow all that much. He gently turned her calf around with one hand until he found a front hoof and latched onto it, pulling it out slightly and attaching the one loop of the calving rope until it was behind the first leg joint. He repeated the process when he managed to locate the other foot. With both loops of the rope securely in place, he stepped back and started putting slight pressure on the rope.

The mama perked up, and using her contractions as a guide, they started bringing her baby into the world. Soon after, two nostrils and a pink muzzle with black freckles on it, made a slimy appearance.

The flaring of those nostrils assured Bran the calf was still alive. "Thank goodness."

"Easy there, big mama, this is going to be the hard part." He was pretty sure trying to pull the calf out on his own was going to be pure torture for his already bruised and battered body, but he also couldn't leave her or the calf to die.

Using his weight and the force of the heifer's contractions, he leaned on the rope at intervals and at other times released pressure to give her a rest. Despite his hand complaining like a bitch and his ribs crying out in agony, he persisted. Lots of swear words came out of him every other second. It was hard, he got sweaty, and he desperately needed a shower. Maybe even in bleach since he was pretty sure that nothing else would kill the smell. But once the calf's head cleared and its body followed to plop down on the grass behind the heifer's back legs, Bran laughed in delighted relief. He removed the ropes from the limbs and picked the calf up and draped it over the top railing by its back legs to help drain the amniotic fluid out of its throat and lungs. The poor thing had possibly swallowed heaps of it with the birth so delayed. Leaving the mucus there could possibly result in pneumonia and a sure death. Bran didn't want that after all his hard work.

Once back on the grass, the poor calf shook its head and snorted to clear mucus from its face. Long lashes framed dark brown sleepy eyes as it looked back at him.

"You're welcome." The sense of accomplishment made him forget all the other crap for a moment. He untied the cow, who immediately turned around to investigate. Carefully picking up his supplies, Bran got out of there, placing the items down outside the gate and giving her time to bond with her baby. Sure enough, a few seconds after sniffing, she started grooming the calf to clean it. Mission accomplished.

By the time Kaden, Trent, and Samuel came back from harvesting the fields, at nearly three o'clock, Bran had already made friends with the little heifer calf. He hadn't showered, since he'd wanted to stay near the calf in case something went wrong with either her, or her mother, but also, it was just nice to sit in the dirt and watch the calf nurse.

"You smell horrible," Kaden said, coming up behind him. "Fall into the manure pile?"

Bran was too tired to rise to Kaden's bait, so he simply shook his head and smiled at the calf that came over to investigate him again. It'd been taking short trips away from its mom every once in a while to come see him. Maybe because it knew what he'd done for it. But Bran was sure it was more likely trying to figure out what the smell was. He really did reek.

"No. I helped her drop her calf," Bran said, not even minding the bit of pride that was in his voice. It felt good, and he was glad that they had both survived.

"Wow. Good job," Trent said.

"Very. That's hard work, especially with you being as beat up as you are," Samuel added.

Bran blushed and got up before Kaden could say something. It was one thing for him to be proud of himself. He was good with that. But he wasn't used to having other people be proud of him for something. He came away from the fence and let himself out through the gate. Kaden stepped forward, to do what he didn't know, but Bran walked away before he could do it.

"I need a shower," he said by way of an explanation.

He didn't wait to hear if any of them said anything as he headed back inside and straight for the bathroom. "Another outfit to burn," he said with a sigh as he shucked off his clothes and tossed them into the trash. Bruised and barely able to hold his head up as exhaustion came straight toward him like a freight train, Bran washed up as quickly as he could, while still making sure that the only smell he carried out of the shower with him was that of the soap.

He hadn't remembered a towel, but he didn't really care as he came out of the shower and darted across the hallway to his bedroom where he got dry and dressed again. This time he only put on some shorts and a T-shirt. It was a new one from Chris, a rainbow unicorn, that he was sure Chris had gotten specifically to embarrass him. Only Bran was too tired to be embarrassed by what shirt he had on at that point.

He wanted sushi but settled for Greek since there was no sushi place even remotely nearby, then headed downstairs. He didn't want their admiration or anything else they wanted to give him, but he did need some water, and since he hated the taste of the well water that came straight from the faucets, that only left him with one option.

"You did really well, mate," Trent said as soon as he was on the first floor.

"Thanks." Bran went right to the fridge.

Trent followed him over, and Bran could hear Kaden and Samuel talking in the living room where the TV was on. "How'd you know to do that?"

Bran really didn't want to talk about that. At all. But Trent stood next to him like he expected an answer. "My dad," Bran said, hoping it was enough. And maybe Trent had heard something about how his dad had died or how he'd made his mother miserable and she'd left him for New York, or something else, because Trent left him alone after that, going into the living room too.

After hearing a car pull up, followed by a knock on the front door, Bran expected to find a delivery person standing on the porch with their dinner. It was only an hour since he'd called, but he figured that maybe they'd rushed it. Instead he got Chris, with suitcases in tow, giving him a massive hug that made him feel like all of his bones were breaking at once.

"Can't... breathe...," he gasped. Chris continued to hang on to him until the pain of having his ribs smashed together in Chris's strong arms finally got to him, and he released a little whimper of pain.

Chris must have heard, because he instantly let Bran go, and the smiling expression he'd worn only seconds before was now replaced with one of concern, and anger. "What happened? Where are you hurt?" Bran let him look and nodded when Chris reached forward to take Bran's bandaged hand between his own. "How the.... No. Who the fuck put their hands on you? I will kill them."

"It's not like that," Bran protested, but Chris was already running his hands over Bran's arms and chest, searching for more sources of his pain. He winced when Chris roughly pushed against his chest, then his ribs, and Bran let him pull up his shirt, because fighting Chris was always useless, especially when he was on a mission like he seemed to be right then.

Chris dropped Bran's shirt and shook his head, looking as miserable as Bran felt. Only his pain and exhaustion didn't come with the anger he could see Chris's did. "This is what you couldn't tell me? Seriously, Bran?" He sounded like he was well past irritated and breaking away toward ready to beat someone up for him. If he hadn't been seriously in need of a nap, he would have thought it was sweet that Chris's protective streak decided to come out and play in a big way. But right now, the only thing he wanted was rest, and Chris was in the way of him getting that. His best friend was being annoying at the moment too. Bran loved him, but he did not like surprises, and he already had more than enough to deal with while he was there. Chris being on the farm was just another added complication that Bran didn't need at the moment.

"What are you doing here?" Bran asked him instead of answering his question as he reached down to grab Chris's suitcases and pull them inside. They were heavy, and he groaned as he realized that he'd be unable to even help that much. "And just how long did you invite yourself to stay too?"

"Don't try to be macho while you're hurt. Here, let me get them." Rolling his eyes, Chris stepped past him and tugged his suitcases out of Bran's arms. "When we talked you sounded off. I asked you what was wrong, and you said you were tired. You weren't fucking tired, Bran. You were being beat the hell up. So me, knowing you as well as I do, got on the first flight out here. And now look at you. I'm taking you home. No amount of money is worth letting someone hurt you like this. I don't care how rich it'll make you. This isn't happening. Pack your things. We're leaving."

Bran tried to rein back his irritation and not snap at his best friend, even if Chris was going crazy. It was so hard to do, though. "You're being dramatic. It's really not like that. And I was tired. I've been tired since the damn taxi dropped me off here," Bran snapped back at him, raising his voice right along with Chris. He saw Kaden and the others get up from the chairs and couches in the living room and remembered they weren't alone. "We're going upstairs. Now."

"Bran?" Kaden said, coming to the doorway between the front hall and the living room. He looked Chris over first, then settled his attention on Bran like he expected some kind of an answer as to what the hell was going on.

But Bran couldn't deal with all of this at once. "Introductions later. Chris, right now, upstairs with me. For the love of God, please follow me to where we can talk for two minutes." Chris continued to stand there, staring at Kaden like he could murder him with only a glare. "Christophori…."

Using his full name seemed to distract Chris from wanting to kill Kaden for a minute. But Bran knew it wouldn't be over until he could actually talk to him. In private. Without everyone staring at them like they were some goddamn roadside attraction.

"Please? I'll tell you everything. I promise. Just not down here."

Chris pursed his lips and looked like he really wanted to say something instead of doing as Bran asked, but he went up anyway after a few seconds, for which Bran was grateful.

"Later," he told Kaden, knowing he had questions too. Bran shook his head and silently followed up the stairs after him.

"The truth, right now," Chris demanded as soon as Bran shut the door behind him. Chris plopped down onto the narrow bed, then made a face when it squeaked. "I cannot imagine you suffering through a bed like this. Not given your current pricey little number back home."

Sighing, Bran lay down next to him. "This was my bed as a kid. It's over thirty years old, though that doesn't really matter since it was always pretty awful. Okay… the truth?" Chris nodded to him as he lay back as well. "A cow stepped on my hand. It's not broken, I don't think, but it hurts all the damn time. And my ribs are bruised all to hell because Kaden threw me into a metal fence."

"I knew it," Chris seethed.

Bran shook his head. "I was in a bull's pen and didn't realize it. Kaden thought he was protecting me, I guess." Chris looked slightly less upset by the details, but he still didn't look happy. Bran was eager to change the subject as he reached over and tugged on the growing scruff that covered Chris's cheeks. "What is this? What are you doing?"

Chris batted his hand away before turning onto his side to smile at him. "I'm growing a beard. I think it makes me look sexier. You?"

Shrugging, Bran mimicked Chris's position but winced when pain shot through him from his ribs. "It's fine. I thought your dad had a no-facial-hair policy at the firm, though."

"Take off your shirt. Let me massage you. It'll help with some of the pain at least. Since you refuse to be rescued from this place," Chris said, bouncing up to his knees. "And Dad hasn't said anything yet. Want to make a bet on how long I can grow it out before he threatens me with another written warning?"

Bran didn't want to bet with Chris, mostly because he never won, but a massage from Chris was something he'd be stupid to turn down. He sat up a little, enough to take off his shirt, then stretched out so his head was on the pillows and his chest available for Chris to work his magic over.

"Overnight me a cheesecake, and I'll massage your hand too."

Grinning, Bran pulled his phone out of his pocket and started searching for a place that could take care of Chris's not-so-odd request. "Deal," he said once he'd found a place. "What do I need to do to get you to rub my feet?"

"Well… first you'd need a shower, because your feet smell, but after that you'd need a personality transplant. I don't touch just any guy's feet, you know," Chris teased him as he started working on his uninjured hand.

Bran smiled at him, knowing full well he wasn't Chris's type, which was a good thing because he made a pretty awesome best friend when Bran didn't want to strangle him. "Thanks for coming out here. Wrong reasons and everything aside, I'm glad you're here. I needed a friendly face."

"You're welcome. You know I'll always come to your rescue. Still, I'm really fucking pissed at you for not telling me you were getting hurt out here. Better get me two cheesecakes to make it up to me."

Nodding, Bran placed the order, then put the phone aside to let Chris take over. All he wanted was some peace and quiet to be able to enjoy what Chris was best at: giving massages and telling him all the ways in which he'd been a horrible best friend over the last week while he'd let Chris worry.

CHAPTER SIX

KADEN COULDN'T believe what he was hearing. At first he thought he imagined it, but when Trent and Samuel glanced toward the stairs, he knew they heard it too.

Every so often the sound of creaking bedsprings reached their ears and a husky voice moaning, "Oh yeah. That's the spot. Right there. Push harder."

How Bran could get it on with Chris, after the kiss they had shared, mystified Kaden. How could he have so badly mistaken the chemistry between them? The attraction? On the other hand, Kaden had kissed Bran first, and Bran ended it too. Maybe his affections were completely unwanted. He must be getting too old to read the signals correctly.

"Chris! That's so damn good, do it again!" This time Kaden blushed. A few times over the last few days, Kaden had wondered what type of lover Bran would be. Silent and intense? Dominant or submissive? Top, bottom, or a switch? Whichever way the thoughts took him, the fantasies he indulged in were hot. From the commotion upstairs, one thing became very clear. Silent and Bran did not go together when it came to bedroom activities.

The whole bloody situation confused the shit out of him. He figured that what Bran and Chris had was similar to his relationships with Trent and Sam. Great friends, but that's it. They'd never had sex before or even had the desire to for that matter, despite ample opportunities to do so. Although he knew of plenty such relationships, friends with benefits or fuck buddies. Maybe that's what Chris was to Bran and vice versa. Even so, Kaden didn't like it but found himself helpless to do anything about the fact.

Having had enough of the audio porn, he turned up the TV volume and tried very hard to concentrate on the show they were watching. Some crime scene investigation sitcom that he usually enjoyed, but not tonight.

About half an hour and a headache later, footsteps sounded on the stairs. Kaden's back faced that way, but Samuel and Trent didn't have to pretend, so they openly glared in that direction as Bran and Chris came into the living room. The food had been delivered, and it sat untouched in the dining room. Kaden also couldn't help noticing that Chris had changed out of the suit and tie that he had been wearing and now wore a pair of khaki shorts and a plain brown T-shirt.

"Okay, time for introductions. Samuel, Trent, this is my friend, Chris. He's a lawyer in Manhattan, where we live. Chris, this is Samuel and Trent. They are friends of Kaden's and also work on the farm," Bran said.

WHEN BRAN and Chris walked into the lounge where the other three men were watching TV, it felt like he was walking into a damn cold room. Especially with the glares they got from Samuel and Trent. What the fuck was their problem? Kaden faced away from them and didn't turn around when they approached. But really, who cared?

Trent unfolded his long body from his seat and reached out to shake Chris's hand, but Chris didn't respond. Bran turned to his friend, ready to tear him a good one, but the expression on Chris's usually animated face stopped him. The man's gaze was riveted to one man. Samuel. Chris apparently saw nothing and no one else.

Bran had to clear his throat twice and elbow Chris hard in his side to get him to snap out of it. "Chris. You're being a rude ass."

Chris blinked and looked at Bran in annoyance before apparently seeing Trent's outstretched hand. "Shit! I'm sorry. Hey. Nice to meet you... errrrr...."

Nothing flustered Chris, and Bran shook his head at this new development. "Trent! That's his name," Bran supplied for him.

Chris gave a nervous smile. "Nice to meet you, Trent." They shook hands, and Bran turned toward Samuel, who watched Chris with a frown between his expressive eyes. Chris stepped forward to greet the big man, and Samuel got up from his chair. The bulk of the man made anyone else look small, including Chris, who didn't seem to mind the difference in their sizes at all as he looked up at Samuel with nothing short of pure, obvious desire.

When Chris looked back at him, his eyes were brighter than ever. "I would love to give him a massage." He looked from Bran back to Samuel. "And I'll do it for free."

When Samuel's frown deepened, and Trent coughed, Bran tried to salvage the situation. "It's not as bad as it sounds, guys. On top of being an excellent lawyer. Chris is also qualified in sports medicine and massage. Among other things." He rolled his neck and loved how his newly relaxed muscles felt. "And he's damn good too. Just saying."

Bran went to find a place to sit, since his bed was in shambles from Chris unpacking, and now that Chris was there, he didn't feel like hiding in his room nearly as much, but the only place to sit that wasn't on the recliner was on the other end of the couch from where Kaden was. Or in the maybe eight inches of room between Trent and Samuel. Neither option was all that perfect, not with Chris also needing to sit down. But he figured Kaden would be more inviting than Trent or Samuel. He could have been wrong, though, since the three of them still looked like they wanted to kill him, Chris, or both of them maybe.

He took Chris's free hand, the one that wasn't still awkwardly gripping Samuel's, and pulled him toward the couch. "I want him," Chris whispered in his ear, his voice loud with his excitement.

"He's not a puppy you can go adopt, and I'm not his pimp. You want him, you work that out yourself," Bran whispered back before plopping down onto the couch a good two feet from Kaden. He expected Chris to sit down between them, but instead Chis had apparently decided his lap was the best option and Bran let out an "oomph" as Chris got comfortable on top of him.

"Fuck you're bony," Bran groaned as he leaned back on the couch and glared at Chris's back. "Elbow me in my sore ribs and I'll dump you on the floor."

Chris turned back to him with a grin. "I forgot how much you like bigger guys. And your ribs are fine. Remember, I just saw them. Few bruises but you'll live. That hand, though," Chris's smile turned into a sudden frown before it was replaced as quickly as it had come on. "It'll be fine too. Given time. And rest. Best friend's orders. So, is farm life any fun?" He turned on Bran's lap and put an arm behind him on the couch.

Bran chanced a glance at Kaden and found him glaring at them both for whatever reason, before quickly looking away. Chris started playing with his hair, running his long fingers through Bran's ungelled and therefore lazy strands. When he looked back at Chris, expecting his best friend to be paying attention to him, he instead saw that Chris was openly staring at Samuel.

"You can't have him," Bran muttered, hoping no one but Chris could hear him. From Kaden's light blush, he could see he was clearly wrong on that. And still Chris continued to stare.

"Hey, rude ass, you're being creepy. Don't make me throw you out," he said a bit louder.

That broke Chris out of whatever the hell had been his attraction to Samuel for the moment. Bran thought he was too intimidating to really be sexy. Kaden was intimidating too, though just enough to be sexy, not in the silently deadly way that Samuel was. Chris did like his guys a lot wilder than Bran did, so maybe that was it. Or maybe his best friend had just straight up lost his mind. Of course, it might have had something to do with Samuel's tattoos. Chris always did have a weakness for men with ink.

"Hey, so about the will and the other option…," Chris started as he turned back to face Bran.

Bran quickly shook his head, hoping to shut down Chris's idea hard. "No. Absolutely not."

"What other option?" Trent spoke up.

Bran looked over at Trent and wished he could duct tape Chris's mouth shut most days. "It's nothing."

"Bran…." Chris tried again.

He narrowed his gaze on Chris. "No. Three more weeks, remember? Then the land can be sold and this house will be torn down. The cows will be slaughtered…." He scowled as he realized that would include the one he just helped bring into this world. "And then I will take you on a two-week vacation to wherever you want to go. Anywhere."

Chris rolled his eyes and let out a giant sigh. "I know. But, Bran, remember those first ten years here? Where you had two parents who loved the shit out of you? It wasn't that bad back then."

He didn't know what Chris was getting at, especially in front of them, but he didn't really care either. The past made no difference, only the present and the future mattered to him, and his decision was set and would not be changed for anyone. And that included Chris.

"It's the six after I'm trying to forget."

Apparently done talking about it, Chris turned on his lap again, so his back was against Bran's chest. Normally Bran would have wrapped an arm around Chris's stomach to keep him from swaying back and forth as he talked, since he liked to talk with his hands, but touching Chris at all felt weird with Kaden right there next to them. Even though it wouldn't have meant anything to Chris to have Bran touching him, he knew. They touched all the time. They'd even lived together for a while. This was nothing new, and it shouldn't have felt any different doing it in front of Kaden and the others. But Bran couldn't shake the feeling it wouldn't have been right, or normal, to rest his hands on Chris's hips while he was sitting on his lap.

"So," Chris began, squirming on Bran's lap and annoying him with every little movement until Bran considered dumping him on the floor. "Quick background. Then you can all share too." Bran groaned. As good an idea as Chris might have had, Kaden, Trent, and Samuel really didn't seem like the sharing type. "Bran and I met when I was eighteen, and he was sixteen. And I thought he was so damn cool for being emancipated and going to college all on his own. My dad chose my focus in college. But my grades stayed up, and I was able to get a few other degrees too. Anyway…. My dad hated him so much. But I adored him. Like a cute little puppy that I got to take out and get stupidly drunk with well before he was legal." He reached back to pinch Bran's cheeks.

Laughing, Bran shoved Chris off of him and onto the couch beside him. It meant he had to sit closer to Kaden but whatever. He was tired of Chris's bony ass digging into his hips. "Your dad still hates me. I'm surprised he even lets me in the door when we have meetings at the firm."

"It's your money. Dad loves money more than he hates you," Chris explained, making Bran shrug. Whatever his dad's issues were with him, and there were plenty of them, Bran had long ago given up trying to get him to be another father figure for him.

Chris was back to staring at Samuel, and Bran reached over and pinched him as hard as he could on the top of his thigh. "You're not in a strip club. Stop staring!" he hissed at Chris. The others could probably hear them, but thankfully they stayed quiet.

"But I want him!" Chris shot back.

Bran shook his head. "Slut."

"Bitch."

Snorting, Bran smiled at him. He felt so much better after Chris's massage, and it was great to have him there, to remind him of why he was doing this. Chris was his rock, the only thing he could absolutely count on in his life besides his money, and he'd needed him there in Montana to keep his head clear while Kaden was always around to screw with him.

"I really needed that massage. Thank you."

Chris gave him a wink. "You're welcome. Your massage noises are so much like your sex noises that I find massaging you to be hilarious. But, Bran, I really think you should reconsider the other option."

Of course Chris wouldn't let that go, and Bran wasn't all that happy about Chris embarrassing him in front of Kaden by telling him what his sex noises sounded like either. It had only been one goddamn time he'd brought a guy back to their apartment in college and hadn't realized Chris had still been home. Chris hadn't left it alone, even ten years later.

"No."

And certainly not because Chris's only reason for wanting him to take the five-year option was because he suddenly wanted Samuel, though for what reason Bran couldn't even begin to guess. Maybe Samuel wasn't even gay. He glanced over at Kaden and saw him trying his best not to look at them. The room felt no more welcoming than it had when they'd come down to what had felt like their deaths.

"Come on, let's go outside, and I'll show you the calf I helped pull out."

He got up, and Chris, thankfully, came with him without any protests. "Now, when you say pulled out, you're not actually saying...." Bran nodded to him, and Chris made a gagging noise as they headed through the kitchen. "Sharing later!" he called back to the guys.

"Don't hold your breath," Bran told him. "They aren't that nice." If his voice was loud enough to reach them, he didn't really care. Sure, he wanted Kaden, but even he wasn't too friendly, and acting like they hated him had made him really not want to spend any more time with them that evening.

He grabbed some dolmades from the Styrofoam boxes left out on the table. It looked like no one had touched the food, which suited him fine, but they could have at least put it in the fridge. Chris took three falafels as Bran put the rest away, and then they headed outside to see the calf.

"Tell me everything you know about Samuel," Chris demanded when they were a good distance from the house and hopefully out of earshot.

Bran wasn't sure why Chris had latched onto Samuel so quickly. It definitely wasn't like him to be so focused on a guy this much and this early on. Sure, he was more of a romantic than Bran was, but neither one of them had ever been really serious about the men in their lives. "He's Kaden's friend. And he works here."

Chris made a face as he waited for more, but that was all Bran had. "Seriously? That can't be it. Is he gay? Seeing someone? How do I get him to notice me?"

That made Bran laugh hard enough that a few of the cows lifted up their heads to see what the noise was. "I don't think getting him to pay attention to you will be an issue here."

"If you let them stay for five years...."

Groaning, Bran let Chris into the pasture where the heifer and calf were grazing. "I will buy you whatever you want, just name it, for you to not mention that damn other part of the will ever again."

Chris just stared at him as they walked toward the cows. "What's with you? I get that you don't want to wait to sell this place, or get your money, but there's something else going on here. I just know it. Gay man's intuition. Don't even try to deny it."

Bran chose to ignore him instead of answering and went to the little calf. She didn't run right up to him or anything like that, but when he crouched down, then pulled Chris down with him, the heifer and calf ventured closer.

"Look at her with her tiny ears and cute little spots. God, I hate you for not telling me how damn adorable cows are. I'm never eating beef again. And especially not veal. What is wrong with you, going out for burgers with me all these years?" Chris swiped at his shoulder, and Bran snorted.

"They're livestock to me. These ones produce milk. Male calves, that aren't sold for breeding, get slaughtered. We had lamb chops at that new Italian place two weeks ago. You think lambs are any less cute than calves?"

Chris shook his head at him, like he was actually disappointed in how Bran saw things. "You're so cold about it."

"That's just how it is." Bran shrugged. He saw nothing wrong with it and would continue to eat beef. Just not while he was surrounded by cows that seemed so capable of staring at him and judging him for not eating grass like they did.

"Don't think I didn't notice you avoiding the issues here," Chris said as they sat down in the grass at the edge of the pasture.

Bran pretended to be dumb. "What issues?"

Chris rolled his eyes and picked up a handful of grass and dirt to throw it at him. "Exactly. Tell me what's really going on here, or I'll go back in that house and give Samuel a blowjob."

"You want to do that anyway," Bran said, snickering.

Chris's smile turned devilish. "Fine. So Samuel isn't your deal, then. Trent?" Bran didn't budge. "Kaden, then. If I went in there, put myself on his lap, ran my tongue over his lips, moaned a little, then touched him on his—"

"Stop," Bran told him, his heart racing in his ears as his mind brought up the images he definitely did not want to see. Chris was a firework, all bright and powerful when he wanted to be, and his sexuality was a big part of that. He didn't want Chris trying anything with Kaden, not even a kiss. It wasn't that Kaden was his, not even a little, but he still didn't want Chris anywhere near him. They'd shared one kiss, which wouldn't have seemed like much, except that one kiss had been seared into him and now it felt like a part of him. No matter what he did, he couldn't forget about the feeling of having Kaden's mouth against his, his warm hands on his skin, his hips pressed into the space between Bran's thighs. He couldn't stop thinking about it, and sometimes he didn't want to.

Chris bumped his shoulder against Bran's. "I knew it was one of them. I told you to have fun. Was it with him? Was he any good?"

Blushing fiercely, Bran looked away from him to focus on the cows. "It was one kiss."

"That's it?" Chris looked disappointed in the lack of juicy, gossip-worthy, details.

Bran nodded. "But it was such a kiss. Like big, forget everything, including my name, kind of kiss. One of those first kisses that doesn't happen all that often."

"And you?" Chris prodded him for more information.

"What do you think? I've got three weeks, remember? That's all. It's over after that." He shook his head and wished he could just burn the whole farm down now and not have to wait until his time there was up. Kaden was a complication he didn't need, or want. He appreciated, no he needed, order in his life. And thankfully, with Chris there, for as long as he could keep him anyway, he'd have a living, breathing, usually obnoxious shield to put between himself and Kaden. Chris nodded, and Bran fell into silence as he focused on watching the calf nurse and pretending everything was exactly as he'd planned it to be, that his life wasn't one complicated mess all because of a sexy, stubborn cowboy from New Zealand.

CHAPTER SEVEN

"IT'S NOT what it looks like between those two." Samuel's deep voice brought Kaden out of his wayward thoughts. The damn man missed nothing, and it was a pain in the ass.

"What?" He tried to appear oblivious.

His friend snorted. "You've never been dumb, so don't even try. You know what I mean. I'm not quite sure what's going on with you and Bran, but it's there and tangible."

"What? What's going on?" Trent leaned forward in his seat, curiously looking between them.

"Nothing," Kaden tried.

Trent chuckled. "Liar. You have your tells, and those red ears right there are one of them."

Samuel stared straight at him, not backing down. "They're only friends. That much I can tell you."

Kaden very much wanted to believe that. Why the hell he cared still escaped him. "Look who's talking," he shot back. "Chris thinks you're a walking piece of meat and can't wait to season and eat you." Strange analogy, but hey, they were farmers.

Samuel didn't even blink. "This is not about Chris and me. It's about you and Bran."

"What?" Trent said in surprise. "You and Chris... and you and Bran. What the fuck? Am I sleeping with my bloody eyes open? Why don't I know about this shit?"

Samuel smiled at Trent. "Nope, you're just a dreamer, mate. There's nothing between me and that outrageous flirt. Kaden and Bran however, there may just be something there. That would depend on what they do about it. Bran is a bit lost, and unfortunately, you can't help him unless he wants to be found. He's used to running away." Sam rose from his chair and walked to the kitchen where he investigated the contents of the bags of takeout in the fridge. "Isn't it great then that you can run for miles without losing your breath?" At that Samuel winked at him and gave them a rare, genuine smile. His gray eyes and mocha skin with a flash of perfectly straight white teeth made him a striking man.

Kaden smiled back. "It looks like you'll be doing a fair bit of running yourself to catch that ball of pent-up energy undressing you with his eyes."

Samuel's smile withered. "I don't run after no one. I stun them with my natural beauty and then tie them the fuck up so they can't run."

Kaden and Trent started laughing. "Natural beauty!"

Samuel scowled. "Shut up. I am beautiful." Then he started shaking with laughter, joining in with them.

"Well, isn't this a merry party? What are we missing?" Chris stood in the back doorway to the kitchen, his eyes 100 percent focused on Samuel, who stood a few feet away from him. Sam's bulk made the fair-sized Chris appear small.

"Where's Bran?" Kaden thought they were glued together.

"Outside, having a come-to-Chris moment. He's got a lot to think about." Kaden didn't want to know what that meant, so he dropped it.

"How long are you staying, Chris?" Trent spoke up.

"Until Sunday. I've got to be in court on Monday, 9:00 a.m. I would've loved to stay longer—" He gave Samuel a heated once-over. "—but maybe another time."

Samuel filled a glass of water from the tap, not looking at Chris. "So Daddy cracking the whip is it?"

Chris's features became dangerously sensual—half-mast eyes, pouty, shiny lips, and a purr in his sexy voice that made even Kaden sit up straight. Chris walked up to Samuel from behind and almost touched him, groin to back. Almost. He lifted one finger, which he dragged down Samuel's spine, and Kaden could see his friend stiffen like a board. No one touched Samuel without an invitation.

"No, my client needs me, and I'm being paid to do my job. Don't worry, Samuel, I will be back. Soon." With a husky laugh, Chris left the kitchen and headed up the stairs. Not long after, they heard the shower go on.

Kaden coughed in the awkward silence. "Well, at least we know he's got balls of steel."

"Or a death wish," Trent tossed out as he left via the front door.

Samuel stood still and said nothing. Kaden wondered what the hell was going through his friend's mind and if Chris had just screwed it for himself.

BRAN CAME in through the back door a few minutes later, then stopped in his tracks, surprised at seeing Kaden and Samuel standing there. "Hi." He'd said it to them both, but his focus was solely on Kaden as he came into the kitchen and poured himself some water. The countertop was the most comfortable seat for him, since the kitchen table put him too near Kaden. So he chose a space away from Kaden and tried not to watch him out of the corner of his eye.

Kaden nodded to him, and Samuel came to sit down at the table. "Hey," Kaden said, appearing to be just as awkward. That made Bran smile a little.

He glanced upstairs as he heard the shower turn off. "Chris?" Kaden nodded, and Bran turned his attention to Samuel. "He's harmless, but if you want me to try to put a muzzle on him, I will."

"A ball gag would be better!" Chris called down to them from the top of the stairs where he stood there with a towel wrapped loosely around his bony hips.

Bran tried not to laugh as he shook his head and heard Chris go into his bedroom. Sharing the narrow bed with him for the next two nights was not an experience he was looking forward to. Add to that Chris's snores and the way he tended to stretch out on beds and Bran was pretty sure he'd end up on the couch at some point.

"It's fine," Samuel said, if a bit gruffly.

Bran shrugged and got up from the table in search of something much stronger than water. He found beer, but he wanted something better while he felt so restless. "Where's the liquor kept in this house?"

Kaden spoke up from behind him. "I've got some bourbon, which I'll share with you for some answers."

Bourbon wasn't Bran's first drink of choice, but it was better than nothing. "I'll take one too," Samuel said.

Bran joined them at the table. "Before you pour me that drink, what do you want to know?" He was a businessman after all, and contracts were a big part of that. He never agreed to anything in writing, which Chris hadn't approved first.

Kaden gave him a little half smile, barely more than the lifting of the side of his mouth. Bran glanced at Chris as he came down the stairs and noticed he wasn't wearing a shirt, and his low drawstring pants clearly showed off he'd gone without briefs too, but he didn't let his attention stray from Kaden for long. It wasn't a hard thing to stay focused on him. Rather, it was harder to not stare at him, to not want him whenever he was close. Even there with Samuel at the table, the big man seemed to fade into the background for him, leaving only himself and Kaden.

Chris was nearly impossible to ignore, though, as he scraped the chair noisily across the floor, intentionally drawing attention to himself as he sat down not beside Bran, as he'd expected his best friend to, but beside Samuel.

Kaden's gaze flicked over to Chris and Samuel before coming back to Bran. "We'll start easy. Why'd you leave here at sixteen?"

That was hardly an easy answer, and if Kaden required a deeper explanation than the one Bran was willing to give him, he would have just gone without a drink altogether. But he could start with the simple, matter-of-fact, truth.

"My dad died that year. Do I get my drink now?"

Nodding, Kaden got up from the table, and Bran was glad it had been that easy.

"Oh, are we trading truths for drinks? I love that game," Chris said as he put his elbows on the table and leaned toward Samuel, who was as stoic as ever.

Bran looked up at Kaden. "Is there more you want to know?"

"Yes." Kaden's answer seemed almost hesitant.

"We can both hold our liquor pretty well, if you're game," Bran offered him. It was a challenge, and he had questions he wanted answered as well. Chris nodded eagerly, which wasn't a surprise. He could drink Bran under the table, and he was curious as hell. Always had been.

Kaden grinned at him. "Sure. Samuel, start thinking up some questions you want to ask them."

"I don't have any," Samuel said as Kaden headed up the stairs.

Chris laughed, though it was far too high to be natural, as he ran his fingertips over Samuel's forearm. Bran watched Samuel closely for any sign that he might need to pull Chris back, but he was as hard to read as ever.

"Surely you want to know *something* about us. Anything you want. I aim to please." And if that wasn't enough of a come-on, Chris flashed a perfect smile over to Bran and tossed his damp brown curls toward him. "Get me something from the fridge. I'm feeling hungry. Something meaty… and thick."

Normally Chris didn't have to try this hard to get a guy to have sex with him, which Bran was pretty sure was all Chris really wanted from Samuel, so the extra effort made Bran laugh.

"Go get your own damn food. I order it, I don't dish it out."

Chris rolled his eyes. "You don't cook either, I see. Which is stupid, because you know how. And you're fairly decent at it." Bran lifted his gaze to see Kaden coming down the stairs, a half-full bottle of bourbon in his hand. The promise of a drink wasn't what made him lick his lips subconsciously, then quickly look away with a blush. "Remember that couples' cooking class we took?" Chris continued as if Bran was still paying any attention to him.

Bran nodded. It was hard to forget the sight of Chris trying to pass off the white glob on his chin that he'd forgotten to clean off as cake icing. "I remember you giving the instructor a blowjob during break. And that you refused to help me bake the cookies."

Chris laughed. "Baking requires rules. I don't follow them well." He turned back to Samuel and practically purred. "Unless it's someone giving them to me in bed. I tend to follow rules quite well when I'm naked. Do you want to see?"

"Whore," Bran coughed out.

Chris rolled his eyes. "At least I'm trying." He shot a pointed look to Kaden, and Bran instantly shut up.

Kaden got out four small glasses for them, then a fifth when Trent came in through the front door. "What are we doing?" Trent asked as he sat down to join them. With Chris pressed up against Samuel, the only empty seat was next to Bran.

"A drinking game," Kaden replied. He poured Bran a shot, which he swallowed the moment it had been handed to him. He saw surprise in Kaden's eyes, but he let it go. If he was going to be telling them some of his secrets, he'd probably need to be pretty drunk to get through it. He didn't open up easily, if at all.

Trent nodded and looked at Bran. "What'd he do for a shot?"

"We're trading truths. I moved out when I was sixteen because of my dad's death." Bran said to him, before going back to watching Kaden. "What if someone refuses to answer a question?"

"They have to do a dare," Chris told him instantly. It was the way they played this game, but Bran wanted to make sure the rules were still the same here.

Kaden didn't look so sure. "Within reason."

Bran smiled as the little bit of alcohol already started working through him to make him more relaxed and maybe even a little bolder. "Of course. No killing anyone or doing anything illegal. Or something that could negatively affect a person the next day when they're sober enough to remember what happened."

"And if the person refuses to answer the question, it can't be asked again, not even vaguely, and not by anyone else. But if two people would know the answer to the same question and one person refuses, you may ask the same question to the other person," Chris added, making Bran glad he had his lawyer around for this. He had plenty of secrets, most of which he didn't want to share with the three of them around, and knew he'd likely be doing plenty of dares.

"And!" Chris bounced excitedly in his chair. "If sex is part of the dare, condoms must be worn. If the dare is sexual in nature and a person refuses, they may do two alternative, nonsexual dares in exchange for the one. That is the only time a dare may be exchanged. If the person that the dare-ee has been told to do something to rejects, they have to answer a truth. If someone forfeits and refuses to play anymore before the bottle is empty, then they automatically lose, and a punishment for them will be decided by the pourer. And no future dares either. All dares have to be able to be completed directly after the dare is decided. If you puke or pass out, you're out, and you forfeit. A shot is given for each truth or each dare completed."

Lawyer Chris had come out to play in a big way. It was funny for Bran to see him both trying desperately to get Samuel to notice him and also outlining the terms of their informational surrender at the same time like he did this daily. Bran nodded, silently agreeing with him on each of his points, though he doubted anyone would be daring them to have sex. That was more of what Chris did, and as crazy as his best friend was, Bran trusted Chris not to cross the line and tell him to do anything to Kaden.

"Do the three of you accept our terms?" Bran asked them. If they did agree, it would open him up for questions, and some of his secrets would have to come out into the light. With the three of them, he also wasn't too worried about their dares, and knew he'd be choosing that option fairly often with them there. Samuel and Trent didn't intrigue him as much, but he had questions for Kaden, and something told Bran getting him drunk would be the only way he could get the answers he sought without fighting him for them.

Chris turned his attention from Samuel momentarily to Bran in order to give him a wide, wicked grin. "This is going to be fun. I love it when we get into trouble together."

Bran nodded to him. "It will be, if we can get them to agree." There was always a chance that Kaden wouldn't want to play his game. He lifted his chin as he turned back to Kaden. "If they aren't afraid of two Manhattan guys drinking some Aussies under the table and learning all of their secrets." Bran saw the tick begin in Kaden's jaw, and knew he was egging him on. He understood they were from New Zealand, but with the bourbon already starting to heat his blood and Chris grinning cheekily at him, silently encouraging him, Bran wanted to see what Kaden would do to him. It was likely dangerous to tempt fate as much as he was, but he'd never been all that smart once he started drinking either.

All three Kiwis snorted, but it was Trent who spoke, "Us Kiwis can hold our own. Let's go and see who drinks who under the table."

Samuel nodded. "Bran, you've just had a turn and answered, so you're up. Ask away."

There were plenty of things Bran could have asked, most of them directed right at Kaden. And of course there was Chris not so subtly pointing at Samuel to get him to ask Samuel some questions for him. But instead he went with the safe option, which was unlike him, but he didn't want to push too hard, too fast and make the three of them leave the table.

"Fine. Trent, how did the three of you meet?"

"Oh, that's easy." Trent smiled openly and leaned back in his chair. "Kaden and I met on the first day of primary school and instantly became best buds for life. We met Samuel a few months later when they became next-door farming neighbors to Kaden's parents. There! Where's my bourbon?" Kaden poured the man a shot, which he swallowed in one gulp, grimacing as it burned its way down.

"Alright, Here's my question to Chris…. Why did you become a lawyer if you were interested in so many other careers?"

It was still very early in the game, but if these were how tame the questions were going to be, Bran had nothing to worry about. Chris shrugged a little. "It's what my dad wanted. He paid for it. He got to decide what I did with it. I'm also an architect, but that's partially because there was this cute guy…."

Bran snickered. "There was always that one cute guy."

Chris stuck his tongue out at him. "Yay. My first drink since the plane ride. They never give out the good stuff there." While Kaden was busy pouring him a shot, Chris turned toward Samuel and seemed to be considering his options. But then, in a surprise move as far as Bran was concerned, Chris refocused his attention directly on him. "Bran, darling, what was the second option in Tobias Wilson's will?"

With an evil smile, Chris drank down the shot he'd been given, and Bran could only stare at him. "Dare," he decided, making Chris pout.

"You're no fun. It's such an easy answer, and we both know it." It was then that Bran realized he'd been outplayed by his best friend, because now that everyone knew Chris had the answer as well, they could ask him the question Bran refused to answer. "Your dare is that you have to kiss Kaden. Your choice of where, though."

"Jackass," Bran muttered to him as he got up from his chair and went over to stand beside Kaden. "Where do you want it?"

"That's not how the game is played!" Chris told him. "You pick, he doesn't."

Rolling his eyes, Bran still waited for an answer from Kaden. When the man looked up at him, Bran knew he was screwed. After their first kiss, Kaden had come across awkward, and he had admitted to it being a mistake, so Bran thought the man would let him kiss him on the cheek or forehead. Anywhere else to avoid kissing Bran again, and still Kaden tapped his own lips with a long finger, not saying one word.

"Ooh," Chris laughed.

Bran shot him a glare. "Would you calm the fuck down already? It's just a kiss." But when he leaned over Kaden, carefully keeping his hands by his own sides to avoid touching him, it didn't feel like it would just be any kiss. He pressed his lips softly to Kaden's unyielding mouth and waited for there to be more, but when there wasn't he immediately began to pull away. Only Kaden's hand balled into the front of his shirt stopped him as the man opened his mouth and slowly granted him access. There was no denying that Bran wanted him, but revealing just how much with the four of them looking on wasn't going to be an option. He roughly pulled away before he could make a mistake and do something he'd regret.

While Kaden was still watching him, he picked up the bottle of bourbon and poured himself his own shot, a double, then went back to his chair and completely ignored Kaden as he drank.

"My turn." And he wanted to get back at Chris for his last stunt. "When was the last time the three of you, in any combination, had sex together? Question directed to Samuel."

Samuel smirked. "Start pouring that shot." Sam turned his dark gaze on Chris. "I don't share very well. At all. I'm a selfish bastard." With the shot glass filled to the brim, his sleeve tattoo stood out in stark contrast on his forearm as he picked it up and tossed it back.

"Chris, why do you feel you have to try so hard?" Samuel sounded genuinely perplexed.

Bran frowned and wished he'd never suggested the damn game. "Chris, take the dare. C'mon, it's not like he's going to make you do anything horrible. You might have to clean dishes or something."

But Chris just shook his head. "These hands don't clean. Remember? And you." He turned his attention to Samuel. "That wasn't really an answer. My boy asked you when was the last time, not how much you don't like to share. Maybe you're exclusive with Trent. Maybe Kaden's your thing, and you don't know about their first kiss."

Of course Chris would start trying to distract people and go defensive. Bran ran his hands over his face and wished he could have another shot.

"But fine, you asked a question, you get an answer. Kaden, pour me another. No one has ever made me work as hard as you are, Samuel. No one at all. So either you're seriously not interested, for whatever reason, or you're not gay. But I've never once had to spend more than ten minutes coming on to someone before they've practically picked me up, thrown me over their shoulders, and dragged me off to some dark corner to fuck me. So excuse me for trying as hard as I do. It's because I want you." Chris downed the shot that Kaden poured him and glared at the table after it was gone.

"Told you to take the dare," Bran said from across the table. Chris lifted his right hand to give him the finger but didn't raise his gaze.

Samuel idly tapped his fingers on the table. "Excuse me for not answering my question to your satisfaction, but I'd assumed we were all in intelligent company here. I don't share, so there never has been a threesome nor will there ever be, least of all with my best friends. About what you said about yourself, you sell yourself way too short. You deserve better than being fucked against the wall in some dark back room or wherever. And maybe it's time that you learn that to want something doesn't mean you always get it."

Without saying a word to any of them, Chris got up from his seat, took his empty glass with him, then sat down on the counter behind Bran. He was Chris's shield, he knew that, and without Chris sitting across from him and next to Samuel, that left him able to openly glare at the much larger man.

"Chris, ask a question," Bran said without looking back at him. He knew his best friend was in a sour mood and also that it would take him a few hours to get over it. Chris didn't like being told he was doing something wrong, and even if Samuel hadn't really meant it that way, Bran knew Chris well enough to know his feelings were hurt, and he was being defensive.

"Kaden, ever been married?" Chris asked him. Bran moved back, screeching his chair over the worn-out tile floor, so that he could be closer to Chris. He'd asked the question for Bran, he knew, and he appreciated him for doing so. He reached back and touched Chris on his ankle, and Chris laid his hand over Bran's chest.

For the first time since starting the game, Kaden looked uncomfortable. "Yes, three times, and I have four kids—Milly, Tommy, Billy and…. Nah, just kidding. Never been married." Samuel and Trent burst out laughing, and Kaden took his drink. When the laughter died down, Kaden looked straight at Bran. "Did you ever or do you still love this farm?"

Before Bran could answer him, Chris leaned down to whisper in his ear. "I want to fly back early." Bran nodded, well aware that Chris would want to run instead of spending more time with Samuel after their little exchange. If he could have left after his first kiss with Kaden, he would have too. He gave Chris's ankle a squeeze to let him know he agreed with him before turning to look at Kaden. He'd asked a question and clearly expected an honest answer. And Bran had just enough bourbon floating around in his system to give him that.

"When I was little, before I turned ten, I did. This place was paradise to me. Then my mom asked my dad to choose between the farm and her, and he chose the farm. She left, moved to New York, and I was stuck here with a grandfather I barely knew and a dad who had chosen cows over his family. I stayed as long as I could, did everything I could to leave, and once I was considered an adult according to the courts, I planned to do just that. I would have left anyway, but my dad's death sealed the deal for me. Now, being here, I can't wait to burn it all to the ground, and I will be the first person in that casino when it's built."

He held out his glass to Kaden, who silently poured him a drink. "Now you, Kaden, why are you so damn willing to fight for this place?"

"My father came to the States years ago as part of a dairy research team, and during several visits to farms in this region, he met your grandfather. They became best of friends in the years after. On one of my dad's return trips, he brought me with him, and I met Tobias. He was a good farmer, a good father, a good grandfather, and an awesome man. So, the answer is simple. This land was his dream and so too his desire to pass it on to you. I will take care of his dream for him until I'm powerless to do so, because I would like to think that if he was my friend, he would've done the same for me. It's because of my love and respect for him that I'm still here." The game was getting too serious by far, and everyone looked on in silence as Kaden drank his well-deserved bourbon.

Bran could only stare at him as the silence stretched between them. He didn't know the man Kaden clearly did in his grandfather. A good man? He remembered being yelled at for playing with the cows and being denied dinner when he didn't get his chores done. His grandfather had been a gruff man who worked all day, and a lot of the night, taking care of the cows and the land for very little financial gain and, from what Bran could see, a whole lot of heartache. His mother had told him stories of a rude man who barely spoke to her and had no real love for the city bride his son had brought home. Bran had only ever seen himself as an extension of that. An unwanted reminder of the mistake his father had made in not marrying a girl more suited to life on the land. He'd been glad to be gone, and he was miserable being back. The next three weeks couldn't go by quickly enough for him.

"Bran, you okay?" Chris asked him as he curled his fingers over Bran's chest, digging into his shirt. Bran got up but not out of Chris's reach and pushed the chair away from himself so that he could lean back against Chris, who quickly wrapped his arms around Bran's chest as if he needed him and squeezed his knees around Bran's hips. Chris wasn't afraid of anything, or anyone, and he didn't need anyone either. But Bran could tell when he was shaken, and he supposed having someone talk to him as Samuel had, even if it appeared it was nothing to Samuel, was enough to unsettle Chris. And he was not happy to see his friend reduced to being vulnerable like this.

Bran continued to stare Samuel down as they waited for Kaden to ask his next question. "Okay, Chris. Do you have any pets?" Kaden seemed to want to lighten the mood, and Bran could almost kiss him for it. Almost.

Bran wasn't sure if he was going to answer or not, until he actually did. "No. I'm not home enough. And they take too much work. We had a dog growing up, though. A golden retriever, great for photo shoots and promo spots to make us look like a great, all-American type of family." He went quiet and gave Bran a bit of a squeeze around his chest. "I give my question to Bran and ask that I not be asked any more."

"That's forfeiting," Bran reminded him as Kaden came just close enough to fill the empty glass beside Chris's hip.

"No. I'm not forfeiting. I'm asking. If I was forfeiting I'd be upstairs and you'd be wrapped around me," Chris clarified for him.

Bran didn't react to Chris's words or the picture of them that they painted. No one had asked if they were having a sexual relationship, so maybe they all just assumed that they were. Really it didn't matter to Bran one way or the other.

"Trent, how long have you all been here?"

"Almost two years now. Kaden came first and recruited us from here when Tobias's staff all bailed when his health declined. So Samuel and I followed about three months later." Trent took his shot and shook his mop of hair as it went down. "I'm getting drunk cheap tonight."

"I have a question for Bran. How do you act when you're drunk? Is the alcohol enough for you to relax a bit?" Trent gave Bran a friendly smile.

It was the kind of question Bran was grateful for, because it was so superficial it barely needed to be asked. It was a wasted question when he could have asked about anything, but Bran appreciated him not bringing down the mood of the game any more than it already was.

"Last time I was truly good and drunk, like fall over curbs and not realize I was bleeding kind of drunk, was at a friend's bachelor party five years ago. It was five, wasn't it, Chris?"

"Four. I did their prenup, and their divorce a year and a half later," Chris reminded him.

"I was slightly off on the time. Anyway, I guess I start getting all deep and philosophical. It's not great for a party, but it beats crying in a corner or wanting to have sex with random people all the time, which I have done too. I do, however, tend to strip down to my underwear when I'm completely plastered," Bran said with a little smile. Kaden poured him a drink, which he chose to ignore for the moment as he tried to come up with a question to ask any of them as they laughed around him. "Chris, suggestions for a question?"

Chris leaned in close to his ear, and Bran was glad no one called them out on cheating, since technically sharing questions was against the rules when they played this game. "Ask Samuel about his opinion of love," Chris whispered.

Bran frowned, having no real desire to know that information. "Why? You don't care about love, so why are you having me ask him that?"

Chris poked him hard in the back, and Bran hissed in pain. "Fine. Fine. Fucking hell, when you actually try to hurt someone, you can do a lot of damage. Samuel, what is your opinion of love?" He felt stupid even asking the question.

Samuel took a few seconds to gather his thoughts. "On the negative side, I believe love can destroy people who don't respect it or confuse love for jealousy or possessiveness. Love is more than a feeling. Above all, it's damn hard work, and it's not fifty-fifty as so many people believe, because then each only contribute half of their capacity to love. It's a hundred or not even worth trying. If done right, love is empowering. It can change your world and the world around you if you choose wisely. God, now I need a drink. Make it a double, please." The only sign of vulnerability was the slow tap of fingertips on the wooden tabletop. When Kaden pushed the shot glass over, Samuel gulped it down and coughed a bit after.

"Right. Bran, have you ever been in a lasting relationship, and what do you think of cheating?" Now that Chris was sitting out, Bran almost felt like running. All the questions from the three Kiwis were going to be aimed at him.

Bran sipped his drink as he considered the answer he wanted to give them. "Your definition of a lasting relationship might differ from mine somewhat, but I was with someone for two years. And cheating isn't something I really have an opinion on. I've been cheated on, I've never cheated, but I've known people who have, and I don't think badly of them. It's something that happens, nothing more."

"Who were you with for two years?" Chris asked him.

Bran frowned, wondering why Chris didn't remember. But it was probably because he hadn't been that open about his relationship with Richard in the latter half of their time together.

"Richard. You probably don't remember him."

But Chris groaned. "Kinky Richard? Yeah, I remember him." Bran felt Chris shudder against his back and smiled because Chris didn't know the half of it, and he never would. "There's a problem." Chris dropped his voice low enough for only Bran to hear him.

"What's that?"

"Samuel is so far out of my league that he might as well be on another planet. I'm going to go upstairs." Chris sounded so sad, so defeated, that Bran turned in his arms and gave his best friend the biggest hug he could, even to the point of hurting his own ribs in the process.

"I'm sorry."

Chris nodded against his shoulder, and Bran moved back so he could get off the counter. "I'm forfeiting. Kaden, as pourer, you get to decide my punishment." He stood there as if in front of a firing squad, waiting for his death.

Kaden sighed, almost looking nervous. "Chris, your punishment is to kiss Samuel. On the mouth."

Chris looked like he was practically shaking as he stared at Kaden. But after a few moments in which he did nothing, hardly even breathed as far as Bran could tell, he went over to stand against the table, right beside Samuel as if waiting for him to make the decision for him.

Samuel swiveled his chair around so he faced Chris and waited for him to make the first move. "In for a penny...," Chris said as he slid himself onto Samuel's lap, the chair creaking under their combined weight. He rested his hands on Samuel's massive shoulders, then leaned in to press his lips gently against Samuel's.

Just as Bran expected, after a few seconds, Samuel placed two hands against Chris's cheeks and pushed him gently away. Samuel scrutinized Chris's features and the next moment pulled him back, joining their lips together in one of the hottest kisses Bran had ever seen. From the side, their lips were parted, and there was no tongue, but dammit, Bran felt his body light on fire at the passion on display before him. Chris moaned and fisted a hand in the front of Samuel's shirt for a moment, before breaking the kiss and almost stumbling over his own feet to get away.

Bran shook his head as he watched Chris practically run up the stairs to his room. He sat back down at the table, and even though Kaden had already poured him his last drink, he poured himself another. Looking at them together, at the want and need he could so clearly see in Chris, he'd thought for sure his friend would stay after that kiss. But Chris seemed determined to run, and Bran knew better than to try to stop him.

"That was fucking cruel as hell," he told Kaden as he threw back his drink.

"Just as fucking cruel as you selling this farm. It seems we have something in common." Kaden glared at him.

Trent gave a half cough, half snort. "And on that note, I think this round of truth or dare is done and dusted." He reached over and capped the now almost empty bottle of bourbon before rising from his chair.

"Well, that was fun. Let's do that again sometime soon. Not. Good night, fellas. See you in the morning," Trent said. The screen door slammed shut, and the ATV started up and Trent drove off, the sound fading in the distance.

Bran looked away from the back door at the sound of Chris on the stairs, his heavy luggage banging on each step. He'd changed out of the casual outfit and into yet another of his many suits and ties, this time a nice dark blue one. Bran got up from the table and, even though he was sore and nearing exhaustion, took the suitcase from Chris once he'd come to the bottom of the stairs.

"Don't look so sad," Chris said, his happy exterior back in place like his own private shield. "I'll see you in three weeks. It was good to see you again. I missed you." He hugged Bran, and if he was okay acting like nothing had happened and everything was still all right with him, then Bran wouldn't question him on it and embarrass him in front of Kaden and Samuel. If he held on a little longer than usual, then no one would have really known but Chris.

"Did you already call a taxi?" Bran asked him. He was aware of Samuel and Kaden staring at them but ignored them.

Chris gave him a little smile. "When I said I had to get back while we were at the counter, I'd actually reserved one online. They should be here at any moment."

If Chris wanted to pretend that he was getting back to work and not just running away, then Bran wasn't going to expose him in his lie. "Sorry you couldn't stay longer. Next time."

"Yep. I had fun."

Bran heard a car pull up outside and walked with Chris to the front door. "I'm sorry," he whispered as they stood in the open doorway.

Nodding, Chris's smile withered a little, like he couldn't force it anymore. "I know. It's just...." He didn't have to say anymore. Bran got it plenty well on his own. "Nice to meet you two. Say bye to Trent for me," Chris called to them.

"Be safe, and call me as soon as you're back in Manhattan. I'll order you new cheesecakes to make sure they get to you there," Bran promised.

"Good. I think Sunday will be all about binge eating and rerun watching as I wallow in my misery."

The saddest part, to Bran at least, was that he knew Chris wasn't joking about that in the least. He really would spend the day on the couch in front of the TV, and Bran wished he could do something about it, but from Montana he was helpless to do much more than try to console Chris over the phone.

"See you."

"Bye." They hugged again, and then Bran closed the door behind Chris to see Kaden and Samuel still staring at him from the dining room table.

CHAPTER EIGHT

KADEN WATCHED Chris and Bran hug, then the door shut behind Chris as he left to return to Manhattan. Talk about acting impulsively, but Kaden sensed more was going on than his eyes could see. Samuel had played a huge role in that, because the cocky, flirty Chris had turned into a scared, vulnerable, and cautious man in the span of a few hours. Enough so to make him take off.

Kaden looked at Bran as the man turned around with a worried frown pulling his sexy brows together. "Is he okay?"

Bran shook his head, then chewed on his bottom lip as he leaned against the wall across from them. "He's…. God, I don't even know how to explain him. But what you did, that was really hurtful. And using him and his attraction to Sam as a way to get back at me makes you an ass in my book." Bran looked between the two of them, appearing to judge them as his green gaze rested on each of them for a few seconds before moving on. "I'm exhausted and fucking pissed that I barely had my best friend around for a few hours because of you two." He started up the stairs, his shoulders shaking as he went like he could barely contain his anger, but stopped halfway up and turned back to them.

"What in the hell were you thinking?" he asked Kaden as he stormed back down the stairs and joined them at the table. He shot Kaden a glare before moving his attention to Samuel. "And you…." He groaned before running his hands roughly through his hair.

Samuel sat forward. "Bran, spare me the drama, please. I know you love your friend, but you and I know he's on the path of self-destruction. He's living the life people want him to and not because it's what he wants or deserves. To help him ignore his issues and allow him to crash is heartless, but I guess with what you intend to do with this place, that should come as no surprise." Kaden saw the blood rush to Bran's face as he got told off.

Bran opened his mouth to lash back out, but Samuel stopped him short by pushing his chair back with a loud scrape and rising to his full height. "No, you shut up and listen. I like Chris and am willing to say it may even be more than that, and I won't stand by while you and anyone else encourage him to live like this. He needs your love, understanding, hugs, phone calls, and whatever else, but more than anything he needs tough love. If you were worthy of being his friend, you would encourage him to get out from under his father's crushing thumb and to leave that stinking job he obviously hates. You would tell him he deserves more than quick fucks and blowjobs whenever and wherever he gets them. And you are the closest person to him and you say you care, but your actions prove differently. You know he's stubborn and will just deny everything and push on and on until he breaks. What then, Bran? Come on—you're so smart. What if he snaps and take his own life, falls into depression, gets hooked on drugs? Gets hurt by some creep during one of his sexual encounters?" Samuel's voice echoed in the room with a boom.

Very few times had Kaden ever seen his calm and collected friend this angry. Samuel had the physique of a beast but a soft heart. Kaden cringed at the harsh but probably necessary words.

Bran blinked and swallowed a few times in the aftermath but eventually looked out the dark window to the night outside. When he turned back, his stunning green eyes swam with tears.

"You don't have any idea what you're talking about," he said, sounding bitter, but Kaden could tell he was lying, even to himself. They watched in silence as Bran took out his phone and began dialing. "Hey. Where are you? Look, when you're back here…. Right, if you come back… there's some stuff I think you need to hear. From Samuel." Though Kaden couldn't understand Chris's words through the phone, he could absolutely hear his tone, and the man sounded nearly irate.

Bran sighed and pinched the bridge of his nose as Chris continued on. "Fine. Do whatever you want, then." He pursed his lips, and Kaden saw his gaze drift between them. "No, don't do that actually. Be safe. For once in your life, just think before you do something. Please?"

Bran got up from the table and leaned back against the wall, then moved to sit on the counter as if restless and unable to get comfortable. And still Chris continued yelling in his ear.

"Uh-huh. Yep. No, I'll make sure to kill him. Don't you worry about that."

Kaden saw him smile and wondered what they were talking about now to make his mood change so quickly. It was hard not being able to hear both sides of the conversation. But when Bran looked over at him, his smile quickly left his face to be replaced by a scowl.

"Have a good flight. I'm going up to bed. Call me as soon as you land. I don't care what time it is. Just call me. Okay?"

He hung up a few seconds later, and Bran sat on the edge of the counter, just looking at them. He sighed loudly enough for Kaden to hear him from the dining room table. "You're wrong about him and me," Bran told Samuel. "I won't let him die."

Bran slipped off the counter and headed upstairs, his head hanging low as he took the stairs slower than Kaden had ever seen him do.

"You're actually a bit scary when you get perceptive like that," Kaden quietly told Samuel as they continued to sit together at the dining room table.

KADEN DIDN'T stay up much longer after that, and when he went upstairs, he saw Bran sleeping soundly through his partially open door. He was shirtless, providing a tempting sight for Kaden. If only he could stand Bran when he was awake, they might have been able to have something together.

He got ready for bed, going through his normal routine, but his mind kept coming back to Bran, and Chris by association. He rarely had a reason to be worried about a stranger, especially one as obnoxious as Bran, but it was hard not to be when he'd seen how affected Bran had been by what Samuel had said to him.

There was a knock on his closed bedroom door, and he pulled his shorts up a little, then tied them tighter, before going to see who was there. The options were pretty limited, though, and he wasn't all that surprised to see Bran standing outside of his bedroom when he opened the door.

"Yes? It's late."

A still-shirtless Bran, wearing only plaid lounge pants, leaned against the doorframe across from him. "I know. Look, I just wanted to say thanks. For taking care of my grandfather. I didn't like him, but I could tell you did when we were talking earlier. I guess it's just nice to know he had someone in his life who could stand him."

"You're drunk, aren't you?" Kaden guessed.

Bran nodded and gave him a sly smile as he hooked his thumb into the waistband of his pants. "Very. I guess the shots you were handing out finally kicked in." His pants slipped down a little, and Kaden couldn't help tracking that movement with his eyes, though he would have rather been touching Bran instead.

Pushing away from the wall with his shoulder, Bran took a step forward and gently pressed his lips to Kaden's cheek. Kaden froze, wondering what the hell Bran was doing now, but while he was still trying to figure it out, Bran was already moving away and going back to his room. At the doorway to his room, Bran put a hand on the wall and looked back at Kaden.

His hair was a mess of loose, blond strands, and the bags under his eyes spoke volumes about the long day Bran had experienced. Despite these things, that some people might have called flaws, Kaden saw only his beauty. It seemed to be lurking there, just below the surface and hidden by an attitude viler than most Kaden was used to facing.

"Good night," Bran said, giving him another little smile before he disappeared into his room, and Kaden was free to attempt to get some sleep, though why he even bothered, when he had to be up in less than three hours, was beyond him.

KADEN WOKE up to an empty house, but he didn't really have time to go looking for Bran when he was needed with the cows. When he got there, though, he found Bran already starting down the aisle, cupping the cows as he went. Kaden noticed him wincing when he used his injured hand, but it was a vast improvement over having him unable to work.

"Morning," he said as he came into the pit and began helping Bran work.

Bran nodded to him but said nothing as they moved through the cows with quiet efficiency. As soon as they were done, he got right back on his phone, which never seemed very far from him, and Kaden went to Trent and Samuel.

"It's a surprise seeing him working again," Trent said as they cleaned up and sprayed everything down with the hose.

Kaden nodded and watched Bran head back inside the house, the phone still stuck against his ear. "Guess his pain wasn't too bad."

"How does he seem today? After last night?" Samuel asked him, instantly reminding him of the drunk Bran who had kissed his cheek so easily, as if it was the most natural thing in the world for affection to exist between them.

Kaden shrugged. "You've seen him as much as I have this morning," he said dismissively.

Trent looked around the yard, seemingly noticing something, or rather someone, was missing. "Where's Chris?"

"He went back last night." Kaden shared a look with Samuel.

"That was fast. I guess when you have money, flying that far for one night isn't too expensive." Trent wandered off to the house for breakfast.

With everyone having a bit of a hangover or waking up late, they all pitched in to make breakfast. All except Bran, who still sat talking on his phone, and by his tone, Kaden assumed it could be only with Chris.

Their plates were almost empty when Bran joined them by the table and uncovered his food to start eating. Then they all stared at him in expectant silence, and he shrugged. "He sounds fine. Chris tends to bounce back quickly from setbacks."

"I would like to think it may be the beginning of something good instead," Samuel said softly as he got up and rinsed his dishes.

Bran looked at Sam as he left through the back door. "He's really scary," Bran mused as he started to eat again, but for one moment, Kaden could swear he saw hope in the man's eyes.

CHAPTER NINE

THE NEXT few days settled into an easy rhythm on the farm and with the workload divided between four of them, the chores weren't as tiring as they normally were to Kaden. If he hadn't known better, Bran would have almost appeared to be taking to farming like a natural and enjoying the work. Bran most definitely smiled more often, and it pleased Kaden to see he got along well with the other two men.

He knew the relationship between Bran and Samuel would be rocky for a while, but not because Samuel was an ass to Bran. After Chris's speedy departure back to the city, Samuel had never mentioned Chris, the game, or the kiss, and he treated Bran with respect and growing admiration. Trent interacted with Bran like he did with Kaden and Samuel—as if they had known each other for years and were good friends. Kaden should thank his friends for making Bran feel at home, because he found it hard to do the same. His intense growing need for Bran clashed with the extreme disappointment in the man's selfish nature.

Those two things couldn't be reconciled, and allowing anything to happen between them meant he was setting himself up for great disappointment and heartache. Bran would walk away back to his life and forget about the farm and the three "Aussies" he worked with for a month.

Later that afternoon the temperatures rose, and sweat ran down Kaden's back as they milked. Bran seemed equally hot, and strands of his hair stuck to his scalp, the back of his T-shirt soaked through. When the last row of cows walked out, they cleaned up with Bran hosing down. Kaden couldn't avert his gaze as Bran stripped his shirt over his head and wiped his face with a dry part before hanging the garment over the fence.

Smooth, strong muscles bulged and rippled as Bran directed the strong stream of water where he needed to wash. His back was facing Kaden, who enjoyed leisurely looking at him while he was unaware. At the bottom of his spine, Bran's lower back dipped before rising again in a perfectly toned ass. Kaden knew because he had admired it several times from a distance, and all he wanted to do was run his tongue along that dip and keep going.

Kaden shook himself out of his fantasy and turned away. Bran wouldn't appreciate being ogled, and Kaden hated being called creepy. With all the cleaning done, they walked together up to the house.

Seeing the ATV standing there, Kaden turned to Bran, "I want to show you something, but you would have to come on the bike with me. Will you do that?"

Bran shuffled to a stop and stared at him. Ready for a denial, Kaden was surprised by Bran's quick nod. "Okay."

Kaden climbed on the bike, and Bran followed, sitting very close behind him and yet not touching him. Disappointment hit him like a punch at Bran's obvious refusal to make contact with him.

He drove the ATV along a track and headed toward the far end of the property where the beef cattle grazed. As they approached the gate of the paddock, Kaden advised Bran to hold on as the terrain would get rough in a second. Warm arms wrapped around his waist, and Bran's weight shifted forward on the seat, flush with Kaden's back. An immense sense of satisfaction and pleasure filled him, making his blood rush to all the wrong places.

At the end of the grazing block, he slowed and came to a stop on a rise and switched the machine off. They both dismounted, and Kaden started walking over the hill to the other side, knowing Bran would follow him. At the bottom of the hill, shady trees lined the border of the farm, and a small stream ran alongside them.

"Oh, wow. I remember this now," Bran whispered.

"Come," Kaden said and walked to the trees. He sat down on the soft grass and took off his boots and socks, putting his hot feet straight into the deliciously cool water. "That is so good. I love coming here." Kaden shared a piece of himself.

Quietly, Bran came up beside him and did the same. They didn't speak, and yet conversation felt unnecessary. Kaden sighed deeply and lay back on the grass with his legs propped up. He almost felt the air move as Bran copied him. Minutes passed, and they didn't move. A wonderful breeze rustled through the trees and helped them cool down. Kaden relaxed and rested his eyes.

He must have drifted off, because when he next opened his eyes, Bran lay beside him and was staring at him. "Sorry, I'm really tired."

Bran smiled gently. "I can see that." They perused each other's features, and Kaden didn't know what Bran was looking for, but it looked like he was searching for something. A few minutes later, Bran sat up, and Kaden followed.

"Wow, look at that." Bran's gaze was locked on the horizon with the sun setting. Hues of red, orange, yellow, and pink painted the sky into a breathtaking piece of art.

"It's beautiful and one of the reasons I love this spot." They admired the sunset for a bit longer before putting their boots back on and walking back to the bike. This time Bran sat glued to him as they drove back.

When they got back to the house, Bran was quick to get off the ATV, but he didn't go far. Instead he leaned toward Kaden and ran his fingers through Kaden's windblown hair while Kaden watched him, wondering what he wanted to do.

Bran lowered himself back onto the ATV, this time in front of Kaden, but there wasn't enough room for them both without Kaden moving back, and he wasn't willing to put more distance between them, not with Bran giving him a half smile that promised wicked pleasure. Kaden rested his hands on Bran's thighs, keeping him close as Bran stretched himself over Kaden's lap.

Without a word, Bran kissed him, his hand tightening in the back of Kaden's hair and pulling his head back until he seemed to get the angle he wanted, the perfect one for pushing his tongue between Kaden's lips. Kaden squeezed him through his jeans, needing him and loving the taste of him against his tongue. With shaking hands, Bran ran the fingers of his free hand over Kaden's chest, touching him everywhere as if he couldn't get enough of him. Which was just fine for Kaden since that's how he felt too.

"We can't," Bran whispered, pulling back a little.

Kaden wasn't listening to him, though as he roughly pulled him closer, fitting him snugly against his lap so that there was no more room between them, no way for him to escape again. "I want you," he groaned against Bran's open mouth.

Bran let out a little moan of pleasure, promising so much more, but just as quickly as the kiss had been started, Bran was apparently done with him as he pulled back and slid off Kaden's lap once Kaden had unwillingly released him. If he didn't want to be there, Kaden wasn't going to make him stay on top of him, but he was damn confused.

"That's it?" Kaden barked at him, feeling frustrated and let down.

Bran laughed as he looked over his shoulder at him. "That was thanks for the ride." He went inside the house and straight up to his room, leaving Kaden shaking his head and wondering what the hell that had been about.

CHAPTER TEN

KADEN NURSED a cup of coffee by the table and heard the screen door open. Samuel and Trent came in and made themselves a hot drink before joining him.

Samuel eyed him warily. "This whole situation sucks, mate. Once this place sells, what are we gonna do? What are your plans?"

Trent gave a weak smile. "I'll go visit my folks for a bit, then get back into it, I guess."

Kaden shook his head. "I haven't thought of it, Sam. I never completely believed he would go through with the sale. I'm starting to believe he is as selfish and egotistical as we'd first thought. I have two farms back home, so I guess I'll go back there and work out the next adventure. You two know you'll be part of it anyway."

Samuel nodded gravely, and Trent beamed. "Sounds good."

"So, do you—" Samuel's words were cut short when Bran's phone on the table started vibrating and ringing loudly. Glancing over, Kaden saw Chris's name on the display. Looking at the stairs, Kaden wondered if Bran would hear it, then decided to answer the thing in case it was important. Soon he'd be taking messages like a personal assistant to the asshole.

"Hello, Kaden here."

"Bran?" Chris said, sounding far away and definitely not himself.

"Chris? Do you want me to get Bran for you? He's upstairs." Kaden could hear nothing in the background.

Chris laughed, and the sound was unnatural and ended on a cough of pain and a groan. "Bran.... With Richard.... Ow. Hits hard."

"What the fuck? Chris, are you okay? Who hit you?" Kaden put the call on speakerphone, covered it with his hand, and jumped out of his chair, charging toward the stairs. "Bran! Get the fuck down here!"

"Chris, are you there?" When he turned around, Kaden ran into Samuel, who had come up right behind him, the worry clearly written on his face.

Bran came out of the room, a sour look on his face, until he caught sight of Kaden on his phone. "What the hell? And who are you calling? Use your own damn phone if you want to call someone."

"Bran... Bran... Bran.... So pretty."

Bran pushed Kaden back as he snatched his phone out of Kaden's hands. "Chris? Are you drunk? What the hell?"

"Richard.... Not Samuel. But can't have him. Richard saw me. Wants me. At the club. Samuel...."

Bran grimaced, and Kaden could see him shaking, as he reached out his hand toward Kaden. "Give me your fucking phone. Now."

Without hesitating, Kaden reached into his pocket and handed it over to Bran. What the hell was going on?

Bran started dialing. "Hello, 911, what is your emergency?" He went over to the dining room table and put the two phones beside each other as he leaned over the scarred wood, his knuckles white as he gripped the edge of the table.

"Connect me to the New York City dispatch office," Bran demanded.

"Sir, this is the south-eastern Montana office. We don't just—"

"You do now. My friend, Christophori Romanoff, is in trouble, and he's in Manhattan. Connect me. Now," Bran said toward one phone before turning his attention back to Chris. "Hey, what club. Where are you?"

Samuel paced up and down in the kitchen, stopping every now and then to stare toward the phone.

Chris coughed. "Hurts.... He said you.... That you liked it like this...."

"Not right now, Chris. We are not doing that right now. I need to know where you are. C'mon, tell me something," Bran practically shouted into the phone, desperation in every word.

"Sir? Where is your emergency?" A new 911 operator spoke up.

"One second. I'm still trying to get it." Bran shook his head. "Fuck, Chris. Just give me one damn clue. Where are you? What do you see?"

"Wooden X. Bran, why no Samuel for me? Why?"

Bran snatched up Kaden's phone. "He's at Club Satyr, it's downtown. Off Ninth and Mill Road. He's in the back playroom. Hurry."

"Thank you, sir. We'll have services there as soon as possible."

Bran tossed that phone aside and picked up his own as he sat down heavily in the nearest chair. "Chris, talk to me. Help is coming. Just keep talking."

They heard footsteps and the shuffling of Chris's phone. "Hello? Who's this?" Kaden didn't miss the way Bran's face drained of color.

"Hello, Richard," Bran said, his voice shaking.

There was laughter on the other end of the phone. "Bran. Beautiful little Bran. You shouldn't have let Chris come out to play alone. The three of us could have had much more fun together."

"Leave him alone, you piece of shit. The police are on their way. If you hurt him any further, Richard, I swear to God—"

"Swear on your money, Bran, at least you believe in that." It sounded like the phone was dropped, and footsteps walked away.

"Bran…." Samuel walked right to where Bran stood, his eyes glued to the screen of the phone, his hand twitching by his side. Bran shook his head slowly from side to side, denying Samuel the chance to talk to Chris.

"Hey, Chris," Bran said into the phone. He wiped at his cheeks. "I'm on my way. Going to book a flight as soon as I know you're safe."

"No. Don't. Stay there. Millions of dollars."

Bran shook his head. "Fuck the money. You're more important to me than money."

"Don't come. Don't want you to see…. Not like this."

The phone was shuffled around again, and the sound of people helping Chris came through.

"Where are you taking him?" Bran said into the phone, but he wasn't answered as the line died on the sounds of a siren. The moment the line went dead, there was chaos around Bran.

"Who the fuck is Richard?" Samuel growled.

Bran looked over at him and slowly closed his eyes before turning back to the phone shaking in his hands. "My ex. He was…." Bran shook his head. "He wasn't good. To me."

Kaden frowned. "He sounded like a creepy asshole on the phone and, from what Chris said, abusive too."

Bran lifted his gaze to Kaden and nodded, giving him all the confirmation he needed.

"What do you want to do now, Bran? Where will they take Chris, and how will we know if he's going to be okay?" Kaden looked over at Samuel, who stood by the large lounge window staring out. Every muscle in Samuel's body radiated tension.

Bran got up from the table and rubbed his hands over his arms. "Fucking Chris. I don't know what to do right now, Kaden. The hospital will call me. I'm his emergency contact. But he told me not to go there. And he was with Richard.... Just.... Fuck." He started calling again. "Misha, what the hell is your number? There we go."

He put it on speakerphone again. "You bastard, I told you not to call me unless it's an emergency with Chris," a gruff voice on the other end of the phone said.

"Misha, Chris was hurt by Richard. I don't know how badly. He's being taken to a hospital now," Bran said quickly.

"What hospital?" Misha snapped at him.

Bran shook his head. "I don't know that."

"Where was he hurt?"

Bran sighed, clearly in frustration. "I don't know that either."

"Well then what do you know?"

Dragging his hands over his face, Bran shrugged. "Nothing. Not a damn thing. I'll text you when I do. Will you go to the hospital and stay with him?"

"Too busy with a dick in your own ass to be with your best friend?"

Bran hung up the phone.

Silence hung in the air. Trent's eyes were like saucers in his head. "Wow, nice guy. Who is he?"

"Misha is Chris's older brother. Half brother. And he hates me. Lots of reasons, but not because I supposedly turned his brother gay, which is really why his dad hates me." Bran groaned and lifted himself onto the counter and looked over at Kaden, seeming desperate for help.

Why Kaden would want to help him escaped his mind. An hour ago he wanted to shoot Bran himself. "If Chris doesn't want you there, you have to respect that. So, all we can do now is wait, either for a call from the hospital or Misha."

"I didn't want to be seen either the first time," Bran quietly revealed as he bounced his bare ankles against the cabinets.

Kaden sighed. "You two scare the crap out of me. You're so self-destructive and irresponsible. It is not surprising someone got hurt."

"And you. You're—" Bran shook his head, and his face fell like he lost all of the fight he'd had in him only a second before. "Never mind. You're probably right." He grimaced as he rubbed his hands together. "You're cruel for saying that. But you're also probably right. I just wish it was me. I'm the one who was with Richard and put up with him for two years, so it should have been me he went after. Not Chris, and not simply because he was in that club looking for someone. I know why he was there, and it's shit, and you're cruel."

"Bran, when last did you actually stop talking to listen to yourself?" Kaden asked him.

Bran stared at him. "What do you mean?"

"You are the one who is cruel, and it sounds like it's such a normal part of how you conduct yourself in business. The sad part is, that it's flowed through to how you treat people around you. I'm not being cruel. It's because I care that I'm saying this, not to intentionally hurt you but in hope of you waking the hell up and seeing what you and Chris are doing to yourselves. Can't you see that?"

"You shouldn't care. In two and a half weeks, there won't be any reason to." Bran looked down at his phone, momentarily distracted by the ringing. "Hello?" he said, answering it.

"Mr. Wilson?"

Bran nodded and held out the phone for anyone wanting to hear the call. "Yes."

"We have a Christophori Romanoff here in the ER at St. Catherine's Hospital. You're his emergency contact."

Bran shook his head. "Put me on the phone with him please. I know he was hurt. I was on the phone with him when the paramedics came. Just let me talk to him."

"Okay. One moment. They were able to rush him through fairly quickly. You're lucky, his procedure normally takes longer than it did."

They all waited through the sounds of beeping machines and people talking in the background until finally there was Chris. "Hello, Chris's house of pain."

"Not funny," Bran snickered. "Not at all. At least you sound a little better."

"They pumped my stomach, and it's like instantly being sober, with all the crap that comes with it. You owe me a new stomach."

"I want to come there," Bran said, sliding off the counter so he could pace through the dining room on his bare feet.

Chris sighed. "I don't want you here. You come here, and I'll check myself out, and I'll get on a plane to Morocco, and you and I both know how much you hate the food there. And camels. There might be camels in Morocco, and you think they look weird. Don't come, Bran. Please. I don't want you here. I don't want to see you like this. I don't want you to see me. I'll be on the first flight to Montana as soon as I'm able to leave here."

"And then we need to talk," Bran said solemnly. "I need to tell you about Richard. I should have told you before. But I didn't, and I was ashamed, and now you're hurt because of me."

Chris was silent for several long minutes. "You didn't enjoy what he did, did you?"

"No. Never." Honesty meant everything right now. "Did he do anything to you besides beating you up?"

Chris laughed dryly, though it ended on a pain-filled groan. "No. Being punched around a bit was bad enough. Not even fucked-up Richard wanted to fuck me. Hating you right now," Chris replied with a long sigh.

Bran smiled a little at the phone. "I know. And I'm okay with that. I called Misha, by the way, he'll be by to see you. I need to text him to let him know what hospital you're in, though."

"Talk to him more. He can yell at you for being stupid while I get better. I will see you in a few days. Promise."

Bran wiped at his eyes. "You better."

"Bye. Don't tell Samuel what happened. I don't want him knowing."

Bran glanced over at Samuel but didn't say anything. "Sure. I won't tell him."

"Good. Bye." Bran hung up the phone and met Kaden's gaze. He glanced away to send a quick text, probably to Misha, but Kaden wasn't close enough to see.

The three of them were staring at him when he looked back up and said, "What now?"

Chapter Eleven

Being stared at sucked for Bran, but not as much as knowing his best friend was hurt, lying in a hospital bed, and unwilling to see him. "I'm being serious here," Bran said when no one answered him.

"Do you make a habit out of lying to people you care about? Why did you promise Chris Samuel wouldn't know about this when he already does?" Kaden said with disapproval.

Bran rolled his eyes and tried as hard as he could to bring his shields up, but he felt cracked open and exposed, in more places than he'd ever been before. It was hard to sit still, to not shake, to simply be in the same room as them and not run like he wanted to, like his mind was saying he had to. Like he was so damn good at.

"If Chris knows, he wouldn't come back here. And I need him here. I need to know he's safe, and I need to make sure he doesn't make any more stupid decisions. But he won't face Samuel again, not willingly. Not after what Samuel said to him and not after what he just tried to do. Once he's here I'll strap him down and make sure he doesn't leave, but getting him here is the important part. And, also, asshole, you don't tell me how to talk to my best friend." He didn't mean the words, but he needed their defense, because if Kaden had let him, he would have run into his arms seeking the comfort he was sure Kaden could give him. If Kaden hated him, was disgusted with him… things were much better like that. Safer for him.

Kaden looked somber. "Okay, that makes sense. For once I understand what you're doing and why."

Bran ignored his words. "Tell me to do something on the farm, or I'm going back upstairs to my room. You've got three seconds."

"I don't think any of us are up to hard work today after the stress this morning. We'll just take it slow today, milk the cows in a little bit while the other two feed the calves and shift the bulls. That'll be enough. Why don't we all sit down here, including you, and enjoy some mindless fun. We can watch TV, movies, or even play games on the console?"

Bran hadn't played video games in years, but the idea of watching TV with them and trying not to care about anything didn't sound too awful. While Kaden still seemed to be waiting for his answer, there was a knock on the front door, and as stupid as it was, Bran hoped it was Chris there waiting for him.

It wasn't, though. Instead he opened the door to the creepy delivery guy. "Hi."

"I've got another package for you. Says it's cheesecake. I could come in, and we could have some. I'd eat it off you and—"

Bran quickly shook his head. "Nope. Counteroffer. You give me my cheesecake, and unless it's marked as cold, or something I have to sign for, in the future you leave my packages on the fucking doorstep and stop trying to hit on me. You saw me in a towel once. Just once. Get the hell over it. Now, my cheesecake." He held out his hands and waited for the now silent, and no longer nearly as cocky, deliveryman to give him the box. Which he did, before backing away.

Bran shut the door behind him with his foot and headed into the kitchen where he opened the cheesecakes. One plain, one chocolate chip. Chris's favorite. "Eat some, if you want to," he said to the three of them. "They were for Chris, but I'll order him more before he comes." For himself he grabbed down a plate and took a fork out of the drawer before taking a precut slice of each and heading into the living room. "Put them away when you're done," he called back to them as he made himself comfortable in the old recliner, which was the only seat that he wouldn't have to share with someone else.

Trent was first to take up the offer for the dessert, followed by Kaden and then Samuel. The TV was on, but Bran found it hard to concentrate on the show as his thoughts circled around Chris and how stupid and, he now realized, selfish, he'd been for not sharing the truth of his relationship with Richard with his best friend. His first slice of cheesecake was gone before he'd really noticed he'd been eating so quickly.

Suddenly Samuel flew out of his chair. "Bloody hell, Trent. Can't you keep your pets to yourself?"

Trent looked around, by his feet, his shoulders, and behind him on the couch. A brown lizard sat on the fabric behind his neck and as Bran watched, it walked onto Trent's arm.

"You let your pets just run around?" Bran asked him as he curled his feet up and under him, afraid of stepping on any little animals now that he knew they were out there.

"No, they let me run around and then find me whenever it suits them. They're not my pets actually, they're wild animals that seem to find me irresistible."

When Bran looked over at Kaden and Samuel, they nodded their heads. "It's been like this all our lives. Critters big and small showing up wherever we go," Kaden said.

Bran shuddered as he thought about wild animals crawling all over him, especially while he slept. It was bad enough sleeping next to Chris, on the rare nights when he crashed at Bran's place, with him stretching out and taking over most of the bed, but the thought of little lizards and things on him while he slept was terrifying.

"That's so cool and scary at the same time." Looking at Samuel, he smirked. "Don't tell me you're scared of that little old lizard there?"

"No. I'm not, but seeing something move behind you out of the corner of your eye is really freaky." Samuel sat back down and resumed eating his cheesecake.

It didn't take long for Bran to relax in their company. Now that he thought of it, the three men were easy to be around when they weren't prying him for information or telling him about his horrible life choices. He wasn't sure when he drifted off to sleep, or how long he'd been out, but he woke up groggy and with his neck protesting in soreness from the angle he'd had it at. It took him a second to realize that he'd been woken up by a phone call, or rather the third phone call from a familiar number.

Bran bit back a curse as he considered not answering the phone altogether, but he couldn't do that. Chris would want him to at least try to be nice. "Anyone want to get to know Chris's dad? Yes? Congrats, then. This is going to be so much fun. Not." He swiped his finger across the face of his phone to answer it and put it on speakerphone as well out of habit. "Hello, Mr. Romanoff. Pleasant day sitting on all your hatred?"

"You little shit. What have you done with my son? He's not answering his phone, and he hasn't been into the office at all today."

Mr. Romanoff was as nice as ever, but the funny thing about it was that having him be such an ass to him, which was actually normal for him, made Bran feel better. A strange constant in this fucked-up day.

"Chris is fine. If he's not answering his phone, it's because he doesn't want to talk to you. Which, let's be honest here, isn't all that surprising."

"I'm sending a car to your apartment. If he's not in that car and dressed appropriately five minutes after it arrives, I will have you arrested for kidnapping."

Bran smiled at his phone. Normally he tried to be nice to Chris's dad, but today he just couldn't muster it. "He's not there, I'm not there, we're off on a drunken orgy together in the middle of the Pacific."

"Of course you are. Fucking faggot. I'll—"

"If you want to know where Chris is, then talk to Misha. Maybe Chris will call you then. I wouldn't, but then again you're not my father. Thank fuck. But if you want to see him, talk to Misha." Bran quickly hung up on him and was glad to be done with the conversation. It was all fun and games until Mr. Romanoff brought out the f-bomb.

Bran looked around the room, waiting for any of them to say something. "Questions? Comments? General abstract thoughts about life?" He settled his gaze on Kaden. "And I swear to God, if you say one thing about how I need to be nicer to people, including him, I will stab you with my fork, and then I will keep eating the cheesecake off of it because I am too lazy to go get a new one right now."

Kaden said nothing, but Samuel got up to walk to the kitchen. "Good on you, mate. That self-righteous prick needed to hear that."

"You're quite the violent person, aren't you?" Kaden mused.

"Says the person who wields a shotgun like a pro," Bran pointed out. Samuel's appreciation for what he'd said made him feel a little better, but it was only momentary. The truth was that he'd been saying the same thing, and worse, to Mr. Romanoff since he'd met Chris's father. Chris chose to hide in the closet, Bran couldn't. This man was responsible for Chris's fucked-up existence in an attempt to please them all, and Bran hated him for it.

"Maybe we have something in common after all." Kaden smiled at him, and for some strange reason, Bran grinned back.

"We both hate homophobic assholes?" Bran guessed. Before Kaden could respond to him, though, Bran was already moving on. "It would have been so much better for him if we'd shared the same father. I didn't have much of anything in common with mine, but I can say that he, and my grandfather too, didn't give a damn about me coming out. They were more concerned with why I was failing math class at the time."

"In addition to despising bullies, we're both good with our hands. For violence I mean." Kaden stumbled over his words, and Bran burst out laughing.

"I know I am, but I can't speak for you," Bran flirted back.

A gagging noise sounded nearby, and Bran saw Trent mimic throwing up like a five-year-old. "That's my cue to leave. Getting sickeningly sweet in here."

"We could go back to hating each other for a moment if it makes you feel better. Kaden, you're an asshole. There. Better?" Bran asked him, though there was no venom in his words.

"Umm, I'd rather not speak about ass and holes in one sentence right now," Kaden teased.

Bran snorted and shook his head. "Fine. You are a fucking asshole." His phone started vibrating again. "Great. Another of my favorite people in the world." He answered it and made sure to put it on speakerphone. "Misha. Are you at the hospital?"

"Why in the fuck would you tell my father to call me?" Misha snapped at him.

Bran sat back in the recliner. He loved Chris, but really, his best friend's family was messed up. "Because I was done talking to him. He dropped that word I hate. You know how I hate that."

"You sound like a pouty, petulant child, Wilson."

Smirking, Bran shook his head. "Yes, Master Sergeant Romanoff." He was too exhausted to try playing with Misha, and the man never played back anyway, so he quickly dropped the act. "Are you with Chris?"

"You think I want to listen to you whine? Why else would I be calling you? Yes, I'm with him. Tell me who hurt him. I feel like hurting them back after seeing his face."

Bran cringed, really not wanting to know. "His name's Richard. He was my ex. You're welcome to break every bone in his body for what he did to Chris. I'll text you his address."

"Do that. I'll make sure to prevent him from carrying on the evil gene." He hung up, and Bran put his phone aside after sending out the quick text. He wouldn't answer it again unless it was Chris. He was done with everyone else in Manhattan for the moment.

Trent strangely stood frozen in the middle of the carpet in the lounge. "He's intense, and his voice turns my knees to fucking jelly."

Bran found himself laughing at the absurd statement and realized he hadn't been this joyful in a really long time. It felt amazing. "That is one man you do not want to handle without safety equipment. And I mean gloves, knee and elbow pads, bulletproof vest, and football helmet. All of it. Because you sure as shit are gonna need all the protection you can get." He shook his head, remembering his first time meeting Chris's older half brother. He'd been scared shitless by a man who hadn't done more than shake his hand before writing him off as soon as Bran had opened his mouth and said something stupid. He had hit on Misha, in a big way, if memory served him right. Actually, come to think of it, he might have even offered to blow him. Probably not the smartest move he'd ever made. But not the dumbest either. That honor went right to fucking Richard Prezinski and the miserable two years Bran had stayed with him, convinced that he needed Richard in his life and that he couldn't do any better because he was simply too screwed up.

THEY TOOK care of the cows a few hours later, then had a quiet dinner of the leftovers from the takeout Bran had ordered over the past few days. By the time he was done with his jumble of mismatched cuisine, he was ready to swear off delivery and actually do some cooking for a while instead. Just not that night. He'd done enough for one day already.

At nearly midnight and with just him and Kaden in the house, Bran got up from the recliner he'd been comfortably resting in while he and Kaden watched a movie. The others had been gone for almost an hour, and he'd considered just falling asleep right where he was. But he needed out of his jeans, and his teeth tasted disgusting.

"I'm going up," he said to Kaden as he pushed himself out of the recliner. Kaden gave him a wave, and Bran began stripping off his clothes before he reached the stairs. It was only his shirt, but when he caught Kaden watching him, it was hard not to feel flattered by the attention. If Kaden had been anyone else, Bran would have probably played with him a little, teasing him in the way his exes had called him on plenty of times.

"What are you thinking about?" Kaden asked him as he remained at the foot of the stairs.

Bran could have lied. He did it easily enough. But telling Kaden the truth was a novel experience for him. "That I could do some real damage to you if only I had a banana to show off my skills." He saw

Kaden's blush, and it made him smile. "I brought a lot of drama into your life, and I'm not sorry about that, but I will say thanks for handling it so well. You're still a jerk about it at times. But you're a mature jerk, so whatever."

Wanting to say more, he instead chose to head upstairs before his mouth could get him into trouble. A quick stop in his bedroom for a pair of lounge pants, then he went across the hall to the bathroom where he washed his face, brushed his teeth, and when he realized he was out of his favorite nighttime moisturizer, he didn't panic. He could get more in Manhattan. Two weeks without it wouldn't kill him any more than this place was already trying to. With his shirt off, he could inspect his bruises, which were mostly faded thankfully, and his hand was pretty normal too. His hair was a mess, but since he slept alone and didn't really care what anyone on the farm thought about his appearance, he left it for the night.

He expected to be alone on the landing when he came out wearing his sleep pants, but instead Kaden stood there, looking ready for bed in a pair of similar, plaid pants as well. "Hi," Bran said, stepping away from the door and expecting Kaden to go through it. But he just stood there looking, and with his shirt off, he was a tempting sight for Bran. If Kaden wasn't going to do anything, Bran wasn't just going to waste the moment.

He stepped closer, judging Kaden's reaction as each second passed and ready to call the whole thing off if he seemed at all disinterested. He'd had enough of everything for one day, he didn't need to be rejected by Kaden on top of everything else. But when he got close enough to touch Kaden, the man was still silently watching him. Bran lifted his hand to drag his fingers lightly over Kaden's chest and down his stomach, following a dark trail of hair that ran below the waist of his pants. Bran desperately wanted to follow that trail down with his hand, and then his mouth, but he stopped himself before he could make that mistake.

"Good night," he said, looking into Kaden's brown eyes. He made himself step away, but he wasn't fast enough to avoid Kaden grabbing him as he circled his hand around Bran's wrist and stopped him from leaving. "Wha—"

Bran didn't have time to finish that sentence before Kaden grabbed him roughly and crashed his mouth against Bran's, stealing his breath and making him freeze at the same time. He didn't stay immobile for long, though, not with Kaden's hands roaming over his chest, pulling him out of his stunned silence. He kissed him back, shoving his tongue into Kaden's mouth and reaching up to dig his fingers into Kaden's shoulders. He was as strong and just as firm as Bran had imagined him to be in all the times he'd thought about him recently.

He didn't get to touch him for long, though, not nearly as much as he would have anyway, because a few seconds later, Kaden had his hands pinned above his head as he pushed him hard against the wall, his face pressed against the peeling wallpaper as he gasped.

"You don't know what you do to me," Kaden groaned out as he pushed hard against Bran's ass, rubbing him through the thin layers of pants between them. Bran smiled. He did know. He'd seen it in Kaden's eyes and the way Kaden watched him. It was gratifying to know he'd been right and hot as hell to feel Kaden take control of him and be rough with him, just as Bran wanted him to be.

He leaned back a little, putting himself in the perfect position for Kaden to thrust against him. Kaden was hard and deliciously built if Bran was correct. Without seeing for himself, though, he couldn't be sure.

He'd been taken against a wall before, so that was nothing new. But being kissed, his mouth ravaged by someone as hungry for him as Kaden seemed to be—that was a completely different kind of experience. With his mouth controlled by Kaden and his chest pressed against the wall, there wasn't much he could do. And for once, for one tiny moment, not having those options was okay with him. He couldn't move, but that was okay. He couldn't make Kaden kiss him, and instead had to wait for Kaden's mouth to come back to his, but he didn't fight it.

Kaden reached around and put one hand squarely on his cock, squeezing him through the front of his pants. The thin material was too much, and Bran wanted it to be Kaden's hand on him alone, not Kaden's hand and his pants, and the fucking buttons that went up his fly. But with Kaden both rubbing him and grinding against his ass, there was little Bran could think of besides how good it felt and how much he wanted him.

He panted and groaned, both rubbing against Kaden and thrusting against his hand in an often awkward dance that brought him pleasure. "I want you," he gasped, the desperation, the sheer wild need, clear in his voice even to his own ears.

Kaden ran his tongue up the back of Bran's shoulder, making him shiver. "Then stay in my room tonight."

The offer was tempting, and if Kaden hadn't slid his hand inside Bran's pants right then, he might have taken him up on it. But something about having him there, touching him, made Bran freeze.

"Stop," he whispered, his body betraying him even as he said the words. It would be so easy to give in, to be with Kaden that night, to let himself have the pleasure he needed.

Kaden pulled away and put a good three feet between them as Bran turned around, facing him and seeing disappointment there in his expression. "I'm sorry." Kaden believed in love. Bran was sure of it. He hadn't asked him, and he doubted that Kaden was the type of guy to go all poetic about it like Samuel had. But still Bran knew. Kaden wasn't the type of guy to sleep around. And Bran wasn't one to commit. "I'm not good for you," he said, pushing off the wall and going straight to his room where he closed the door behind himself. Bran leaned his forehead heavily against the wall as he shook with a hot, painful mixture of need and regret.

CHAPTER TWELVE

THE CALL he'd been hoping for came in at five in the morning, and Bran came away from the milking pit, despite Kaden's protests, to answer it. "Chris?" he asked excitedly.

"No. It's me." Misha calling from Chris's phone. Never a good sign in his book, though this was the first time he'd experienced it.

Bran tried to take a deep breath. "Is he okay? What's wrong?"

"He's fine. My phone is dead. We'll be stopping by his apartment, then mine to grab a few things, before we get on a plane to Montana. First class with all the extras. All on your credit card. I thought it would be fitting, considering you got him into this mess."

Bran wasn't about to start arguing with him. "That's fine. I'm glad he had one of the numbers on him. Can I talk to him?"

"No," Misha said harshly, making him scowl. "Not until you and I talk first. He'll be in Montana, on your farm, for a week. It's been cleared with my father. He will be there to relax and recover and get his head on straight, because this will not be happening again. Until I say otherwise, you are not to touch him, speak to him, or come anywhere near him."

Bran wanted to argue, but he knew from experience doing so with Misha would be a wasted effort and only leave him feeling frustrated and on edge. He had enough of that, though of a different sort, with Kaden at the moment and didn't need it from Misha as well.

"Will you tell him I miss him, then?"

"Depends on how our talk goes. You fuck it up and I'll make sure that you never, ever see him again." To some people Misha's threat might have seemed silly, or idle. Bran knew to take him seriously.

"I'll be here," he promised. Not like he could actually leave anyway.

"I know you will. We'll be at the farm by sundown." Misha hung up on him, and Bran was left standing there, staring out at the cows in stunned silence.

BY THE time the sun started setting, Bran could hardly sit still. Instead he chose to pace in front of the big windows in the living room as he watched for a car to pull up. Pacing there meant that sometimes he ran into Samuel, who was also pacing, but he tried his best to avoid running into him. He'd done it once and had gone flying to the floor, while Samuel had just looked on. At least he'd been a gentleman and had offered Bran a hand up.

"They'll be here soon," Kaden promised him, for probably the dozenth time.

Bran believed him, in a way, but he knew he would feel much better about it once Chris was actually there where Bran could see him for himself. It was nearly dark, though, when a car did pull up in front of the house. He swung the door open and charged out there. If it was anyone else, he would have told them they were late. For Misha he stayed silent and hugged his arms around his chest, waiting for Chris to come out.

Misha got out first, then came around the front of the car to get Chris. Even in the bad lighting, Bran could see the bruises, the bandage on his cheek, and the sling over his left arm. He wasn't walking well, or at all without help, and Bran quickly moved to support his other side, but Misha shook his head at him.

"What did I tell you? Stay back there until we've talked."

Bran wasn't a child, and he did remember, but the need to help his best friend was very nearly overwhelming to him, especially when he saw Chris slip a little in Misha's arms.

"Get back!" Misha barked at him as he lifted Chris into his arms and brought him sideways through the front door. Bran trailed silently behind him, all of his attention focused on the drowsy Chris and the bruises he could see purpling his face.

"Where am I taking him?" Misha asked him, but Bran wasn't paying attention to him. He was too focused on Chris. "Bran!" Misha snapped at him, bringing him to attention in his commanding way. "Where am I taking him?" Misha asked him once he'd lifted his gaze to meet Misha's steel gray eyes.

"Upstairs. First door on the right."

Misha gave him a nod, and Bran followed him to the bottom of the stairs where he watched Misha take Chris up.

"So that's…." Trent shook his head. "Still fucking jelly. My knees. They're going to be useless with him around," Trent explained when Bran looked back at him.

He nodded, understanding. Misha scared him shitless, but maybe he had a different effect on other people.

"Are you okay?" Kaden asked him as Bran took a few steps away from the stairs to come back to the wall so he could use it for balance.

Bran looked at him briefly, then quickly looked away. "You saw his bruises. I'm nowhere near okay." His hands shook, so he stuffed them into the pockets of his jeans to hide them. He couldn't get rid of his hot, angry tears so easily, though, so he turned his head away from them all to hide them the best he could.

"You are a fucking ignorant, selfish, conceited child," Misha spat at him as he came back down the stairs. "Sit down at the table, Bran. You and I are going to have a chat."

Misha's idea of a chat never ended well for Bran, and he'd been through plenty of them. Normally he balked and tried anything he could to get out of them. But nothing ever worked on Misha, and this time Bran knew he deserved whatever Misha wanted to dish out to him.

With Misha there, watching him from the other end of the table while he sat down, it was like they were the only ones in the house. Misha was that big, that imposing, and Bran felt completely drained of any will to fight back against him after seeing the state Chris was in.

"Thanks for bringing him here," Bran said, putting his arms on the table.

Misha shook his head and tapped his fingers roughly on the table. "You don't speak. You listen. I'm so fucking tired of hearing you run your mouth. Understand?"

Bran nodded.

"I need a 'yes, sir' from you."

Bran narrowed his eyes at Misha. "This isn't the Army, you aren't my superior officer, and if you try to make me say it, and actually get me to do so, it would be a lie. So how about treating me like another man, instead of a new recruit in boot camp how you normally do, and let's have that talk?"

The surprise was there in Misha's eyes, though it didn't last long. Through the kitchen door, he saw Kaden, Samuel, and Trent come closer. If they were worried about him, they didn't need to be. Misha could tear him a new one, but he would never actually lay a hand on him because of how much Chris cared for him. There was no malice in Misha that he knew of, only a protective streak that extended solely to Chris and meant anyone who hurt his little brother was in for a world of trouble. It was one of the things Bran respected about him, because he knew no matter what Misha thought of him, he would always be there for Chris. It was something he couldn't have said about their father.

"Let's get started, then, without the sir this time."

Bran tilted his chin toward him in thanks.

"You are a spoiled little child and a selfish one. You act like a whore, you have sex with anyone you please, and you think you can have anything you want because you have a nice ass, lack any real gag reflex, and have enough money to toss at anyone who doesn't instantly agree with you."

Bran wasn't about to deny any of that.

"And because of your stupidity, Chris is now in a lot of pain. Richard was your ex. You were the one who found him, who introduced him to Chris. And, Bran, I want you to know, I know everything. The man chose to talk, to beg, while I was working him over. I could kill you myself for not warning Chris about him. You disgust me, and I know you are horrible for my brother. I wish he'd never met you. You were sixteen and giving out blowjobs to anyone who even smiled at you. You were a whore then, and by all accounts that hasn't changed at all. You're a lost cause, and I'm only sorry that my brother got mixed up with you. Whatever problems you have, whatever damage was done to you to make you the fucked-up person you are today, my brother didn't deserve any of that."

The truth in his words hurt, but they were still the truth, and it was high time Bran started admitting that. "I know."

"You are…. Hang on. What did you just say to me?" Misha actually looked shocked for a whole two seconds before doubt came over his features.

Bran lifted his chin defiantly. He was done lying and pretending, and Misha, as much as he didn't like him, was right about him. "I said that I know. You're right. My money only increased my problems, and two weeks ago, I still would have gotten down on my knees for little more than a smile and a cute face. I didn't care if the man was married or a client. If I wanted them, then I had them. It was that simple. Sex and money are both tools to use for power, and I'm used to using both to get what I want. I'm saying that I know. I'm saying that you're right. And I'm saying I'm trying to be better."

Misha didn't look as if he believed him, which wasn't surprising. Two weeks wasn't about to be enough to change over a decade of behavior, but it was enough to start making him see things a little differently.

"Why?"

That was the easiest answer of all. "Because I don't want to see Chris hurt any more than he already is. Because I won't bury my best friend. Because if I'm better, then I believe he will be too. Because if I don't go to clubs, if I don't fuck random guys in bathrooms, if I make an actual effort to know who it is that is in my bed, and if I try to actually care about myself more than my money or how I'm going to get off, then maybe, just maybe, Chris will too."

He shook his head at Misha's stunned expression. "I won't lose him. I love him too much. You don't have to believe me, and I wouldn't blame you for thinking I'm still a lying prick. I've lied to you a few hundred times since we've met, and those are just the times that I remember. But I am going to try, Misha."

Misha sat back in the chair and gave him a slight nod. "For once I actually believe you're serious. I don't know if you'll be able to change your ways, but I think you might want to. Go upstairs. He's been asking about you nonstop. But Bran, if you cause him to get hurt by your own stupidity again, I will take him away from you, and I will hide him somewhere that even you, with all of your money, won't be able to find him again. I will not spend another night in a hospital with my brother lying beside me because of your actions. Do we understand each other?"

"Perfectly." Bran slid his chair back from the table and was careful to avoid Misha as he walked past him and out the kitchen door. If Kaden wanted to say something to him, and he looked like he might have, he didn't get the chance because after touching him briefly on his wrist, only enough to acknowledge he was there, Bran headed up the stairs and disappeared into his bedroom.

Chris was a fucking mess. There was no better way to put it, and Bran sat down heavily on the floor beside the bed with his back to Chris. There was enough room beside him if he'd wanted to spoon him, but it didn't feel right. After Chris getting hurt, all because he hadn't told him about Richard, he didn't feel worthy.

"I'm sorry," he quietly said as he leaned his head back against the mattress.

"I know you are. I love you, but I'm mad at you, and I don't know how long I'll take to forgive you for this," Chris told him just as softly. "I am glad I'm here, though. Misha tried to convince me to get better in the city, but I didn't want to be there. Not when you're here." He did bring his hand down to Bran's shoulder, though, and Bran was grateful for that contact. "Tell me about you and Richard. Not the good stuff, not the stuff you used to say. Tell me about him hurting you. Tell me the truth."

Bran turned so he could see Chris's face. His right eye was swollen, his lip was cut, and Bran wished he could take it all away. "I never wanted you to know about that part."

"It's too late now," Chris said, smiling at him, then wincing as he reached up to touch his lip. "Ow. Okay, so no smiling for a while. Or laughing. My ribs hurt so much, even with the pain medicine. It makes me stupid, so if I say something really out of character, blame it on the pills."

Bran smiled at him and reached out to touch Chris on his shoulder. "I missed you. I was so scared."

"I missed you too. Stop avoiding the question, though. I need you to tell me about you and Richard."

Bran really didn't want to, but if Chris needed to hear it, he'd say the words he should have years ago. If he had, Chris wouldn't have been in this sorry state. "Richard and I.... It didn't start out horrible. You know that. We used to go on double dates, and he would take us to expensive restaurants and buy us really nice clothes. Then...." Bran shook his head.

The words were too hard to say, the memories too vivid when he brought them back up. "Sometimes abuse starts slowly, like a whisper of doubt where you know something is wrong, but you don't know how wrong until it's very wrong. When I stopped calling you all the time, when I broke lunch dates with you, when I said I couldn't go out because I had to work late, that was almost always because of him. Because if I really loved him, I would stay with him, I would spend more time with him, because if he mattered that much to me, I wouldn't choose you over him."

Chris moved his hand to Bran's neck, and Bran turned his face to kiss Chris's palm. It looked to be one of the few unblemished parts of him. "I should have fought harder. I should have told him to fuck off, that you were more important to me than he would ever be. But I didn't. I was young and stupid and thought for sure I was in love for the first time. When he told me I was fat, that I was lazy and ugly, I started to believe him. He said I couldn't do anything right, and I started letting him do things for me because I was so fucked up in my own head that I actually believed what he was saying. When he hit me…."

Bran licked his lips and wished he didn't have to say the words, but Chris was looking at him expectantly. "When he hit me, I thought it was what I deserved. I thought I'd done something wrong. When he told me he loved me, that if I was better he wouldn't have to kick me in my stomach or smack me across my face, I thought he was right. And Chris, the stupidest, worst, most fucked-up part of it all was I actually started to believe love was only that. That if I loved someone, then I endured whatever he wanted to throw at me because the more you put up with, the more it showed you cared about them."

Chris closed his eyes. "That's such a crock of shit."

"I know that. Now. But back then? I thought Richard walked on water. I thought everything wrong was because of me. I thought I was the one needing help, not him. He was in my head and in my life for so long, and there didn't seem to be a good way out of it. I laid there, and I let him use me. I began to expect the beatings when I'd done something wrong. And all the time you were less than five blocks away from me, and I didn't have the guts to walk over to your apartment and tell you everything."

Though it was a struggle, Chris managed to sit up with Bran's help. "You should have told me. When you came back after that time, telling me how you'd gotten so wrapped up in Richard you'd forgotten all about me, that hurt. You've always been my best friend and like a brother to me. Even more than Misha is. He's great, and I love him, but not like I love you. And I felt like you threw me away. Like I didn't even matter to you anymore. I couldn't take it."

Bran laid his head over Chris's lap and hugged his legs tightly as Chris rested his head on top of Bran's head. "I'm so sorry," he whispered.

"I never meant for you to feel like that back then, or for you to be so hurt now. You're all I have."

Chris smoothed his hair back from his face, and Bran closed his eyes. "How did you leave him?"

Bran kept his eyes closed, not wanting to see Chris's face when he told him the last of the secrets he'd been harboring for years. "He told me he was done with me. That I'd become useless and boring. I practically lived for him, and he threw me away like trash." Bran wiped at the shameful tears that tracked down his cheeks. "A few months later, he came back, but by that time you and I were inseparable again, and even though we were slutty, I saw the difference between what we did and what I had allowed him to do to me. We slept with people because it was fun. Richard had wanted complete control, and that had never been fun for me. I told him never to come back, to lose my number, to forget all about me. And I thought he had."

"And that's when you stopped believing in love," Chris figured out. "I was wondering when that happened."

Bran sat back on his heels and gave Chris a little smile, followed by a nod. "It started with my parents' divorce, but it ended with Richard. He was the first and last person who ever said they loved me. And the same went for me. He ruined me for the good guys of the world."

"Guys like Kaden?" Chris asked him.

Bran nodded. Just like Kaden. "Don't let the crap we've been through and the choices we've made ruin you for Samuel. Please?"

Chris grimaced. "Things aren't as easy as you want them to be."

"They never are." He got off the floor and kissed Chris on his unbruised cheek. "Get some rest. I'm going downstairs to make sure Misha hasn't killed them all yet." He helped Chris lie back down in bed and covered him up to his shoulders with the sheet.

"You know, I can actually walk and come downstairs and do things for myself. Right?" Chris asked him.

Bran shrugged. "Maybe. But I like taking care of you. Need anything?" He made sure Chris had his phone within easy reach in case he needed one of them later on.

"I'll take a shot of bourbon if there's any left and a pillow to throw at your head."

Chris smiled, despite his grimace, and Bran laughed. "Night. I'm glad you're back here."

"Yeah, yeah. You really think I'd let Misha take me anywhere else? He tried. Believe me. Paris was an option there for a little bit. You know how much I like crepes. But I had to come back here and be with you. Close the damn door when you leave."

Bran laughed as he did just that.

CHAPTER THIRTEEN

WHEN BRAN reached the landing upstairs to go to Chris, Kaden faced the big badass at the table. "Misha, I'm Kaden Barker. These are my two best friends and coworkers, Samuel Mealamu and Trent McCarthy. It's nice to meet you, but I just want to make you understand that the way you just spoke to Bran will be the last time you do so. He may be a little shit sometimes, but none of what you blamed him for was intentional, and making him feel any more guilty than he already does is unnecessary."

From his sitting position, Misha glared at him, a tiny muscle ticking along his jaw. Steel-gray eyes, which Kaden could imagine would reduce some men to a whimpering mess, scrutinized him from head to toe.

When the man looked at Samuel, his shoulders squared, and he stood up. Trent appeared on Kaden's other side. "Fair enough. I can see I'm outnumbered. In opinion anyway. I'll back off, but only if you keep him in line. And, if you really love him, which it's clear you think you do, then I suggest you get your head examined. That boy is toxic." Misha shook his head as if he felt sorry for Kaden.

"Your opinion of him is just that—an opinion. Maybe if you bothered over the years to get to know him instead of grilling him for every little thing, you may have discovered there is an actual human being in that cocky, selfish, conceited body. And that man hurts, and thanks to you and dickhead Richard, even more so tonight. Not everyone deals with life's shit the same way. Some of us are lucky enough to come from loving homes, but other's lives may be hell. I know yours has probably not been moonshine and roses, seeing as I've had the pleasure of hearing your sperm donor speak to Bran on the phone the other day. And by the looks of you, you chose to handle your pile of crap in your way. That does not mean you are any better than anyone else."

Misha stood ramrod straight during Kaden's speech. "But, if you can ease up on him, I'm sure we can all get along fine, even if it's just for the duration of Chris's stay here on the farm."

Samuel cleared his throat. "I guess now it's my turn." Misha swung his gaze over to Samuel, but not before Kaden saw his stare linger on Trent.

"I know Chris is your brother, and you clearly love and protect him, but here's just a heads-up. Chris is mine." Samuel dropped the words like a hand grenade right there, and Kaden wanted to run and hide.

"The hell you say!" Misha gritted out.

"It could be hell, for you anyway, or like my good mate, Kaden, said, we can get this stuff out of the way now and all get along. Your choice."

Misha came around the table and got into Samuel's face. If the situation hadn't been so dire, Kaden would've taken a moment to appreciate the two gorgeous and strong beasts squaring off. Misha had a few inches on Samuel, but his friend made up for it in sheer muscle mass. Kaden would buy tickets for that match.

"What gives you that right?" Misha asked.

"The fact that he told me he wants me and because I know, and you better not tell him I do, that he went to that club and got picked up by that abusive fucker because he thought he couldn't have me." Samuel rumbled back, not appearing to be intimidated by Misha at all.

Kaden watched as Misha looked Samuel up and down even as close as they stood to each other.

"What the fuck does he see in you?" Misha retaliated, his nostrils flaring.

"And you call Bran conceited. Maybe he sees his future. I'm no walk in the park, but I can tell you that if it works between us, he won't find anyone on this earth, including you, who will love and protect him as I will. And that won't mean I'll curb his freedom like your asshole of a father has done. You want to lay any blame for Chris's physical and mental brokenness, there's the person you're looking for. For the record, tell that man if he ever sets foot near Chris again, I will beat the crap out of him!" Samuel's voice rose a little. Kaden knew the man was about to lose his cool completely, and that would be really bad.

"Tell me when it's going to happen. I'd pay to see that," Bran spoke up from behind them. Kaden turned to see him drinking straight from the bottle of bourbon he kept in his room.

"That's...."

Bran nodded to him. "You should keep your door shut and your bourbon locked away when people have especially hard days. Better yet, buy two next time if you don't want to share." He looked from Kaden over to Misha. "Don't screw with Samuel. You hate me, fine. You fuck with Kaden, I'll do my best to hurt you back. But you screw with Samuel, you're messing with Chris. What he said is true. Chris cares about him. Deeply. More than I've ever seen him care about another person romantically. If you hurt Samuel in any way, you'll have Chris to deal with. So, Misha, I suggest you shut the fuck up, sit the fuck back down, and learn how to deal with this because you're not the only person in this house who gives a damn about him."

Misha shook his head. "The whore grew some balls," he snarled at Bran.

"The asshole can't learn to shut his fucking mouth," Bran snapped right back at him. "And don't call me a whore. Not again. Slut, fuck bunny, whore—they're all off the table. You don't actually fucking know me, and unless you've been a saint, which I know you haven't, sit down and zip it. Now, you're blocking my way to the cheesecake. Move your ass."

Though it looked like it pained him, Misha did take a step back, making a path for Bran to the fridge. He got out the cheesecake, along with a few plates and silverware.

Kaden stepped forward and reached out his hand. Misha stared first at it then into Kaden's eyes, before reaching out slowly to shake it. Next Misha surprised the fuck out of him by extending the gesture to Samuel, who smiled slightly as he made peace with him. When those gray eyes landed on Trent however, Kaden swore they came to life. They actually lightened and the handshake was more of a handhold.

"I wouldn't say it's nice to meet you all, because that's a lie, but hey, tomorrow may be different," Misha spoke as he disengaged from Trent and took his seat at the table, next to where Bran was indulging in a slice of cheesecake.

"Fuck, I'm tired." When Misha saw Bran eating, he moaned. "And hungry. Can I please have something to eat? Those peanuts on the plane just don't fill the hole in your stomach."

Bran passed him over some cheesecake. "Here. It's from the place down the street from my apartment. I had it flown in."

"Of course you did," Misha said sarcastically, but he started eating anyway.

"Anyone want a cup of coffee or tea?" Kaden decided to play the host. All four mouths were chewing, but their hands shot up to tell him yes.

"You five had better have saved me some of that," Chris spoke up from the doorway, making Bran shoot to his feet well before Misha even got out of his chair. They didn't have enough chairs at the table for Kaden to sit down too, so Bran gave Chris his chair and moved to sit on the counter. "Most of my cheesecake is gone, Bran," Chris grumbled.

Bran rolled his eyes, but Kaden did see him smile. "I'll order you three tomorrow. You're going to be so sick."

"That's fine. I don't mind being sick from eating this," Chris said, digging in.

Kaden scanned Chris's features, taking in the scrapes, bruises, and cuts on his skin. Before his anger could reignite, he shut it down. "So, Chris, when are we playing truth or dare again? At least it's a good excuse to get roaring drunk, and apparently some people start taking their clothes off, so we may even get a show if we're lucky."

Bran snorted and shook his head as his gaze met Kaden's. "Didn't know you were such a perv. You and delivery guy would get along well." He gave Kaden a wink, then put his empty dish into the sink.

"I'm up for a game," Chris announced.

"You can't have alcohol with your pain medicine," Misha said almost immediately.

Chris pouted and took another slice of the chocolate chip cheesecake for himself. "Yes, yes, I know. I'll be having water. And guys, let's not make it the pain fest that it was last time. Please?"

Bran nodded. "Agreed."

Kaden looked over to see Bran staring at him, as if warning him not to do anything to Chris this time around. Like he had any intention of hurting him.

"Misha, are you in?" Chris asked his brother.

"Yeah, I need a drink or ten, but that bottle is almost empty." Misha sighed dramatically, but a hint of a smile pulled at the corners of his mouth.

"Don't despair," Kaden reassured the man. "I have more where that came from." He left to fetch another bottle before rejoining them.

Bran was first to speak up with a question. "Kaden, when did you lose your virginity?" He got off the counter to start handing out glasses to everyone, then waited for Kaden to pour him a shot. He sipped it as he went back to the counter to sit.

"Well, us Kiwis love rugby, and I was playing first team for our school at the time. I think I was sixteen." Kaden didn't say anymore, because the age was all Bran asked for and helped himself to a shot.

"Almost the same age as you, Bran," Chris said, turning to look back at him.

"Shush. You can't spill my secrets," Bran chided him. "Besides, you don't even remember who it was with, so there's no way you actually remember what age I was."

Chris laughed, then put a hand to his side as pain shot into his expression. "If you expect me to remember who your first was, you're shit out of luck. I barely remember who mine was. Kaden, hurry up and ask your question already."

"Chris, do you like kissing? As in a lot? Some guys skimp on that, they don't seem to like it, but how about you?" Kaden asked.

"You better as hell not be asking for yourself," Bran growled at him.

"You're interrupting my answer time," Chris said, turning in his chair to look back at Bran. "And he's not asking for himself, whacko. Don't be a silly head."

"Pain meds galore, huh, Chris?" Bran teased.

"I do love you. You're so pretty when you aren't being an ass. Back to Kaden's question, though!" He turned his attention from Bran to Kaden. "If I was with a guy who let me kiss him as much as I wanted to. And if he had brushed his teeth. And if he didn't bite my lips like some kind of rabid animal. And if he actually smelled nice. Then yes, I do like kissing people. Assuming they meet all of the above criteria. A shot for me!"

Bran poured some water into his glass.

"And… a question." He looked around at them, but Kaden saw his gaze skip over Samuel almost immediately. "Misha! What are you going to do now that you're retired from the army? Do tell us. Inquiring minds want to know."

"How many pain pills did you take?" Bran asked him. "I think you're high."

"I think you're still pretty. Not as pretty as some people at this table, but still pretty," Chris shot back at him.

"I haven't decided yet. Maybe I'll do some traveling. I haven't been to a country outside of the US where I wasn't shooting at people in forever. Might be nice to see something before it gets blown up." Misha held out his glass for Kaden, who poured him a drink.

"Trent... are you seeing anyone right now?" Misha asked him.

Trent blushed beet red. "Other than a bunch of critters stalking me, no I'm not seeing anyone at the moment. I apparently have this natural magnetism, but it's restricted to animals only."

"Bran! I think Misha likes Trent!" Chris whispered loudly to him.

Bran just shook his head. "I think you need to lay off the pain pills. You're hilarious when you're high."

Trent swallowed his bourbon and pursed his lips in thought. "Chris, what is the strangest place you've ever had sex in?"

Chris turned back to Bran. "I'm sorry. You're not going to like this answer."

Bran frowned back at him. "Why not?"

"Because you know that classic truck you bought at auction, the one you spent an entire summer fixing up? I sort of kind of maybe had sex with your boyfriend at the time in the back of it."

Bran stared at him for all of three seconds before laughing hilariously. "You had sex with Jonny Crooked Dick? Why in the hell.... No. Don't tell me. It was the tattoos. It had to be the tattoos. You've always had a thing for guys with ink. You know what, thanks for coming clean, I still love you, but don't ever tell anyone you had sex with him again. You've got a reputation to uphold of actually having some taste in men. And Jonny Crooked Dick doesn't count. That's just embarrassing."

Chris smiled at him. "You're really not mad?"

Bran shook his head. "No. Not even a little. Unless, of course, this was before I tried to have sex with him and then you didn't warn me so I could have avoided that miserable night. But no, I'm not mad. Ask your question."

"Get me some water." Chris held up his glass for Bran to refill, which he gladly did. "I choose.... Hmm. Samuel. I choose you." Bran snorted behind him. "Are you a top, or a bottom?"

Kaden expected Samuel to balk at the personal nature of the question, but his friend just smiled and beckoned with his fingers for his glass of bourbon. "Many guys think because of my size, I like to top, but I don't prefer one or the other. I'm a switch, because there's nothing better than giving up control every so often and being taken. I love it."

Chris covered his blush with his hand and got up from the table to go stand facing Bran. "I still want him," he whispered loudly enough for everyone to hear him.

"I know you do. Go back and sit down before you fall over. Do you need anything?" Bran asked him.

Chris shook his head. "A way to make him like me?"

Kaden saw Bran look at Samuel over Chris's shoulder. "I think you'll be okay. Go sit before you fall on your face and your brother threatens to kill me." Chris gave him a kiss on his cheek, which Bran promptly wiped off, before going back to his seat.

Samuel eyed Misha. "What do you look for in a guy?"

Misha held up his glass for Kaden to refill. "Someone who can handle my military past and doesn't judge me for what I did while I served, including the people I shot and the cities I helped bomb." Relief filled Kaden when he heard Misha's words, because there wasn't a more nonjudgmental person on this planet than Trent. Misha drank back his bourbon as soon as Kaden had finished filling his glass. "Chris, what in the hell do you like about Samuel so much? And don't say the tattoos. That's not an answer."

"Take the dare this time," Bran urged from over his shoulder.

Chris shrugged and looked down at his water before looking back at his brother. "He makes me feel better. Somehow. Like it might be okay to just be me. Like that might be enough." He turned back to Bran. "Hit me, barkeep. And make it a double."

Bran gave him a little smile and refilled his glass with more water. "Here. Do you need to lie down or something?"

"Stop worrying. It'll give you wrinkles," Chris said, smiling at him. "Wrinkles and crow's feet, and then you'll get more spa treatments, and then the girls will hit on you again, and it'll be awkward, again, because you never go in with any guys, and then I'll have to pretend to be your husband, again, and it's just a mess. Stop getting worried, Bran.

Your turn. Think you'll ever change your mind about love? If the right person came along?"

Bran frowned and slowly rolled his glass between his hands. "Dare."

"It's a yes or no question!" Chris scoffed at him.

"And I still choose dare," Bran said with a snicker. "Choose it for me, or the pourer has to. Them's the rules."

"Kaden can dare you to do something. Right now there's too many of you for me to focus on at once."

Kaden knew he shouldn't, but he couldn't resist. "Bran, we've heard about your nonexistent gag reflex plenty of times now. Trent went grocery shopping for us today, and I asked him to bring a bunch of bananas. Your dare is to show us your talent."

Chris looked like he couldn't contain his laughter, but Bran only hopped off the counter, went to the pile of bananas across the kitchen, and pushed Kaden's chair back with his foot so he had enough room to sit on his lap but still lean back against the edge of the table.

"You want to see my talent?" Bran asked him as he slowly started peeling the banana. Kaden could only nod, realizing far too late he was in deep shit.

With sensually slow movements, Bran stripped the banana bare, leaving only the flesh, which he ran his tongue over the top of while looking up at Kaden. Smiling, he closed his lips over the tip of the banana and released a soft moan only loud enough for Kaden to hear. At least, that was what he hoped. But the way everyone was staring at them, it was hard to be certain.

Chairs scraped across the floor as the others stretched to see the show. Instead of being good about it and taking it all down, if he was actually capable of that, Bran slid his mouth seductively over the banana, sucking on it just as Kaden had imagined him doing to his dick. And all the while he kept looking up at Kaden with a little smile playing over his full lips. Bran rested his free hand on Kaden's thigh, his thumb lightly brushing over the zipper of his pants, making Kaden almost vibrate under him with need.

"Just eat it," Kaden groaned out.

Bran pulled his mouth off the banana, releasing it with a "pop." "But I thought you wanted to see my talent. This is part of it. If you wanted me to eat a banana, you should have just said so."

"I'm learning my lesson," Kaden snapped at him.

Bran grinned and ran his tongue up the underside of the banana. "I'm sure you are." He gave Kaden a wink, then mercifully stuck the full banana into his mouth, easily closing his lips over it. He opened his mouth back up, released the banana, then bit off half of it, making Kaden grimace.

Before getting off his lap, Bran leaned forward to whisper in Kaden's ear so only he could hear him. "Next time you want to play, give me something harder to swallow." While Kaden turned bright red, Bran kissed him on his cheek and went back to the counter, giving the other half of the banana to Chris as he walked past him. He didn't forget to pour himself a drink, though, while Kaden watched him in stunned silence.

"Chris, your turn, what kind of a lawyer would you be if you weren't at your dad's firm?" Bran asked him.

Chris beamed a smile back at him. "How'd you know I'd still be a lawyer if I ever left?"

"Because I know how much you like power and bossing people around," Bran said, smiling at him. "So, c'mon. Share."

"I think nonprofit. Something fun."

Bran made a face and shook his head. "You think nonprofit work would be fun? Have you ever met a lawyer who enjoyed it?"

"No, but it could be. Better than handling the divorces of people who have no idea what marriage is. And not everything is about how much money you can make," Chris grumbled, sounding almost defensive.

Leaning forward over his knees, Bran looked like he was considering something as he pressed his lips together then nodded. "Fine. You leave your dad's firm. I'll give you the capital to start up your own nonprofit one."

"You know I'm not broke right?"

"You won't have fourteen million in liquid assets in two weeks," Bran said, smirking at him.

Chris shrugged. "True. You can pay for my firm, then. Assuming I ever actually leave him. My next question is to Bran. Aside from what happened with Richard, is there anything else you were keeping from me?" Chris suddenly took the game into a much more serious tone.

Bran frowned and shook his head. "I thought this was supposed to be a lighter game. And besides, you don't want the answer to that question."

Chris got up from his chair and came over to stand in front of Bran, facing him. "Why not? No more secrets. I want to know everything. Is it that you cheated on that paper for literature your first year of college? Because I already know about that."

Bran glanced over at Kaden, almost as if he wanted to say something, then quickly looked away. "Stop asking me this. You don't want to know. I promise. I choose to go with a dare."

"No. I want to know. You have to tell me. Now," Chris demanded.

Bran pressed his mouth into a hard line. "Then I forfeit," he said, not looking away from Chris. "Kaden, choose a punishment for me."

Chris shook his head and laid his hands on Bran's shoulders. "What are you so worried about, so ashamed of, that you can't even tell me? You know I'll still love you. So what is it?"

Sighing, Bran slowly nodded. "Maybe you do need to know. Maybe it's time. Go sit back down. I can't say it with you right in front of me. It's too hard. I'll tell everyone. I promise you, though, Chris, you will not like this answer, and I was trying to protect more than just me. But maybe you do have the right to know who your best friend really is. Maybe that's part of finally growing up and trying to be better. If you end up hating me for this, then at least it's because you'll know the whole truth about me and what I've done."

Chris frowned, but he did retake his seat after a few seconds of hesitation. "It can't be all that bad. I don't care if you've killed people or—"

"Or been paid for sex?" Bran asked him quietly, making Chris's mouth drop open. "I was nineteen, and you were about to turn twenty-one, and I wanted to make it special for you and my part-time job wasn't paying nearly enough. So I went to someone who might have had the extra money, and they said that they couldn't spare it. Then I went to the only other person we knew who had a good job and could afford to give me some. I asked for a lot, because I wanted your birthday to be fantastic. And when they wouldn't give me a loan, I offered myself. I got paid, you and I went crazy, and we had a great time, and you were never, ever supposed to know where that money came from."

Chris was still staring at him. "Bran...."

Misha moved back from the table and shook his head. "You should have told me what you wanted the thousand dollars for. I would have just given it to you."

Bran stared at him for a long moment before getting off the counter to pour himself a double, which he quickly drank down, looking like he needed it. "You are my best friend's absolutely terrifying older brother. You were nearly thirty. I didn't think to talk to you about it at all, and you never asked what I was going to do with it, I just wanted Chris to be happy. And besides, you already had your opinions of me by that time. I thought you wouldn't believe me even if I had said something."

Misha frowned and crossed his big arms over his chest. "And I was only doing it to prove a point about the kind of person you are. That you would so easily sell your body, that you acted like a pro about it, like you'd been doing it for years already. I wanted Chris to never speak to you again after that night, but he didn't listen to me and even when I told him that you were a slut and a whore, he never believed that you'd actually sell yourself."

"That's because he loves me," Bran said with a soft, sad smile. "And really, you have met me, haven't you? I can fake just about anything if I need to. I needed money to take him out, my mom couldn't afford it, I hadn't spoken to my grandfather in over three years, and your family was out of the question. So I went to you, because I knew even if we did have sex, you would have never hurt me, and I did what I had to, to get what I needed. It was that simple. You started calling me a whore that night, and I let you because you knew the truth about me. I'd whored myself out to you, so I deserved it."

"My opinion of you went drastically down after that night. Before then, you were just the slutty, irresponsible best friend of my little brother. You two partied, and I worried about him while he was with you, but I didn't hate you until that night. I was afraid that if he hung around with you much longer, you would get him into prostitution too, or he would die in some gutter with a needle in his arm and all anyone would ever think of him was he was some senator's son turned junkie hooker who died while trying to get a fix."

"That's some imagination you've got there," Bran said sarcastically.

Misha shook his head. "Don't do that. Don't use sarcasm to defend yourself. Just talk for once in your life."

Bran's expression turned hard. "Fine. I would have never done that to him. I wasn't a prostitute. I needed one favor, and by that time

I'd figured out plenty well that sex got me a lot of the things I wanted in life. So when you said I couldn't pay you back for the thousand dollars, I used what I had to get it, which has always been my mouth and my ass. It was a one-time thing, and I'm ashamed of it. It was supposed to be a secret I took with me to my grave, and now it might have not only cost me my best friend, but also someone I was starting to really care about. So, Misha, back off and let me go upstairs. I'm done with this game."

"You want to run when things get tough for you like you always do? Like you're so good at?" Misha challenged him. "You should have told me the truth."

"You shouldn't have asked a desperate kid to have sex with you for the money so you could prove a point," Bran shot back at him. "I was nineteen and had already spent three years practically unsupervised, learning all about what it meant to use my body in all the ways I needed to in order to get ahead in the world. I was at an all-boys college where it was routine to give blowjobs to get out of doing essays, and no one batted an eye about the parties we had in the dorms. Most of the time, the RAs joined in, and it was normal for me to wake up with strange people in my bed and no memory of the night before. I hadn't even figured out what my boundaries might have been before they'd already been pushed aside. My first kiss was during a tutoring session with a teacher's aide who then asked me if I had any condoms with me because he was out."

Bran took a shuddering breath before continuing. "I was a broken, screwed-up teenager, and all I wanted was to take my best friend out for his birthday. And you needed to prove some point about me being horrible for him. Well, we both got exactly what we wanted, then, didn't we?"

As if Bran had slapped him, Misha stepped back. "You're right. I'm sorry for that."

"It's done. Your apology doesn't make any difference now." Seeming to completely ignore Misha, Bran focused his full attention on Chris. "Say something. Please? Even if it's that you hate me, that you never want to speak to me again, I just need to hear you say something."

Silently Chris got out of his chair and went to stand in front of Bran. When he put his arms around him, Bran wrapped himself around Chris and laid his head on Chris's shoulder.

"You are a great guy and the best friend I've ever had. I love you."

Bran smiled and hugged him tighter. "I love you too."

"What do you say we blow this game and go into the living room with the rest of the cheesecake and binge until we feel like puking while we watch the worst TV imaginable? There's got to be some infomercials on for crap we don't need but are going to end up buying anyway. Maybe they'll even have faster shipping options so we can be disappointed even sooner," Chris offered.

"Deal."

Chris took his hand, and Bran slid off the counter.

"Why do these games always get so depressing when we play with other people? When it's just us, we're never this miserable while playing them."

Chris shrugged. "Maybe it's because they're masochists. Or sadists. Which is it?"

"Like I'm supposed to know the difference?" Bran said with a snicker as he took the rest of the bourbon from in front of the silent Kaden, and Chris grabbed the cheesecakes.

"Won't they need that?" Chris asked him.

Shrugging, Bran took a sip straight from the bottle as they walked out of the kitchen. "I'm sure Kaden has more hidden somewhere."

"Do you think, if we'd been able to actually date before going to college, that we wouldn't have been as screwed up?" Chris asked him.

"Maybe. It's hard to say really. It might have made a difference in how easy we were, since that place practically encouraged random sex, but I don't know," Bran replied, sounding sad. "It doesn't matter much now anyway."

"No. I guess it doesn't. Credit card at the ready?" Chris asked him in an obvious attempt at trying to chase away their shared misery. He lay down on the couch with the best angle for viewing the TV, and Bran sat down on the floor in front of him.

"The numbers are all in my head," he said, tapping his temple. "Let's see who buys the most useless crap tonight."

Chris laughed and laid his hand on top of Bran's head. "I can't believe you had sex with Misha. That's just…. Ew."

Bran snorted and covered Chris's hand with his own. "Yeah. Let's not talk about that anymore. Or ever again. I think we've had enough sharing for a long time. My drama level is overflowing at the moment."

Chris tugged on his hair, and Bran turned on the TV, both of them seemingly ready to get lost in it as Kaden watched them from the kitchen.

CHAPTER FOURTEEN

AFTER BRAN dropped the bomb about what happened between him and Misha, everyone else seemed shocked and subdued. Misha avoided making eye contact with all of them while he stood up and started clearing the table by placing the shot glasses in the basin.

Did he like the fact that Misha had used Bran and deceived him? Hell no. Considering the hatred in Misha's voice when he spoke to Bran over the phone and in person, Kaden found it hard to imagine the two of them having sex. Pleasurable sex anyway. How could anyone make love to someone they so obviously despised?

He glanced at Trent and saw his friend idly drawing imaginary pictures on the wooden surface of the table in front of him.

What was going through his friend's head, Kaden couldn't guess, until Trent got up and muttered, "I'm starting to hate that game. Come on, Sam, let's go." The two of them left via the back door, and Kaden heard the ATV start and drive off.

Misha stood by the kitchen sink, staring out the window into the darkness. Kaden sort of wanted to feel sorry for the man but couldn't quite muster the energy to do so. He wasn't a saint after all.

"I'm gonna go to bed. The couch is the only spare bed we have at the moment, so please help yourself to some linen and blankets in the cupboard below the stairs. Good night." His head felt light from the bourbon, but his feet felt like lead as he walked away from Chris and Bran where they watched TV. He wanted to talk to Bran but knew now was not the time.

Having had a shower earlier, he just stopped by the bathroom to brush his teeth before going into his room. In the dark he took off his clothes and climbed naked under the sheets. He couldn't remember the last time he'd been too damn tired to put on pajama pants, but tonight he was, and the work on-farm wasn't to blame. All the bloody drama in his once-peaceful life was the culprit.

Despite being a bit drunk and exhausted, his brain refused to switch off, and more than an hour later according to his phone, he still stared at the ceiling in boredom.

Soft footsteps came closer, and his door opened. "I told you I wasn't good for you," Bran quietly said. It was a statement, and a resigned one at that, without any of his usual snark or venom.

Knowing Bran was punishing himself for things of the past, Kaden remained silent. Bran walked into the room until he stood beside the bed. The light from the hall shone into the room, making it easy to see each other.

Bran looked down at him as if waiting for something, some secret to reveal itself to him from Kaden's eyes. "Have you ever had sex with someone you didn't love?" Bran asked him after a long moment.

"Yes, when I was young, horny, and stupid," Kaden admitted.

Bran looked around the room, and Kaden saw him replace the vulnerability with his flirty mask. Kaden was sick of seeing this artificial side of the man.

"Want some company?" Bran asked him. Bran wore only a pair of low-slung boxers barely staying up on his hips. Bran seemed unsure and scared as he stood waiting for Kaden to give him an answer.

"Guess not," he said, turning around when Kaden hadn't said anything to him one way or the other.

"Bran," he spoke softly as the man walked back toward the door. "I do want you, but not like this. We've both had too much to drink, and once again, emotions are flying high all over the place. You feel guilty, and you're angry, and as usual you're trying to cover it up with pretending everything is okay for you. I don't care what happened between you and Misha. That's in the past. We've all done stupid shit, but if we make love, it will be for the right reasons. Not because of guilt, anger, alcohol, insecurities, or whatever else. Nothing's changed for me, but you need to ask yourself what it is you want from me, because I don't take this stuff lightly. Think on that, and we can talk tomorrow." Kaden spoke the words as softly and kindly as he could, knowing Bran to be very fragile right then.

"Okay, sleep well. I'll see you in the morning." Bran padded out on bare feet and pulled the door mostly shut behind him.

WHEN KADEN woke up, he expected to see at least Bran, if not Chris downstairs. But instead he heard snores coming from Bran's room, and since he knew Bran didn't snore, he decided to let them sleep in. Misha on the other hand, was ready, and along with Samuel and Trent, they got to work.

The work was harder than usual because of how tense everyone still seemed to be, but at least Misha seemed to pick it up quickly. And he stayed silent, not at all complaining like Bran had. That was one blessing as far as Kaden could see.

When they returned to the house, to the sweet smells of breakfast laid out for them and the sight of Chris and Bran sitting at the dining room table with a bottle of orange juice and two shot glasses between them, it seemed like the most pleasant, most normal thing in the world.

Until Bran looked over at Kaden and explained what they were doing. "Refresh of what we're doing. Since you all weren't here to hear the rules the first time around—"

"Because we were working, which you should have been doing," Kaden said, coming into the kitchen, followed by the others, and helping himself to some of the eggs benedict, pancakes, and sausage. He hadn't thought they had enough food to even make all of this, but maybe Bran had found yet another place he could bribe into delivering food to them.

Bran rolled his eyes. "I was. I made breakfast. Back to the rules. Chris and I are playing truth or dare, only us. The rest of you complicate things. Dares are off the table, any question can be asked and will be answered, and the person who has the last shot of orange juice wins and gets a foot rub. Don't worry, I ordered more orange juice when I ordered the extra groceries."

"Again?" Trent asked them, shaking his head. "Haven't you two learned your lesson about this game yet?"

They ignored him. "Now that they're caught up, it's my turn," Chris said with a smile as Kaden tried to bite back his sigh of frustration. What was it with them and this game? It only ever seemed to bring them misery and frustration. He shared a look with Samuel and Trent, who both seemed to be thinking the same thing, as they all finished grabbing food for their breakfasts and found places to sit around the table, though Misha did have to pull a metal folding chair out of the closet.

"Bran, ever jacked off while thinking about Kaden?" Chris asked him, making Kaden choke on his food.

Bran blushed, but only a little, and took his drink. "I have. Did you ever even want to be a lawyer, or was that just your dad getting into your head?"

"That would be thanks to my dad. I don't mind it so much now, though. And if I ever kill one of my stupid clients, I'll be able to defend myself," Chris said, taking a drink of juice and grimacing. "This is a lot more sugar in the morning than I'm used to."

"There better not be vodka in there," Misha spoke up from the end of the table.

Bran rolled his eyes, and Chris smiled. "Nope. No screwdrivers this morning. I think we're both off alcohol for at least a day. But I'm also off pain medicine. Just as long as I can stand it. Bran, do you actually need the money from selling this place?"

"No. Not really. I'm breaking apart a company in six weeks that is going to make me double what the sale of this place will. But I like money, and having more of it is always nice," Bran said with a little shrug. The bottle hadn't been that full to begin with, and Kaden was glad to see that it was going down quickly. He hoped to never see them playing this game again. "Have you ever jacked off while thinking about Samuel?" Bran asked Chris. Samuel coughed, and Kaden ate faster, hoping to avoid hearing anything else that could be considered extremely personal.

Chris bit his bottom lip, and Kaden saw him look to Samuel before refocusing on Bran.

"I'm going for a walk. I really don't want to hear about my brother and sex," Misha said, getting up from the table.

Kaden saw Bran grin and wondered what he could possibly be thinking about. Bran and Chris stayed silent until the screen door had closed behind Misha. "I knew that would get him to go away," Bran said, sounding like he was pretty proud of himself.

Snorting, Chris shook his head. "If you hadn't thought of something, I was going to."

"Don't like him right now?" Bran asked him.

"Not really," Chris admitted. "Now, about your last question…. Nope. I haven't."

Bran looked surprised, and honestly Kaden felt the same way. It seemed like such a strange answer coming from what little he knew of Chris. "Wait. What?" Bran asked.

But Chris only waved a finger at him. "Wait your turn. And pour me my shot."

"Pour it yourself. The bottle is only three inches from your hand," Bran snarked, but he tipped the bottle over Chris's glass anyway.

"Bran, what do you see when you look at Kaden?" Chris asked him, sounding fairly melodramatic. "With your heart?"

Bran snorted orange juice out of his nose as he laughed and had to get up to get a cloth for his face. "What in the hell were you watching after I went upstairs?"

"Really sappy movies. I'm serious, though. Gruff, sexy, cowboy? Someone you can't stand? Share with the table. We're all not really friends here, but we tolerate each other, even without alcohol, so open up your soul and other random shit, and answer my damn question. You know I've got the patience of a two-year-old."

Grinning, Bran shook his head, but when he looked over at Kaden, for only the briefest of seconds, his smile instantly dimmed.

He slumped forward, rounded his shoulders a little, then answered him. "Don't laugh. If you do I will show you where the psycho bull lives that wanted to kill me, and I won't save you from him. But, okay. He's...." Bran licked his lips. "So you know he's sexy. And let's face it, the accents do something to a person after a while."

Chris nodded and blushed a bit. "Yeah, they do."

"But he's kind and loyal and willing to help someone even when he knows I'll be selling this place out from under him in two weeks and sending him and his two best friends back to New Zealand. So, to me that makes him a really decent guy. Probably one of the few I've ever been interested in." Bran grabbed the bottle and finished it off straight from the spout while Chris protested. "Game over. I win. You owe me a foot rub."

"You cheated!"

Bran grinned at him. "Cheat to win seems like a decent motto for the moment."

"Where do you want it?" Chris grumbled.

Bran met Trent's gaze from across the table. He sat next to Chris on one side and next to Kaden on the other. Kaden wondered what could possibly be going through his head as Bran flicked his gaze over him, appearing to decide something as he slowly smiled.

"Trent, can I trade places with you?"

"Uh. Sure," Trent said as he rose from his seat. Bran got up and moved around the table, taking Trent's vacated spot.

He was barefoot, so it didn't take much effort to get his foot into Chris's lap right after he'd sat down. "Fucking cheater," Chris grumbled as he began massaging Bran's foot.

Apparently ignoring him for the moment, Bran twisted around so that he could look at Kaden. "Mind if I stretch out and lay my head on your thigh?" It might have been an innocent question, except Kaden thought he knew Bran well enough by then to know that nothing was innocent about him. Especially when his grin was as wicked as it was right then.

"You have something planned," Kaden accused him.

"Nothing at all. So, can I get comfortable, or are you going to let me get a backache here without any kind of support?"

Kaden said nothing as he moved back from the table a little, giving Bran enough room to rest his head on top of Kaden's thigh. He put his left arm up, resting his elbow against Kaden's sternum as he moved his hand behind his head.

Bran left his right hand lying across his stomach as he closed his eyes. "Tell me if you change your mind," Bran told him. Kaden was already starting to.

"How's the pressure, your majesty?" Chris snarked at him.

Bran smiled and turned his head against Kaden's thigh, appearing to get more comfortable, but it brought him right against Kaden's zipper, making him freeze as he pretended not to notice Bran's movements on his lap.

"You could go a little harder. Just like—Fuck yes. Right there. Just like that." Bran groaned a little, and Kaden wished he'd never agreed to let him lie there. He was too close and looked far too good with a light blush covering his face and his blond hair a wayward mess over Kaden's thigh. "How's your pain level?" Bran asked Chris.

Chris shrugged. "Not too bad. Enough to notice it, but not enough to make me want to be a loopy mess again. I remember saying you were pretty a lot last night, but it was like I couldn't stop myself."

Bran chuckled, and Kaden wished he could reach down and touch Bran's smiling lips right then. "You did say that," Bran replied.

Groaning, Bran sat up next to him, but before he was completely off his lap, he reached down to give Kaden's inner thigh a squeeze.

CHAPTER FIFTEEN

BRAN FELT Chris lay his hand over his shoulder, gently pressing against his muscles, and he turned to look back at him. "Can I get some help?" Chris asked him softly, his words coming out in a breathy whisper.

Nodding, Bran got up from his chair. "You okay? What's wrong?"

Chris gave him a weak smile. "Pain's back. And I'm a little dizzy. I think I overdid it." He took Bran's offered hand and his help up from the chair.

"Bed or couch?" Bran asked him, taking in Chris's sudden paleness and becoming instantly worried about him.

"I want to get more comfortable, so it'll have to be the bed."

The others might not have understood what Chris meant, but to Bran it made perfect sense. "Sure thing." He glanced over his shoulder at the others but specifically Kaden, knowing they still needed to talk and intending to do just that. "I'll be right back." He didn't wait for any kind of acknowledgment from them, only wrapped an arm around Chris's waist in case he lost his balance and started heading for the stairs.

"I'd like to help," Samuel offered from behind them, but Bran turned and shook his head at the much larger man. Chris might have liked him, and even wanted him, but being seen as vulnerable was a big deal to them both, and Bran knew, with absolute certainty, that Chris would have rather pretended he was perfectly fine than get help from Samuel right then. It might not have made a lot of sense, but that was their way.

Chris was okay until Bran got him to the bed, where he sat down as he trembled with a grimace. "Shit."

"Yeah. Let's get your shirt off. We'll go slow." Bran hated this part, hated seeing what Richard had done to his best friend, and as he slowly worked the loose shirt over Chris's head, it was no easier seeing the bruises then as it had been that morning when he'd helped him get dressed. He shook his head and tried to bite back his curses as Chris's myriad of bruises were exposed to his view.

"They look worse than they are," Chris said, reaching up and covering Bran's hand on his unbruised shoulder with his own.

Bran slipped his hand from Chris's skin and got him a pain pill from the little bottle Chris had brought from the hospital. A glass of water still had a little left in it, and soon Chris was medicated with some of the strongest stuff Bran knew of. If the people downstairs thought his face was a mess, then the morbid art that Chris's body had become would have shocked them, and he was glad they weren't all crowded around him to stare.

"I hate myself for what he did to you," Bran said as he helped Chris lie down and covered him with a light blanket.

"You should stop blaming yourself," Chris replied sleepily.

Smirking, Bran shook his head. "Only a saint would let me off that easily."

"Then I'm a saint. The saint of sluts and sinners. That's me."

Bran leaned over him and brushed some of Chris's loose, wild curls off his forehead. "You could have a good thing here with Samuel, even if it's only temporary. Don't screw it up."

Chris gave him a weak smile before closing his eyes. "Says the hypocrite to the slut."

"That's what I mean. Don't call yourself that. He obviously cares about you. Give it a chance," Bran told him. It would only be for two weeks, which was hardly anything, but maybe it could be the thing his best friend needed in order to think he was worth something too, more than a willing mouth in a bathroom stall in some random club downtown.

Chris didn't say anything to him as he quietly left the room, only closing the door slightly behind him. When he came back to the table, Trent, Samuel, and Kaden were still there.

"Everything okay?" Trent asked him, to which Bran nodded.

Bran turned his attention to Samuel. "Did you mean what you told Misha earlier? About how Chris was yours?"

"I mean everything I say," Samuel replied, making Bran believe he might actually do such a thing, which would be a novel experience for him. Very few people in his life could even say such a thing with a straight face, much less stick to it.

He drummed his fingers over the back of the chair as he looked at Samuel, weighing how much he wanted to help Chris against whether or not he wanted Chris to be pissed off at him again. Helping him won out.

"Chris and I, we've got our barriers. We've had them for years, and they work for us. Usually. They keep people from hurting us, my dad and grandfather before they died for me, his dad for him, but they also tend to turn people off. People we might actually find could be good friends, if we were willing to try."

Bran forced himself to absolutely not look at Kaden. This was not about himself, and it most certainly wasn't about Kaden either. This was about Chris maybe getting a chance at something, someone, who could be good for him.

"Sometimes we even have our barriers up around each other, as much as we try not to. I think it's because we've had them for so long they're practically a part of us. It's easier for me to pretend than it is for me to be like this. That's why we play truth or dare. It helps us with our truths and generally doesn't let us hide from each other. My point with all this is that he won't open up easily, but he could use another friend, and he likes you too. He's upstairs right now, highly medicated, and half-asleep. If you wanted to talk to him and get to know the Chris without all the bullshit, the one that I'm best friends with, and I will kill you for if you hurt in any way, now would probably be a pretty good time. Just saying."

Bran shrugged as he finished talking. The ball, as some people liked to say, was in Samuel's court. If he chose to blow off the idea of talking to Chris while he rested, then Bran knew he'd never bring it up again because Samuel was unlikely to get another chance like this. It was his one shot, and Bran really hoped Samuel took it.

Bran got up and went to the fridge to look for any leftover cheesecake or anything sweet he could find. He almost threw both his arms in the air and yelled, "Yes!" when he turned around and found Samuel missing from around the table.

He smiled at Kaden and Trent. "Wise man."

The look Kaden gave him surpassed intense, and Bran's skin warmed, and other parts of his body responded to the heat in the man's gaze. How long could he fight this thing between them? Did he really want to deny himself the little bit of ecstasy and happiness he would find in Kaden's arms, if only for a short time before he destroyed their lives?

Someone cleared their throat, and Trent slowly unfolded his tall frame from his seat. "Time to go… have a chat with the bull or the birds or even the bloody pigs." When the screen door slammed shut, even such a harsh sound didn't break the connection between them.

Kaden pushed his chair back, came around the table, and approached Bran, who momentarily wanted to run like a rabbit in the face of a dangerous predator, but he stood his ground. He was fucking tired of running away. Maybe he wanted to stay and face the threat head-on, but he knew this gorgeous man standing before him would never hurt him.

"You drive me insane with wanting you. See what you do to me?" Kaden grabbed Bran's left hand and cupped it over his rock-hard erection below his faded pair of jeans. Bran glimpsed a flash of insecurity in the dark brown eyes he stared into and could have kicked himself. He was responsible for that self-doubt Kaden had, because of his tendency to play selfish games. His hot and cold behavior, his kiss me, then "don't touch me" game had done its damage.

"I'm sorry," he whispered, tears stinging the back of his eyes. Kaden started removing his hand and swallowed hard.

"I can't do this anymore, Bran…." Kaden meant to turn away, but in desperation Bran grabbed his arm and spun him around, pushing his broad back against the stainless steel door of the fridge. Hard.

"No, you misunderstood. I'm sorry for leading you on and not making good on it. I want you so bad I'm aching for you all the time. This." He cupped Kaden through his jeans again, firming his grasp and rubbing up and down. Kaden's head clunked back against the fridge, and a soul-deep groan left his throat.

Bran pushed in as much as his hand between them allowed, the other planted next to Kaden's head on the metal, and kissed him. Like he'd wanted to for so long. Like he meant it.

In a split second, Kaden spun them around and reversed their positions. Bran found himself pinned to the steel, his legs parted, and Kaden's knee flush with his hard-on, grinding deliciously against him.

"If you keep that up, I will come in my pants. I've been so wired the last few days it's almost embarrassing." Kaden laughed when he kissed and sucked on the side of Bran's jaw, before sliding over to his lips and taking them in a wet kiss. Kaden kissed him like no one ever had before—slow, urgent, hungry, and possessive. Every part of his mouth, tongue, and teeth received attention, Kaden's taste driving him wild. Bran grabbed one handful of hair and the other of T-shirt fabric and gave himself over to Kaden. This man wouldn't let him fall, but would take him on a wild ride he would never forget and catch him when he came back down. Bran ground down on the rough denim between his thighs, the pressure almost deliciously painful and knew he was closer than he'd thought.

Breaking the kiss, he gasped for air. "I'm gonna... stop, Kaden!"

"Yeah, stop, Kaden. I really don't want to do this, but Beefsteak broke out, and I'm gonna need a hand, even with my supernatural skills, to get the damn thing back in." Trent's words were the ice-cold bucket of water Bran needed to send his orgasm packing for another time.

His first instinct was to push Kaden back, to put as much space as possible between them. He didn't like becoming a spectacle in general, but this thing with Kaden was too new, too personal, for him to feel comfortable being caught with him. He wanted to brush it off, to pretend Kaden didn't make his blood boil with need and his heart race with uncertainty.

But he couldn't. Kaden didn't deserve that from him, and he'd hurt him enough already. He loosened his grip on Kaden's T-shirt, but he refused to let him get too far away from him.

"One of the cows has a name?" he asked Trent, hoping to distract himself, and Trent, from what he'd just been doing with Kaden.

Kaden nodded to him and slid his hands down Bran's sides, leaving a trail of heat wherever his fingertips touched. Though he was still fully dressed, Bran felt as if he might as well have been naked with how raw and exposed he felt under Kaden's hands.

"The bull. Coming out to help us get him back in his pasture?"

"Is this the same bull that wanted to kill me?" Bran asked him, trying to figure out which of the hundreds of animals on the property he was talking about. When Kaden gave him a quick nod, Bran was instantly very sure of his answer. "Um, not only no but hell no. Good luck with that, though. Try not to die."

If Kaden was disappointed in him, he didn't show it. Instead he moved back, releasing him to lean against the cool metal of the fridge on his own. "See you later, then."

They were almost to the back door when Bran decided to change his mind. "Wait. I'll come with you two. Just give me a second to tell Chris where I'm going." Kaden smiled back at him, and he knew he'd made the right decision as he headed up the stairs.

The bedroom door was slightly open, and since it was his room, and it was Chris, he would have just pushed the door open and barged in. But he heard Chris quietly talking to Samuel before he'd even gotten to the top of the stairs, and when he saw Chris sitting up in bed, his bruises and scrapes on display for Samuel, who sat in a chair across from him, Bran knew he would be interrupting.

He knocked on the doorframe and waited for Samuel to look up at him. Chris turned a little toward him too but winced and had to look away again just as quickly. "Hi. The bull got out, so I'm going to help Trent and Kaden get him back in. Hopefully without any of us dying."

"I should help too," Samuel said, starting to get up, but Bran shook his head.

"It's okay. We've got it covered." Bran took a step away from the door. He could have just as easily texted Chris to let him know where he was going to be, but he'd wanted to see him too, to make sure sending Samuel up to him really was the right decision. He could see now that it was. Chris was so private about any kind of pain, or vulnerability, he had, and seeing him sitting there, where Samuel could see all his injuries, hurt. Chris really did feel comfortable around Samuel, and Bran naturally relaxed and trusted Samuel as well.

"I'd like two minutes alone with Bran," Chris said, sounding small and making Bran frown at the unusual tone. Chris threw people out of his bed, his room, his office. They were his spaces, and he decided who was in them. He didn't ask for permission, from anyone.

"I'll be right outside," Samuel said, getting to his feet.

When Samuel was within a few inches of him, Bran whispered, "thank you," to Samuel, who nodded. Bran closed the door and took Samuel's vacated spot across from Chris in the old, uncomfortable chair. He was glad to see a lot of the color back in Chris's cheeks and the smile back on his face.

"He came up to check on me," Chris told him.

Bran hoped nothing showed on his face, revealing to Chris that he'd practically told Samuel to go upstairs to see him. "That's nice of him."

Chris blushed a little. "I thought so too. Surprised me. He's a good guy. I think he could be a nice friend to have. I'd like to maybe keep in touch with him, after these two weeks are up."

"There's this fantastic new invention called e-mail…" Bran offered him, earning himself a smirk from Chris. "I think they're all decent guys. And good for you wanting to stay in touch with him."

"And, don't laugh, but I think I've decided something else," Chris quietly confessed, leaning toward him. "And you can't tell anyone. Not even Kaden."

Bran rolled his eyes. "We're not really at the sharing-our-friends'-secrets stage. We're not even at the middle-name-sharing stage. Kissing, that's it."

"That's so unlike you," Chris said as he smiled at him.

It was, but Kaden was unlike anyone he'd ever been interested in, so maybe that fit. "What did you decide?" He wasn't rushing Chris, not at all, and if Kaden and Trent got bored of waiting for him, then they could go deal with the bull themselves. But he was curious about what seemed so important to his friend.

Chris glanced back at the closed bedroom door before coming even closer to Bran. "I'm going to try celibacy for a while. Not forever, but at least for a few months, I think. If not longer."

It was so strange, so completely out of character for him, that Bran thought he was joking at first. But Chris's gaze never wavered from his, and how serious his best friend was slowly started to sink in.

"I didn't think you even knew what that word meant," Bran softly joked.

"When I'm not a bruised mess, I will hit you for that. Not really hard, probably with just a pillow, but I will be hitting you," Chris promised him.

"Fair enough. So…." What was there to say to something like that? "Why?"

"You're trying to be less of an asshole with Kaden, I'm trying to be less of a slut around Samuel. It won't matter in the grand scheme of things with him, since I don't chase people across the world, but maybe being thirty-four and having six months as my longest relationship isn't the greatest achievement in the world. I'm not saying I'll ever get married, because we both know how pointless I think that really is, but something more solid than what I'm used to might be nice. Don't tell anyone. You promised."

Bran got up and ruffled Chris's hair. "I won't say a single thing. And for you. I'll help however you need me to. No more clubs, then?"

Chris frowned. "No, I'm not giving up going to clubs. I like to dance too much. But maybe just one drink instead of five, and you watch me to make sure I don't go off with the first cute guy who grabs my ass? And I'll do the same for you?"

"I can do that." Bran leaned over him and gave Chris the gentlest of hugs he could manage. "Want some time alone, or do you want me to let Samuel back in?" Bran asked him.

"He can come back. I like his company." Bran let him go, though he would have rather stayed right there with him. "This place is screwing with us."

Laughing, Bran completely agreed with him. "It's like the outside world doesn't really work here. It's refreshing but also scary as hell."

"So fucking scary," Chris agreed with him.

Bran gave his shoulder a light squeeze, then headed back to the door. "Get some rest," he called to Chris as he opened it to see not only Samuel standing there, waiting on him, but also Trent and Kaden. They looked between them as if he'd interrupted some whispered conversation, which made Bran curious but not enough to actually demand an answer from any of them. Not wanting Chris to hear every bit of what he was about to say to Samuel, he closed the bedroom door tightly and kept his voice low while addressing only Samuel.

"If you bring him down before I get back, he'll want to wear a shirt to hide his bruises. Third drawer down on the dresser has some shirts that are a size too big for me, so they're about three sizes too big for him and are easier for him to get on and off. But he'll still need your help. Start with his right arm first, his ribs there are worse off than on the left, and he can use his other hand to help some. He can have another pain pill in two hours. They're on the nightstand. If his stitches start to bother him, there's a cream he can apply in a pot next to the pill bottle." His instructions complete, Bran moved away from the door and started heading down the stairs.

"Did you ever look like he does now?" Samuel asked, surprising him with not only his words, but also the concern, and underlying anger in his tone.

Bran tightened his hand on the old wood bannister, his knuckles going white with remembered pain as he turned back to look at Kaden, then at Samuel. "I was with Richard for two years." The truth was he thought Chris had gotten off easy, all things considered, but he wouldn't ever say that out loud. Trying to calm the panic in his heart, Bran quickly headed down the stairs. They could make whatever assumptions they wanted out of what he'd said. But they were smart, he knew, and they'd come to the truth all on their own without him having to say anything more.

Misha was coming in through the front door when he reached the bottom of the stairs, and Bran moved aside so Trent and Kaden could come down too and not run into him. "Where's Chris?" Misha asked him as soon as he seemed to catch sight of him.

"Upstairs with Samuel," Bran said, waiting for Misha to say something about them being together, just one thing, that would justify Bran snapping at him. Samuel's question had put him on edge, and he knew Misha would be someone he could take his anger out on who wouldn't shy away from an argument with him. If anything, most days Misha seemed to be as ready for their spats as Bran was.

But Misha only nodded, taking the moment away from him and denying him the outlet he sought. "Were you three heading out?" Misha asked them.

"The bull got out, so we need to get him back into the right paddock," Trent said.

Misha smiled in excitement. "Sounds interesting. Can I help?"

Bran saw Trent nod out of the corner of his eye and glanced back at Kaden to see what he thought, considering the rocky start between Misha and them. Instead, Bran found Kaden's gaze fixed solely on himself and he blushed under that attention.

"Sweet. Could be fun," Misha said. Bran laughed despite himself. His own and Misha's idea of fun were worlds apart.

He looked back at Kaden and Trent. "Is it too much to hope the bull got tired of waiting on us to go get him and decided to put himself back in the pasture all on his own? I'd really like that to be the case."

CHAPTER SIXTEEN

OUTSIDE, TRENT and Kaden got on the ATVs, and Kaden beckoned to Bran while Misha moved behind Trent on his. "You can sit with me." Bran seated himself behind Kaden and wrapped his arms around his waist. Before pulling away, Bran laid his cheek against Kaden's back, and Kaden felt the soul-deep sigh the man let out.

Reaching down, Kaden gave Bran's thigh a squeeze in support. What the two friends had been through in their lifetimes was utter crap. Chris's parents should've nurtured and protected their son, and Bran's parents should've sorted out their shit and not made their son suffer for things he played no role in. The realization made him understand for the millionth time how fortunate he was for his parents.

"Tell me about your family," Bran said, just loud enough to be heard over the noise of the ATV. "Anything at all. Seems like you know all about my drama. Tell me yours."

"There's not much drama, except the bit my younger sister caused when she hit her teens. She's all grown up now, so she luckily outgrew that hormonal stage. Thank God, because we couldn't live with her." Kaden chuckled. "My mom and dad are both in their sixties, and my father is the best dairy farmer I know. My mother is the strongest woman I know, and my dad rules by her permission only."

"They're still together?" Bran sounded genuinely surprised by that.

"Yes, they are, and I don't think that will ever change. If you see them together, you will understand they were meant for each other. Without the other, each one of them would wither and die, I think."

Before they could talk any further, Trent stopped by a paddock gate and opened it for them to drive through, before closing it again.

"Right, he's broke through the fence at the back end, and I've already fixed it, so if we can stop there and open the corner gate, we should be able to herd him back in here," Trent explained.

"Okay, let's do it." Kaden nodded and turned to look at Bran over his shoulder. "Don't get off the bike. No matter what happens, you hold on, okay?" He waited for wide-eyed Bran's confirming nod before following Trent to where the paddock opened into the next one.

As soon as they drove into the next pasture, Kaden spotted the beast toward the western side on a slight hill. He communicated with Trent that they would split up and each would come up behind the bull from opposite directions.

Beefsteak watched them approach and tossed his head and scuffed his front legs in the dirt. The faster they moved, the better, so they rode in from behind and spoke to him to get him to start moving forward, and once he was, they slowly sped up a little. If they slowed down or stopped, the bull would have time to think of them as a threat and turn on them.

"Freaking hell, he's massive," Bran whispered against his neck. "Look at all that muscle."

"He's a big one," Kaden agreed but kept his eyes on the animal. Things could turn to shit very fast.

The process went surprisingly well until they almost reached the gate and Beefsteak realized they were attempting to curb his newfound freedom. The big bull came to a dead stop and turned on Kaden and Bran, lowering his head and pawing the ground, sending grass and dirt flying behind him. Kaden knew to retreat would spur him on, so he nudged the bike forward in little spurts, trying to get Beefsteak to turn around and keep moving, but no such luck.

The bull moved forward and nudged the bike with his massive head as if warning it to back off. "Hold on, Bran. If he backs up and charges, I'll act fast. He's just pushing his luck for now." With that weight against them, they didn't move, although Kaden kept the throttle going to give them ground if Beefsteak let up.

However, when the bike bumped slightly against the curly haired forehead, Beefsteak was not happy. He withdrew and turned around, and Kaden almost whooped until the beast turned back around and took a run up.

"Shit!" Kaden yelled.

"Hey! You big chunk of steak!" Trent had lost his damn mind, Kaden thought. His friend had discarded his bike and was running with arms wide into the space between Kaden's ATV and the angry bull.

"Trent! Get on the fucking bike!" Kaden yelled.

The bull came a few steps forward and stopped, staring at Trent. "Yeah, asshole, Come through me." Trent bellowed at the quivering mass of muscle ahead of him.

Beefsteak tossed his head a few times but stayed where he was. "I'll be damned, Trent. Even he loves you," Kaden whispered behind Trent's back, feeling Bran's fingertips digging into his own shoulders.

When the bull just stared at Trent, the man swung his arm toward the open gate. "Get out of here!" The scene was so absurd, Kaden had a strong urge to burst out laughing, but he shut up.

Beefsteak lowered his head again, looking at Trent from below heavy brows, but Trent didn't back down. Trent took a step forward. "Out!"

Kaden knew Trent was scared shitless by the wet patch of sweat on the back of his shirt and the way his outstretched hand shook as he commanded the animal to go through to the next paddock.

Beefsteak looked at the gate opening and almost grudgingly trudged over there and through to where Trent had sent him. As soon as he went in, Trent shut the gate behind him and sank to ground in hysterics.

"Oh my God! That was intense!" he howled.

"Intense? Are you fucking crazy, going head to head with that bastard?" Kaden growled, but Trent's laughter was infectious, and they both joined in.

"Gotta go change my pants," Bran informed them dryly from behind him on the bike and set them off again. Misha looked incredulous as he stared at Trent, but he stayed silent as if he couldn't think of a single thing to say in his shocked state.

"No worries, mate. Me too." Trent chuckled as he got up from the grass. "I had no bloody idea if that would work."

Kaden sighed. "Next time you test your theory in a non-life-threatening situation, okay?"

Trent snorted. "Let's get out of here." They went out the top gate of the paddock they were in and drove around to get home, instead of tempting their fate with Beefsteak twice in one day.

WITH CHRIS up and around, it seemed like Bran was in a great mood, despite having to milk the cows with the rest of them when they came back from getting the bull in his pasture a few hours later. At least Kaden thought he looked like he was feeling better. He was smiling, and though he gave Kaden a flirty wink a time or two when Kaden was caught watching him, it was all genuine, lacking any of the mask Kaden had grown so tired of seeing Bran wear.

"It is so fucking hot out here," Bran said as they finished cupping a row of cows. He lifted his shirt up, exposing his stomach as he fanned himself, drawing Kaden's attention.

Trying to focus back on his work, Kaden looked away from him, but it didn't do much good when Bran put himself between Kaden and the cow he'd been about to cup. "Faster we get this done, the faster we can get inside," Kaden reminded him.

But Bran smirked at him and refused to move. "You like to look."

Shaking his head, Kaden moved around him. "You already know I want you. I think that's been made pretty clear. So what's your point?"

Bran didn't seem turned off at all by his abruptness. He wasn't trying to be rude, only wanting to get done as quickly as possible and out of the sudden blast of evening heat, which had seemed to come out of nowhere as soon as the clouds scattered, revealing a pale blue sky and a scorching sun.

"I don't mind you looking. I like to look too. Though, I'd like to see you without the shirt on sometime. The pants can go as well," Bran said, moving away from him with a teasing little smile that had Kaden shaking his head and wishing they weren't in the middle of milking, so that he could grab Bran and kiss that smile right off his face. How one man could make Kaden want him so completely with just a little lift of his lips was completely beyond him. He'd never been affected this badly by someone so quickly before.

He worked swiftly and was glad to see that Bran had decided to get back to milking as well since it made the work go faster when he wasn't so distracted by him. They moved the last of the cows out of the bales and started rinsing the cups off and hanging them up in preparation for the wash cycle. Kaden was happy to be done for the night as he stripped off his apron and gloves. He saw Bran go speak to Chris off to the side, where he stood with Misha, smiling as if he wasn't in pain and didn't have bruises splattered all over his face.

Kaden went to get the hose, and Samuel turned on the water. Right up close the spray from the hose was a powerful stream, but at the distance Bran stood away from him, it wouldn't hurt him at all. And, Kaden thought, Bran had complained of being too hot.

"Bran, come do your job!" he called to the man, pulling him away from Chris. He didn't want to accidentally spray Chris.

Bran came toward him, a cheeky smile on his face, but it was quickly replaced with shock as Kaden pointed the hose toward his chest and sprayed him down with the icy water. Soaking wet and laughing, Bran sprinted toward him and tried to wrestle the hose out of his arms, getting even more wet in the process and soaking Kaden as well until he could hardly see through the rivers of water streaming into his eyes.

Kaden wrapped his arms around Bran from behind, fighting for control of the wildly spraying hose as Bran tried to spray him back with it. They laughed and often ended up coughing on the water as it sprayed into their mouths.

It was fun to play with Bran like this, to see him laughing and hear no sarcasm behind the sound. But having him rubbing against him, pressed tightly against him from chest to hip, that was something Kaden couldn't ignore for long. He managed to pry the nozzle away from Bran, but when Bran spun around, Kaden was instantly distracted by the sight of him dripping wet with long lines of cold water running down his chest and stomach, outlining every muscle, every inch of skin Kaden had been desperate to touch.

It didn't matter that Bran still had on a shirt as Kaden caught sight of his nipples, hard from the cold water and practically begging for attention. He grabbed Bran by his wrist and pulled him flush against his chest, the hose forgotten as it sprayed over their feet, filling their gumboots to the top.

Bran smiled at him, the laughter still on his lips and in his eyes, though there was want there too, as obvious as any other expression Bran was capable of having. Kaden fisted a hand in his T-shirt and kept the other clamped around his wrist, keeping him close as he crashed his mouth over Bran's. There was no hesitation in Bran's response. No insecurities or worries. There were only his soft moans and the play of his tongue against Kaden's mouth, begging him for more.

Pulling the soaked Bran tight against his body, Kaden cupped both of the man's tight ass cheeks in the palms of his hands and ground their groins together. Kaden made sure to rock his hardness against Bran's.

"Feel that, Bran? I can't wait to slide it home in your hot body or over the wetness of your cocky tongue."

Bran sucked a spot on Kaden's neck and moaned against his skin. When Bran nipped his earlobe and breathed heavily into his ear, Kaden lost touch of their surroundings. Sliding his hands up, he grabbed two handfuls of wet fabric and peeled the shirt off of Bran's body, letting it drop where it wanted to.

"God, you're so fucking sexy. I can look at you all day," Kaden growled, taking in the feast before his eyes. A defined chest, small juicy nipples all puckered and ready for his lips to taste, and a treasure trail disappearing below the waistband of soaked denim.

Dragging Bran closer by a hand behind his neck, Kaden kissed him like Bran belonged to him. He claimed his tongue and reached with one hand to loosen the button of Bran's jeans, pulling the zipper down slowly.

Bran huffed in frustration and pushed Kaden back a little as he wrestled Kaden's equally drenched shirt off. When Bran's eyes landed on his chest, he licked his full lips and stroked his hands down Kaden's pectorals. Kaden had no shortage of hair on his chest, and it appeared Bran approved.

"I love your hairy chest. It gives me a serious hard-on when I see it." Bran kissed him again, his mouth open, hot and seeking. Kaden liked Bran this out of control, so hot with need for him and open about it. Not running like he had before, because he had been too scared to face his feelings.

With Bran's button and zip half-undone, Kaden slid his hand into the back of Bran's pants and in the process pulled them down even more as he lifted Bran against his own body. Looking down he could see Bran's cock clearly through the wet blue fabric of his briefs, the hardness pushing in between the elastic and Bran's stomach as it fought for freedom.

As Kaden reached down between them, a couple of throats cleared nearby. Loudly. "As much as we love the show, guys, it's time you remember you have an audience. You might not think so right now, but you will feel embarrassed after, so head on to the house and get a room!"

Bran's stiffening against him made it clear the younger man had forgotten where they were, and Kaden pulled him closer to cover him up as best he could. Kaden feared the moment interrupted and gone, until Bran took his hand and pulled him along as he started walking toward the house.

"Let's get the fuck out of here."

They hurried past their snickering friends as fast as wet denim allowed them to go, but it seemed their friends were enjoying this too much. "Ooh, Bran!" Trent joked in a high-pitched tone.

"Kaden, darlin'. You're so hard…." Samuel snorted through bouts of laughter.

"And think of us poor bastards out here going high and dry, you hear?" Chris yelled as the screen door slammed shut behind them.

"Fuck, it's like having four kid brothers who have never grown up." Bran laughed before Kaden pushed him against the wall leading upstairs. "Wait, let's go upstairs. I want to wrap my legs around your waist, but they're in a vise of wet fabric right now, and it's making it hard to even walk in them."

"Dammit, Bran. Hurry!" Kaden pushed him ahead up the stairs.

"Okay, okay. I'm so gonna climb you like a tree when I get you naked," Bran promised huskily.

"I'll keep you to that," Kaden promised.

When they cleared the top step, Kaden led Bran to his bedroom, and once inside he closed the door and leaned against it.

"Now I have you right where I've wanted you for so long." Kaden grinned.

"Believe me when I say, I have no desire to run. I'm done with that," Bran said solemnly. "I don't want to go another day without knowing how you taste and feel." With that, Bran started undressing himself as Kaden watched the best striptease of his entire life.

Bran went slow, whether from how wet his jeans were, which made them difficult to get off, or because he was intentionally moving at that speed, Kaden didn't know. But he enjoyed it all the same. Bran had been fit before, but now he looked really amazing and much healthier.

Kaden shoved his hands inside his own jeans, heavy from the water and tight against his legs. He wanted them off, but he wanted to stroke himself more, especially as he saw Bran roughly force his jeans and briefs down his thighs, exposing his thick cock.

He had the look of a man not at all ashamed of his own nudity, lacking all shyness about his body, as he kicked off his pants all the way before coming toward Kaden as if stalking him.

"You have too many clothes on," he said, leaning over Kaden and pushing him back against the bed with one firm hand on the middle of his chest.

Bran cut off his words with a fierce kiss and the flick of his tongue against Kaden's teeth. Kaden moved to help him get his own pants off but found Bran's hands already there, and it wasn't long before he was naked as well, his chilled skin flush against Bran's as they lay together on the bed.

Kissing him was wonderful, the heat of Bran's tongue against his, the wild taste of him in Kaden's mouth. He could have lain there for hours just kissing him. Another time, though. When he wasn't desperate to finally have him and his heart wasn't racing wildly out of control. He reached down to squeeze Bran's ass with his right hand, pulling him closer until he felt Bran's thick head rubbing against his own shaft.

"Fuck, I want you," Bran groaned, pulling his mouth away from Kaden's. He missed the contact for a moment, until he felt Bran move his lips to the side of his neck. Bran kissed down his chest but seemed to be moving too quickly. Kaden wanted to spend far more time on Bran when he had him under him. Bran's nipples, still hard from the cold, begged him for attention.

Bran knelt between his thighs and wasted no time sliding his mouth over Kaden's cock, taking him in fully before Kaden could have said anything otherwise. Not that he would have. He groaned and fisted his hands in the sheets beside his hips, wanting to grab onto Bran but not knowing him well enough to know if he could, if that was something Bran would allow him to do.

His cock hit the back of Bran's throat, and he gasped. The sound from his lips quickly turned into a groan as Bran moved one of Kaden's legs over his shoulder and began playing with his sack. He was rougher than anyone Kaden had been with before, as if he needed to feel every inch of him, to play with him and couldn't waste time with being gentle.

Bran lifted his mouth off Kaden's cock, releasing him and grinning up at him, his cheeks stained a dark red. "We should have done this sooner."

Laughing, Kaden brought his hand to Bran's bare shoulder and gave him a squeeze. "If you hadn't been such a bloody prick, we could have." He brought his hand up to the back of Bran's neck, then his hair, waiting for Bran to tell him to stop. But Bran only smiled at him before opening his mouth again and sliding his full lips over Kaden's shaft. Taking a chance, he curled his fingers into Bran's wet hair and pushed him down a bit. Not far, only enough to test the waters with him. But the groan that filled the bedroom wasn't from his throat, it came from Bran's, and Kaden closed his eyes on that sound.

"You like that," Kaden said, smiling as Bran slid his wet, warm mouth over his shaft. He received a hum in reply, before Bran lifted himself off Kaden's cock, finishing with a swirl of his tongue over Kaden's tip.

"You're delicious." He moved back up Kaden's body, kissing him as Kaden rolled over him, pinning Bran beneath him. Putting his hand between them, Kaden kept his mouth locked on Bran's as he squeezed his fingers around Bran's cock, tugging him up against Kaden's stomach. He couldn't wait to be inside of him, to feel Bran move against him, to hear his moans as Kaden rode him.

"Fuck yes," Bran grunted against his mouth. "Fuck me. I want you to put your big cock in me, to stretch me and—Oomph."

Kaden pressed his hand firmly over Bran's lips, silencing him. "How much of that is you faking it and saying things you think I might want to hear?"

Bran's cheeks darkened, not from lust but rather from embarrassment as he looked away from Kaden and stared silently at the wall for at least a full minute, if not longer, interrupting his need. Kaden released his mouth and held himself above Bran, refusing to move until he got an answer.

After releasing a long sigh, Bran turned back to look up at Kaden, and he was relieved to see that the mask was gone, leaving only Bran below him. "I don't know how to have sex without sounding like I'm in porn. I've never done it before, and normally the guys I'm with love it. What do you want to hear, then?"

Shaking his head, Kaden pressed his lips gently to Bran's. "Just you. Your moans, your sighs, you telling me what feels good for you. I want to be with you, not yet another act you think you need to put on when you're around me. Just feel what I do to you and be honest about it. Think you can do that?"

"I can try," Bran promised. Kaden nodded, knowing that was the best he could hope for with him.

Kaden bent his head and took one of Bran's tight nipples between his teeth and nipped it. When Bran moaned deeply and grabbed a handful of his hair, Kaden knew he had it right—Bran loved nipple play.

"Hurry," Bran urged him. "And you better fucking have some condoms, because I don't want to have to go to Chris for some right now."

"I do have some in the bedside drawer, but they may be expired or rusted from old age," Kaden teased.

"Don't care. Just want you in me." Bran arched his hips up to meet Kaden's, giving Kaden a feel of everything he had to offer as he pressed his cock against Kaden's. "You know you want to. If you think you can handle me."

"Oh, I can handle you, but I've been known for my stamina, so let's see how much of me *you* can handle." Kaden moved lower over Bran's deliciously hard abs, licking as he went along, with the tempting treasure trail leading him to heaven. When Bran's cock bumped his chin, he pulled away slightly and just had a good look at perfection. Bran trimmed his pubic hair, and Kaden never imagined it could be such a turn-on. Everything neat and tidy and so… accessible.

Without waiting any longer, he took Bran's hard shaft in hand and placed it on his tongue, looking Bran in the eye as he slowly lowered his head and took him in as far as he could go. Bran brought his hand to Kaden's hair, showing none of the hesitation Kaden had struggled with, as Bran pushed him down. Kaden's abilities weren't as well developed as Bran's, and he wrapped a fist around the root of Bran's hardness to avoid gagging.

"I can't wait until I get to fuck your mouth. I think I want you on your knees in the kitchen," Bran groaned as he tightened his hand on Kaden's hair, controlling him.

Kaden smiled and pulled off. "As long as I get to have you on the counter after." Sucking the head of Bran's cock into his mouth, he swirled his tongue around it, probing the slit with the tip, and Bran's wild reaction drove Kaden to the point of shooting his load. Bran's sounds of pleasure were amazing, but Kaden's control was shit today.

"More later. I want you now," Bran practically begged him as he let go of Kaden's hair to dig his fingers sharply into Kaden's shoulder.

"Hell, yes! My stamina has taken a hike today. I can't wait anymore either." Kaden pushed away and reached for the drawer, almost pulling it clean out of the cabinet, and managed to catch it before it fell to the carpet.

He retrieved the small bottle of lube and a condom and placed them beside Bran's hip where he kneeled between his spread thighs.

Bran put one hand behind his head, and Kaden caught him watching. "What?"

Smirking, Bran shook his head. "Just admiring. How long's it been for you?"

Kaden felt his cheeks heat up. "A while. There hasn't been anyone since I've been in the States." He was pretty sure he didn't want to ask Bran that same question, but he did anyway because Bran brought it up. "How about you?"

Bran moved his hand from Kaden's shoulder to drag his fingers down the side of Kaden's neck, making him shiver as Kaden watched a slow smile come across his face. "Three weeks. A few days before I came here. Want to know who with? I'll tell you if you do." The challenging, overtly sexual mask was back over Bran's features, and Kaden wanted to sigh at the sight of that barrier Bran had brought back out, as if Bran wanted to remind him that he'd been with numerous other men, and Kaden would be just another one of them.

"No, I don't want to know, because it's in the past. This here is now, and I believe you're no longer the same person you were back then. I want this Bran, the real one who doesn't feel the need to hide." Kaden stroked a hand over Bran's stomach, down one long leg, trying to soothe Bran's distress away.

Kaden saw the change come over Bran's features and the insecurity slowly leave his eyes as his smile turned far less flirty and much more genuine. "Okay. We're naked together, and in less than two weeks, I'll be sending you packing back to New Zealand, so I guess I could try to be myself with you for right now." Kaden leaned down to kiss him and felt Bran melt against his lips, turning from a stiff body under him to someone warm, and welcoming.

Kaden felt the sharp pain in his chest when Bran so easily mentioned sending him away when they were on the verge of sharing such intimacy with one another, but he filed the emotion away for a later time.

"That's all I'm asking."

Bran wrapped a warm hand around his cock, and Kaden sucked in a breath.

"If you touch me much more, I won't be able to fuck you into the mattress." He uncurled Bran's fingers from around him, grabbed for the lube, flicked the cap open, squirting some onto his fingers.

Bran opened his thighs wider for him, giving Kaden more room to get him ready. "You're being too slow," Bran complained.

"I'm enjoying myself," Kaden disagreed as he ran a lubed finger around Bran's pucker, wetting it before applying gentle pressure to allow Bran's body to let him in. Kaden felt Bran stiffen under him as he slowly pushed first one finger inside of Bran's tight entrance, quickly followed by another. "I don't want it to hurt, so speak to me. I like to play rough sometimes, but I don't do pain." Kaden looked away from the captivating sight in front of him to Bran's face, checking to make sure Bran was doing okay.

Bran frowned up at him. "You actually care if I'm enjoying this. Don't you?" He shook his head. "Weird."

"It's called making love because it involves more than simple gratification. If I wanted self-pleasure, I can jerk off, but this is different. I get my kicks out of your enjoyment." Kaden had some of those lovers in the past—the "I've had what I wanted, so see to yourself" type of guys.

Bran said nothing to show he understood what Kaden was saying, only wrapped an arm around Kaden's shoulders and pulled him close for a kiss. "More," he whispered against Kaden's lips. "Now."

Kaden swallowed Bran's gasps and moans as he added a third finger and gently stretched Bran to take him inside his body. When Bran's hole relaxed and Kaden felt the resistance ease, he pulled away from Bran's lips with a last soft kiss. On his knees he tore open the foil packet and rolled the condom over his straining hardness. He leaned forward on one palm and lined himself up to breach Bran's heat.

He went slowly, waiting for Bran to show any sign of discomfort, to give him any clue of possibly being in pain, but there was none. Only his soft gasps, and his fingers digging into Kaden's back with each gentle inch.

"How are you doing?" Kaden asked him before placing a kiss on Bran's cheek.

"I'd be a lot better if you'd actually fuck me instead of treating me like I'm some goddamn piece of china," Bran growled.

Knowing Bran's past was filled with nameless, quick fucks and quicker orgasms, Kaden took his time pulling out and sliding back into the hilt. This was one bout of sex Kaden wanted imprinted on Bran's mind so he'd never forget it.

He covered Bran's body with his own, plastering their skin and lips together as tightly as their bodies were joined, and made love to him. As Bran's body accepted his possession, Kaden picked up the speed and intensity of his thrusts, making sure to bottom out because he got the most amazing sounds out of Bran when he did so.

Bran was art and beauty as he moved below him, meeting him with each thrust, with each breath, each begging cry as Bran asked him for more as if he couldn't get enough of Kaden, as if Kaden was everything he'd ever wanted or needed.

Kaden knew Bran was all he would ever want or need, but unable to say the words, he showed it to Bran with every slide of his body, every brush of his hands or touch of his lips. He sucked on the side of Bran's neck, knowing he would leave a mark but not caring. Bran needed to see it every time he looked in the mirror and remembered this moment.

He felt it the second Bran went from enjoying him, to when his frenzied body neared release. It was in the shaking of his hand against Kaden's spine, to the way Bran arched his neck and closed his eyes so tightly as if he wanted to push his orgasm back, to keep it away for as long as he could.

Kaden felt his own orgasm looming and slowed his movements, stopping completely. He took Bran's face between his sweaty palms, looked into his gorgeous green eyes, and kissed his mouth. He claimed Bran's mouth and tongue, their breathing hard and fast as they fought to keep kissing and not give in to the need to breathe. Bran's ass spasmed around his erection, and Kaden moaned into Bran's mouth at the delicious tightness.

When they were both calmer, Kaden started thrusting again, staring into Bran's eyes with every move. When Bran's eyelids slid shut, Kaden kept watching him. The man was so beautiful to him. Beautiful and wild.

"I'm so close," Bran whispered. "Don't want this to end."

"It doesn't need to. We always have more time." Kaden knew his words had a double meaning, but whether Bran would catch it in the moment, he wasn't sure.

Lifting away a bit, he reached between their bodies and took Bran's dripping cock in his hand and started stroking him in time with his penetration. Giving himself up to the ecstasy of finally having Bran to himself, Kaden let go and gave all he was to the man he had come to care for deeply, despite fighting it all the way.

He stroked at the angle he found drove Bran crazy and loved him hard. Bran wrapped both long legs around Kaden's hips, pulling him even deeper. Kaden felt Bran's orgasm break, the man's back lifting off the bed in a beautiful arch and his lips opening for a yell, which Kaden took into his own lungs to share.

Kaden let go and joined Bran in orgasm, knowing anyone other than Bran Wilson would never be enough for him, ever again. If only Bran wasn't so insistent on pushing him away.

CHAPTER SEVENTEEN

BRAN SLOWLY untangled himself from Kaden's arms and tried to control his shaking. But what started as a shiver and quickly turned into tremors that went through his whole body, was uncontrollable.

"What's wrong?" Kaden asked him, sitting up beside him. Of course he would be able to tell something was off with him. He was far too perceptive. Bran shook his head, hoping Kaden would leave it alone as he reached for his pants. They were still soaking wet, so he grabbed the discarded sheet and wrapped it around his waist as he rose from the bed. It wasn't much of a barrier, but it was something, and it was all he had at the moment as he turned and looked down at Kaden, who stared at him like Bran had somehow screwed things up for him. Again.

He wanted to run, but knew he shouldn't. Still, everything inside of him demanded he leave Kaden's room, go straight to his own, get dressed, and pretend this never happened. Only he didn't want to brush it aside. He didn't want to forget.

Bran leaned against the wall across from Kaden's bed and slid heavily to the floor. "What comes next?" Bran quietly asked him.

"Do you want to talk about this?"

Frowning, Bran shrugged. "What do you normally do when you finish with someone?" he clarified his earlier question.

Not seeming to give two fucks about his own nudity, Kaden came off the bed and sat down across from him on the floor. "For starters, I don't really finish with people. Just because we've been together, doesn't mean I'm suddenly done. To me this means I want this to continue."

"For the next two weeks," Bran reminded him, and as he saw Kaden look away, he felt like he had stabbed him. Some people may have been fine flying around the world for someone they cared about, but Bran had simply never wanted to be with someone enough to make that kind of an effort. He rubbed his hands over his bare arms.

"Was this a mistake?" Bran had never once asked anyone he'd been with that question. He hadn't even considered asking any of them that. But he knew Kaden wanted more than someone to fuck for the next few weeks, and Bran wasn't sure if he knew how to be that for him. He'd never had a time limit on a relationship, and now that he was starting to realize that Kaden might matter to him, he wasn't happy about only having the limited amount of time with him.

A small voice in the back of his head reminded him if he so much as walked twenty feet out the front door, leaving the Wilson dairy farm property, Kaden, Samuel, and Trent would be entitled to stay there for another five years. For Bran, though, that just wasn't possible. He wouldn't have the farm hanging around as a reminder of everything he'd lost for so long.

On the other hand, if the farm sold, he lost Kaden as well. And Samuel and Trent. The whole thing was a huge fucking mess.

"I should go," Bran said, looking toward the door.

"You don't have to leave," Kaden told him.

Bran frowned, wondering what else he would do. "Then what?"

"You could come back to bed. We could talk."

"Okay." He could manage to have a bit of a conversation, he supposed, as he came back and lay down on the bed next to Kaden. "We were good. Let's do that again."

Kaden chuckled and shook his head, making Bran think he'd said something wrong. "No. We'll talk about something other than sex." He stretched out next to Bran and laid his arm over Bran's stomach, and Bran tried to relax and not feel like Kaden was holding him trapped with the simple contact.

Bran had no idea what to talk about other than sex after sleeping with someone. He'd never even tried. "Cows are good?"

Kaden rolled over on top of him, and Bran spread his thighs, letting Kaden get more comfortable on him if he wanted to. "Yes, the cows are fine. Are you okay?"

"This is new for me, so I'm trying. But I don't mind it. If that's what you mean." Bran lifted his lips to place a soft kiss on the underside of Kaden's jaw. "So… something to talk about. Does your sister have any kids? Family all back in New Zealand? Looking forward to seeing them again?"

The soft smile curling Kaden's lips told Bran all about a brother's love for his sibling without saying a word. "My sister is married and has two kids, a boy and a girl. Thank God for that, because at least my parents won't bother me for one or the other. If it wasn't for Kylie, they might not have been so accommodating of my sexuality," Kaden joked.

"What's it like being an uncle?" Bran asked.

"So much fun, because you can teach them all the naughty stuff, let them bake or play in the mud and get dirty, but then send them home to their parents to clean." Kaden laughed with glee.

"You're an evil uncle." Bran grinned in reply.

"Nope, I'm the bestest uncle in the world, and those are their words, not mine," Kaden swore solemnly before dropping a quick kiss on Bran's sensitive lips. "And I miss them of course and am looking forward to seeing them again when I go home. Whenever that may be." Kaden's words reminded Bran of the present and the going-nowhere-fast situation they were in.

He pushed against Kaden's shoulders gently, and the man let him up. "I'm going to get dressed and go make us something to eat. I'm hungry."

"Don't do this, Bran. Don't push me away," Kaden pleaded.

"I've got to go." Bran slipped out of the room and hurried to his own. He'd promised Kaden he didn't want to run anymore, but the truth was that running was the only thing he'd ever been really good at when it came to being with other people.

Bran was glad he found Chris alone in the bedroom they were sharing when he came across the hall wearing only a sheet and quickly closed the door behind him. Chris gave him a knowing smile and put his phone aside. The game he'd been playing continued to make noise, but they both ignored it.

"So. You and Kaden, huh?"

Bran quickly pulled out a pair of loose drawstring shorts from the dresser and slipped them on. It was amazing what just getting one piece of clothing on could do when he was naked and wasn't feeling quite like himself.

"I guess the sheet kind of gave it away."

Chris rolled his eyes and sat up in bed. "And the bite mark on your neck. What's wrong? You don't seem happy about it at all."

Bran flopped down onto the bed next to him and wondered why it was so easy for him to lie in bed and talk to Chris, while it had felt completely foreign to do the exact same thing with Kaden only a few minutes before.

"He thinks it's normal to talk after sex. That's weird, right?"

"Like about what he could do to improve on if he ever got the chance to be with you again?" Chris asked him, looking just as confused as Bran felt.

He shook his head. "No. We talked about his family, his sister. Whether or not she had kids. You ever do that?"

Wide-eyed, Chris just blinked at him. "Weird. No. People actually talk about that kind of stuff after sex?"

Bran rolled off the bed. "I don't know. I've never really hung around to find out. Maybe they do. Maybe we're the weird ones."

"Well, we already knew that," Chris said, grinning at him.

Bran went back to the dresser and began riffling through his shirts. "Shirt or no shirt? For going downstairs, having dinner, seeing Kaden again...." He blushed and turned around to find Chris watching him. "What?"

"You look good. I'm glad you're filling out a bit. Do you want to be tempting, or do you want to be modest? I'm sure you'll be comfortable either way, so that's not even a question."

Bran wasn't really sure what he wanted to be. When he was alone in his apartment, or even when Chris was there, he went without a shirt on all the time. It wasn't a big deal to him, and it shouldn't have been now. Why in the hell did sex have to go and complicate everything for him?

"Tell me what to wear," Bran grumbled.

Getting off the bed, Chris came over to the dresser too, and when Bran didn't move, he shooed him aside with a wave of his hand. "First of all, those shorts don't do anything for you."

"These shorts are my loosest ones," Bran protested as Chris handed him another, tighter pair.

"Yes. And they look like pajamas. Put on the khakis." Bran hesitated, and Chris shook his head. "Come on. Get naked. I'm hungry, and you have to make me dinner."

"Oh I do, do I?" Bran joked with him as he pulled the other shorts down and stepped into the new ones. They fit him better at least.

"There. Your ass looks great in those. Now. As for the shirt problem. Hmm. No, I don't think you'll need one tonight. Ever considered piercing your nipples?"

Bran laughed as he opened the door and stepped out of the room. "Misha has pierced nipples, therefore I will not."

Chris was right behind him as Bran headed down the stairs. "Misha has tattoos, you had one. The world didn't implode."

As soon as he stepped foot on the main level, Bran realized Kaden was watching him from the living room, and he tried not to blush. "I had a tattoo. And I spent thousands getting it removed. Not the same thing."

"You had a tattoo?" Kaden asked him from the living room before Bran could make it to the kitchen.

He shot Chris a glare, which he laughed off as he went to sit beside Samuel on the couch. "I did," Bran hedged. It wasn't his favorite topic by far. And the way everyone was looking at him didn't really help.

"I don't remember you having a tattoo," Misha said as he came out of the kitchen with a bottle of beer in his hand and leaned against the wall across from Bran.

"It was after you," Bran said dismissively, not wanting to think about that night again. "Dinner orders? Ideas? Suggestions?" Anything to get them off the topic of his tattoo.

Kaden smiled at him, and Bran easily returned his smile, until Kaden started talking again. "I want to hear more about your tattoo."

"No. It was a stupid, drunk mistake. Back to dinner." When no one had any suggestions, Bran turned around and headed into the kitchen. "I'm making chicken cacciatore!" he called back to them, hoping they at least had the ingredients for something as simple as that.

He was kneeling in front of a lower cabinet when Kaden walked up behind him. "Are you going to ask me about my tattoo again?"

"I was actually going to offer to help you cook dinner, seeing as how you milked, and the rest of the guys are being lazy right now," Kaden said, coming over to stand beside him. "But if you wanted to talk about your tattoo, I am curious."

Bran smiled and rose from the floor with a couple cans of diced tomatoes in his hands. "Here's the deal. If you chop up an onion for me, because I always cry a lot when I have to do it, then I will tell you about the horrible tattoo I got when I was twenty-two."

"I can live with that," Kaden said, plucking an onion out of a basket on the counter. He got to work on the dicing while Bran went to the stove and started heating up the oil to cook the chicken.

Bran really wanted to have something nonembarrassing to tell Kaden about someday. "I was already pretty drunk when I followed this guy upstairs and we had sex. I guess it was his friend's place, and he was crashing there or something. I don't know. I never got all that many details about the situation, or him."

Kaden grimaced, and Bran nodded to him. It was another one of those awful things he'd done that was fun at the moment but not for much longer than that. "After we do our thing, he starts talking about how he's a tattoo artist and how I'd look great with a tattoo on my lower back. To show off my ass, he said."

"That's...." Kaden shook his head. "Really? You went for that?"

"I really wish I hadn't," Bran said as he put the chicken into the largest pot he'd been able to find in the kitchen. He was amazed everything was right where his grandfather had always kept it, like Kaden and the guys hadn't changed a thing. "Of course he had his kit there, and me being all excited about my first tattoo, couldn't wait. He tattooed me, I went downstairs where Chris was making out with someone, showed him, everyone at the party laughed, and Chris got me out of there before I could kick the guy's ass."

"Was it that bad?" Kaden looked as if didn't believe it could be as horrible as it had been.

Bran snorted, remembering how mortified he had been. "Oh, it was far worse. This guy had tattooed 'Insert Here' on my lower back with an arrow pointing to my ass. I used all of my savings at the time to get that sucker removed as quickly as possible. If you look closely, there are still a few little marks from the laser, but at least the original mess is gone."

"No more drunk tattoos for you," Kaden practically ordered.

It was an easy thing to agree to, and Bran quickly smiled at him as he moved on to chopping the vegetables. "So what about you? Any stupid, drunk memories you feel like sharing? I already know you don't have any tattoos. You had to have gotten into some kind of trouble, though, when you were younger. And when you're done with the onion, go ahead and toss it into the pot with the chicken. Please."

Kaden got to work, and Bran settled in beside him, working together to make the dish. It was nice, Bran realized. He didn't often make meals with other people, but this might have been something he could get used to.

"I have a few," Kaden drawled with a slight grin. "We all suffer a little bit of stupid, especially after hitting puberty. One night we had a disco at our school. Now it's a damn small school compared to your schools here, the student enrollment totaled just over a hundred."

"That's really, ridiculously small. I know here in Montana we didn't have a lot of people my age, but the school I went to had closer to a thousand. Chris's high school had almost four thousand people in it." Bran shook his head, not quite believing what he was hearing.

"So, as you can imagine, everyone in the community knew everyone, or let's say, everyone's business anyway. At this disco, Trent, Samuel, and I were bored out of our minds—all these girls gave us wide eyes, begging us to dance and mingle, but hell, all three of us were gay." Kaden snorted. "Trent came up with this brilliant idea for us to do the obstacle course at the back of the school property in the dark. Stark naked. And hey? Who were Sam and I to argue?"

Bran snickered, imagining the three of them. "How much trouble did you get into?"

"Heaps! We had a great time doing it, though, until we got called into the office the following Monday to see photos of our bare asses all over the principal's desk. The best one was of us crouching down, asses in the air to start the belly crawl across the sandpit. Well, all three of us got to wash the school toilets, windows, and water fountains for a whole year." Kaden chuckled.

Bran laughed until his stomach hurt from it, and he had to grab the island to balance himself and keep from falling over. "You three sound like you were crazy back then. It would have been fun to see you. I think if I hadn't been so shy, I would have liked being your friend."

Kaden walked up into Bran's private space. "Even then, you and I would've never been just friends. I would've reacted the same way I do now that I know you," Kaden said softly, his breath fanning across Bran's hot cheeks.

Bran blushed and looked at the stove, judging the time they had left before looking back at Kaden. "We'll have about fifteen minutes where the chicken just has to stew in the sauce," Bran said, coming away from the stove after putting a lid over the pot. The smell of the rich tomato sauce, with the vegetables slowly working into it, made him hungry, and he was glad he'd thought to make it. And also that they had most of the ingredients in the house. He'd had to skimp a little on the green peppers and would have much preferred to use fresh tomatoes and cook them down as opposed to the cans he'd used. But all in all he didn't think it would be a bad dish, and there was plenty enough in the pot to feed everyone, especially when he added in the pasta.

He smiled over at Kaden, who had finished washing his hands and looked as if he was ready to go back to the living room and watch TV with everyone else. Bran had been glad for his company in the kitchen, and his help, but he wasn't ready to release him quite yet.

With Kaden's back leaning against the large island, Bran moved in front of him, putting a hand on his lower stomach, right above the button of his pants. "I know we just came down, but do you want to go back upstairs?" Bran asked, pressing his lips to the side of Kaden's neck, right over the pulse he could feel racing against his mouth. "We could have some more fun." He lowered his hand a little, running his fingers over Kaden's zipper, before cupping him through his pants. If the man didn't get what he was suggesting by then, Bran was pretty sure there was no hope for him. Fifteen minutes wouldn't be enough for sex, not the way Bran liked to play things, but it would be enough for him to get on his knees in front of Kaden and really enjoy him. Even though he'd just had him, Bran was practically humming for more. Sex he could do, and do well by all accounts, and as long as Kaden didn't expect anything more from him, he was pretty sure things would be okay.

Kaden leaned his head back, closing his eyes and looking very much as if he liked what Bran was doing. And for a second, he thought he'd get his way as he kissed around to the front of Kaden's throat and dragged his wet lips down his skin to gently suck at the hollow in Kaden's throat.

It was fun, and Bran was more than ready to take Kaden's hands and pull him upstairs, that was, until Chris came into the kitchen, interrupting them. Bran took his mouth from Kaden's neck, but since Chris couldn't see around the island to get a look at where his hand was on Kaden's pants, Bran had no intention of letting him go.

"So…," Chris began, leaning his elbows on the table and giving Bran a knowing smile, as if he could tell where Bran's mind had been, and also how annoyed he was at the sudden interruption to his plans. And worse, that Chris had come over at that precise moment intentionally. Bran had never once thought to call Chris a cockblocker, but in that moment it was only one of the many unfortunate names he was calling his best friend in his head.

"What?" Bran tried not to snap at him, and failed, earning himself a grin from Chris, as if he was laughing at him and his mounting frustration.

Chris gave him a little shrug. "I was just wondering if you'd like to go outside with me. I was going to go walk and see the calf you helped deliver. Maybe you should name her, you know, before you send her off to slaughter or something. Whatever people do with female cows. But, since I see that you're busy, I guess I'll just go for that walk myself."

He loved Chris, really he did, but even he had to see how obvious he was being. "Subtle. Really fucking subtle. Why don't you name her for me while you're at it?"

"Oh could I? Maybe I'll call her Diamond. Remember that kitten you had in college, when we got our first apartment together, and her name was Diamond? I think that would be a good name."

Bran shook his head. He did remember Diamond and how much he'd adored her for the eight months they'd had her before they'd had to put her down. That had been the first, and last, time he'd had a pet of his own.

"Go ahead," he told Chris, no longer wanting to play since Chris had gone into unhappy memories. Chris seemed to realize he'd come up to the line, at least, as his smile lost some of its brightness, and he backed away from the island.

"See you."

Bran gave him a wave as he left, but his mood was gone, and he let his hand fall away from the front of Kaden's pants.

"What was that about?" Kaden asked him as they stood together.

Bran figured Kaden wouldn't be asking about the kitten. "Chris doesn't want me to sell the farm in two weeks." That wasn't really why Chris was annoyed with him, and not the entire truth about selling the farm, since Chris wanted him to hang on to it for another five years, but as much as he liked Kaden, he wasn't interested in getting into all the details with him.

"Maybe he likes it here," Kaden said idly.

Bran shrugged. Maybe he did. Or possibly just wanted to be away from Manhattan for a while, and anywhere Samuel was would have been just as good for him. "I'm not sure." Because he didn't want to be a tease to Kaden, he then added, "My offer to go upstairs is still on the table." They'd have fun, Bran would make sure of it, but his heart really wasn't in it anymore. At least not for the moment.

Kaden leaned forward to give him a soft kiss on his lips, which Bran hesitantly returned. "As much as I'd like to take you up on your offer, I'd want more time than that with you."

Bran nodded and pulled him close for another kiss.

CHAPTER EIGHTEEN

THE FOLLOWING afternoon Bran successfully persuaded Kaden, Samuel, and Trent to allow him and Misha to milk the cows while Chris supervised. Bran knew the three friends worked hard every day and rarely got a break from the continuous grind of farm work. Since Kaden had taught him how to do the milking plant wash cycle, Bran could do most of it on his own now. So, his good deed was to give them the milking off and pray like hell everything went smoothly.

Chris spent the whole time with his nose scrunched up because of the sights, smells, and sounds of the cows. Misha just got on with the job. When the last cows left to walk out to pasture, they made quick work of the cleaning and walked toward the house, but a yell and laughter in the paddock stopped them in their tracks.

Kaden, Trent, and Samuel, all shirtless ran around like crazy people in the long grass, chasing each other and then diving over some invisible line, sometimes tackling each other to the ground.

"What the hell?" Bran said as they walked over to the fence to watch. After some scuffling and wrestling on the ground, Trent jumped up with a ball in his hand and started running like hell in the opposite direction from the other two. "Fuck, he can run!" Bran said in awe, watching Trent's legs pump to run away from his buddies who watched him go, not even making an effort to pursue him.

Kaden and Samuel spotted them and leisurely walked to where they watched from the fence. "What kind of football is that?" Bran asked.

"Football is for pussies, that's rugby!" Samuel teased, his eyes crinkling at the corners. With his shirt off, Samuel's tattoos were on display, and they were mysteriously beautiful—tribal Maori designs decorated his forearms and biceps, reaching over his pectorals and shoulders, all the way around to his back. The art almost came alive with the movement of his muscles as the big man took his T-shirt and wiped off the sweat on his skin.

Looking at his friend beside him, Bran saw Chris admiring Samuel, a telling flush staining his neck and cheeks, his eyes too bright.

Kaden cleared his throat and threw out both his arms, putting his chest and abs on show. "What about me? Why isn't anyone staring at me?"

Bran snorted a laugh. "You know you're sexy, so why even ask?" Kaden stepped closer, and Bran dragged a palm over his sweaty stomach. Trent seemed to have discovered in the meantime he was playing by himself and joined them by the fence, the always-friendly smile in place.

"You boys all done playing your little game?" Bran teased. His question might have been directed at the three of them, but his gaze was solely fixed on Kaden, who, with his shirt off and his shorts slipping down his hips, made Bran want to drag him back inside and upstairs by his belt loops and strip him down.

"Just think, Bran, if you weren't selling the farm in two weeks, you could learn how to play rugby," Chris whispered loudly in his ear.

Rolling his eyes, Bran batted Chris away from his ear without answering him. But Chris did deserve an answer, if only to stop him from dropping constant hints. "I'm selling. I know you don't want me to, but having Samuel within a four-hour flight of you in case he decides to someday have sex with you is not enough reason for me to keep around a piece of property I absolutely cannot stand and wish I could take a tanker of gasoline and a flamethrower to. So please, I love you, I know what you're doing, but please just stop with the hints and the suggestions." Chris looked like he'd slapped him, and Bran shook his head. He wouldn't apologize, not for this.

"What about me being a four-hour flight away? Is that not reason enough for you to keep it?" The joy had faded out of Kaden's eyes, and Bran felt it like a punch to the stomach, but he ignored it. That's what he did best.

"I don't have the time, or the energy, to fly four hours for sex. As good as it was," Bran said as coldly as he could manage. It hurt to say such a thing to Kaden, especially when he saw how much his words affected him. But it was better that he remembered this was just sex between them, and their affair had an expiration date, rather than assume this was going to continue between them as if they had a future together.

Trent bent over and picked up the rugby ball and stalked off, clearly pissed off with Bran. Misha shook his head sadly at Bran and followed

Trent to wherever it was the man was headed. Samuel's expression was equal amounts of sadness and disgust.

"Chris." Samuel addressed his friend. "Let's go and feed the chickens and check in on that calf and its mama." Chris didn't even spare Bran a look as he walked away with Samuel.

Kaden was next, stalking off in the direction of the back porch of the house. The screen door slammed shut, and Bran was alone. "What the absolute fuck?" he grumbled, shaking his head as he headed into the house after Kaden. He supposed if they were really going to have this argument now, which seemed pretty unavoidable at the moment, then at least they'd be alone for it. He was so tired of having an audience for everything.

Inside the house, Kaden was nowhere to be seen, but Bran heard the shower and knew he had a few minutes' reprieve until they would sort this out. He poured himself a glass of orange juice and stood looking out the kitchen window, seeing Trent and Misha in the distance where they appeared to be talking.

Why they'd all been so pissed off was beyond him. Sure, the guys were being thrown out in a couple of weeks, but they weren't going to be staying on forever. And Chris would get over it. Misha, whatever his issues were, had no bearing on Bran. He'd stopped caring about Chris's half brother a long time ago. Right after Bran had been stupid enough to have sex with him if he wanted to get precise about it.

A few minutes later, he heard the shower turn off and soon after, footsteps on the stairs, but Bran didn't turn around. If Kaden wanted to fight, he wouldn't make it easy on him. Kaden stopped behind him, and before he knew it, the man grabbed him and pushed him over the closest piece of kitchen counter.

"What the fuck are you doing?" Bran gasped in shock as he started to struggle against Kaden behind him.

"You like no strings attached sex, so that's what we're doing." Kaden reached around and unbuttoned his jeans and yanked them down to his knees.

"Finally, you're seeing this my way."

Bran felt Kaden's cock line up, and the next moment it slid in deep. Bran curled his fingertips over the edge of the counter and held on. Other than the rough withdrawal and pumping, Kaden almost didn't touch him, and for the first time in his life, Bran didn't like it one bit. His body experienced the pleasure, but his head wasn't quite there with it all, and he didn't know why.

KADEN HAD never had unattached, mindless sex in his life, but he did his best to imitate what he knew about it while his heart ached. He fucked Bran like a nobody, the way Bran preferred all his sexual encounters to be. No softness, no affection, no sweetness. No love.

When he heard Bran gasp, he knew the man was close to coming and pulled out. Shaking like a leaf, he pulled Bran up and turned him over, reaching to the ground where he had dropped his towel and laid it behind Bran's hips before pushing him back down, on his back this time. Face to face.

"That," he said in a shaky whisper, "I hated every damn second of that."

"Me too," Bran said, just as softly. When Kaden looked up at him, he saw unshed tears hiding behind Bran's eyes before Bran quickly looked away from him. "That was sex, but this, this is how I do it, Bran. Because you're not just a piece of ass to me. This is how I show how I feel about you." Bending his head, Kaden took Bran's leaking cock into his mouth and sucked him in. He tasted the essence of who Bran was and filed the memory away with all the other precious ones. Bran grabbed his hair in two tight fists and used his mouth, and Kaden let him. Using his fingers, he caressed Bran's ass, fingering him in time with the movements of his mouth.

"Stop," Bran said, suddenly releasing Kaden's hair. "Please. I can't. Not without you." Kaden understood the broken words. Together.

"Look at me!" Kaden growled, and when Bran opened his eyes, he laid his heart bare. "I love you, Bran." He entered Bran's body and took him. Lifting Bran's legs over his elbows, Kaden angled his thrusts to give Bran the most pleasure possible, and Bran went wild underneath him. The next moment Chris came around the corner in the lounge and saw them, Bran completely unaware.

"I don't know how to love someone, though, Kaden. I don't even know what that really means. If I could love you, if I was any good for you, then I would." He put one hand on Kaden's chest, and the other over his eyes, hiding what Kaden was pretty sure were tears.

"That's enough for me. No more running and pretending this isn't happening." Kaden assured him. Using his eyes and head, he told Chris to leave. That he would take care of Bran. That Chris could trust him with Bran, and with a slow nod, Chris acknowledged him and left the room as quietly as he had appeared.

Bran dragged his hand over his face, and Kaden saw he had been crying but was no longer doing so. He still looked sad, though, which was never something Kaden had intended to make him.

"Why did it have to be you?" Bran sighed as he curled his fingers over Kaden's chest, biting his nails into his skin nearly to the point of pain.

Kaden kissed him, trying his best to drag Bran out of his misery. "Be with me, right here. No more games, just us. I want you. I've been wanting you since I first saw you looking like a proper gentleman in a suit standing in the dirt."

Bran wiped at his eyes and gave Kaden a watery smile. "I did look good. Didn't I?"

His ego was astounding sometimes. "And I kept wanting you right up until you opened your bloody mouth." He slid into Bran's tight body, groaning with each passing inch. "Don't fight this. Just enjoy it."

Bran moved his hands to Kaden's shoulders, then his arms, squeezing him tightly. "Harder," Bran gasped as Kaden pushed into him, and Bran clamped his legs around Kaden's hips as Kaden gave him his wish.

"I'll give you everything you want," Kaden promised him. He wrapped his forearm under Bran's neck, holding him up, so that he could kiss him in time with each rapid thrust. Bran closed his eyes, and Kaden leaned over him, pressing his forehead against Bran's as he pumped into him as quickly as he could. "All I want is you," Kaden whispered against his lips. He felt Bran tighten around his cock and heard his soft moan a second before Bran dug his heels sharply into Kaden's back, forcing him to go deeper.

Bran bucked against him, going wild against his chest with each racing heartbeat and every loud groan. He was beautiful in his desire, in his pure need to reach his own pleasure, and Kaden covered Bran's mouth with his own, sharing each of his sounds of pleasure and his whispered words of need. When Kaden reached down a hand to stroke

Bran's shaft, he touched Bran's fingers and joined their hands to give him a tighter grip.

Bran's hot cum erupted between their sweaty bodies, and Kaden wasn't far behind him as his climax ripped powerfully through him. Through it all he held Bran close to his heart with their lips joined as intimately as they were in body.

It took them a long time to separate, neither of them seeming to be in a hurry to let the other go. But being caught together, postsex, in the middle of the kitchen, wasn't all that enticing either, and eventually they did move apart.

"What now?" Bran asked him as he pulled his pants back on before following Kaden upstairs where he could get cleaned up and dressed.

Kaden had no idea and still didn't have a good answer even as he closed the bedroom door behind them before discarding his towel in a laundry hamper. "I don't intend to let you go so easily."

Bran smirked and looked like he wanted to make a joke, but the words seemed to quickly die on his lips with a shake of his head. He took a deep breath. "You won't have a choice. In two weeks I'm gone, back to Manhattan and then on to San Diego a few days after for a business meeting."

"And I'll be on a plane back to New Zealand." Kaden had no idea what he could say to make Bran change his mind or if it was even possible. But he wasn't willing to just give up so quickly, not like Bran seemed to be. "What would it take for you to keep the farm?"

"A whole new childhood full of memories," Bran said, sounding miserable as he sat on the bed next to Kaden and banged his head against the wall. "I can't make myself love this place like you do. Or even tolerate it. I really do want to burn it all down. What about you? How can I make you forget all about it? How can I get you to move on?"

"This place doesn't hold any of us captive, Bran. Samuel, Trent, and I are here, because it gave us a break from what we do back home. Different scenery, an adventure, a challenge—call it what you like. If you go ahead with the sale, don't feel bad because you're leaving us homeless and jobless, because we are far from it. Feel terrible because you're destroying a dream of someone who built it and left it for you to take care of," Kaden said firmly, but gently.

Bran didn't know why, but for some reason he had imagined exactly what Kaden just described. If he sold the farm, they'd pack their backpacks and get on a plane to go home with nothing to show for their dedication, loyalty, and hard work to his grandfather. His absolute selfishness and pride hit him straight between the eyes. Why did he assume Samuel, Trent, and Kaden had little money? Nothing about the men spoke of hardship or lack, but still, Bran, who practically swam in money, had assumed he was the only rich one.

"You, Sam, and Trent would've spent the next few years or more working here and had bargained on it, until I showed up. So if I sell, you will all be without an immediate job and—"

Kaden interrupted him. "Bran, listen. I wanted to avoid ever speaking of this, but Trent, Sam, and I? We are fine, financially anyway. We won't be destitute. I promise." A small smile pulled at Kaden's lips, his eyes teasing.

"What do you mean? I'm taking it out from under you," Bran stammered.

"Yes, over here you are, but we have our safety nets back home. We are all in some way involved in businesses back in New Zealand. We'll be fine," Kaden assured him.

"Really?" Bran asked.

"Absolutely. Trent and Samuel are partners in a large two-thousand-cow dairy farming operation, and I own two smaller farms myself and share another one with Sam and Trent. Like I said, we will be fine. It just means we'll have to go back there and play the role of super-hardass bosses like we mean it." Bran's mouth wouldn't close after Kaden's admission.

"You own two farms? Why didn't you tell me this before now?" Bran asked in amazement.

"It never came up, and it wasn't important." Kaden shrugged.

Bran shook his head as a smile shaped his lips. "You're freaking amazing—you know that?"

"I do now." Kaden walked closer. "Because you just said so."

Bran wrapped his arms around Kaden's neck and landed a soft kiss on his lips.

"Would you come visit me in Manhattan? Stay with me for a couple of weeks sometimes?" Bran asked him, already knowing the question was unfair since he wasn't willing to do the same. And he'd never once been willing to put in that kind of commitment.

"For love, I would."

He slipped his hand into Kaden's. "I don't even know what that word means. I've only heard it from one person, and I've only ever said it to them. And if that all-consuming need to never screw up and always please them, regardless of what it meant for myself, is love, then I want nothing to do with it."

"Richard?" Kaden quietly asked him. Bran could only nod, and Kaden moved so he was lying down next to Bran, and Bran lay his head on Kaden's muscular upper arm. "Seeing Chris, and knowing that at some point that was you, makes me want to kill Richard."

Bran smirked and curled in against Kaden's chest, resting his forehead in the hollow of Kaden's neck as Kaden wrapped his arms around him. "Get in line." Lying as he was, Bran couldn't see anything around him, and his entire world, for that moment at least, was made up of just Kaden. It wasn't difficult for him to relax and simply be there with him, with the world outside of the two of them cut off like it was.

"That wasn't love. I know you probably thought it was, and he was a horrible person for making you believe him. But love doesn't hurt like that. It doesn't leave you feeling broken and miserable."

It was a nice sentiment, but Bran knew how wrong Kaden really was. "Love always causes pain. That seems to be the whole point. You love someone until they leave you, or if they don't leave you and you get forty or fifty years with them, eventually they die, and you're still left alone and hurting."

He felt Kaden sigh a second before he tightened his arms around Bran's back. "You're so cynical. I'd rather have those years with someone I loved, and who loved me back, rather than go through life without ever having even tried."

"Have you ever been in love before me, then? Is it as great as you seem to think?" Bran asked him, trying, and generally failing, to keep the challenge out of his voice. He wasn't sure when he'd turned so antagonistic with the people he cared about, but he wished he could stop it. Just because he didn't put any stock in love didn't mean Kaden was stupid for still thinking there was something to it.

"Yes, I have been in love twice as far as I can remember. The first time was absolute puppy love and the relationship doomed from the start. I was only sixteen and almost idolized him but soon realized he was a closeted asshole taking advantage of a willing kid. The other time was about nine years later. We were together for four years, moved in together, and did the whole nine yards, but it didn't work out. We didn't fit." Bran imagined he could hear echoes of the pain at the lost relationship in Kaden's voice.

"Do you still talk to him at all?" Bran quietly asked him. He was a little jealous, not of the person Kaden had been with, but that Kaden had been able to have that kind of relationship with someone, something that lasted that long, and didn't leave him as messed up as his time with Richard had left him.

"We split up with the condition of doing it like mature adults, so yeah, we did speak for a time after, and then he moved away to pursue his art career in London. I get an occasional e-mail from him, and he has since gotten married to the man of his dreams, and those were his words, not mine." Kaden smiled as he spoke those last words.

Bran tightened his hand on Kaden's side self-consciously. He was glad the guy had moved on, that there wasn't a chance of him coming back into Kaden's life and staking some kind of a claim to him. Not that Bran had any reason to feel that way. He knew he'd be saying good-bye to Kaden in less than two weeks and only had their short time together to really enjoy him.

"You don't sound jealous."

"Why would I be? I told you we didn't fit. We tried to make it work and were as miserable as two wet cats together. Not like you and me." Kaden growled before rolling over and pinning Bran to the mattress. "Because we fit just right."

"When we aren't fighting you mean?" Bran asked, smiling up at him as he brought his hands to Kaden's neck.

The next moment Kaden bit his neck and sucked the spot. "Oh, but fighting means great make-up sex all over the place—the barn, the ATV, the paddock, the creek...." Kaden's words trailed off as he kissed Bran's hot skin again.

Bran's phone started ringing in his pocket and, groaning, he rolled out of Kaden's arms and sat up to answer it. "Shit," he quietly cursed before answering it. "Hello, Mr. Romanoff."

"Where's my son? He's not answering his phone."

Bran didn't have the energy to snap back at him or to care all that much about Mr. Romanoff's continued anger toward him. "Which one?"

"The one you turned into a faggot."

The word hurt, as it always did, but right then it hurt most because Bran knew, while he could hang up on Mr. Romanoff and not have to speak to him again for a while, Chris didn't have that choice, and he heard abuse from his own father every day at the office.

He reached back to give Kaden's hand a squeeze before he slid to his feet and started heading out of the bedroom. "When I see him again, I'll tell him to call you."

"That's not good enough. I need to speak with him immediately."

Bran bit back the nastiest retort he could think of and went down the stairs. "It's a big farm. I'll have him call you. Bye." He hung up the phone as quickly as he could, cutting off anything more Mr. Romanoff might have said.

"Their dad?" Kaden asked, coming down the stairs with him.

Bran nodded. "Yeah." The side of his neck felt warm, and he reached up to touch it. "Did you leave a new mark on me?"

Kaden didn't look at all ashamed. "Yes."

"Okay." He didn't mind having Kaden's bite marks on him. They were reminders of the fun they had together, and now he knew how Kaden felt about him, he supposed they were also reminders of Kaden's love for him. Almost like a ring on his left hand, only significantly less terrifying for him to bear.

Finding Chris was luckily the simplest thing he'd had to do so far that day, as they were all talking in the living room. The TV was going, but no one really seemed to be paying attention to it.

"Hey. Call your dad back," Bran said as he leaned against the wall and met Chris's gaze.

Chris rolled his eyes. "I was avoiding his calls for a reason. But fine. I'll talk to him. After I get an apology from you."

"What the hell for?" Bran scoffed.

Kaden shook his head and went to sit down next to Samuel. "You aren't serious. Are you?"

Bran wanted to sit down too. But the only option was next to Misha, and he was absolutely not going there. So he shrugged and got as comfortable as he could against the wall.

"Yes. I didn't do anything wrong."

"You were an asshole," Chris snapped at him. "Even more than usual."

Bran didn't think he had been, but he wasn't willing to fight with Chris either. "Sorry, then."

Apparently that wasn't good enough for Chris as he shook his head. "Not even close to working. Try again."

"Chris…." Bran shook his head. He really didn't want to apologize, especially since he hadn't done anything he needed to apologize for, and he certainly wasn't comfortable apologizing in front of everyone. If Chris was mad at him then they'd handle this privately. Like they always did. "Come outside with me instead?"

Chris sat back and crossed his arms over his chest. "Start talking. Or I tell everyone about the time I got you drunk and you gave me a lap dance. While wearing a pink thong."

Bran's cheeks flamed, and he swallowed thickly. That wasn't something he wanted to share with the rest of them. "You still have the video?"

Chris nodded. "And I'll break it out if you don't make me happy within five minutes."

Well, that was more than enough reason for Bran to give Chris anything he wanted. "I'm sorry for wanting to sell the farm," he tried. But Chris shook his head. "For not caring the calf is going to go somewhere else to be milked and some of the others will be slaughtered?" Chris frowned but didn't let him off the hook, so Bran kept thinking of what Chris could possibly be mad at him for, trying to come up with something. "I didn't buy you more cheesecake. I let that spider plant you got me last year die, I stared at Samuel with his shirt off."

Kaden cleared his throat, and Bran looked over at him. "You don't control who I look at."

"Didn't think I did," Kaden replied, looking unamused. "I don't know Chris all that well, but I'm pretty sure you're nowhere near the mark when it comes to why we were all mad at you."

Bran looked to Chris for confirmation, and he nodded. "Fine." Bran blew out an irritated breath.

"You're nearly out of time," Chris told him pointedly.

"I know." Bran tried to think, to come up with whatever Chris wanted him to say. Finally he thought he had something. "I'm sorry I've been refusing to listen to you about the farm, about how much you want me to keep it. And I'm sorry I snapped at you and made it seem like the only reason you want me to have it is because you want to be closer to

Samuel. I'm also sorry I made it seem like what Kaden and I have started is nothing. It won't last, but it's not nothing."

"You don't know how long we'll be together," Kaden argued with him.

Bran nodded, conceding the point, though mostly because he wasn't willing to argue with him and Chris at the same time, but his focus was on Chris. "Better?"

Chris got up from the couch and came forward to give Bran a hug. "Sure. I forgive you for being more of an asshole than usual." He moved back but didn't go far, as he laid his head on Bran's shoulder and wrapped his arms around Bran's back from the side. "So, my father called?"

"Yes. Which reminds me. Misha, does your dad know you're gay?" Bran asked him.

Misha frowned and seemed to stiffen. "I don't know what you're getting at."

Chris lifted his head from Bran's shoulder to look at his brother. "He doesn't know? How the hell is that even possible?"

Bran knew it wasn't any of his business, but it bothered him that both Chris and Misha were gay, but only Chris was strong enough to come out, to bear the brunt of their father's anger and homophobic bullshit.

"How'd you figure it out?" Misha asked Bran.

Bran shrugged and wrapped his arm loosely around Chris's waist. It was familiar and intimate, and he looked to Kaden to see if he was jealous or not. But Kaden wasn't paying attention to him anymore. Instead he and Samuel were quietly talking to each other.

"He asked to speak to the son I turned gay. Now, that doesn't usually mean a lot, except it got me thinking that he doesn't really use Chris's name. And he does use yours. So...." Bran shrugged.

Misha frowned and glanced over at Trent, who sat beside him looking quietly interested in the conversation but choosing not to be a part of it. "No, he doesn't know. My mom does, but since she isn't speaking to our dad, it's not an issue for me. To him, I've had a girlfriend for the past five years, and when he insists I bring her out of hiding, I have a neighbor who lives two doors down from me. Her name's Sarah. She's a lesbian and in a long-term relationship with a lovely woman who makes the best damn double chocolate chip cookies. But her parents are homophobic too, so when they insist on seeing her boyfriend, I play that role. It isn't ideal, but it works for us."

Bran shook his head as disappointment came over him. Misha had always been this larger-than-life figure to him, someone he was terrified of and looked up to. It saddened him to realize Misha was just as scared of Mr. Romanoff as everyone else was.

"Your whole fucking family needs to get out from underneath his thumb. How much do I need to pay you to kill your dad?"

"You don't mean that," Chris said quietly as he balanced his chin on Bran's shoulder.

Bran glanced around the room and realized he had everyone's attention again. "Yes, actually I do. Misha names a price, I'll do the transfer, and he can hang him up by his balls and light him on fire for all I care. I'm so fucking sick of seeing him hurting you, and now Misha, who fought in wars and got shot for crying out loud, is afraid of him? No, I'm not sorry I want him dead. I want him really, super dead." He turned back to Misha. "Name your price. Anything."

Misha wouldn't stop staring at him. "I'm not going to kill my dad for you. He's a bastard, and I can't stand him. But I'm not going to do that."

"Coward," Bran muttered, much too quietly for Misha to hear him, but Chris bit him hard on his shoulder, making him cry out in pain as Chris let him go. "What the fuck?"

"Be nice. I'm going to go call him back." Chris took out his phone and went into the kitchen.

"Want me in there with you?" Bran asked him before he could go too far.

"No. And if you're not sitting on Kaden's lap when I get back, I'm breaking out the video."

Bran gritted his teeth together and sat down heavily on Kaden's lap without asking for permission. "Fucking blackmail. I'm not some goddamn child who has to sit on a lap." He looked back at Kaden. "And you're so far away from being Santa that this whole thing is ridiculous."

Kaden said nothing, just wrapped his arms around Bran's stomach to hold him in place and went back to talking with Samuel about the cows. Trent came over a few moments later and took Chris's vacated seat, leaving Misha sitting alone on the couch. Bran almost felt sorry for him.

"Hey, Misha, what happens when you fall in love with someone? What, then?" Bran asked him, his curiosity getting the better of him.

Misha snickered, but Bran could see the sadness there lurking behind his expression. "Finding a man who is capable of loving someone like me, who can take out a target at four hundred yards without a second thought and go out for beers and hot wings after, is pretty much impossible, so I haven't given it much thought."

Bran was pretty sure he wouldn't be able to do it. He kept part of his attention on Kaden and his conversation with Samuel and Trent, but he couldn't help focusing a little on Misha too.

"Have you ever wanted to come out to him?"

Misha leaned forward over his knees to answer him. "And go through the same kind of crap Chris is? Not really. I don't need my dad in my life, and I don't like him, but I can't completely write him off either. I've tried. I considered coming out to him plenty of times, but I guess having a dad who knows so little about me and sometimes even seems proud of me is better than not having one at all. And I think that's what would happen. Chris is a lawyer, so dad has to see him all the time. They work together. But me? I'm ex-military. I went to college because the government paid for it. I went against what he wanted for me. If Chris hadn't come out, he would have been the favored son because of his career path. If he'd have married a nice woman, someone he could put down like dad did to my mom, keeping her below him, then add in a couple of kids, I'm pretty sure dad would have thought Chris was a saint. I'm fairly certain dad only calls me when he can't get ahold of Chris, or when he wants a photo op with his all-American son, or when Chris's mom guilts him into reaching out to me. She likes me for some reason."

Shrugging, Misha kept eye contact with him, as if challenging Bran to say something to contradict him. But Bran wasn't willing to do that. "If you ever do decide to come out, I'll back you up however you need."

"Because you hate him that much?" Misha asked him with some surprise.

Maybe that was part of it, but Bran shook his head, because it wasn't everything. Not even close. "Because you're Chris's brother. Because you're there for him. Because he's brave and strong, and through him you're part of my family too. I've only got him. Or at least I did until I came here. Now you and I are talking like we don't want to kill each other like some barbarians with wooden clubs, and—" He glanced back to find Kaden watching him. "Maybe I have something special here too. And Trent and Samuel are pretty decent as well. Samuel's scary protective, and I think Trent is crazy with the animals, but they seem like good guys."

Kaden pulled him closer, and Bran smiled as he felt Kaden's lips on the back of his neck, right below his hairline, tickling him a little.

CHAPTER NINETEEN

BRAN WAS the perfect mix of muscle and softness, making it comfortable for Kaden to hold him on his lap, as long as Bran stopped shifting his weight, rubbing against Kaden's dick. He really didn't want to get hard with his two best friends sitting next to him, but it seemed like he wasn't going to get a choice if Bran didn't start sitting still.

A phone beeped, and Bran pulled his phone back out. Kaden heard him groan and frowned at Bran's back. "What's wrong?"

"Frank's buyer is being impatient." Bran leaned back against Kaden's chest and crossed one leg over the other. The position was no more comfortable for Kaden than the last one had been. "He wants to know what date he can start getting his demolition crew out here." Bran turned his head, and Kaden met his gaze. "Not to sound pushy, but this is business. How long will it take you three to be ready to move?"

"You didn't seriously just ask them when they're going to get out. Did you?" Chris asked, coming back into the living room. "You can get off his lap now."

Bran put his phone back into his pocket and brought his hand up to run his fingers over Kaden's neck, leaving a trail of heat in his wake and making Kaden shiver. "You can stay right where you are," Kaden murmured against his ear.

"I know I can." Bran sounded incredibly smug. "Enough about Frank and moving and other crap. What'd his majesty want?"

Chris sat down next to Misha, though he kept looking at Samuel, and especially at his lap, like he wanted to be in the same position Bran was in. "I need to go back to Manhattan tomorrow."

Bran nearly vibrated on Kaden's lap with his sudden bout of anger. "What the hell? You were supposed to get two more days here!"

Chris didn't look any happier about the new development than Bran sounded. "One of my clients got his nanny pregnant and has to up the date his divorce is going to be finalized before his soon-to-be ex-wife finds out about the proof of infidelity and he loses half a billion dollars."

Bran slumped back against him. "Fucking hell. And people wonder why you and I can't stomach the idea of marriage."

"It's utter bullshit," Chris agreed with a heavy sigh. "I'm going to miss you."

"Me too."

Kaden didn't have the heart to tell Bran that Chris wasn't just talking to him, but also to Samuel.

"I'll see you as soon as you're back in Manhattan. We'll rent a bunch of movies, buy all the good stuff at the liquor store, and get a whole pile of ice cream," Chris promised him. Bran got off his lap, and as much as Kaden wanted to keep him right there, he let him go over to sit next to Chris and cuddle up next to him on the couch. They were affectionate together, much more so than he was with either Trent or Samuel, but he was sure Samuel had been right in his first assessment of them. There was nothing sexual between them, and Kaden doubted there ever had been.

"Who's hungry for BBQ?" Trent asked in an obvious attempt to lighten the mood as he got up from the couch. "Tough if you aren't, because it's my turn to cook, and that's all I can make."

"The rest of you can come up with salads or whatever, and Misha and I will sort out the meat. Come, Misha," Trent said as he left the lounge and headed toward the back door through the kitchen. Misha got up and followed him out.

Kaden went into the kitchen to see what he could find for salads or side dishes, and soon the others joined him there. "What are we making?" Samuel asked.

"I can open a can of baked beans and heat them up," Chris offered as he sat down at the dining room table.

"Oh, hell no! I'm sleeping in the same bed as you, remember?" Bran rolled his eyes and went to stand next to Kaden. "I can help, if you want. You helped me with dinner last night."

Kaden smiled in thanks. "I'd like that. Make a salad for us?"

Nodding, Bran got to work. "Does everyone eat everything?"

No one spoke up to complain, so Bran got to work, and Kaden started going through the cabinets to find some quick sides to make since the meat wouldn't take long to cook up. At least they could trust Trent not to burn the whole lot.

In the end Bran threw together a good salad from ingredients they had in the fridge, though they definitely needed to go grocery shopping again, and Kaden had managed to find a bunch of frozen ears of corn shoved way into the back of the freezer. There was instant pudding for dessert, courtesy of Chris, and Samuel quickly boiled some baby potatoes, which apparently, the Kiwis enjoyed sliced open with a dollop of garlic butter and sour cream. All in all, it made for a delicious, really quick dinner, and they ate it in comfortable silence around the fire pit in the backyard, with the sun setting around them and the cows calling to each other in the nearby pastures.

"We need to play a game," Chris said, getting up after the plates had been cleared away. "I make the rules, and I decide what alcohol we drink, since I'm leaving tomorrow. Well, Misha will be going with me, but I'm the special one who has to go back to make my clients happy."

Trent almost choked on the last bite of food he was chewing. "Every time we play your bloody game, it ends in disaster."

"Not true," Chris argued. "Okay, so maybe true. But new rules. Starting with no serious questions. Only sexual ones, stupid ones, or playful ones. And we're drinking… Bran, how much orange juice is left? And do we have any vodka?"

Kaden felt like he was watching a nightmare unfold right in front of him as Bran replied, "We're good to go on both. I'll start mixing them." He got up before Kaden could stop him.

Chris clapped his hands together, looking nearly gleeful. "Excellent. And, if you break the rules and ask anything serious, you have to get naked and stand on your head for five minutes. No exceptions."

The two friends disappeared into the kitchen, Kaden presumed to go fix the drinks. Samuel looked so serious when he glanced at Kaden that he barely withheld the urge to laugh.

"Is this wise?" his friend asked gravely.

Kaden chuckled. "Probably not, but are you gonna stop them?"

"I suppose if they're entertained…," Misha added, shaking his head. "It's the stupidest game I've ever seen them play. I'd prefer they play spin the bottle, since it seems much safer, but then I'd likely end up kissing one of you two." Kaden noticed he didn't include Trent in that equation.

"Hey, what are you trying to say?" Kaden asked in a mock serious tone.

Misha's grin turned nearly feral. "That I don't know, or want to even hazard a guess, as to where your mouth has been lately."

"You did not just say that. What are you? Five years old?" Samuel laughed, and so did a blushing Trent.

"I think we're already missing the fun," Bran said, coming back to them with a large pitcher of what looked like orange juice but clearly wasn't, judging by the smell of it, in one hand, and a couple of shot glasses in the other.

Chris shook his head and gave the shot glasses he carried to three of them. "Damn bastards. Couldn't even wait for me. And by me, Bran, I do mean us."

Bran gave him a wink and handed out the rest of the shot glasses. "Of course you do. Now, before we get too carried away, I feel like I've got to warn you that this here pitcher is a little more than a half-and-half mixture. We don't play lightly when it comes to vodka. So drink responsibly and use protection or something like that."

Trent cleared his throat dramatically. "I would just like to officially announce that since you two were too hungover after the last two games to drag your asses out of bed to milk the cows, it's you who are milking in the morning. Not me and Samuel. We're sleeping in." Trent ended with a satisfied grin.

"Thanks, mate." Samuel nodded toward him.

"Question, though." Bran spoke up as he got comfortable next to Kaden. "What if one of us, meaning not me, is sleeping in next to one of you, meaning not Trent. Then does that person get to sleep in, since by not sleeping in they would wake the other person, meaning Samuel?"

Chris rolled his eyes, but he was smiling. "I would love to sleep in tomorrow."

"You have a flight to catch right after you get done milking, though," Misha reminded him, almost evilly.

"You're such a spoilsport. I bet, if we were closer in age, you probably would have told me Santa wasn't real and the Easter Bunny was made up."

Shrugging, Misha snorted. "Yup, and don't forget the Tooth Fairy. That's kind of what older brothers are for, I'm told."

"On to the first question!" Bran announced, apparently forgetting about his other question and filling Kaden with dread as he leveled his gaze at him. "Kaden, darling, favorite sexual thing to do to another person?"

Kaden had quite a few favorites, so he took a bit of time to think. "Make them beg." He was glad to see Bran blush deeply and stumble over whatever else he was going to say. Kaden reached over to pour himself a shot of what smelled far more like vodka than any kind of fruit juice.

"You know the rules, ask the next question," Chris reminded him, sounding impatient.

Kaden decided to let go and just have fun. "Misha? Do you spit or swallow?"

"Swallow. It's far less of a mess," Misha said, not looking at all embarrassed as he took his shot and grimaced after downing it. "You two drink like you're in a fraternity. Damn that's strong. Fine. Trent, what's the most sensitive place on your body?"

Trent blinked a few times and went redder than Kaden had ever seen him before. "My back."

Misha frowned. "Your back? So where on—"

"Nope," Trent interrupted him. "That was one question, and one answer is what you got. Wait for another turn." Misha did not look at all happy about that.

Trent took his shot and gave a little cough as the strong liquor hit his throat. "Chris, have you ever been rimmed?"

Bran snorted. "Clearly he needs to pay better attention."

Chris nodded and started pouring himself a shot. "Not only have I been rimmed, I've been rimmed by two guys at once. There was supposed to be a third guy, but he bailed. Sadly. I think he had to study or something. Or maybe he was doing Bran. Do you remember?"

"Dark hair? Glasses?" Bran asked him, to which Chris nodded. "It was a little bit of both actually."

Chris drank his shot down and grinned wildly as he put his glass back down in the grass by his feet. "Wow those are good. So yummy. My turn! Hmmm. Who shall my victim be? Samuel! But what to ask you? Keeping along the rimming line, do you like to rim the guys you're with?"

"I've only been in three serious relationships in my life, and yes, it's something I can do."

Chris's mouth dropped open. "Wait, what? So that means you've only been with three guys? Ever?"

Bran smacked him on his hand. "You can't double ask." Samuel took his deserved drink and sat back in his chair, ready to ask his question.

"I was getting clarification!" Chris argued, but Bran shook his head, denying him, and Chris began to sulk. "Bastard."

"Princess," Bran retorted, grinning. Kaden laughed at their play.

"Misha, what is it that you have never tried before when it comes to sex?" Samuel grinned at the other big man.

He looked around at them all, then shifted uncomfortably. "It's a bit embarrassing, especially considering I'm always on top, but sometimes it seems like it might be nice to be tied up, you know, to be at someone else's mercy for a while, for someone else to be calling the shots. Even if it's only play like being tickled or something. Bondage doesn't really appeal to me, but being played with does." Bran poured him a drink, which he downed quickly. "Kaden, I can't believe I'm about to ask you a fucking sex question, but how many guys have you been with?"

"This game is much more fun," Bran said, interrupting Kaden's answer.

Chris nodded. "We should do it this way all the time. Only, Misha, I do mean this in the most respectful way possible, I don't want to ask you anything sexual."

Snorting, Misha raised his empty shot glass to Chris, agreeing with him.

"Well, thank you for yapping when it's my turn to talk," Kaden moaned.

"You're welcome!" Bran said, grinning at him.

"Misha, to answer your question. I have been with five guys in total, but not all were full-on sex," Kaden answered at last.

"I demand clarification!" Bran said, nearly jumping to his feet before Chris pulled him back down to the chair.

"You can't have it! No double questions!" Chris said gleefully as he poured Kaden's shot. "Here, Kaden. Drink up."

Kaden drank it down and shook his head a little to clear it. "Chris—what is your one secret sex thing you feel too embarrassed to tell your lovers about?"

"Shit," Chris grumbled loudly, and Kaden saw him look to Samuel before quickly looking away again. "So. Um. It was to be kinky stuff, but after what just happened to me, that's not going to work. Ever."

"Sorry," Bran said, looking miserable.

Chris gave him a small smile and reached over to hold his hand. "You tell me you're sorry for Richard one more time and I will kiss you on the mouth. With tongue." Bran shuddered, and Chris laughed. "But now I guess my biggest kink, which isn't really a kink at all, would be for someone to say they loved me while they were having sex with me. I think it would feel nice. You know? Like not if they said it for the first time during sex. Because that would be a bit ridiculous, and I wouldn't believe them anyway. But in the sappy late-night movies, they're always saying it while they're having sex. Which is usually right before the secret baby plot point arrives, or the presumed dead ex-wife with amnesia comes back, or some other utter bullshit like that."

Bran sniffled, and Chris swiped at his shoulder. "Shut the fuck up."

"You're such a sappy romantic," Bran teased him.

"Video of you in a thong is only a swipe of my finger away, and I swear I will use it," Chris threatened, instantly shutting Bran up and making him press his lips together. Chris took his time pouring himself a drink as he seemed to survey the men gathered around him, choosing his prey much like a lion might. If the lion was clearly buzzed and well on his way to being drunk. "Bran. If you were going to get something pierced, what would it be?"

"Well…. If Misha didn't have pierced nipples, I might go for that."

Chris rolled his eyes. "You can pierce your fucking nipples. I told you the world wouldn't implode, and it won't. There's no law that says you can't do the same things to your own bodies."

Bran snickered and stared over at Kaden. "I might just do that, then. In case I ever meet someone who likes to play with my nipples. Might be fun to make them all shiny for him. In case they get lost along the way and need reminding of where two of my most sensitive areas are."

"How about a room for you two? From those of us not getting laid regularly on this trip, I'd like to say that you both suck," Chris nearly whined, making Bran laugh.

"Not my fault I'm irresistible," Bran said as he poured himself a shot and sat back to drink it down. "I'm sexy, and I know it."

Chris would have fallen out of his chair while laughing if Misha hadn't grabbed him by the back of his shirt and yanked him back into it. "When we're ninety and all wrinkled, you'll probably still think you're sexy enough to get some young, cute nurse. Probably the one that gives you your enemas."

Bran didn't deny it. "Hey, if he's hot." He raised his voice a little. "Oh, nurse, I think I need a sponge bath. I'm just oh so dirty."

This time Chris really did fall out of his chair, landing in the dirt, and Bran looked like he would have fallen right along with him if the fire pit hadn't been in his way.

"I get to ask a question!" Bran announced, as if he'd only just remembered it was his turn. "Trent. Sexiest thing about a guy?"

"His voice. Especially as he speaks against the back of my neck." Trent nodded decisively, his eyes very bright from the potent vodka.

"Misha—are you a top or a bottom or switch?" Trent hiccupped at the end of the sentence, and they all laughed. Kaden thought the fun was about to start with everyone completely sloshed.

Misha downed his shot before answering, which might have been cheating, but no one called him out on it. In fact, Chris tried to give him another one as if he'd forgotten he'd already filled Misha's shot glass the first time.

"I'm…. How do I put this? No one wants to top me. It could be fun, but no one ever has. Maybe they're afraid I'll shoot them. I'd like to be topped sometime."

Chris made a gagging sound, and Misha tried to club him over the head, but Chris was luckily fast enough to duck. "Trent. Back to you. Wildest fantasy you have that no one has ever given you?"

Trent leaned back in his chair, all inhibitions gone as he stared straight at Misha. "I'd love to be fucked on the back of the ATV." Then he almost giggled. "I can't believe I just said that."

Misha leaned forward in his chair, staring right at Trent. "I could do that. I'd fuck you so hard, I'd slide right into you and—" His words suddenly died as Trent's head rolled to the side and he bolted from the chair. Before any of them could get up to go after him, the sounds of someone puking came back to them from the tall grass by the side pasture.

"Never mind," Misha grumbled, sitting back and looking disappointed.

"Sorry, mate. He's never been able to hold down much alcohol," Kaden explained. "Good thing he's not working in the morning."

"Thank fuck he just got sick. Because the two of you together was not an image I needed," Chris said happily. "Trent is gone. We need someone to ask the next question in his place. Oldest person here, speak up now."

"Samuel, you're older by two months. You ask," Kaden piped up.

"I'm forty-two if that matters," Misha said. "But I pass it to Samuel if I'm the oldest."

"Damn, what to ask." Samuel sighed. "Bran, what were you and Kaden doing this afternoon after our rugby game?"

Bran grinned, and Kaden dreaded his answer. As much as he cared about Samuel and respected him, he didn't really want the other man knowing he'd had sex with Bran in the kitchen.

"Perv. Wouldn't you like to know? I choose dare. Dare, dare, dare. So much dare. What are you going to make me do? Do you want a kiss? Want me to kiss Kaden? Want to watch me eat another piece of fruit?"

"Nope, I think you should give Kaden a lap dance in a pink thong. Or any thong if you have one. We'll watch and critique your performance." Samuel grinned like a cat that caught a bird.

"I hate you. I really superly hate you right now," Bran said, shaking his head. "Anyone here have a thong?"

When no one spoke up, Bran shrugged and got up from his chair to begin stripping off his clothes. It wasn't until he got to his jeans and unfastened them enough to show off that he was obviously not wearing any underwear that Kaden stopped him. "Go put something on so you're not naked. The point isn't to be naked in front of one of my best friends."

"You think a thong is any amount of not naked?" Bran challenged him.

Kaden frowned at him and reached forward to unbutton Bran's jeans and pull his fly down a little, exposing some of him but keeping a small shred of his modesty. It was hard to resist not putting his mouth on the thin trail of blond hair disappearing below his open zipper, though.

"There. Now you can start."

Bran dropped his voice a little and leaned over Kaden so his mouth was right next to Kaden's ear. "Sure. And tonight, when you're complaining about how much of a tease I am, you can remember this moment and how you're the one that unbuttoned my pants." He gently closed his warm mouth over Kaden's earlobe and sucked it between his teeth, making Kaden bite back a groan and grip the arms of the chair to avoid grabbing at Bran's waist and risk pulling off his pants in front of everyone.

He stood up with a knowing grin. "Chris, music please. If you would. Something soft, slow, sexy. You know what I like."

Chris took out his phone. "Oh, I do. Too bad I didn't bring any dollars. You have a card reader tucked away in those jeans?"

Bran ran a finger down Chris's cheek. "Not this time, baby cakes." Seconds later a soft song started playing through Chris's phone, and Kaden watched, nearly mesmerized, as Bran began to move his body to the beat as if giving lap dances was what he did every night and this song was his playlist.

He moved his hips and ran his hands down Kaden's chest, teasing him with each touch, each sensuously slow movement, each lick of his lips and coy little smile. "You want me," he whispered in Kaden's ear as he bent forward before sliding to his knees in front of him and dragging his fingertips over the top of Kaden's thighs.

"You're never allowed to do this in front of someone else again," Kaden groaned out, barely able to resist dragging Bran back inside and tossing him onto the bed.

Bran climbed onto his lap and began moving against him, grinding to the slow beat of the music. "Oh? You think so?" He slipped a finger between his full lips and began sucking on it, teasing Kaden even before he began to softly moan. "What do you want to do to me?"

"You know what I want," Kaden said, bringing his hands to Bran's hips and controlling his movements, bringing him close in the way he wanted, pushing them together. He could feel Bran's bulge even through the thick material of their jeans and couldn't wait to have him again. He pulled one hand off Bran's right hip and started to slide it into Bran's open fly, but Bran grabbed his wrist before he could.

"Nope, nope. You want to touch there, you need to pay. I'm not cheap." Bran brought Kaden's thumb between his lips and began sucking him, sliding his wet mouth over Kaden's thumb, teasing him in a way that drove Kaden wild.

The song ended, leaving Kaden feeling both denied and spared, as Bran gave him a fierce bruising kiss, before sliding off his lap.

"I need to bring cash next time," Chris joked, grinning at them both.

Bran retook his seat but left his pants unbuttoned and open. "Samuel, was that satisfactory for you, or would you like your own demonstration?"

"No. Thank you. I think we're all suitably or unsuitably horny. I think I'm ready to crash in my bed now. If my dick ever settles down." The usually calm and reserved Samuel chuckled like a young girl, and the whole group held their stomachs as they laughed.

"Chris isn't going with you," Bran spoke up, sounding stern.

Chris frowned, looking instantly sad and as if Bran had stolen his puppy. "I'm not?"

Shaking his head, Bran frowned at him. "No. You're not. Remember? We talked about this."

"We did?" Chris looked completely confused. "Oh! That's right. Nope, sorry, Samuel. No blowjob for you tonight. Not from me. Or anyone else here. I will kill you all."

Bran looked like he was trying to hold back his laugh but didn't quite succeed. "You're outweighed by everyone here. Even me. There's no way you could actually kill us all. But okay. I'll take you up to bed. C'mere, drunkard."

"You're such a party pooper, Bran. Couldn't you have pretended to be too drunk to remind me of our big talk?" Chris whined as Bran grabbed him by the arm and lifted him out of his chair. Kaden watched as Bran and Chris weaved their way into the kitchen almost hitting the doorframe, before breaking apart to go through it one by one.

"It amuses me so fucking much that you two think you can handle them," Misha said, shaking his head as he looked between Kaden and Samuel. "Playing with fire, both of you. Big fire. We're talking volcanoes here. You'll be splattered."

"Well, at least this game didn't end in an emotional wreckage. That's a plus, but I haven't been this drunk in a bloody long time. Time for bed." Kaden got up and had to steady himself for a second as the alcohol ran from his stomach to his head now that his circulation was flowing again.

Samuel got up and stumbled two steps forward, almost face-planting in the remaining embers of their fire. Kaden pointed and laughed at him.

"Shut up, dickhead. I'll volunteer to go peel Trent off the ground wherever he fell asleep. Good night." Samuel couldn't quite manage to walk in a straight line as he wandered off into the dark.

Kaden yelled at his retreating back. "Walk home! Don't want to find you two wrapped around a fencepost in the morning."

Misha didn't bother getting up, instead choosing to sit there and stare up at the stars above them. "I'll be in when I can manage to walk a little," he told Kaden, not that he'd asked. "You three drunken idiots are more than enough without me adding to the mix."

Kaden shook his head. "You're in that drunken-idiot pile. Don't get eaten by coyotes out here." He headed inside, stumbling up the stairs until he was practically on all fours because the stairs kept moving under him, before he crashed into bed with his clothes still on.

He was almost asleep when he heard his bedroom door open and saw Bran come in, the light from the hallway lighting him up from behind. "Chris is kicking me, and Misha snores. Also, I don't want to sleep next to Misha even if I'm on a different couch than him." He slid in behind Kaden and slipped his hand into Kaden's pants. "Want some company?"

Kaden started pushing his pants over his hips before his brain had even connected with his tongue. "Yes. Stay," he said, the words coming out in a drunken slur.

CHAPTER TWENTY

BEING HUNGOVER, and half-asleep, made Bran feel mostly dead when he and Chris trudged back into the house well before anyone else woke up. Milking three hundred cows by themselves was hard work. Doing so when every little noise made him feel like his head was being broken apart from the inside out, though, was nearly torture.

"I think you made those drinks extra strong last night," he grumbled to Chris as he flopped down on the bed. He could have fallen asleep right then and there, except Chris was going to be leaving soon, and Bran didn't want to miss saying good-bye to him.

Chris shrugged. "Maybe I did. Maybe I didn't. Maybe those damn cows are so freaking cute I want one as a pet."

Bran rolled over onto his back and snickered. "I'm sure that would go over well in your apartment building. I'm sorry you have to go. I wish you didn't."

Chris gave him a sad smile and pulled out his suitcase. "Me too." He hadn't really unpacked and hadn't brought much with him anyway. But they stared at the open suitcase for a long time, getting lost in their own thoughts.

"Is there nothing you like about this place? Nothing at all?" Chris finally asked him.

As much as Bran loved Chris, he really didn't want to do this with him right now. "What do I need to do to get you to drop this? Just for today? I know you won't stop for more than that right now."

Chris reached over and patted his knee. "A bargain?" Bran nodded. He could do that. "You find one good thing about being here, one actual solid thing that has nothing to do with Kaden, and I'll tell my dad not to call me a faggot, or even use the word around me, the next time he does. If you do that, then I won't mention you keeping the farm again for a whole forty-eight hours after you tell me what it is."

Bran's eyes went wide. "You serious?" He'd wanted that for years, ever since the first time Mr. Romanoff had said it when Bran and Chris were together in his office. Chris had just been starting out, they'd been setting up his office, and Bran had wanted to kill his dad as soon as he'd said the word.

Chris didn't look too sure, but he nodded anyway. "It's time I start sticking up for myself. Right?"

"Absolutely," Bran easily agreed with him.

Getting up to start tossing his clothes haphazardly into the suitcase, Chris was nearly shaking. "So that means I need to tell him that. I doubt he'll listen, but I'm willing to do that if it means you'll actually find one thing you like here."

Bran sat up to help him finish packing. "Thank you. That means a lot to me. I worry about you with him."

"Want to hear something stupid?" Chris zipped up his suitcase and went to the suit he'd had the strength of mind to lay out the night before.

Bran shrugged. There wasn't too much stupid Chris could say that they hadn't already shared over the past decade. "Sure."

When Chris looked back at him, he was blushing. "I'm a tiny bit insecure with you being here around Samuel and me being gone. I mean, I know I'm not going to have sex with him. And I know we wouldn't be good together anyway. Not with my issues. But I wasn't so drunk that I didn't see him watching you while you were on top of Kaden last night. And I just—"

Bran got off the bed and hugged Chris as tightly as he could. He was relieved to feel Chris wrap his arms around him as well, despite the fear he was feeling. "You have nothing at all to worry about. Last night we were all drunk, stupid, and horny. Anyone would have watched me with him. I'm just that good. But Kaden is more than enough for me to worry about right now, and Samuel really cares about you. Get yourself better, and be friends with him."

Chris stepped back, putting some space between them, but he didn't let Bran go entirely as he kept his hand pressed against Bran's ribs. "If you and Kaden stay together, maybe I'll come visit you in New Zealand, and he'll be there, and we can try again."

Bran didn't have the heart to tell him there would likely be no him and Kaden past the thirty days, which were more than half-over. He was coming up to the final stretch, and finding something he liked about the place wouldn't be enough to make him want to take up farming permanently. Still, if it meant that Chris wouldn't let his dad push him around for a while, then Bran was more than willing to put in the effort too.

"Maybe. I've never been there. It might be fun to see if all the people there get pissed off when you call them Aussies like these three do."

Chris grinned. "Did they really?"

"Oh yeah. I thought Kaden was going to punch me. That was my first day here. Seems like forever ago." Nearly three weeks on the farm, practically cut off from the outside world, and he felt like things had changed so much for him. Like his whole life had been broken apart and was slowly being put back together.

"I would have loved to have seen that. Samuel being all sexy and angry. Sounds yummy."

Bran rolled his eyes.

With a sigh Chris shook his head and moved away from him, letting him go as he headed toward the bedroom door. "I need to get a shower so I can get dressed and go on a plane and head back to the real world."

Bran knew he was right, and he did have to go, but so much of him wished he could kidnap Chris and keep him there with him. "Want me to make you anything for breakfast?"

"Sure. Surprise me? I'll be down as soon as I get dressed." Chris didn't sound at all happy about it, but he left the room to go shower anyway. He was responsible like that. Bran knew he probably would have tried to get out of it in some way.

As soon as Chris was gone, he changed out of his latest muck-covered outfit and put on a pair of sweatpants. He hadn't been for a run in weeks, having felt like he'd had enough of a workout from daily farming chores, but if he was really going to try to find something to like there, then he knew he would need a clear head for it. Even though it was barely after six, he figured the sun would get hot while he was out, so he left his shirt off and headed downstairs wearing just the sweatpants and sneakers over his bare feet.

No one was awake when he started pulling out skillets, but that changed soon enough as Misha glared at him from the living room before he'd even started scrambling the eggs for french toast.

Since he was going for a run, he needed a playlist, which he started to make while the bread soaked in the egg mixture. Hip-hop and pop were usually his favorite go-to choices when he wanted to get energized.

Rap, he had on his phone for when he needed to wake up on time and wanted something he'd be desperate to turn off as his alarm. Rock could have been a viable choice too, but for some reason, maybe because he'd be running around seven in the morning, he didn't want to listen to something with a lot of drums and guitars in it.

He moved the bread to the skillet and glanced up at Misha as he came into the dining room, blearily hanging his head. "How's the hangover?" Bran asked him, making up some more egg mixture so there was enough for him to have too.

"I'm never, ever drinking with you two again," Misha growled at him. "How are you even still functional right now?"

Snorting, Bran shook his head and went back to making his playlist. For some reason he found himself going to a group of songs he hadn't listened to in at least five years. They were pop songs from the seventies, ones his mom had helped him pick out, and she'd called them her pregnancy album. All the songs she'd listened to while she'd been pregnant with him and then had wanted to share with him during the long hours he'd spent sitting beside her at the hospital.

Chris had meant so much to him during that time as he'd not only brought him notes from the classes they'd shared, that's what most friends would have done, but he'd watched over her while Bran slept. He'd helped feed her when she was too weak to do it herself. And Chris had been right there beside him when she'd slowly slipped away.

"Hey, what's wrong?"

Bran looked up to find Kaden standing in front of him and wondered when he'd come downstairs. But Samuel and Trent were also there, and something was definitely burning beside him.

"Shit," he grumbled, tossing the burned french toast into the trash and pulling down a new skillet. "Sorry. I was thinking."

Kaden nodded. "You looked like you were about to cry."

Bran wanted to laugh, to joke, to say he never cried. But that would have all been a lie. "I was thinking about my mom. How she died, how much I loved her. How she adored Chris."

"Your mom was a freaking saint," Chris said, coming down the stairs as he expertly wound his fingers around his tie, securing the knot into place at the hollow of his throat. "She used to tell the best stories of you as a kid out here. Coming in covered in mud, bringing home a baby coyote you'd found and wanting to keep it because you thought it was a puppy."

Bran gave him a watery smile as Chris sat down at the kitchen table with everyone else. "I'd forgotten about that. Mom shrieked and thought I needed rabies vaccines. She was yelling so loudly Dad thought someone had come to try to murder us or something."

"That's a good memory," Chris said. "But it doesn't count for what you need to do today."

Bran nodded. He hadn't been trying to get out of his promise to Chris.

"Do you want some help with breakfast?" Kaden asked him as Misha got up and went upstairs, probably to go shower and get ready too.

Kaden was sweet for asking, and even sweeter for being worried about him. Bran leaned forward to give him a gentle kiss. "Thanks," he said, pulling back. "But I've got this. My hangover isn't so bad that I can't manage to make a bit of food for everyone."

Kaden frowned, looking concerned, but went to sit by the other men where they waited for their food. Bran quickly made enough for everyone, then sat down at the table to join them for the last breakfast he'd have with his best friend in his childhood home.

"Hey, Bran?" Chris spoke up between bites of breakfast. He sounded sly, like he was up to something, and Bran smiled, wondering what it could be. Chris's schemes almost always promised fun.

"Yeah?"

"How many guys have you kissed in the last three years?"

His smile died on his lips as he flicked his gaze over to Kaden before coming back to Chris. Of course most of the table were looking at him again, including Kaden. At least he was fairly certain if everything else in his past hadn't turned Kaden away yet, then this little revelation wouldn't either.

Bran put his fork down softly on his plate. "Define kissing?"

"You know… when you put your mouth on someone else's and stick your tongue in…." Chris said with a wink.

So, Chris was choosing to get technical. Fine. He wanted to play, but his need to be honest, especially when it concerned Kaden, won out. "Exactly…. One. Which, really, you already knew."

Chris grinned at him and took another bite of his food. Sometimes he forgot his manners and spoke with his mouth full when he was excited.

Apparently this was one of those times. "And who is that?"

Bran rolled his eyes, smirking as he glanced over at Kaden. "He already knows he's special. There's no reason to start giving him an ego. I think he's fine as he is."

"You're so fucking adorable," Chris said, giving him a big grin before he quickly ate, in a hurry to finish his breakfast. Bran couldn't help blushing as he looked away from Kaden. "You've also only spent the night next to one person in a lot longer than that."

"Uh-huh." Bran went back to eating.

"And—" Chris continued.

Bran pinched the bridge of his nose. "He gets it. He's special. This is different for me."

Kaden chuckled, and Bran was sure it was probably at his embarrassment. "I'd like to hear what Chris was going to say."

Bran shot a glare at Chris, who opened his mouth revealing a mess of half-chewed french toast, making Bran shudder.

He turned to Kaden, in the interest of honesty and not being a bastard anymore, and said, "Probably that I touch you a lot more than I generally touch people, even the ones I'm regularly having sex with. And it's not that I don't kiss people, or haven't recently, it's that kissing is important to me, and it's stupid, but opening my mouth on a kiss leaves me feeling vulnerable, just like when I fell asleep next to you last night, and I don't like being vulnerable, so I carefully choose the people I decide to be like that with." He took a deep breath and knew damn well Kaden was staring at him as he turned back to Chris. "Did I forget anything, or were those all of my secrets you wanted him to know before you left?"

Chris twirled his fork a little, splashing droplets of a mixture of maple syrup and honey, which was the only way Chris ate french toast, over the edge of his empty plate. "You cook for him too. And you're smiling more. Don't fuck this up."

"I'm not leaving Manhattan to become a farmer," Bran said, already getting annoyed with him, despite promising himself they wouldn't fight on Chris's last morning on the farm.

But Chris rolled his eyes and got up from the table to clear his dishes. "Figure out a compromise, then. Don't let the first good person in your life get on a plane with nothing and no one to show for what you two started."

"I was going to give them severance pay," Bran argued. The figure he had picked out was substantial.

Chris noisily put his dishes into the sink right behind him, making Bran jump. "I know you have a heart somewhere in that way too buff chest, even though you're making a shit showing of it right now. Jesus, you're pretty when you get all muscly. Come into the living room and cuddle with me until Misha tells me we have to go. I want my Bran time. And then I can tell you all about how you're being a jackass, and you can insist, again, that leaving him will be okay, and easy for you, because you don't get involved and blah blah blah lies. All lies."

Bran tried not to look at Kaden as he got up from the table, but it was hard not to know he was being watched by at least one pair of eyes. Trent also looked at him but more in disappointment. Or disgust. He was pretty sure those two emotions went hand in hand with these guys when it came to him and when they thought he had screwed up.

Samuel was watching Chris, which wasn't a surprise, and Bran didn't know how his friend was going to handle not being able to see Samuel again after he left for his plane that morning. Chris took his hand and yanked him into the living room, where he pushed Bran into the recliner, then sat down on his lap.

"You're going to wrinkle your suit," Bran warned him.

Chris shrugged. "And you think being on two planes, even though I'll be in first class, won't do the exact same thing? I'm giving the plane a head start."

Bran wrapped his arms around Chris, holding him close. It should have been Samuel he was sitting on top of. Bran would see him in twelve days, but Chris would have no reason to go to New Zealand, and Bran didn't have the heart to tell him that no matter what Chris said, and no matter how much Bran cared about Kaden, this wouldn't ever be more than one intense, emotional fling. And it was going to hurt so fucking much when they got into the car he'd be renting for them and they left for the airport.

This was why he didn't do love. This aching pain was already starting to grip his heart at the mere thought of Kaden leaving. He was a realist. He knew he wouldn't be getting on a plane to New Zealand anytime soon. If he happened to have business there and Kaden took his call, then he probably would try to visit. But he hadn't been willing to drive an hour for a guy before, and New Zealand was on the other side of the planet.

"You got quiet," Chris said, turning on his lap so his legs dangled over the side of the recliner.

Bran nodded. He couldn't wipe at his eyes without letting Chris go and alerting him to something being wrong. As long as Chris kept staring at Samuel while he and the others ate, then Bran knew he was in the clear.

"Just thinking." And before Chris could ask, he added on a lie, "About how much I'm going to miss you."

"You'll miss me a lot more when you're in New Zealand," Chris said, as if reminding him about some secret life choice Chris had already made for him. Bran said nothing, only continued to hold him tightly. "What if I bought the farm?" Chris asked him, surprising Bran.

"You're going to pay millions just to be able to visit Samuel until his work visa expires in a few years?" Bran couldn't believe what he was hearing.

Chris shrugged and turned back to him. "Would you accept my money? I'd need a few days to sell my stocks and get it all together. I don't have the liquid capital you do."

Chris was looking at him so intently, like he needed Bran to say yes, that Bran couldn't flat-out shoot him down. He'd tell him no later, when he couldn't see how much his words were going to hurt Chris.

"I'll consider it."

"Give me a well-thought-out pros-and-cons list of me owning the land by tomorrow at noon, Manhattan time, and I'll meet with a therapist."

That surprised the crap out of him. "Therapists are useless. You've never even considered one before."

But Chris didn't seem to be backing down. "Deal?" He offered Bran his hand, even though he couldn't shake his palm without letting go of Chris.

"Sure. If you think it'll help you, and this bargain will make you go, then I will make a good list for you. I can't shake your hand, so give me your palm, and I'll kiss it like I did the time we argued about whatever household chores neither of us wanted to do and I had a broken arm."

Chris pressed his palm gently against Bran's lips, and he gave his palm a quick kiss, sealing the deal. "I remember. I got out of toilet-scrubbing duty and had to do dishes because you didn't have two hands, and the lasagna had to be scrubbed off the pan. That was right after you went hang gliding, right?"

Bran was surprised he remembered that much detail about the incident. It had been at least four years ago. "Yes. And I broke my arm in two places and had to figure out how to type only with my left hand."

"And I made fun of you and your funky handwriting."

Snickering, Bran shook his head. They were good memories, despite the pain he'd been in and the amount of frustration he'd had to go through. But his memories with Chris had always been good, which was probably why they'd never considered getting together. Being best friends was better than any relationship either of them had ever had.

"Time to go," Misha said, coming back down the stairs, freshly showered and looking far more awake, though also a lot more sour, than he had when he'd gone upstairs to get ready. He dragged two suitcases behind him, one for himself and one for Chris, who slowly slid off Bran's lap as if he'd rather do anything but leave.

"I'll see you soon," Bran promised him, already seeing the sadness in his eyes. Chris gave him a weak smile, and Bran hugged him close. "We'll go to that restaurant that just opened. The one that serves chicken hearts that are still beating and crickets in lollipops."

Chris buried his face against Bran's shoulder. "Sure, we will. Then, because we'll both be too freaked out to eat anything, we'll go have burgers after. Though, not cow. Bison for sure."

Misha put a hand on Chris's shoulder, silently letting him know they were running out of time, and Bran let him go. It was always so fucking hard to say good-bye to Chris. "Yep. We'll find the best damn bison burgers in Manhattan. It can't be that difficult. You'll be okay. Right?"

"I'll look after him," Misha promised, and Bran nodded to him, trusting Misha wouldn't be going anywhere for a while. Not when Chris still needed help.

"And you'll be back home to visit soon," Chris said. The rest of his words were implied, and Bran didn't acknowledge them. Chris thought he'd come back, visit him in Manhattan for a while, then be off to New Zealand or back to Montana, either way, Chris clearly thought Bran would be seeing Kaden again soon. The hope was there in his eyes and in his gentle expression. Bran wouldn't kill that hope just yet. There'd be plenty of time for Chris to tell him just how stupid he'd been to let Kaden go, how he'd never find someone like him again, later on. And Bran would take every word, because he knew Chris would be right when it came time for that argument.

They let go of each other, and Bran frowned, wishing Chris could stay, that he could keep him away from his dad. He needed Misha for that, though, just until he could get back to Manhattan.

"Say good-bye, Chris," Misha said, reminding them all, again, that they had a plane to catch.

Kaden, Samuel, and Trent entered the lounge from the kitchen, and Bran appreciated the privacy they had been given to talk. He saw Chris look to Samuel and stepped back, giving his best friend some room to say good-bye to the three of them. Samuel's normally dark complexion looked pale suddenly, and fine lines pulled at the corners of his mouth as the big man watched Chris get ready to leave.

Bran shook his head and turned away, unable to watch this thing between them. He knew Chris didn't get like this about guys, and it was all his fault his best friend wouldn't be able to keep Samuel.

But when he heard Chris take a few steps, he turned back and was surprised to see Samuel coming closer to him as well. It was the longest and most intimate hug Bran had ever witnessed as he saw Chris close his eyes and lay his cheek against Samuel's chest. It was nearly frightening seeing that kind of affection and such emotion from the usually playful Chris. He knew Chris could feel that way, because he'd felt it himself a little sometimes when he and Chris were especially close, but to see Chris with someone else made him both happy for his best friend and afraid for him as well, because only heartbreak waited for him at the end of that path.

Samuel pulled away and took Chris's cheeks between the palms of his hand and stared into his eyes. "Take care of you," he almost whispered, before gently kissing Chris on his mouth.

Bran watched, in shocked silence, as, instead of grabbing Samuel like he expected Chris to, he simply returned his kiss, then stepped back, giving him a nod as if he was promising to do just that. And Bran hoped to hell he would keep that vow.

They drew apart, and Kaden and Trent stepped up and gave Chris quick hugs good-bye. "You have to come see us back home so we can keep playing truth or dare. It's not good to let too many months go by without some shots," Kaden teased Chris.

Chris laughed, and Bran wondered if anyone else heard the tears behind the sound. "I will."

Misha walked right up to Trent, who surprisingly stood still as the other man invaded his personal space, almost to the point where their noses touched.

"This is not over between us. I will see you soon." Then Misha wrapped his fingers around Trent's chin and lifted his mouth to meet his own in a kiss that was as fierce as it was brief. Trent was left blushing deeply and staring at him, as Misha stepped back.

"We've got to go," he reminded Chris, who nodded dumbly before sighing. Bran grabbed him in one more tight hug and kissed his cheek, before he went to the front door to see them off. Bran felt the three of them come up behind him, and he glanced back at Kaden, hoping his worry over Chris, and his sadness at seeing his best friend go, wasn't as obvious as he felt it was.

He waited until Misha and Chris got into the rental car and drove off his property, before he turned and began putting his headphones in his ears. "I'm going for a run," he told them, and was off before any of them could say anything to stop him.

CHAPTER TWENTY-ONE

AFTER BRAN took off for his run, Kaden and Samuel cleaned up the kitchen while a subdued Trent fed the chickens and did a few chores he probably fabricated in his mind. Like Kaden and Samuel, Trent had somehow gotten hooked by a crazy Manhattanite, and his disappointment at Misha leaving was hard to hide.

"I'm beyond worried about Chris being back in Manhattan and working all day, every day with his ass of a sperm donor," Samuel growled.

"I know what you mean. Bran is not in the same position, but I hate the idea of him going back there anyway. When the fuck did life get so complicated?" Kaden chuckled, but the sound was almost sad, rather than funny.

"I would book him a ticket, drug him, abduct him, and take him home with me," Samuel suggested dryly.

"Yeah, as if that would go down so well with Bran. He's got to want to be with me, Sam. I'm no one's fool. My heart wants him with me, wherever, but he's got to be in it too. Otherwise, I'm wasting my time. Again." Kaden sighed.

Samuel sadly shook his head. "If Bran is playing with you, and I don't believe he is, that's on him. He'd be blind not to see what he has in front of him. It's always easier to lie to yourself than it is to be honest and change. Especially when you're scared shitless, and that's the place Bran finds himself in."

"In the meantime, I'm hanging in the balance here, not knowing what the hell is going on. It's damn hard, mate. A bit like a rollercoaster ride," Kaden said in frustration.

"I know, and it's shit. I don't know how you do it," Sam agreed.

In silence they continued to clean the kitchen, and while Samuel mopped the floor, Kaden tidied the lounge. Everyone seemed to leave their cups behind after finishing drinks, and he gathered them up and took them into the kitchen to be washed.

Kaden turned toward the sound of the back door opening and couldn't help his instant reaction to seeing Bran shirtless, sweaty, and grinning like a fool as he came into the house. He stopped in the kitchen, and Kaden openly stared at him as he leaned against the counter.

"You're being obvious," Samuel said as if he found Kaden's distraction hilarious.

"Yep."

Bran came to the archway that separated the living room from the front hallway and leaned against the wall with Kaden still watching him.

"How was the run?"

"Really good. I just wanted to stop and say hi before I headed up to take a shower."

If his friends hadn't been there, he would have been following Bran up to join him in the shower. While he didn't mind them knowing he was having sex with Bran, he drew the line at doing so while they were in the house and likely able to hear every sound.

Bran turned around, and Kaden frowned as he caught sight of a large red mark on Bran's left shoulder. "What is that on your shoulder?" he demanded.

"I'm showering!" Bran said instead, giving him a wave and heading up.

"I wonder how he got hurt this time," Samuel said, shaking his head. "He's accident-prone."

That was one way to put it. Another was that Bran seemed to often act without thinking. At least it didn't look so bad, or like it hurt him at all. Unlike how badly his hand had been messed up or the bruises that had bloomed over his ribs weeks ago.

Bran was back down within twenty minutes. He was freshly showered, wearing only a pair of comfortable-looking sweatpants a size too big for him, and still grinning as he sat down in the recliner. There was room next to Kaden on the couch, and he wished Bran had come to sit next to him. But before Kaden could invite him over, Bran was already pulling out his phone.

He sent off a text, then looked surprised as his phone started ringing before he could put it back into his pocket. "Hey. I thought you'd still be on the plane."

Kaden wasn't all that surprised when Samuel muted the show they'd been watching. "Chris?" Samuel asked him, to which Bran nodded. "Would it be rude to have him on speakerphone?"

Bran smirked. "Samuel wants you on speakerphone. You okay with that? Sure. One second." With them all able to hear Chris, Bran came off the recliner to sit next to Kaden, just as he'd been hoping. But instead of simply sitting next to him, Bran hung his legs across Kaden's lap and balanced his phone on his knees. The only place Kaden had to put his hands were on Bran, which wasn't exactly a hardship as he laid one hand on Bran's calf and the other on his hip.

"You're on speakerphone. What city are you in now?" Bran asked him.

"Minneapolis. And St. Paul. This is weird. People say JFK is a weird airport, but this place is like two airports mushed together, and each city has their own side. And, also, remind me not to take morning flights again if I can help it. I like getting my free alcohol when I'm in first, but I'm not one of those people who can drink gin before noon like the guy next to me could. Just no."

Kaden smiled and moved his hand to Bran's firm stomach, wishing they were alone. Bran caught his gaze, making it clear to Kaden he knew exactly what he was thinking and wanted him too.

"How's Misha handling it?"

Chris laughed. "I'm rolling my eyes over here. Misha has been skydiving, but for the army so I bet it's not actually called that, so he was fine. Anyway, he put on his headphones and told me not to disturb him if I had to get up to piss. He was across the aisle from me, but I guess he thought I might have fallen into him or something. But enough about me, I want to know if you found a thing yet."

Kaden had no idea what they were talking about, but he did notice how Bran's smile lost some of its brightness. "That's actually why I texted you. I'm going to go into the other room and take you off speaker."

"No. You're not," Chris argued. Kaden pressed his hand against Bran's chest, keeping him there too. Not because he was in league with Chris and whatever plan they'd had, but because he didn't want Bran getting up either. "Samuel, is he still in the room?"

"Yes, the four of us are in the living room," Samuel confirmed for him.

Bran rolled his eyes. "Fine, you want to hear it and embarrass me at the same time? So be it. I was on my run, which was fun actually. I can't stand running in Manhattan, too many people, so I use the treadmill, but here it was nice once I got into the flow of it. I even visited the crazy bull, which, let me tell you, was such a rush."

"You did *what*?" Kaden snapped at him. Bran twisted his fingers against his over his own chest, which helped relax Kaden a little, but he couldn't believe Bran had been so reckless. "Wasn't one time of him trying to kill you enough for you? You can't be that crazy around him. You could have been seriously hurt. He could have killed you."

Bran gave him a soft smile. "Thank you for giving a damn. That means something."

"Yes, it's very sweet. I want to hear more from Bran, though." Chris sounded upset at being forgotten about.

Laughing, Bran shook his head. "Yes, princess, we will all bend to your whims."

"You better."

Kaden caught Samuel's smile. Trent shook his head. "They're both nuts," Trent said.

"So… back to the bull. I was running, and he was coming after me, but I was only maybe ten feet from the fence. I got over it, but I slipped on the way down and hit my shoulder. But then this cow came over and started licking me, and her tongue was weird and slimy and long. It was so gross. I was covered in the most disgusting cow spit."

Kaden couldn't believe Bran looked so happy about that.

"I thought you were going to tell me about something you liked about the farm," Chris said, sounding like he was a little annoyed.

Bran nodded. "I just did. I thought it was hilarious."

"Really? Whatever works for you, then, I guess. So, as per our arrangement, I won't be mentioning you keeping the farm for the next forty-eight hours. Enjoy your reprieve."

Kaden knew he should have realized him selling the farm should have worked into this somehow. Bran and Chris kept talking, but Kaden was no longer listening in on them. He didn't understand how Bran could want to sell this place, even after seeing the beauty of it every day and spending nearly three weeks on it. He didn't stop wanting Bran, or loving him, but he couldn't help the flood of disappointment that washed through him. He'd thought, or rather he'd hoped, that Bran had started to come around. Apparently he'd been wrong, and the realization hurt him like a kick in the gut.

Their phone call over, Bran got up and slid himself onto Kaden's lap. His mouth was crushed a second later as Bran rubbed against him. "Go upstairs with me," Bran said, pulling away just enough to nip at Kaden's jaw. He wanted to, and it would have been so easy to, but he wasn't feeling like it right then.

"I'm going out for a while," Samuel offered, already getting up.

But Kaden shook his head. "There's no need. I won't be going up."

He knew the second his words had hurt Bran, because he pulled his arms from around Kaden's neck and got to his feet. "Bran...."

But Bran only shook his head and went back to the recliner. He was back on his phone, quietly typing away this time, while Kaden tried to think of something to say to explain things to him. Samuel turned the sound back up on the TV, and eventually Kaden looked away from Bran's sour expression.

He kept typing, annoying Kaden more and more with each tap of his finger against the screen.

"Are you trying to prove what a cold hardass you are to those around you, or are you trying to convince yourself, Bran?"

"I don't have to convince myself, or you. I know who I am. Do you?" he asked Kaden, but he didn't look up from his phone.

"Okay, but do you like being like that? Because I can't imagine how you sleep at night. You take from people without a second thought and carry on as if it's normal. I know it's probably part of being a businessman, but I'm in business too, and you can still be successful at it while having a heart." Kaden got angrier at Bran's refusal to even look at him.

This time Bran did put his phone aside. "I'm giving you all a severance. It's more than I've given anyone else in any business I've ever broken apart before. What do you need from me to be able to move on and for us to be able to enjoy each other for the next few days before you leave and I go back home?"

Kaden seldom got blindingly angry, but when he heard the word "severance," his control left him, and his blood roared through his veins like a steam train. He stepped closer to Bran, where the cold man stared at him from the recliner where he sat.

"Stuff your severance pay up your ass, Bran! Money can't buy me or Trent or Samuel's respect or friendship! I'm not for fucking sale, and I don't need your bloody money. I have enough of my own, so don't put yourself out with the kind gesture just to make yourself feel better. I'm not your highly paid whore." Sarcasm laced his every word.

"You're blocking the TV. I actually like this show," Bran snapped at him. He had the nerve to smile, though it looked like a mask. The fact that he couldn't even be honest with him pissed Kaden off even more. "Oh, don't you like the person you're fucking? Did you really think this would end up with me flying twenty-one fucking hours, with a layover in Dubai of all places, every time I wanted to see you?"

"You rate people's importance and the value of a relationship on the cost of a plane ticket and how long a flight may or may not be? You're nothing like your father or your grandfather. I'm actually wondering if you were even related," Kaden spat out in disgust.

Bran flinched back. "Maybe I'm not. Would you fly twenty-one hours for me? If I called you up and said, in my best sex voice, 'Kaden, I need you, and I need you now,' would you drop everything just for a screw?"

"If it's still a bloody screw to you, then we have nothing further to talk about. I am saying this one last time—I don't do just sex. You know what? I'm done wasting my time and breath with you. I mean fuck-all to you, because I'm just a screw, right? Bran, sell the farm, build a bloody casino, go back to your ice palace or what the fuck ever in Manhattan, because I don't need this shit in my life. I know one thing for damn sure, I will die one day with a clean conscience about how I treated people I crossed paths with, but you will be all alone because you used people and treated them like crap! If you've made up your mind, I'm not sticking around to be your fuck buddy, so as soon as I'm calmer, I'll come pack my shit and get off your fucking land. Samuel, you and Trent are welcome to come with me. I'm done here!" Kaden whirled around and left the house, slamming the screen door behind him and feeling slightly bad when the top hinge broke off and the whole thing hung askew on the doorframe.

To get his mind off what just happened and to help forget the coldness in the man he'd come to love, Kaden fetched the pressure washer and started cleaning the walls around the milking shed. He might as well clean it before the bulldozers came to tear it apart. His mind drifted away from the awful present, and he concentrated on his life back at home, Kaden started planning his next season and how he could get into business with his two mates in their growing enterprise.

INSIDE THE house, Bran flinched when the screen door almost came off the hinges as Kaden stormed out. Unbelievable. He had no idea Kaden could get that angry, because no matter what Bran dished out until now, Kaden had always handled it calmly.

Bran looked at Samuel, who sat on the edge of his seat, staring holes in Bran's head. "Is he for real?" he asked Samuel.

"As real as he's gonna get. I know you're a little bit messed up like Chris, but I don't appreciate you messing with my friend's heart like this." Bran could sense the anger brimming just beneath the surface of Samuel's words.

Bran shook his head. "This has nothing to do with you, Samuel. I respect you for how you feel about Chris, but this, what Kaden and I are fighting about, isn't anything you need to have an opinion about."

Samuel got up from his chair. "Excuse me, but fuck you, Bran. Just like you and Chris are a package deal, because your friendship was forged through difficult times, so too is this friendship of three. Just as you won't stand back and watch me mess with Chris, I won't with what you're doing to Kaden. Neither will Trent, because you don't actually know him at all, but he's not only the kind, smiling, happy bloke you perceive him to be. Kaden's a damn good man, and he deserves better than this from you or anyone. Do whatever you want with this land, but treat Kaden like a human being, not a piece of ass."

"I know he's good," Bran snapped at him. "He's fucking wonderful. So what would you have me do? Walk away even after everything because that's what he deserves? Or tether him to me in some attempt at a long-distance relationship that will only ever be damned?"

"It's damned because you say it is. Unless you change your attitude, that's all it would ever be, but you're a big boy, Bran. Figure it out." Samuel walked out of the room, and then the front door shut quietly, leaving Bran behind in shocked silence.

Bran got up and went to the back door. The screen panel, barely hanging on its hinge, squeaked as he pushed it open. He frowned as it closed loudly behind him. He hadn't meant to make so much noise.

Kaden stood by the milking shed, the pressure washer in his hands. Bran could have asked him what he was doing, but there were better, far more important questions to ask him.

"Are you really leaving? Are you actually done with me now?" He held his breath, waiting for Kaden's answer. Waiting to hear the words he knew so well. He wasn't worth the time, the flight, the cost of having a real relationship with.

But when Kaden turned around, the naked pain in his eyes almost slapped Bran in the face like a physical touch.

"Bran, I can't do this anymore, and I take my hat off to you who can, but I can't touch you and kiss you and love on you, when I know it may possibly be the last time. Or that I'll wake up in a few days' time and say good-bye to you, and you'll walk away as if I never was. A notch on your bedpost or something. You are looking out for yourself, and I think it's time I do the same. I am worth more than this, and I need more from you. If you're incapable of thinking beyond selling this place and walking away from me, then yes, I'm done with you, because my heart is already broken enough." Kaden's brown eyes shone with tears he held back.

Shaking, Bran stepped up to him, waiting for him to back away and put distance between them, but when Kaden stood there, as if expecting Bran to hurt him again, Bran reached out to him, running his fingertips down the front of Kaden's shirt.

"I think we need to talk about this. I would like to," Bran said quietly. Kaden walking out had been a wake-up call. Samuel's anger had been the nail in the coffin for him.

Kaden swallowed hard, and Bran watched the movement of his tanned throat. "Why? You have made up your mind already."

Bran shook his head, refusing to believe Kaden had finally given up on him. He'd pushed Kaden so hard, tried everything to get Kaden to give up on himself, and none of that had worked. Bran knew he was a bastard, but it couldn't be over.

"Please? I will beg you if I have to. I know you like that. I'm only asking for a few minutes."

Kaden quietly searched his eyes, running over his face and stopping on his lips. "If you walk away, you'll never know how I can make you beg. What do you want to say to me after all that?"

Bran licked his lips and tried for courage, but he was shaking far too much to feel like anything more than a child asking Kaden for one more chance, which he would probably end up screwing up anyway.

"I would want you more than every few months, but I know that's impossible. I don't have the time to fly a day to see you as often as I'd want to."

"Bran, how have you been conducting your business since you've been on the farm? You're not in Manhattan, and I've seen you stay up to date with everything using your phone and a laptop. We have phones and laptops in New Zealand too." Kaden offered him a little smile, and the gesture gave Bran hope.

Smirking, Bran knew he was right, and he felt ridiculous for not seeing that sooner. "I'd have to get a work visa to spend any kind of real time with you. And you'd have to get one here. And there's this farm and my apartment in Manhattan and…." He shook his head. It was all too much for him to figure out. "I've never even tried to date someone who lived in Jersey. And that's only a few hours away. How in the hell could I make something work with you? I want you so much, but I feel like starting something more than just sex will end up disappointing you. And yet it seems like I've already hurt you at every fucking turn." He took a deep breath. "Tell me what to do. How to fix this. Tell me how to make you happy, because I'm out of ideas, and I don't know how to make this work."

"Just be honest about how you feel about me and the other guys. Stop acting like you don't give a shit, because it hurts. And just be willing to try. I don't have all the answers and I didn't plan on falling in love, but I'm sure if we wanted to make it work, there's nothing in this world that can stop us."

Bran offered him a tentative smile. "I'd like that. And I'd also like to kiss you now. If I can."

Kaden pulled him forward and mashed their mouths together, Bran tasting the desperation in his kiss. Bran pushed him up against the wet wall behind them, wanting him completely, but he pulled back before he could do anything more than kiss him.

Stepping back, Bran licked Kaden's taste off his lips. "I need to tell you something else."

"I hate those words." Kaden glanced away. "What now?"

Bran tried to control his shaking, but he found it nearly impossible. "If someone like me can love, someone with my history and my messed-up ideas on sex and relationships, if I can love, then I believe I love you."

"Now *that* I can work with," Kaden growled before spinning Bran around and pinning him to the wall. The water droplets soaked through his pants, making him shiver. "If I wasn't so jealous of showing off your body, I would fuck you against this wall right now. If you haven't figured it out yet, I like a little bit of exhibitionism every now and then."

"I'd let you." Bran roughly ran his hands down the front of Kaden's shirt, loving the feeling of having him so close again and needing to feel connected. He started to let himself believe maybe this thing between them could work somehow, like maybe this would be one relationship of his that wasn't absolutely doomed from the start. It was a risky thought, and he knew it opened himself up to getting hurt, and badly too, but hearing Kaden go off on him had made him realize he couldn't keep running anymore. Not if he ever wanted to have someone of his own, and he was sure there was no one better out there for him than Kaden.

Being so honest, so open, so very vulnerable with Kaden was painful. But he knew they both needed him to be, as much as he could possibly manage. "But…." This part sucked. "I think we shouldn't. I think, and this is going to sound insane, that I would like to go watch TV with you right now instead. Maybe. I'd like to sit next to you on the couch, with Trent and Samuel there, and I'd like to not be an asshole around them for a while. I'd prefer it if they didn't hate me. They're important to you, and Chris matters to me, and Samuel is special to him, and Misha and Trent are something or other. Anyway. Making this work with you means I should probably work things out with them too." He really didn't have the first fucking clue about being friends with people who were friends with a guy he was with, but he'd try his best. For Kaden.

He leaned forward to rest his forehead against Kaden's neck. "God, I want you, though. I don't want to be good right now. I should be, but I love being with you, having you inside me, feeling you moving under me. What do you want to do? You tell me you want me against this wall, and I'll pull my pants down myself. You want me upstairs—I'll lead the way." He really wanted his hands to stop shaking. It was one of his biggest tells when he was nervous or worried. And in that moment, he was both. "Tell me what to do here. Please."

Begging, in a sexy way, could have been fun. But Bran knew that wasn't what he was doing as he reached for the front of Kaden's pants and wrapped his hand around his stiff cock. He needed Kaden to give him some direction, to tell him how to make this right, how to make what he'd done up to him. It wasn't Kaden's fault he had no idea how to have a real relationship, so Bran could only grasp blindly at straws, feeling like he was in complete darkness, and at Kaden's mercy. Not knowing what to do or what Kaden needed from him, left him feeling afraid. It wasn't a feeling he enjoyed, but he knew if he was going to put in any kind of real effort, he needed to let himself become vulnerable around Kaden and to let his defenses fall away. No matter how hard or terrifying that might be.

Kaden kissed him once, gently. "As much as I want you, I think you may have the right idea. We should go reassure Trent and Samuel that I haven't murdered you yet and tossed you in with the pigs."

Bran laughed, but something in Kaden's expression stopped him. "You haven't actually considered that. Have you?"

"Only once or twice," Kaden said with a wink, which only made Bran laugh harder as he followed him back inside, his hand tightly locked around Kaden's.

CHAPTER TWENTY-TWO

TWO DAYS later Bran came into the kitchen and sat down across from the three of them as they ate their breakfasts. "You oversleep again?" Trent asked him, smiling as if he'd made a joke. He'd patched things up with both Trent and Samuel, and things were peaceful. Kaden was even letting him sleep in the same bed as him, even though he didn't have Chris kicking him as an excuse to sneak off to Kaden's room.

Shaking his head, Bran pulled out his tablet, turned it on, and opened up a video call with Chris. He was at the office, Bran knew, but he'd also be waiting for his call. Making an appointment to speak with his best friend seemed mildly ridiculous, but this was a business meeting. He'd even worn a button-down shirt to get himself in the right frame of mind.

"Romanoff and Associates, Mr. Romanoff speaking. Good morning, Mr. Wilson," Chris said, making Bran smile.

"Hey. We're all here at the table. I'm glad you got the pros-and-cons list I sent you. Are you ready to run some numbers with me?"

"What's this about?" Kaden asked him, putting down his fork, still full of scrambled eggs.

Bran waited until Chris nodded and gave him a thumbs-up before he looked at Kaden. "I want to see the numbers for the business of farming. I need to run them. It's a favor to Chris, and he'll be helping me keep them all straight. We can trade truths if you'd like to exchange information, after all this is a business dealing, but I do need these details."

Samuel gave him an odd look before leaning toward the tablet. "Chris, how are you doing?"

"Sorry to be curt, Samuel, but currently I'm working. Bran, I've got thirty minutes for you right now. Get the numbers, or call me back when you have them." Chris sounded impatient, not that Bran blamed him for being so. They both had business dealings to attend to. Or maybe he was just trying to put up a front since everyone else was there.

"Deal?" Bran asked them, making eye contact with each of them.

Trent was the first to respond to him, giving him a shrug. "Sure. Whatever."

Samuel nodded but said nothing. Kaden didn't look so sure. It was good enough for Bran since he was in a bit of a hurry. "Yearly average income?"

"For three hundred cows milking two hundred and ninety days, you're looking at about one point eight million per annum," Kaden confirmed.

Bran nodded and typed in the figure. "What brings in the most money?"

"The milk sales to the dairy company and sale of surplus high-quality heifer calves and also the beef we rear on the farm. There's also the possibility of growing corn for feed or biofuel."

"Lots of pots, lots of figures. I don't need them all just yet. Ballparks are good to help right now. Yearly average expenses? Including your salaries and any contingency money for sick cows and stuff like that." Bran looked up at him before going back to typing. On the screen Chris was writing down numbers as well, his head bent over a notepad.

Kaden tapped his fingers on the table as he thought. "About eight hundred thousand to a million, depending on what happens in the year, providing there are no major disasters such as drought, flooding, or disease outbreak, which could make costs spiral out of control."

Bran frowned as he looked down at the screen of his tablet and saw the unbelievably low numbers staring back at him. "No one can survive on these margins." They weren't awful, as far as farming went, but he didn't know how to make them better. Not without spending a lot more time learning about farm budgets than he was willing to at that moment.

"Your grandfather did just fine," Kaden said, clearly annoyed with him, despite how early it was.

"Bran…," Chris said in warning, as if he didn't already know he had to tread lightly with Kaden. They were better, but perfect would take time and work. Over the past few days, he'd realized he was willing to put in both when it came to Kaden.

Bran rolled his eyes as he glanced up at Kaden, wondering why he was getting pissy. "Fine, most people can't survive on these margins. Most people I know back in Manhattan would be miserable on them. Happy?" Kaden didn't look at all pacified, but Bran wasn't interested in making things up to him right then. He'd do that later, when they were alone. If Kaden was still speaking to him at that point of course. With his sour expression, there was no telling what kind of mood he'd be in when the sun went down. Since their explosion things had been smooth, but he knew things wouldn't instantly be roses and chocolates between them, especially when they got annoyed at each other. He had a lot of making up to do before they'd be anywhere near a normal relationship.

"How many cows can this land support?"

Kaden pursed his lips as he thought. "Three hundred cows, the hundred head of beef we have, rearing the 25 percent replacement heifer calves annually and we're able to grow corn crops. Including the horses, pigs, and chickens."

Bran nodded to Kaden before turning back to his tablet. "Chris, what are my margins if I double the size of the dairy herd?"

"They stay approximately the same. You'd have to raise the size of the herd exponentially to be able to see any real difference in the margins, and at that point you'd need to buy out one of the farms close to you and begin to have a much more factory-farm operation. However, when looking at those numbers compared to others in the area, the profits appear to be above average. In fact, for a dairy farm of its size, the profits seem to be steady and decent. I'm not talking anywhere near the amount of money you're used to, but it isn't poverty levels either. Far from it."

Bran smirked. There was a massive difference between poverty and multimillion dollar profits coming in. He looked away from the tablet to the three men sitting around him. "Thank you all for your input. It was insightful and valuable. This meeting is now adjourned." He went back to talking to Chris. "Hey, out of lawyer mode now please."

"Get out of business mode first," Chris retorted with a grin. Bran quickly unbuttoned the top three buttons of his shirt. "There. That's better."

It was good to relax a little now that he had the information Chris had wanted him to get. He'd promised to consider keeping the farm, again, after seeing the numbers. He'd give it a solid effort and really look at it from all angles, but he didn't expect to like the numbers any more than he did at that moment.

"Mind telling us what that was about?" Samuel asked him.

"You can tell him our deal," Chris said, surprising him. He wouldn't have thought that Chris wanted any of them, including Samuel, to know he was getting help. It showed his weakness, his vulnerability.

"One second, Chris," Bran said, lifting his gaze from the tablet to give Samuel his attention for a moment. "Chris asked me to take a look at the business side of farm life. In exchange he will continue to see a therapist for the next month."

"Melanie," Chris said, pulling Bran's attention back to himself. "Dad's hoping she'll turn me straight."

Bran tightened his hand on the table and hoped Chris didn't see how angry that made him. "What is she really doing?"

"She says I need to love and respect myself before entering into any kind of a relationship, which includes strictly sexual ones, even when they're anonymous."

Nodding, Bran was glad someone was there to give Chris the right kind of advice. "I like her already. I'll let you get back to work. Thanks for the help."

"Anytime. You pay me well enough to spare half an hour to do some simple math with you. You know my opinion of the farm, regardless of what the numbers say."

Bran did know, but he was also sure whatever Chris thought about the acreage, and the cows—it had almost nothing to do with what was actually there, and far more to do with Samuel.

"I will see you in just over a week."

"I'll stock the liquor cabinet in preparation for your imminent arrival. *Paka.*"

Hearing Chris use a couple of Russian phrases here and there wasn't all that weird for Bran, but he could see the confusion on the faces of the men around him. "Ciao."

The screen went dark as Chris hung up the call, and Bran turned off the tablet. "What?" he asked Samuel, who was watching him closely.

"Chris is in therapy?"

"Yes." Bran got up from the table and poured himself a glass of orange juice. If Samuel wanted to ask him anything else, Bran wouldn't be answering him. Chris had already said Samuel wasn't to know anything more than the basics. He was in therapy and it had to do with relationships. Misha was only allowed to know the basics because he'd been the one to recommend her. Bran had never put all that much stock in therapists in general, but if Chris thought she was helpful, then he'd be as supportive as he could possibly be.

Samuel nodded. "That's good." Bran frowned at him, expecting Samuel to say something about how much Chris needed therapy or about how it was high time he got in there. Bran was ready to snap at him, to defend Chris against Samuel if he so much as said one snide thing, but Samuel did none of that. "I'm glad he's taking steps to help himself."

Really there was nothing Bran could respond with, so he simply nodded and drank his juice.

"You planning on joining us for the rest of the workday?" Kaden asked him.

Shrugging, Bran realized he really hadn't thought about it. Beyond making Chris happy and ensuring he continued therapy for another month, as was their deal, Bran hadn't really decided what he would be doing that day.

As he thought, Bran sipped his orange juice. He still had questions for Kaden, ones he should have thought to ask while he had Chris on the phone to keep track of the numbers for him.

"I suppose so. Is four farmhands a good number to support the herd of cows on this farm, or what would be the most efficient? Assuming each of those men is experienced in such work, is accident-free for the year, and makes the average income."

While he was thinking about the farm and looking at Kaden, he also realized he needed to make another call. He could have waited, and probably should have, but he didn't want to forget either.

"One second. Hold that thought." No one looked particularly enthused when he took out his phone again.

"Anderson Realty and Investments," a fairly familiar voice answered the phone as Bran put it on speaker and glanced over at Kaden.

"Now, Dillon, don't hang up."

At least that made Kaden smile before his expression turned into a snicker. Samuel didn't look at all surprised that there was yet another person on the planet who didn't want to talk to him.

"Bran Wilson. Now, why would I want to hang up on you? Could it be how we were dating for about a month before you decided to have sex with my neighbor?"

Frowning, Bran realized he probably should have warned Kaden about that, since he was shaking his head and looking like he was fed up, again. But, in all honesty, he hadn't really been dating Dillon.

"We went out three times, there was no form of commitment expected on my end, and—"

"And I was in such deep trouble the second you smiled at me. What do you want? You've got four seconds before I hang up on you."

Good old Dillon, always getting right to the point. Bran respected that about him. "I'd like to start subletting my apartment. The parking space will come with it. Rental management commission is yours if you want it."

"Is this the million-dollar apartment with that gorgeous view of Central Park?" Of course now Dillon sounded excited.

"Yes. I've only got one apartment. You interested? You've got four seconds to decide."

It felt good for him to be able to surprise Dillon like this, like he had the power again. "Yes. Of course I want it. Are you insane? Your building is one of the most coveted, most—"

Bran knew how good his location was. "I'll be back in Manhattan in a week and a half. We'll set up a meeting then and get all the details worked out. Bye."

"Thank you, Bran. Seriously, just, thanks."

Bran hung up on him and put his phone away. He really was done this time.

"An ex?" Kaden asked him.

Bran wouldn't have called him that. "I think three dates doesn't really make the guy an ex. He was nice enough, I guess, but I didn't feel much chemistry, so it wasn't a real big deal to me."

Kaden sighed, and Samuel caught his attention. "And you're subletting your place?" Samuel asked him.

"Yes. I'll be in New Zealand much of the time. At least that's my intention. If that's where Kaden would prefer to live. I need to wrap up a few things in Manhattan, but once everything is taken care of, I plan to get on a plane, the one with the absolute shortest flight possible, and spend some time there." He looked to Kaden, realizing they hadn't made any kind of definite plans, and he'd essentially invited himself into Kaden's home without exactly asking him if he could stay there.

"Is that all right with you?" Bran asked him, suddenly feeling uncomfortable.

But Kaden simply nodded and came forward to give him a gentle kiss as he wrapped his arms around Bran's waist. "Yes. I want you there. And it would be nice to be home for a while. I think Samuel and Trent can stay here for a few months to oversee things and get some people hired for us after we're down there too. Then after a bit, they'll come down as well."

"Good." That was very good. Trent smiled at him, and Samuel nodded his seeming approval of Bran and Kaden's decisions. Their approval meant more to him than he would have thought possible. "So, about farmhands. Is four a good number? Does the farm have the income to support a fifth? What if the fifth was an intern from a local college or something along those lines? Unpaid but getting valuable life experience spraying cow shit off the walls of the milking shed."

Kaden tightened his arms around Bran's back. "You sound like you're considering keeping the farm."

"It's only to satisfy Chris's curiosity." Even as Bran said it, he was pretty sure he wouldn't be selling the farm. He still had his doubts, though. There was a lot left to work out one way or the other.

"Four people is fine," Trent said, adding his opinion to the mix.

Bran nodded and pulled out his phone to leave a message for himself. "Will need to hire more people then. If keeping. Kaden will be in New Zealand. Tell Chris to make him happy," he mumbled as he looked at his phone and sat back down at the kitchen table.

An e-mail had come for him while he'd been making his notes, and it should have made him happy, since it was from Frank and showed him the plans for the farm, but looking at where the casino buildings were going to be, where Frank's buyer was going to be putting a fucking spa, it made him curl his fingernails over the scarred wood in his anger.

"What's wrong?" Kaden instantly saw his mood change.

Bran handed the phone over to him. "Look at where the spa is going to be." He waited for Kaden to see it, until recognition darkened his features, and he became as angry as Bran was.

Kaden practically bristled in his seat. "Are you fucking kidding me? On Tobias's grave site? That's... just wrong, man." He pushed his chair back from the table, the screeching sound making Bran flinch.

"What?" Samuel and Trent asked at the same time.

Kaden hadn't returned his phone, and Bran didn't mind him sharing the drawing with both of them. He was too stunned to really process it all. Before coming there, selling the farm had been simple, easy almost. A business transaction. Now he could see where the casino was going to go, and the home his grandfather had built for his grandmother, a woman who had made the best sweet tea, was going to be torn down to make way for a parking lot.... He shook his head and felt sick as he looked up at Kaden. He wanted Kaden to have the answers, but he knew Kaden's answer would involve him keeping the farm, and Bran simply was no farmer, even if it was only on paper.

"This is what I wanted," Bran whispered, knowing he sounded as if he was trying to convince himself of that fact and not any of them.

Kaden covered Bran's shoulder with a warm hand, giving it a squeeze. "Wanted is past tense. You're not the same person you were when you came here three weeks ago. You have changed, so don't be too hard on yourself. Take time to think things through, and make the decision you can live with for the rest of your life because regret can be a relentless master."

"Changing my personality was the only way to get you to have sex with me," Bran joked, not meaning a single word of it. He felt worn out and torn apart as he got up from the table and took his phone back from Kaden. "I'm going to go upstairs."

Kaden look worried but let him go. This was something no one could help him with, and he loved Kaden a little bit more for giving him the space he needed to deal with his roiling emotions. Maybe he could have a nap too, and things would hopefully be clearer when he woke up.

He could only hope.

WELL PAST midnight, Bran turned away from watching the cows graze as he heard Kaden come up behind him. "You're out here late," Kaden said, leaning his arms over the fence as well. "Couldn't sleep?"

Shaking his head, Bran went back to looking at the cows. "I had a lot on my mind. Only a few days left until the sale." If he decided to go through with it.

"Then you'll be a millionaire, and all of this will be a casino." Kaden sounded resigned, as if he expected Bran to sell the farm and knew there wasn't anything he could do to stop him if that was his final decision.

Bran nodded and lifted his foot to rest it on the fence. "I'm already a millionaire. And…. Something about a casino being here, on my family's land doesn't feel right. My father died in this pasture. Did my grandfather tell you about it? He was on the ATV, and it rolled, crushing him. My grandfather was milking, and I was sulking because I'd been grounded and my father hadn't allowed me to go out with some of the guys from school. I was supposed to be out here with him, but I was being a brat. It took me three hours to go looking for him, and by that time it was too late. They told me it wasn't my fault, but they also said that he'd laid there, slowly dying, for at least two of those hours. My grandfather didn't bother looking at me again after that, and I left as soon as I was able to."

Sighing loudly, as if he was tired of it all, he shook his head and tightened his hands on the fence. "The idea of people gambling over his ashes, over my grandfather's grave, doesn't make me happy. But I can't be on this farm either. I can't own it myself. I can't live here full-time, and I won't force myself to try. A short time is one thing, but I can't do this like you can."

He took a shuddering breath. "And there's going to be a hotel where my mom taught me how to whistle to the cows in the pasture. And the creek I loved as a child? That's going to be filled in. My dad taught me how to fish there." His hands were shaking, and he tucked them into his jeans to hide them.

"Maybe that's why I couldn't sleep," he said, looking over at Kaden. "Just the idea of a casino being here…." He shook his head as disgust rolled through him. "Every good memory I have of my mom here will be destroyed if I go through with the sale. I don't know that I can do it. But I can't be a farmer, and I don't see any other choice here."

"I might have an idea. But let's talk about it in the morning," Kaden said, taking his hand.

"I'm awake now," Bran protested.

Kaden nodded and pulled him away from the fence. "So am I. It's late, though, and right now I'd rather have you back in bed."

Grinning, Bran stopped, refusing to go any farther. "I'm curious. Is it the idea of being caught that turns you on with your exhibition fetish or just being outside? Because it's not so dark out here that I can't see how hard you are."

He could also see Kaden's quick blush. "It's a bit of both, actually. But right now I want you in a bed and not just on your knees in the grass."

"As long as I get to be on top this time," Bran said, easily agreeing with Kaden about their need for an immediate bed. Sex was a good distraction, and one he welcomed, but he knew the problems would still be waiting for him in the morning.

RIGHT AFTER milking the next morning, the four of them sat down for a talk at the kitchen table. Kaden knew what he wanted and exactly what he planned to say, but with Bran giving him a soft, sleepy smile, Kaden had a hard time concentrating.

"Still want to talk?" Bran asked him.

Kaden slowly nodded and pressed his hands together on top of the table. He looked to Trent on his left and Samuel on his right. He hadn't spoken to them about his plan, since there hadn't been time, but he was sure they'd be on board with his decision.

"Yes. I have a proposal for you, regarding the farm."

He should have expected Bran's barely concealed look of annoyance, he supposed, despite that it wasn't even seven in the morning yet. He wished he could reach across the table, put his fist in Bran's shirt, and pull him close for a kiss to wipe away that sour expression of his. He couldn't, so he chose to lay out his proposal instead and hope Bran had an open enough mind to listen to him for a few minutes.

"I'm listening," Bran said. He took a sip of his orange juice, then a bite of cereal. Samuel had taken out cereal for them all. They'd all been too tired, likely from the drama over the past few days, to really put in any kind of effort when it came to breakfast. The cows were another story, they would always do right by the livestock on the farm, but taking care of themselves was completely different.

Kaden hoped he really was. "I would like to partner with you on this farm, to go into business with you. Whatever the casino buyer was offering to pay you, I'll buy myself in by paying half."

Bran only laughed at him, until the sound was abruptly cut off. "Sorry. I thought you were kidding. You are, aren't you?"

Kaden shook his head. "No, I don't joke about stuff like this."

Bran pushed his cereal aside so he could lean forward over the table, coming toward him. "My answer is no."

"What?" Samuel quickly asked him. Trent looked equally surprised.

Kaden couldn't believe his instant refusal either. "If it's about the rest of the money, I'll pay it." He wasn't prepared to spend the whole sum of money right this minute, but he could come up with it, and if he needed to borrow some from Samuel and Trent, then he would. That way they could all be partners in the venture.

"It's not that," Bran said.

"Then what?" Trent asked him. "We would all rather see the farm stay with Kaden than end up being the site of some damn casino."

Kaden didn't understand it either, and Bran's rejection without even taking the time to think it through, instantly annoyed him. Was Bran so determined to sell the farm that he wouldn't even consider his offer? But Bran looked right at him, all traces of the sleepy Bran that he'd woken up next to were gone. This Bran was all business, despite the dirt smeared across his cheek and how much Kaden knew he needed a shower.

"The farm isn't a sound business investment. I don't want you to waste your money on it."

That was his reasoning? Kaden chuckled as he ran his hand down his face to get rid of some of his own traces of sleep. Bran had been… enthusiastic during the early hours of the morning as they'd both found good reasons for staying awake, despite knowing they had to get up to work in the morning.

"While I appreciate you trying to look after my money, please don't. You're not my business advisor, Bran, and I don't want you putting yourself in that role. I want to share the farm with you. It would belong to us both, and you wouldn't have to worry about the operation of it, because I can take care of that part. What was the casino builder going to pay you for it?"

"Close to nine million," Bran said, not surprisingly. Kaden knew what land went for in the States, especially when there were four hundred acres of it.

Kaden had a figure ready before he'd even really considered it. "I'll give you five, if you split the farm with me."

Bran gave him a shrewd look, and Kaden waited for him to say something, to argue with him, anything. But he only pulled his phone out of his pocket and put it on the table between them. A few swipes across the screen and Kaden saw it dialing Chris.

"Hey. What's up?" Chris said as he answered the phone. Kaden saw Samuel sit up a little straighter beside him, and Kaden smiled, knowing how much Chris obviously meant to him.

"How much time do you have? I need you to draft a business deal for me, with all the usual legal language in it. Things I would not think to put in when it's only seven in the morning."

Kaden reached across the table to move some wayward hair off Bran's forehead, earning himself a smile and a kiss on his fingertips. "Hi, Chris. We're all here too."

"Fun times. Wish I could be. Bran, you've got ten minutes. Talk fast. I've got a meeting coming up. Divorces. Everyone wants them, and they want them immediately. And when they're not trying to end their marriages, they're expecting me to get their kid out of their third DUI like I'm some kind of fucking genie. So, Bran, hurry. This might just be the most interesting thing that happens to me all day, and I don't want to miss any of it for one of these damn boring meetings."

Kaden smiled and realized he missed having Chris around. Even Misha had been good company after their rocky start. They all seemed to understand one another and worked together as friends.

Bran nodded. "Get something to write with because this is going to be a lot. Kaden wants to share the farm. Here are the terms. I sell it for the total sum of two million dollars." Kaden started to argue with him, but Bran held up his hand to silence him. "That sum is to be paid in installments of ten thousand dollars per month into an account we'll open up for this purpose and both have access to."

"That's not at all what we talked about," Kaden said in disapproval.

Bran looked away from his phone to shake his head at the three of them. "You want to make a stupid business decision, that's on you. My job, as someone who gives a damn about you, is to make it the least amount of stupid possible."

Kaden heard Chris laughing through the call. "You two are priceless. I love this plan. Keep going with the terms. What happens if you two break up?"

He didn't want to think about that and planned on it never happening, but he could see Chris's reasoning.

"If we break up before the sum is paid off, and stay broken up for at least a month, then Kaden owes me no more money because, let's face it, the breakup would be because of me doing something stupid," Bran said, surprising him once again. "And, if we break up at any time, the three of us, meaning you, Misha, and I, still get access to the farm as a vacation spot outside of the rest of the world."

"What?" Trent and Samuel exclaimed, both equally shocked at Bran's generous offer. This was not the scheming, selfish, self-centered businessman they had met a few weeks ago. Kaden shook his head in amazement as he stared at Bran, their eyes locked as Bran spoke to Chris. Kaden should've known his heart wouldn't lead him astray to fall in love with an inherently bad person.

A small smile pulled at the corners of Bran's mouth, his eyes very bright, and all Kaden could think of was to drag him back upstairs and have his wicked way with him.

"I love you," Kaden said softly.

"Oh, I know that," Bran said in his sexy voice.

Chris laughed loudly over the speaker, "That's my boy! Knew you would come to your senses, but thank goodness it was earlier than later. That's a great deal. I'm proud of you. Now before my time is up, can you go outside for a few minutes, Bran? I'd like to talk to you in private, please."

"Okay, sure. Give me a minute to leave the house. Thank you three for joining in the meeting. I'll be back soon." Bran left via the front door, and Kaden heard his steps fade as his walked off the deck.

"Kaden, are you there?" Chris's voice came over Kaden's speakerphone after Kaden had answered the unexpected call.

"Yup, I am."

"Bran doesn't know you're hearing this, so don't ever say I don't do you any favors, okay? Now shut up and listen."

Kaden gestured to his friends to remain quiet as Bran's voice reached his ears over the phone. "Okay, Chris. I'm alone, so shoot. What's going on?"

"I wanted to get you to myself so I could say that I admire you for this major change of heart, which I knew you had in you from the start, by the way. You're so used to conducting business deals, and you thought a true relationship would offer you some sort of guarantee or something. Some insurance against anything ever going wrong. See, this thing with Kaden is a high-risk investment—it's almost painful to take the chance on it, and your palms are sweaty, and your heart is pounding out your chest, but boy oh boy, isn't the return so sweet if you're not too chicken shit to take that first plunge. The rewards you will earn could never be measured in monetary value, because nothing will ever compare." Chris's voice almost broke at the end.

Bran sniffed. "Look at you. When did you get so wise? Or such a fucking sap? You should go have a daytime talk show. You're pretty enough for it."

Chris cleared his throat. "What can I say? I'm a late bloomer. And Samuel likely had a hand in it as well. You pay attention to him for more than a few minutes and you might learn something. That man…. Well, I don't want you to know, actually. I'm not ready to talk about it, I don't think. Another time. You can thank me later, maybe pay for my ticket to come see you in New Zealand."

"Actually, about that, I want all six of us to have access to that account for the purposes of travel. Misha is stubborn, and I don't know Samuel or Trent well enough to know how they'll take the offer, but I don't want finances to be the reason you two can't see the men you're interested in. A few more things, all profits stay with the farm, meaning with Kaden. He can't sell the farm or give it away, but the livestock he can do whatever he wants with. I'll own it in name only, but I don't want to work it, and as soon as he signs the papers, I'm sleeping in, staying up late, and never working this hard again. And I need so much fucking chocolate I might just buy that company to keep me in supply. I hate working this hard."

Chris laughed. "Amen to that. I've never worked so much in my life."

"Exactly. Please draw up the contract for us as I specified and get it to me overnight if you can?" Bran asked.

"I'll do my best. Gotta go. Love you, bye." Chris's lawyer voice was back.

"Love you too. Bye," Bran said seconds before the line went dead.

Kaden switched his own phone off before Bran came back inside. With the way Bran avoided feeling vulnerable, Kaden wasn't sure how he would react to knowing Kaden had listened in on that whole conversation.

As Bran came around the corner to join them again at the table, Samuel got up. "Anyone for a cup of coffee or tea?" They all responded with their preferences, and Kaden looked up in surprise when Bran stopped next to his chair.

Trent pushed his own chair back. "I'll go see if we have some biscuits left in those empty cupboards."

Bran watched as Samuel and Trent walked into the kitchen before looking at Kaden. "Can you please move your chair back a little?" Kaden did as he asked, and Bran promptly climbed in his lap, wrapping his arms tight around Kaden's neck. Kaden put his own arms around Bran's waist and pulled him closer.

Bran buried his face against Kaden's neck, and he felt him shiver. "Are you okay?" Bran shook his head a little.

"Give me a few seconds. I want to tell you something." Kaden smiled but waited him out. When Bran obviously felt ready, he pulled back and looked into Kaden's eyes. "Why is this so damn hard?"

"What is?"

"I want to tell you how I feel about you, but it's… difficult. I've never felt this way before," Bran said haltingly.

"I know, and that's enough for me," Kaden soothed.

"No, you deserve better, and I want to do better." Bran looked around, appearing to think hard. "Wait. I know." The next moment, Bran's palm slid over Kaden's eyes. "Close your eyes for me please." Kaden grinned at the man's silliness, because his eyes were already shut.

Close to his ear, he felt Bran's hot breath stir his hair. "Kaden, I love you. I'm so shit scared I can hardly sit still, but I want to say it to you, so you know. I never want a day to go by in which you doubt what I feel for you, and more than that, I know life can be shit, and things go wrong. Whatever happens, I love you." Bran's voice started quivering halfway through his confession, and Kaden tightened his arms as the words he longed to hear filled his heart.

He reached up and slowly pulled Bran's fingers away from his eyes and drew back his head until he could look at him. "And I love you, Bran, no matter what. Shit can happen, we will fight and disagree, we may get sick or even pass on, but we would've had this until then. Us." He pulled Bran's face forward and kissed him with all he had.

CHAPTER TWENTY-THREE

NONE OF them were excited to find out that Frank would be coming over at noon, but the three of them chose to stay in the dining room, quietly eating the chicken Samuel had cooked for them and the macaroni and cheese Trent had managed as Bran got up to answer the door. Kaden quietly watched him, his appetite a lot less than it normally would have been after a hard morning of milking the cows and cleaning all of the outbuildings.

"Mr. Conns, thank you for coming over on such short notice. Please, join us in the kitchen. Can I get you something?" Bran asked him as he returned with the small man.

Frank shook his head. "No. I'm fine. Thank you. However, I am surprised that you wanted to meet with me now. I thought our next meeting to finalize the sale of the property wouldn't be until next week."

Kaden was relieved when Bran took the empty seat next to him, forcing Frank to be between Samuel and Trent across from him. Next to Samuel, Frank looked even less impressive, and Kaden tried not to grin. He knew what was coming and looked forward to seeing the smug expression wiped off Frank's round face.

Bran rested his elbows on the table, and Kaden dropped his fork to be able to wrap his arm around Bran's back. He rested his hand on the small of Bran's back, right above his pants, and wished he didn't have such a formal-looking button-up shirt on because the material was too stiff to allow Kaden to slide his hand under Bran's shirt like he could with a tee.

"That's why I wanted you to come here," Bran began. "I won't be going through with the sale after all. I appreciate your buyer's offer and wish him the best in the future, but he will have to buy the land for his new casino closer to all the other casinos in Montana. I hear Billings still has some room for one or two."

Frank's face lost all color. "You can't do that. There are provisions in our agreement that say—"

"That if I breach the contract and back out of the sale, I owe you 5 percent of the sale, because that is the commission you would have received had I kept up my end of the bargain. That total is just under four hundred thousand dollars. Do you have an account number handy where I can send the bank transfer?"

Kaden turned and stared at Bran, just as Trent and Samuel were doing. "You have to pay him how much?" Kaden couldn't believe the figure he'd heard or that Bran was so completely calm about it. "He hasn't done anything!"

Bran gave him a smile and turned to kiss his cheek, as if that would stop him from asking. "It is a fair deal. And one which I signed. The account number, Mr. Conns? I'm tired and hope to get on with my day as quickly as possible."

But Frank didn't look pacified in the least. "My buyer will not be happy, Mr. Wilson. Not at all. You must reconsider."

Shrugging, Bran ran his hands through his hair, making the blond strands lay even more wildly than they usually did when he didn't put any of the sticky stuff in it that cluttered up the bathroom sink. Kaden couldn't wait for the day when Bran realized he looked much better without his hair slicked back away from his face.

"Please feel free to give him my phone number. I will explain everything to him, in as much detail as I can, until he hopefully understands this decision, as much as it is a business one for him, it is a far more personal one for me. Now, I would appreciate the account number to do the transfer. If you have it with you. If not, please e-mail it to me, and I will pay you for the work you've done. Either way, though, your time on my family's farm is winding down, and I am becoming irritated. You receive the same amount of pay either way, so why you insist I think about going through with this deal is beyond me."

"Have they bullied you in some way? Coerced you into not selling?"

Kaden scowled at him. "You think Bran does anything he doesn't want to do?" Samuel snickered, and Trent shook his head. "You're out of line, mate."

"And out of time," Bran added on. "Trent, please see Mr. Conns out."

"Here is the account number," Frank quickly said, as if he thought better of being escorted out of the house without getting paid first. Bran took the man's phone, which had a long number clearly displayed on it, then started tapping away at his own phone. A few minutes later, Bran handed the phone back to him, along with his own, and Frank nodded as if he was satisfied, before passing the phone back to Bran.

"I suppose we're done here, then," Frank said as he got to his feet.

Bran nodded. "I believe so, yes."

Kaden thought Bran should kick the man out himself but soon found himself changing his mind as Bran slid his hand onto Kaden's inner thigh and squeezed him through his pants. He was shaking, Kaden realized a second later, and not simply wanting to tease him as they all waited for Mr. Conns to leave the house. Kaden wrapped his hand around Bran's wrist, silently letting him know he was there for him.

As soon as Trent closed the door behind Mr. Conns, Kaden turned and cupped Bran's face with his free hand, pulling him in for a kiss. "You are a bloody nutjob," Kaden said when he'd needed a second to breathe between their fierce kisses. "I can't believe you are going to pay him that ridiculous amount of money. For doing nothing."

Bran smirked and looked like he was going to say something, probably full of sarcasm judging by his expression, but then he shrugged, and he was just Bran without any of the mask or attitude.

"I signed the contract. Chris drew it up. It is a fair deal, and 5 percent is the going rate for someone like him. He was less real estate agent and more intermediary, but he served the same purpose. And I breached the contract. I expect to get a call from the casino builder later and will do my best to placate him as well, but in the end here, I know I was the one who backed out of the deal, so there should be penalties involved."

Kaden shook his head, not knowing what had made Bran grow up so quickly over the last three and a half weeks, but he absolutely loved the change in him.

There was a knock on the front door, which Kaden ignored, and if Bran thought he was going to be getting up, Kaden stopped him by twisting his hand in the front of Bran's shirt, keeping him close.

"It might be for me," Bran mildly protested.

"Then they can wait. Right now you're mine."

Bran grinned wickedly at him, and even though he hadn't meant for his words to come out that way, looking at Bran now he couldn't help wanting to drag him upstairs with him.

"Overnighted envelope for you," Trent said, coming back into the dining room and putting the thin package in front of Bran on the table.

Kaden let him go as Bran's smile turned from teasingly wicked into one of sheer delight. As if it was Christmas morning, Bran tore into the envelope. "Perfect timing. I love getting new contracts from Chris," Bran explained.

Kaden thought that was odd, but he didn't say anything as Bran handed them each a copy of the contract. "Please read through it completely and carefully, mark anything you don't agree with or have questions about, and if you like everything, then go ahead and sign where it says to," Bran instructed them as he got up from the table, went over to a wire cup at the edge of the counter, and came back with a handful of black ink pens.

Bran sat back down and began silently reading over the contract, his head bent as he went, and Kaden supposed he should do the same. Everything Bran had spoken of the day before was drawn up in the contract, word for word. Beside him, Bran signed his name at the bottom of the last sheet, then neatly put the packet back together and recapped the pen. He took out his phone and began playing with it as if he was content to simply sit quietly and wait for the rest of them to be done.

Kaden knew Bran would never back down, so he signed the document where required and sat back. Samuel and Trent stared at the two of them across the table, their expressions a bit shocked.

"Why are we part of this?" Samuel asked.

Kaden wrapped his arm around Bran's shoulders as Bran gave Samuel a slow smile. "You told me you three were a package deal. I choose Kaden. I guess I get two new friends in that mix."

That made Kaden smile, and he trailed his fingers through the back of Bran's hair.

"Any questions?" Bran asked the three of them.

Trent shook his head. "This is too much, Bran. You don't owe us anything or have to prove something to us. As long as you treat Kaden good, we'll be friends anyway."

Kaden nodded, agreeing with Trent, but Bran didn't budge. "This is part of me being good to him. And, also, because I can't be on this farm all the time and not hurt. But I don't want it to be more than that. Just a farm. Having it here, having you three on it, or some people you trust working it, however you want to handle it, means when I need a break, I can come here. When I miss my dad or my grandfather, they're here, and it's not a casino, or a shopping center, or whatever else. And, it also means when Chris needs to escape, there's a safe place for him to be. Even if you aren't here, Samuel, I still need him to be able to come here. He's not great, he tries, but he's messed up. Having him here made me realize he needs a place to go so removed from the rest of our normal lives, and this is it. So think that I'm doing this for you or for Kaden or whatever else you want to. It's all true. But I'm also doing this for him and for me, and I need this, so sign the damn contract if there's nothing you absolutely disagree with." He looked over and gave Kaden a smile. "Please."

Trent and Samuel looked at each other in silence before opening the contract and signing their names on the last page. "Thank you, Bran." Trent spoke softly as they slid the paperwork back to Bran across the table, who put them back into the second return envelope Chris had included.

"He'll get these tomorrow, after I arrange a pickup. Kaden, come with me please?" Bran said, getting up from the table.

"Ooh. I like it when you get all bossy with me." Kaden chuckled as he rose from his seat. Bran laughed and took his hand, tugging him into the lounge where he pushed Kaden lightly onto the couch before sitting on top of his thighs.

Trent and Samuel came into the lounge too but hesitated as if sensing they'd be interrupting something. Kaden waved them in, though, and they sat down nearby. They were his friends, and they lived on the farm too. He appreciated when they gave him privacy with Bran, but he was pretty sure, given Bran's current mood and the way he was still slightly trembling, that he wouldn't be pressing Kaden to do anything more than sit together.

Kaden stroked Bran's thigh. "You made the right decision, babe. Your grandfather would be proud of you, and I know you don't remember much, but he spoke of you often. He loved you and constantly wondered if you would ever come back to the farm."

Bran frowned down at him and rested his hands on the couch behind Kaden's head. "He talked about me? Really?"

Kaden nodded. "I promise, he did. I knew a lot about you before even meeting you for the first time. I knew that you were intelligent, strong, hurting, and stubborn. He probably didn't know you would return to the farm, but I would like to believe he knew you would do what's right."

Bran's bottom lip trembled, like he was close to tears, and Kaden leaned forward to give him a soft kiss. "Thank you. I didn't know any of that. I hadn't spoken to him in half my life and had written him off completely. I should have been there for the funeral at the very least."

"Maybe, but that's over now. We move forward, and besides, Tobias knew you were going through a hard time. He may not have liked you leaving the way you had, but he understood, and he cared." The ornery old man had a soft heart, Kaden remembered.

Nodding, Bran looked like he might have been feeling slightly better, though there were still shadows in his eyes. "Moving forward. Right. I can do that. So, you sexy Aussie, tell me what I need to know about your family so I don't make them hate me like you did five minutes after I get there." Bran gave him a wink, letting him know he'd been joking about the Aussie part, and it took him right back to the first morning he'd found Bran standing in the dust, looking angry enough to strike out like a snake in the grass.

"My family is the easy part." Kaden smiled. "With my parents, it's quite simple—you love me, they love you, and my mother will mother you until you want to pull your hair out. My dad, he's an extremely laid-back, easy-to-please man of few words. My sister, Kylie, on the other hand, she's a handful."

"No," Samuel jumped in.

"A pain in the ass," Trent finished for him. "She drove us insane in high school." They all smiled as they said it, though.

Kaden laughed. "Yeah, right. And still you wanted to beat the shit out of the man she is married to today when she brought him home for the first time."

"Well, she's like a sister to us, so we had to act the part," Samuel argued.

Bran smiled at them all. "Loving parents, a sister with kids, and two friends who wanted to kill me right away. Don't deny it. I could tell what you both were thinking." He leaned his forehead against Kaden's. "I can't wait to meet these people who mean so much to you."

Kaden kissed him softly on the lips. "Not too long now and you will. I have some staff to hire, and you have an apartment to sublet. When everything here is taken care of, we can fly out and relax properly without worrying over loose ends. Trent and Samuel will stay on to train the new people and oversee things. I think I've been away from home long enough and my parents and sister will want to meet you right away."

Bran was fine with all of that. He'd have to cut back a bit on his work, since there were some things he just couldn't do from New Zealand, but for the most part, his business would go on as usual.

"Wait till you taste a hangi," Trent teased.

"A what?" Bran asked in confusion.

Trent laughed. "A hangi. The Maori people make a hole in the ground and put large stones in there before making a fire in it. Once the stones are heated, they place food like roasts, vegetables, and even pudding in there and cover it up with soil, and the food cooks over a few hours before it's ready. It's the best meal you'll ever have, and Samuel here, is the best hangi chef I know." Trent waggled his eyebrows as he bragged about Sam's cooking abilities.

Bran grinned. "That sounds so good. Okay, Kaden, put that on the list of things we're doing in New Zealand. Or rather, things I'm eating. I don't dig holes. Thank you." He hugged Kaden tightly, nearly choking him. "For everything. I mean it."

Kaden pulled back to see his face, searching his eyes. "I know you're probably a bit scared, and most of this is all new to you, but I promise you won't regret the choices you made with me. With us." Kaden glanced at his friends, including them in his words. "You took a dare to risk all you were familiar with and stepped into something completely different, and I love you for it."

"I love you too," Bran said, not shying away from the words at all as he looked right at Kaden. "We'll be good together, for as long as you'll have me."

"And if I want you forever?" Kaden asked him.

Bran gave him a soft smile. "Then forever is what you'll have."

Exclusive excerpt

Dare to Hope

Dare: Book 2

By Kara Nash and Caitlin Ricci

Christophori Romanoff is an expert at being the perfect son for his homophobic father. But maintaining the facade comes with a heavy price, and when he swears off anonymous sex and getting drunk every night, he needs his friends more than ever. Only he's convinced they're busy with their own lives and better off without his interference. On the surface Chris is fine, but underneath the expensive suit and the law degree he got only to please his father, he's breaking apart from the pressure, and he falls back on his oldest—and most dangerous—coping mechanism.

Samuel Mealamu hoped to hear from Chris soon after their last good-bye in Montana, but as the months go by without a word, he realizes what they started was one-sided. Still, he worries about the destructive path Chris was on and hopes the silence means he's doing better. But nearly a year later Chris finally calls, and it's obvious he's in trouble. Samuel thinks he's seen Chris at his worst, but this new, far more broken man might be too much for even Samuel to help.

CHAPTER ONE

SAMUEL SHOT out his hand to grab his phone off the bedside table before the device even had time to ring properly. Being a light sleeper had its perks at times. In the dark the screen's brightness almost blinded him, but not enough for him not to see the number was an overseas one—an American one, if his memory served him right.

His heart sped up as he put it to his ear. "Hello, Samuel speaking."

"Hey. So…. It's Chris. And I just remembered it's pretty late there. Shit. Sorry."

Samuel sat straight up, leaning his bare back against the headboard. "Chris? Hey, how are you? Is everything okay?"

Chris laughed, though for some reason Samuel couldn't quite name, it sounded a little off. Maybe eight months of not hearing Chris's laugh—or even his voice, for that matter—had begun to mess with his memories of the sounds. "Of course things are okay. I'm good. Just hating winter here in New York, as usual. There's snow everywhere, and the cabs can't drive even half the speed limit because of it. I've been late to three meetings this week because of the traffic and accidents. We get snow every year, but it's like people suddenly forget how to drive the second those flakes start to come down or something. It's insanity. Tell me you have gorgeous weather or something. Please?"

"Actually, we do at the moment. It's summer here, so maybe it's time to make use of Bran's kindness and come pay us a visit?" The idea of seeing Chris actually made him look forward to something, because settling into life back in New Zealand hadn't been as easy as Samuel had thought it would be. Too much had happened to them in Montana: new friendships were formed and lives changed—some dramatically, like Kaden's, since he'd now hooked up permanently with Bran.

"That's kind of what I wanted to talk to you about. I've got some time away from the firm and I was hoping to come see you. If you'll have me. But the catch is, I don't want Bran, or Kaden, or anyone else in New Zealand—except you, of course—knowing I'm coming there. If you snitch, it'll be a lot longer than eight months before I decide to talk to you again." His laugh was back, but it sounded even worse this time, almost desperate.

For Chris to hide something from his best friend was huge, because the two men were practically joined at the hip. How they had survived the last eight months without their cuddles and twisted passion for the game truth or dare, Samuel would never know.

"Chris, keeping anything from Bran spells disaster. You know that, right?" Samuel would respect Chris's wishes, but he had to at least try to get Chris to do right by his friend.

This time there was no laughter in Chris's voice, only a hint at something painful that Samuel couldn't even begin to guess at. "I do know. He's my best friend. His mate, as he's taken to calling me since moving full time down there on the other side of the fucking planet. But I need a little time with just you." The brightness was back in his voice a second later, as if Chris had flicked a switch. "Gotta try to get into your pants again, this time without an audience. You know? So, what do you say? Can I come visit you, or are you going to make me continue to freeze my ass off in this snow?"

It didn't take a genius to know something was wrong, but Samuel played along. He had to until Chris was where he could see him in the flesh to determine what the hell was up with the man. When it came to acting, Bran and Chris used to be masters at it, and Samuel knew pushing anything over the phone would drive Chris away. And he didn't want that, not when Chris had finally reached out to him for help. Yeah, the sexual innuendos were still there, but they were what Chris was hiding behind at the moment.

"Please? I'll be good. I promise."

A fist clenched around Samuel's heart, and he went cold. Chris did not beg for anything, and he was doing almost exactly that. Something was seriously wrong, but Samuel kept his voice calm, despite the sweat breaking out on his forehead. "You? Be good? Ha-ha, but of course you can come and see me. Getting in my pants on the other hand.... Let's just say, good luck with that." It pained him to joke with Chris, but he had to keep things light or Chris would never board a plane to New Zealand.

"Yeah, we'll see. So. Tomorrow work for you, then? I'm looking at a flight that gets me into Auckland at six, and I can take a cab to you if you text me your address. They are called cabs there, aren't they?"

Samuel chuckled. "Nope, they're called taxis, and you'll do no such thing. I'll pick you up at the airport. Fortunately, I am the boss here, so I can take the milking off."

Chris sighed loudly and sounded very much like he was getting frustrated. "Not gonna work. Please? I'll take a taxi—it's not a big deal. Just don't fight me on this. I can't argue with you right now. Not about a fucking taxi from the airport to wherever you live. Text me your address or just tell it to me now. I'm heading out to JFK. And remember, no telling Bran."

The pleading in Chris's voice stopped Samuel from arguing any further. "Okay, have you got a pen or online maps ready? Have a look at taking a shuttle to here because it'll be cheaper than a taxi."

"Shuttle. Right. Pen. Go for it."

Samuel gave him the farm address, making sure he understood it was the driveway with the purple mailbox with the cow painted on it. "Think you can find it?"

"Purple box with a cow. Pretty sure I still have my eyes and can spot it," Chris said sarcastically but still playfully. "Thanks. See you tomorrow. Don't bother putting clothes on before I get there! They aren't part of my plan!" Chris blew him a kiss through the phone, then promptly hung up.

Like an idiot, Samuel lowered the phone and stared at it while still sitting in the dark. It was almost one in the morning and he had a whole workday to get through before Chris would arrive in Auckland the next day. New Zealand was roughly seventeen to twenty hours ahead of the states, so Chris's tomorrow would be the following day for them. Chris's flight would take a good twenty-three hours or so, excluding any stopovers for the aircraft to refuel.

He placed his phone back down and lay back onto his pillows. With his eyes closed, he tried to go back to sleep, but the effort was futile. His thoughts traveled back to their time spent working on Tobias Wilson's farm in Montana for about two years before Bran, and by default Chris, stormed into their lives and changed almost everything. Kaden fell hard for Bran, a guy who made their blood boil for a long time with his selfishness and greed. In the end, however, and fortunately for Kaden, Bran redeemed himself by revealing he had a heart of flesh and blood after all.

The two lovebirds lived on the larger of Kaden's two farms, about a twenty-minute drive away from where Samuel and Trent co-owned a large two thousand-cow dairy farm stretching over seven hundred acres of Waikato country. They saw the other two men regularly when having meals together or when they went out for a night of drinks, fun, and dancing. Surprisingly to all of them, Bran had easily adjusted to living in a rural town after the hectic lifestyle of Manhattan. Samuel had at least expected Bran to have some withdrawal symptoms from the five-star lifestyle he used to have, but apparently Bran's finances were still flourishing even with him living on the other side of the globe.

On the downside, Samuel found it hard to hang around them for too long at times, to see the love, passion, and affection they shared, because Bran reminded Samuel of Chris so much that a phantom ache started in his heart for a man he would probably never have.

Even the lighthearted, often absent-minded Trent hadn't walked away from Montana unscathed after laying eyes on Chris's crazy, dark, ex-army half brother, Misha Romanoff. Forgetting he was lying down, Samuel tried to shake his head but didn't quite succeed. Trent needed all the bloody help he could get with that nutcase if they were to ever pick things up where they left off after saying good-bye in Montana. They were such opposites, and if it wasn't so ludicrous to imagine the two together, Samuel would've found it totally hilarious.

Samuel would never again think of Montana as the green, flat, peaceful, crop-growing, blue-skyed land of promise as they always depicted it on television or in movies. No way. To him, Montana brought back memories of shit-loads of drama, fighting, worrying, and confusion. Not to mention a healthy fear of truth or dare, but whether the fear came from the drama that unfolded during the stupid games or the raging hangovers the next day, he wasn't quite sure.

Hell yes, they had heaps of fun too. But there had been so much heartache and self-destruction in the midst of it all, mostly centered around Chris, and Samuel hated the moment Chris returned to Manhattan at his homophobic father's command. Samuel hadn't been sure Chris had been healed up physically or emotionally enough to deal with his controlling family, but Misha had left with Chris and promised to keep a close eye on him. Despite the latter, Samuel had been uneasy since then.

His thoughts returned to the unexpected phone call from Chris and the strange request for Samuel not to let anyone know Chris would be in New Zealand. He couldn't help the dark sense of foreboding rising within him. For Chris to not want Bran to know he was in the same country, or even the same town—only twenty minutes away from each other—was not only strange, but a big deal on so many levels. Not only would Bran feel betrayed, deceived, and hurt if he ever found out, which was bound to happen with them living in such a small community, but Samuel worried over the impact this would possibly have on their very special friendship. Furthermore, Samuel's concern grew at the possible reasons why Chris would want to seek refuge with him, at his home, when his best friend lived almost down the road. What was so bad for Chris to want to hide away from the person who knew and loved him best?

From all he had heard tonight, spoken and unspoken, during their long-distance call, Samuel concluded Chris was in trouble. What kind of trouble and the damage to Chris because of it, he couldn't decide. Some time later, still without any easy answers for his questions, he fell into a restless sleep.

KARA NASH makes her home amongst the stunning islands in the South Pacific. Writing is a passion, but so is reading, a good cup of steaming coffee, and the love and company of friends and family. While life carries on around her in a bustle, her mind is filled with the voices and antics of the characters in her next creation. Kara is an absolute romantic at heart and happy endings are precious, which is why she chooses to tell stories of couples fortunate to find and hold on to love. And cats! Kara adores these furry creatures and the sense behind "too many" escapes her when it comes to them.

CAITLIN RICCI was fortunate growing up to be surrounded by family and teachers who encouraged her love of reading. She has always been a voracious reader and that love of the written word easily morphed into a passion for writing. If she isn't writing, she can usually be found studying as she works toward her counseling degree. She comes from a military family, and the men and women of the armed forces are close to her heart. She also enjoys gardening, hiking, and horseback riding in the Colorado Rockies she calls home with her wonderful fiancé and their two dogs. Her belief that there is no one true path to happily ever after runs deeply through all of her stories.

Website: www.CaitlinRicci.com

A Thornwood Novel

About *Last* Night

Caitlin Ricci

A Thornwood Novel

Before jumping into his first semester of college, Thomas Maloney decides to lose his virginity at a party to a stranger he's sure he'll never see again. Only the next day, he's surprised to learn the same one-night stand will be sharing his dorm room. Thomas considers himself lucky, but his new roommate—not so much.

Closeted as they come, football jock Remington "Rem" Daniels is on track for a shot at the pros. Rem tries to play it cool and avoid falling for the confidently gay Thomas, which could hurt his chances. Dealing with their constant need to get in bed together wouldn't be so hard if Rem didn't have a girlfriend and Thomas didn't have a conscience.

When she delivers news that will change Rem's life forever, Thomas knows it's time to move back home to Thornwood, Colorado. But neither the distance nor knowing Rem belongs to someone else helps Thomas get over him. Rem's feelings haven't changed either. When it comes down to love or football, Rem will have to make the hardest choice of his life and hope Thomas will still be waiting for him when he does.

www.dreamspinnerpress.com

reckless

caitlin ricci

When his best friend, Lee, offered him his sub as part of a bet, Colton Prier never expected more than a clean condo from the boy. But Tate Nicholson is well-trained, eager , and he likes rope play as much as Colton enjoys tying him up. It should have ended after one night, but they begin meeting in secret, and Colton can't stop thinking about Tate. It's a betrayal of his friendship with Lee to fall in love with Tate, but Colton can't help wanting the sub for himself.

He's not alone in his feelings, either. Tate thought he was happy with Lee. Not completely fulfilled, but happy enough. But as he spends more time with Colton, he realizes Lee isn't capable of giving him what he wants anyway. Lee demands his full submission, but Tate doesn't want to be a lifestyle sub. Colton expects his obedience at times but gives him his freedom more often than not, which is more in line with what Tate wants.

When Tate really needs his Dom and Lee isn't around to help him, he reaches the tipping point and needs to choose who he wants to give his submission to, and to accept the consequences of his choice when he does.

www.dreamspinnerpress.com